WOLF’

DON BALDWIN

First published in 2024 by Blossom Spring Publishing

ISBN 978-1-0687765-8-8
E: admin@blossomspringpublishing.com
W: www.blossomspringpublishing.com

DEDICATION:

I would like to dedicate this book to my family: my wife, Sheela, my daughter, Orlaith, and my son, Lorcan. The jewels of my life!

IN MEMORY:

In memory of my sister Brenda and my brother Dermot, both sadly missed but never forgotten.

IRELAND
c950
Viking territory
Maximum area of influence of Dublin Vikings.
PROVINCES
Lesser Kingdoms
Cenél Conaill
Dál Riata
Cenél nEógain
Dál nAraide
NORTHERN UÍ NÉILL
Dál Fiatach
Airgialla
BRÉIFNE
Conaille Muirtemne
CONNACHT
SOUTHERN UÍ NÉILL
(Meath)
Tara
Dubhlinn
(Dublin)
LAIGIN
(LEINSTER)
Dal Cais
Limerick
Osraige
Uí Fidgente
MUNSTER
Déisi
Vadrefjord
(Waterford)
Weisfjord
(Wexford)
Desmumu
Cork
Eóganacht
This map created for The Ireland Story. It may be used elsewhere provided a link is given to www.irelandstory.com, the site is non-profit and the map is not modified in any way.

Chapter One

BEGINNINGS

A sudden gust whipped the top of the pine trees and then died just as quickly, leaving a strange, pensive silence hanging over the forest clearing. Approaching from the south of Ireland, a dark-haired figure quietly broke the tree line and headed towards the centre of the summer glade, his sure, easy balance and the slim sword strapped across his back clearly marking him out as a warrior.

From the east and then the west, two more figures emerged from the trees and walked with fluid grace towards the centre of the small enclosure, and while these women wore no swords, both concealed daggers beneath their dark green cloaks. The last figure, caped in a similar cloak, arrived from the north. And although she wore no insignia of rank, she had the obvious bearing of nobility. The four gathered in the centre of the grassy tract, and it was clear from their refined features, almond shaped eyes and sylvan-coloured clothes that they were not of the race of men.

"So it begins," said Eiru without preamble, sliding back the hood from her golden hair. "The islands of Inishbofin and Rathlin off the north coast have both been attacked by Norse pirates, their monasteries plundered and burned, while a fleet of Viking ships prowls Strangford Lough with the ravenous intent of winter wolves."

"There have been similar attacks in the west," added Folda. "Both the monastery on the island of Inishmurray and the religious centre at Roscam have been destroyed, with many people butchered and a great many more carried off into captivity."

"It's the same sorry tale in the east," lamented Banba. "The monasteries on the islands of Saint Patrick and Lambay have both been decimated with great slaughter, while a host of Viking craft has also moored in the sheltered waters of Dublin and show little sign of leaving."

"The south is likewise afflicted," reported Midir. "The sea seems to vomit forth these ships, both Norse and Danes alike, and there have been raids all along the southern coast. The valleys are filled with the smoke of destruction and the anguished cries of fathers and mothers who have lost their loved ones to the slave ships. The monastery on the jagged island of Skellig Michael has also been desecrated, and one unfortunate monk was nailed to the church door and left for the gulls. The hungry birds started on his eyes; he had still been alive."

"It seems that these Vikings have little love for the new religion," said Eiru after a heavy silence as the shrill outburst of a startled blackbird suddenly punched the air.

"Are we to oppose these barbarians?" asked Banba.

"No, not at this time," answered Eiru. "We must let the contest between the Sons of Odin and the Milesians run its course, for now. This war between the White Dragon and the Red Dragon is an age-old conflict, and now it is to be waged on a new battlefield. Still, we must be ready to act when the time is right. For as the Sons of Odin grow in strength here, so too will the power of their dark gods, and that we must not allow."

"Why should we concern ourselves with the plight of the Milesians? Didn't these Gaels dispossess us of the land?" asked Folda.

"Yes, that is true," answered Eiru patiently. "But the

Tuatha De Danann only conceded the upper realm to the Milesians. Ireland's underworld still belongs to the Ever-Living Ones. And besides, the Gaels have honoured the ancient accord agreed between our races. They still accept our hidden presence here and revere our sacred places. Can we be sure that these Sons of Odin would do the same?"

"Not all these mortals respect our sacred places," countered Folda peevishly. "What about this wild child that violates a sacred grove with impunity in Midir's domain? Is he above our law?"

"Midir?" asked Eiru.

"It's a peculiar situation indeed. An orphan boy seems to have been taken in by a wolf pack whose den is in the heart of a sacred grove," explained Midir with a nonchalant shrug.

"Wolves are of course free from our laws, but a mortal, child or not, who trespasses into a sacred grove must be dealt with accordingly," stated Eiru.

"Death does seem a little harsh for a boy who is, well, part wolf after all," reasoned Midir.

"It is the law, Prince Midir," said Folda dogmatically.

"And yet the law is not inflexible, Folda," responded Eiru, offering Midir a little latitude to make his case.

"Perhaps…" Midir paused to choose his words and try to enlist an ally.

"Perhaps what Prince Midir is trying to say," Banba continued, offering her support, "is that nature has strived hard to keep this child alive, and maybe we should not be so quick to kill him. Could nature have some special purpose for this boy?"

"Besides howling at the moon?" muttered Folda.

"What do you have in mind, Prince Midir?" asked

Eiru, ignoring Folda's barbed remark.

"Adopt the boy and bring him to our underworld until he is no longer a child. As Folda has rightly pointed out, if nature has some future role for the boy, we cannot simply leave him to the company of wolves," suggested Midir.

"It is your right according to your rank to do such a thing, Prince Midir, but it is not without its risks," cautioned Eiru.

"Among the other dangers, time runs differently in our world, and mortal memories can easily fade away and be lost," warned Folda.

"Perhaps the loss of some memories might be no bad thing for this child," reflected Eiru. "And if you are prepared to assume the full responsibility of the task, you may adopt this human child, Prince Midir, being mindful of the swift passage of mortal time. Also, as it is a time of war, you will need to train the boy well in the martial arts, and you may also teach him a little of our secret craft. When he is fully grown, you must then return him to the race of men. From that time on, you too shall watch over him, Banba, for he will then be a part of our race too."

"And what are we to call this orphan child of ours?" asked Folda without rancour.

"It seems that nature has already had a hand in that," offered Banba.

"It has indeed," agreed Eiru. "Then so be it. Let this human child be named Wolf."

*

Downwind, concealed by the undergrowth, Midir quietly watched the unusual scene in the sacred grove below. Near the wolf den stood a large, isolated boulder, on top of which squatted the feral boy, taunting his wolf-sister, Willow, and her darker brother, Shadow, who could not climb the steep rock. Then he would pounce down on his siblings, wrestle with them on the ground and then start the game all over again. A litter of two was small, thought Midir; perhaps that's why Storm and Ash had made room for the lost boy. Storm's ears pricked up, sensing Midir's presence. Seeing his reaction, Ash sprang to her feet. Midir knew he had little choice now but to end the happy scene and life for the boy as he knew it.

I mean no harm, said Midir with the mind speech as he walked from the bushes, his empty hands raised high.

Have you come for the boy? asked Storm, his instinct to attack tempered by his fear of the tangible power of the Ever-Living Ones.

No, Storm! We cannot, protested Ash, moving to defend the child.

We knew this day would come, said Storm, knowing resistance was futile.

I only mean to care for the boy, as you have done, reassured Midir.

He has suffered much, said Ash, looking softly towards the boy, who was still perched attentively upon the rock.

It has made him strong, reasoned Midir.

There are better ways to make cubs strong, reproved Ash. *Will we see him again?*

Not in your lifetime, mother. Perhaps in theirs, answered Midir, looking towards the two cubs peeking out from behind the boulder, one coloured black, and the other grey. Ash called her two cubs to her. She took a last tender look at the boy cub and then followed Storm into the undergrowth as the child stayed hunkered down on the rock, transfixed by the stranger before him. A moment later, Willow's gangly grey figure came crashing back through the bushes to get the boy cub, who had obviously not heard their mother's call, and after yapping at her brother several times, hesitantly went off to find her family.

I will not harm you, boy, communicated Midir.

Alarmed at hearing these strange sounds in his head, the boy's hackles went up and he started a low, rumbling growl.

Unfortunately, there seems to be no easy way to do this, continued Midir as he walked forward, the boy's growls now becoming menacing as spittle flew from his mouth. *And this will definitely hurt!* said Midir, whipping up his hands and hurling out a shockwave that knocked the boy clear off the rock, leaving him sprawled on his back on the ground. Pinpricks of light exploded before the child's eyes as a thick black cloud seeped down over his vision. The sensation of Willow's wet tongue frantically licking his face, the very last thing that he vaguely remembered.

Chapter Two

AGREEMENTS

Amergen pulled his cloak tightly around him; this Oakwood was a strange place, a cold place, even though it was noon and still high summer. The locals mumbled about the old spirits of the land, guardians of the forest, and the unsettled ghosts of an old hill fort nearby that had suffered a brutal and mysterious end. The two wolves that had shadowed him on either side since he had entered the sprawling woodland did little to lift his sense of unease. It wasn't that Amergen was unaccustomed to wolves. Ireland was rife with them. But there was something unusual about the way that these two stalked him, not menacingly, but rather in an attentive, curious way, the lighter wolf occasionally venturing a little closer to Amergen, while the darker one stayed in the background weaving its way smoothly through the shadows. Amergen brandished his staff towards them, muttering beneath his breath and shaking his head in disbelief.

His crucial search through the wilds of Thomond had Amergen on edge, but then, these were strange times. Frightening fireballs had been seen burning across the sky. The moon too had flushed an unsettling blood red, while the skies had thundered as if the very gods themselves clashed. The new religion claimed that these ominous signs and the upheaval throughout the land heralded the end of the world. The Christian priests were always keen to peddle that idea, mused Amergen, ever ready to prepare you for the next life, for a hefty price of course, while they industriously built their sprawling monasteries to endure in this one. The people had certainly warmed to this new religion, but their hearts remained firmly rooted in the old one. Still deeply connected to the hidden deities of the land, the silent providers of fruitful harvests and fertile flocks; to these ancient gods, the Irish people now quietly turned for protection during these most turbulent times.

Ireland had, of course, always been a violent land. Too many kings and too few kingdoms, even fewer now that these Vikings had forced their way onto the land, carving out their burgeoning strongholds. Setting Irish kingdom against kingdom, fomenting strife and then swooping down like ravenous hawks to snatch up the spoils of war. Little wonder that the Viking port town of Dublin was now the slave capital of the Western world.

Amergen tried to push these dark thoughts to the back of his mind and focus on his surroundings and the deer trail that stretched out before him. Bluebells had overpowered the ever-present fern wherever a chink of light had managed to break through the congested canopy, from where a noisy jay safely railed against Amergen's unwanted presence in the forest. Amergen suddenly stopped, as he had unexpectedly entered a small clearing surrounding a massive oak tree. Beside this ancient timber, bathed in a shaft of sunlight, stood a solitary deer rooted to the spot. The pair stood motionless, their eyes locked together in a rare moment until the doe thought better of it and bounded casually back into the woods.

He walked on towards the old tree, its immense girth supporting an array of weary limbs which were draped with moss and ivy, forcing the branches almost to the ground. Amergen laid his hands gently upon the bole of the tree, absorbing its silent history. "We have been in this world a long time, my friend," said Amergen softly and then instinctively jolted back as a black arrow thudded into the tree trunk beside him, barely missing his hand. Amergen snatched his hand away and looked back along the flight path of the arrow towards the undergrowth, where a tall, powerfully built figure silently emerged from the bushes. The man walked with the easy balance of a hunter. His dark green buckskin clothes, tousled black hair and intense amber eyes all combined to give him a distinctly feral look, coupled with an unmistakable aura of danger.

"Don't worry, Grey-Beard, if I had been aiming for your hand, I wouldn't have missed," joked the archer with a barb of dry humour as he carefully worked the arrow free from the bark.

"My hair is white, not grey!" retorted Amergen indignantly.

"There's a difference?"

"There most certainly is, young man," snapped Amergen. "And if you do manage to live long enough, you might learn to tell the difference. Is this how you treat all the travellers who pass through these woods?"

"Only the ones who scare the game for twenty miles in all directions," answered the hunter calmly, returning the arrow to its quiver.

"Are you Wolf?" asked Amergen, getting straight to the point.

"Who's asking?"

"My name is Amergen. I am a counsellor to Mahon, King of Thomond, which includes the territory of all North Munster," said Amergen rather pointedly. "I am also a special advisor to his younger brother, Brian Boru, commander of Mahon's troops. I, or should I say we, have learned that you are a man with, shall we say, a particular set of skills. We would like to avail of those talents, for a price, of course."

"I think you are mistaking me for someone else," answered Wolf casually, shouldering his bow and preparing to leave.

"I do not believe that I am," continued Amergen, undeterred. "Indeed, it is my opinion that you are, in fact, Captain Wolf, an officer in the secretive Rangers: a stealthy cohort of mercenaries, saboteurs and assassins who operate in every dark corner of this country, plying their nefarious trade for very handsome rewards."

"It seems that you are well informed," conceded Wolf. "Life makes of us what it will, Counsellor. The Rangers make no excuses for what they are or for what they do. Perhaps many of these men might have been farmers or fishermen, maybe even priests, in some other lifetime, but not in this one; hard winters breed hard wolves. In any case, I no longer pursue that particular profession."

"Perhaps what you say is true," granted Amergen. "But let me remind you that you have been hunting in the territory of Thomond for quite some time now. And without the king's permission, I might add, which is a most serious offence, Captain. Commander Boru is a reasonable man and has no desire to make life here difficult for you. Or your wolf friends," said Amergen with subtle menace, looking directly at the two unusual wolves that still lurked nearby. "He simply asks you for a small service in return for his forbearance, for which, of course, you will be well rewarded. However, consider this carefully before you give me your answer; slighting royalty is a perilous business, and once refused, the powerful seldom ask for something twice."

“A small service, you say?” asked Wolf warily.

“A minor action, really. Nothing too taxing for a man of your rare abilities,” said Amergen casually as he slowly sat himself down against the tree. “A score of men should suffice.”

“Can Boru not undertake this minor action himself?” suggested Wolf. “Surely he can gather up twenty warriors a lot quicker than I?”

“It is imperative that Brian not be connected to this undertaking in any way,” stressed Amergen. “That’s why we thought it best to use mercenaries. They’re independent, professional and...”

“Expendable?” offered Wolf.

“Something like that,” admitted Amergen, unabashed.

“Alright then, let me hear what it is that you have to say,” relented Wolf, taking the longbow from his shoulder, wedging one end into the ground and leaning lightly on the other. “But I make no promises, Counsellor.”

“King Mahon has betrothed his younger sister, Aoife, to Jarl Ivar, king of the Limerick Vikings,” began Amergen bluntly, “in order to form an alliance: a pact to promote peace in North Munster and allow the Dalcassian tribe time to regain their strength after many years of hard fighting against these Danes.”

“So that the O’Kennedy clan can then challenge for the Munster crown?” ventured Wolf.

“It seems that you are also well informed,” commended Amergen with a slight tilt of his head. “Brian, however, is opposed to this marriage. As Mahon’s younger brother and commander of his troops, Boru has no desire to openly oppose Mahon or defy his king. Nor indeed does he want to antagonise Ivar at this particular time; this is where you and your Rangers come in."

"I'm listening," prodded Wolf, starting to see the bare bones of Amergen's plan.

"Princess Aoife is to be escorted to Limerick very soon. Boru simply requires you to abduct the girl, keeping the bloodshed to a minimum; King Mahon would not tolerate the loss of any of his precious Royal Guard. However, the ambush must look convincing, as there are spies everywhere and we cannot run the risk of Ivar suspecting some sort of underhand plot."

"Even if it happens to be one," commented Wolf dryly. "But why can't Boru simply go along with this peace pact? Surely sisters and daughters are traded in hard bargains every day of the week?"

"This is a deeply personal matter for Boru," said Amergen simply. "These Limerick Danes slaughtered Brian's father, mother and brother when he was just a child. As a young warrior, Brian would not make peace with the Danes as his brother Mahon had done, and he took to the hills with a score of warriors to continue the fight. For two gruelling years, Brian and his men waged brutal guerrilla warfare against these Vikings. Hit-and-run raids mostly, sabotage, assassinations; they gave Ivar and his men a right bloody nose and caused them no end of embarrassment. But in the end, starvation and exposure got the better of Brian and his band. Ivar has been sore about that humiliation ever since, and Brian believes that Ivar and his men would gladly take their revenge out on Aoife. And he does not intend to hand them the opportunity."

"Perhaps Brian's skills as a shadow warrior would have been better served in the Rangers," said Wolf, with respect.

"Brian learned a lot about the darker arts of war during that hard time," explained Amergen. "He knows better than most commanders that all wars aren't won with shield walls and pitched battles. And that shadow warriors such as yourself and the Rangers also play a vital, often unsung role in the course of any war."

"Still, this is hardly a task for the Rangers. As I'm sure you know, we tend to operate as highly trained individuals or within small compact units," reasoned Wolf. "Using twenty skilled Rangers on a simple ambush operation would not be cheap. Surely a competent officer and a platoon of well positioned foot soldiers would serve just as well?"

"No. There can be no mistakes, no risk of injury to the princess or loss of life," stated Amergen firmly. "But it must be convincing. This has to be handled by professionals; there is far too much at stake here. Do not concern yourself about the cost, Captain Wolf. Brian Boru has deep pockets. But remember this: the powerful pay for results, and they have little tolerance for failure. Well, will you do this small service for Boru? Will you undertake this minor action for the kingdom of Thomond?" asked Amergen gravely, having given Wolf a quiet moment to digest the facts.

"I'm not sure that you have left me with very much choice, Counsellor," answered Wolf soberly, stealing a glance towards his wolf-sister, Willow, and her brother, Shadow, who prowled attentively in the background. His refusal would fall heaviest on them and on all the other wolves that roamed this forest. "But then I suppose that was the whole idea. So yes, Amergen, I will do this thing that Boru asks of me."

"Good," said Amergen, getting stiffly to his feet. "Here, this should get you started," he said, tossing Wolf a heavy purse of gold coins to seal the deal. "Now it appears that we both have arrangements to make, and quickly. We will meet at the ruins of that old hill fort near here called the Fort of the Two Ravens, at the next full moon. I will bring the final details of the ambush and the rest of the payment. You know of this place?"

"Yes, I have heard of it. But surely you don't intend to have any part in this abduction?" asked Wolf, detecting a little too much involvement from Amergen. After a down payment, most wealthy clients were usually happy to get well away from the whirlwind that their scheming invariably unleashed.

"I will need to stay close. Obviously, I cannot be seen during the ambush, but Princess Aoife will need to see one friendly face when this is all over," reasoned Amergen. "And besides, 'he who pays the fiddler, calls the tune!' does he not?"

"There may well be a grain of truth in that saying," conceded Wolf, "but know this, Amergen: when I lift that fiddle and the dancing starts, it's I who will decide how that tune is to be played. Is that understood, Counsellor?"

"I know better than to try and teach a cat how to drink milk, Captain, especially one with claws as lethal as yours."

"Then we are agreed?" said Wolf, offering his hand. "And the wolves of this forest will come to no harm?"

"Yes, we are agreed," answered Amergen, gripping Wolf's hand, the trace of a sly smile hidden beneath his beard. "Until the next full moon, Captain."

"We shall await you at the Fort of the Two Ravens. And *White-Beard*, you had better be ready to dance!"

poked Wolf.

"Do not let my scholarly looks mislead you. I am well versed in the songs of war," said Amergen enigmatically. Wolf did not doubt the counsellor's words for a moment as he watched Amergen hurry off to the south. There seemed to be some sort of twisted honesty about the small man. But a great deal of mystery too, concluded Wolf warily. Then he turned towards Willow and Shadow and pointed towards the northeast and the stronghold of the Dublin Norse.

Chapter Three

CONNECTIONS

A brisk easterly breeze swept in from the Irish Sea, rippling the heather on the lonely hill as Wolf leaned on the pommel of his saddle and surveyed the Viking town of Dublin down below. Balor was restless, but then the black stallion usually was when he sensed danger. And besides, the big horse was never really at ease with the two strange wolves that travelled with his master. Dublin was unlike most other human habitations in Ireland at that time, towns being a Viking concept and relatively new to the land. The large town's predominant colours of roof-rush cream and darkened timber walls seemed to be totally out of place in the green countryside that surrounded it. And the town's long linear streets seemed to be completely at odds with the natural contours of the land. Dublin Town fairly burgeoned inside its timber and rampart palisade, so much so that untidy shanty towns had begun to mushroom outside the town's defensive walls.

The din from the town was endless. Blacksmiths forged and hammered as carpenters cut and shaped timber for houses, ships, storehouses, taverns, footpaths and wharfs, while both trades co-operated to fashion holding pens and chains to secure livestock and slaves alike. Mixed through this incessant noise was the endless chatter of people, punctuated by the occasional peel of laughter or a sharp scream, but more often than not by anguished cries of pain. The screech of raucous gulls only added to the cacophony of sound as they wheeled through the plumes of smoke above the sprawling town in their endless search for the refuse discarded by this congestion of people: a fair-haired race who seemed to grow by the day, their numbers augmented by the succession of longships that entered Dublin port from every part of the Irish Sea.

Balor shifted impatiently as Wolf assessed his options. "I know, Willow," said Wolf to the fair-coloured wolf standing beside the horse, well clear of any flying hooves. "I don't much like it either," he added, turning in the saddle to see if his wolf-brother, Shadow, was still lurking in the shade of the trees, true to his name and in keeping with his nature. "But this is not a job for a lone wolf," he went on to say. "It is a task for a pack, and that's where I can find one, in the heart of the foreigner's stronghold." Willow gave a quiet whimper, then lay down and rested her head on her forelegs; she knew her human brother only too well.

Wolf could leave his horse and gear in one of the many safe houses that the Rangers had dotted all around the country, but his sword was another matter. A good sword could take a blacksmith a year to make and might cost as much as a dozen cows. Wolf's doubled-edged sword with its black leather handle and silver pommel, combined with its matching dagger, had attracted many envious eyes over the years. The dilemma was always the same in these situations: carry the sword into the town and attract unwanted attention or leave the weapon behind and feel extremely vulnerable in a very dangerous place.

"Away, Willow," ordered Wolf as he put his heels to Balor's flanks. His course of action determined, he headed cautiously down the hill towards Dublin as Willow went to rejoin her brother, who was waiting at the tree line.

Having stabled Balor at a nearby safe house, a farmstead west of Dublin, Wolf approached the Viking stronghold on foot, pulling up the hood on his dark green buckskin tunic and blending in with the assorted mix of Norse, Irish and other foreign merchants all keen to get into the safety of Dublin Town before the gates were closed at dusk. As he neared the opened gates, Wolf snatched up a basket of turf and carried it over the sword strapped across his back, passing unnoticed beneath the two guardhouses mounted on either side of the wide gateway.

Wolf slipped off the busy thoroughfare and went down a narrow side street, ditching the basket of turf as he went. As night slowly fell, Wolf quickly continued to weave his way through Dublin's familiar back streets to the tavern called the Dirty Dog. The inn was a seedy place and best avoided, but Wolf had not been active in the Rangers for a while, and contacting a secretive organisation was not a straightforward business. However, the grubby tavern was just the place to do so. Using the less frequented backstreets to avoid announcing his presence to the powers that be was a sensible precaution, but it meant falling under the shrewd scrutiny of the ever-watchful residents of Dublin's poorer quarter.

The congested rows of wattle-and-daub houses left little room for the rickety timber footpath that weaved its way between the shacks. Tired women herded unruly children indoors as the night closed in, firing the stranger a sullen look as he passed, with the brooding air of trouble written all over him. The dogs were uneasy with his presence too, some growling, others barking, while a few braver ones came towards him with hackles raised and tails high to tentatively sniff at his leg, only to beat a hasty retreat with their tails between their legs and the peculiar scent of wolf lingering in their muzzles. As he neared the bustling wharf along the River Liffey, the appearance of the buildings improved considerably, becoming larger and more solid. Some served as workshops, others as stores, while a few had been converted into crude taverns to cater for the basic needs of sailors, soldiers and merchants alike.

Wolf instinctively checked for an easy extraction of his dagger, and then he pushed open the door of the Dirty Dog tavern and was met by the overpowering smell of stale ale, old vomit and the unmistakable stench of menace. The innkeeper had just finished lighting the oil lamps and was making his way back to the counter, while the rest of the patrons seemed to be consumed with a game of dice at the other end of the long room.

"What can I get you, stranger?" asked the innkeeper amiably. "Food, ale? A girl, maybe?" He added the last with a quick glance at the heavy beamed ceiling, which obviously supported other rooms up above.

"Just ale," answered Wolf, tossing a few copper coins onto the tacky counter. The innkeeper soon returned, gave the counter a cursory wipe with a greasy cloth, then planted down the horn of ale. And Wolf suddenly stood a gold coin on its edge on the counter between them. The innkeeper snatched it up immediately, throwing a furtive look towards the dice game, which had just drawn to a noisy conclusion, with the inevitable collection of winners and losers.

"'Life on the edge', eh?" said the innkeeper cryptically.

"'It's all about balance'," responded Wolf, reciting the rest of the simple code.

"Toke!" The innkeeper summoned the tavern boy, then went off to confer with him in a corner as three of the dice game's losers arrived at the other end of the bar.

"You should have held, Bjorn," offered one, trying to console the big redhead whose name, which meant 'bear', certainly suited the man for size.

"Yeah, double or quits, that was a crazy bet," added the other, thinking aloud, then thought better of it when he saw the scowl on Bjorn's face. "But a brave one all the same," he quickly clarified. Bjorn gave Wolf a disgruntled look and then loudly called for more ale.

"Hey, you! Is your head cold, 'Green Man'?" called Bjorn, finding offence at Wolf's drawn-up hood and homing in on a new target for his angst.

"Don't start, Bjorn!" warned the innkeeper as Bjorn's two companions began to subtly shift like two well-trained hunting dogs sensing that there might be a new game to be played — with better returns than the last one. Wolf took a last sip of his ale and then calmly turned to leave, but Bjorn's sidekicks had quickly moved to cut him off.

"What's your hurry, Green Man?" asked Bjorn, stepping in between his two heel hounds. "We only want to see your sword."

"We'll trade you for it," suggested one sarcastically.

"Yeah, we will give you a fair price," added the other, which gave the three of them a mirthless laugh.

"Don't lay a hand on him, Bjorn!" ordered the innkeeper. "Well you know that Jarl Kanarvan has decreed that all tribes are to be afforded safe passage while conducting business in this port. And you're on your last warning, Bjorn. One more breach of the peace and the jarl will ship you back to Norway for sure!"

"Look!" answered Bjorn insolently. "I will only place a finger on him so." And then he poked his left forefinger hard into Wolf's collar bone and slowly began reaching for Wolf's sword with his other hand. In a blur of movement, Wolf stepped back, snatching his dagger with incredible speed and swinging it up in a backward arc, cleanly severing Bjorn's forefinger in an instant. Wolf then quickly stepped to the left and brought the hilt of the dagger crashing down on the bridge of another's nose, smashing his face in a gush of blood. A knife had made a wild slash at Wolf's throat, but Wolf had expected the move and gone down on one knee, and he drove his dagger into the other companion's foot until the tip of the dagger bit into the timber floor beneath. Wolf yanked his knife free as the man screeched in pain, and then he moved swiftly to the door, leaving a discordant mix of moans, groans, curses and screams in his wake. The innkeeper loudly berated the injured trio for bleeding all over his floor as Wolf stepped out into the torchlit street and slammed the door behind him. He knew that he had only moments before the other patrons of the Dirty Dog recovered their senses, and then he heard the sound of angry voices, the scraping of chairs and the thud of a knocked-over table.

"Hey, Irish!" called Toke the tavern boy, who had been sitting waiting on a barrel across the street. "With me, quickly!" Then he took off down a narrow backstreet as the tavern door was flung open and light spilled out onto the empty street. Wolf quickly followed the boy down the well-worn rat run as the patrons of the Dirty Dog chased after them in close pursuit. Residents shouted in alarm and anger as guard dogs furiously barked. Women screamed obscenities as frightened children began to cry and heavily laden clotheslines were trampled to the ground. Toke suddenly lurched to one side of the narrow path, and Wolf followed his lead as a vicious dog on a short lead lunged at him and barely missed his leg. Enraged at missing his first two targets, the slavering mongrel set his sights squarely on the third man and bit down hard on the man's forearm as he went to pass, stopping him and his fellow pursuers dead in their tracks. A press of outraged women armed with clubs and spades took care of the rest.

Toke led Wolf to the back door of a warehouse and then disappeared into the night with a grin as bright as the silver coin that Wolf had pressed into the boy's grimy hand. Wolf eased himself into the storehouse and gently closed the door behind him. He adjusted to the complete darkness and sensed that the building was empty by the scuffling sound of rats as they hunted down whatever gleanings of grain remained.

"Bjorn will have to train a new finger to pick his nose," said a familiar voice from the darkness at the other end of the storeroom.

"He's fortunate that I left him with so many options," responded Wolf with mock seriousness, adjusting his vision as the light from a candle slowly filled the large room.

"Please, Captain Wolf," said a grey-haired man, gesturing towards a stool placed at a makeshift table. "I'm sure that this is not a social visit."

"Commander Sten," greeted Wolf as he sat, but Sten used his free hand to brush aside such formalities as he filled two small bowls with wine. Ranger officers usually shunned such observances of rank in the field, as it quickly signalled them out as leaders, and as such, prime targets. Besides that, all Rangers had undergone the same hard training and so had duly earned the respect of their peers, regardless of their rank. Subsequently, the distinction between officers, NCOs and privates was not as pronounced in the Rangers as it was in other military units.

"You appear fit," complimented Sten as he handed Wolf the beaker of wine.

"Probably the result of having to chase my dinner," reasoned Wolf. "Hunting keeps me active."

"Ah yes, you never were one for the creature comforts," recalled Sten. "Something to do with that shady past of yours, no doubt," added the commander with a little pointed humour.

Most men and the occasional woman came to the Rangers with a troubled past. Some talked about it, others didn't. In any case it mattered little; all were stripped of their past life and identity and moulded into Rangers, if they made it through the training. After that, it was of no consequence if they were Irish, Norse, Dane or otherwise. As Rangers, their first duty was to the unit, and just as importantly, to each other.

"So, what brings you back to our sordid little town, Captain?"

"I need twenty Rangers," stated Wolf, getting straight to the point — already eager to leave the stifling confines of the congested town.

"I thought that you had turned your back on our way of life?"

"I had," admitted Wolf, "but circumstances have changed."

"I see," considered Sten, sipping his wine. "And what makes you think that I will give you these men?"

"This," said Wolf, tossing a heavy bag of gold coins onto the table.

"You make a persuasive argument," allowed Sten, casually poking through the glittering coins.

"And there will be more," encouraged Wolf.

"Who is the client?"

"A prince of Thomond named Brian Boru is the paymaster, but I am to deal with a middleman named Amergen, some sort of advisor."

"Amergen, I vaguely remember that name. A strange character, as I recall," responded Sten. "I have also heard of this Brian Boru, an ambitious man by all accounts, and ambition can be a very dangerous animal. Can we trust him?"

"Since when could anyone trust the rich and the powerful?"

"True," conceded Sten. "Still, we would do very little business without them and their kind. What exactly do you need?"

Wolf laid out the warp and the weft of Amergen's plan as Sten studiously listened.

"You suspect something?" asked Wolf when Sten seemed reluctant to respond.

"Sometimes you sniff a piece of meat and you cannot say with complete certainty if the meat is off, or the meat is good. Hunger persuades you one way and caution the other, until you finally devour the meat and hope for the best," concluded Sten as he slid the bag of coins off the table. "It is wise to be careful in this business. There is little merit in running blindly onto a waiting blade, like so many tend to do. Still, life is risk, and it is unlikely that many Rangers will die at home in a warm bed. That being said, move forward cautiously on this one, Wolf. The powerful tend to make and break the rules as they please, and they have little regard for those that they use along the way. And so to logistics, Captain. I'm fairly sure that Lieutenant Godfridsson is here on leave. Perhaps we could appoint him as your second-in-command? I believe that you two worked together before— that job on the lakes, as I recall? Sterling work and very cunning indeed."

"Godfrid is a fine officer, solid under pressure. I would be happy to have him."

"I could also give you Sergeant O'Neill; he's still as tough as ever. I think that warhorse was around when you were a young man forging your way up through the ranks?"

"A good man to have at your back," agreed Wolf, remembering the seasoned campaigner. "I'd be glad to have the benefit of his experience."

"Sound thinking. 'A wise king has many counsellors'. Give me a week to organise the rest of the men," concluded Sten, rising to leave.

"Better make one of them a woman," added Wolf as they walked. "It might be advisable to have a female operative along to control the target. We don't want to risk damaging expensive goods."

"Blade is in town," suggested Sten as they neared the door, "but maybe —?"

"No, Blade is fine," answered Wolf, quickly dismissing any suggestion of reticence on his behalf. He and Blade had history, a brief romance, but that was long ago. First and foremost, Blade was a Ranger and lethal with a sword. As to whether her name could be attributed to the sharpness of her blade or the quickness of her tongue, few could say; fewer still had been prepared to ask her over the years, reflected Wolf with a rueful smile as he quietly slipped out into the night.

Chapter Four

PREPARATIONS

A small church bell chimed softly, insistently, summoning the monks to evening prayer as Amergen followed Brother Kevin across the monastery grounds in the fading light of day. Amergen noted how well Saint Finbarr's monastery had continued to flourish under the protection of its most unlikely allies, the Danes. Thirty years before, the Danes had attacked the Cork monastery, along with much of Munster. Its savage work in southern Ireland completed, the Danish fleet had then headed off towards mainland Europe. But a small number of those ships later returned in peace and held talks with the monastery and the leading McCarthy clan.

These Danes were granted lands near the monastery, an arrangement that proved to be advantageous to everyone concerned. Over the years, the Danes had kept the peace and provided vital trade links between Ireland and Europe, exporting animal hides, wild animal pelts and wool, while importing essential salt from England and highly valued wine from France. In addition to this lucrative service, the Danes also provided safe sea-passage to the monks and local Irish nobles throughout Europe while secretly performing other more clandestine tasks, all for a healthy profit, of course. In addition to this mutually beneficial business and perhaps just as important, all three parties shared the same common enemy: the wild, unpredictable Norse. And whenever possible, the Danes, the Irish and the Church were all happy to work together to hasten their enemy's demise.

Brother Kevin knocked gently on the door of the small

monastic building, and on hearing a vague mumble, led Amergen into the congested room. Here, surrounded by shelves packed with scrolls and books, stood a cluttered desk where Abbot Ultan industriously scribbled, barely aware of his guest.

"Ah! Amergen, my favourite pagan," beamed the aged monk, finally tearing himself away from his work. "And how are you, my old friend?" asked the abbot, pouring Amergen a cup of wine.

"Tired."

"Well, Counsellor, did you find your wild man?" asked the abbot eagerly.

"Eventually. He's not an easy man to track down. And then, there were the wolves."

"Wolves?"

"Never mind. It's a little hard to explain."

"So, will he do it?" pressed the monk.

"It took a little persuasion. But yes, he will do it."

"Does he suspect anything?"

"No, I don't think so. But even if he does, he knows his options are limited."

"Excellent!" purred Ultan. "And is there any news of the girl?"

"I think I finally know where she is," answered Amergen wearily, daring to hope that his long search was almost at an end.

"But surely that's wonderful news!" responded the abbot excitedly. "Is there still time?"

"I hope so."

"I will pray for you both, even though you are an obstinate pagan and she is… well... I will pray for you both nonetheless," offered the elderly monk with sincerity.

“And what of your tame Dane?” asked Amergen tentatively. “Will he do what we have asked?”

“The Danes are pragmatists and businessmen first and foremost. He will carry out your plans precisely as you have laid them out, for a price of course. But Jarl Arne is a curious man. A clever man, even, and he would like to meet the man who pays him such vast sums of gold. Have no fear, Amergen; I have only told him what he needs to know. Brother Kevin!” The door creaked as it opened wider. “Please bring in our Danish guest.”

Jarl Arne, a Danish word which meant ‘eagle’, was aptly named. Dressed entirely in black as was the custom of the Danes, the tall man seemed to glide into the room, his sharp eyes scanning all before him like a wary predator. The abbot handed the Dane a cup of wine and indicated a seat, then introduced Amergen to the Danish leader.

“So, this is the spider that spins such intricate webs,” said the Dane, not unkindly, with a small salute of his cup. “It seems that we are to do business together.”

“And this is acceptable to you?” asked Amergen, trying to gauge the jarl, who was quite clearly a highly intelligent man.

“Your requests are, shall we say, a little peculiar. But your gold is most acceptable,” stated the jarl with a small nod towards the abbot, who had facilitated the transaction.

“You have secured the Norse ship, equipment and clothes that I have requested?” asked Amergen, boring down into the details of the deal.

“Indeed. A fine vessel, even if it is Norse,” conceded the big Dane. “We found them prowling along the Irish coast. So we relieved them of their ship and everything else, even their golden locks. Now they are our thralls and dig our fields, all dreams of gold and glory long forgotten. The captain had even taken along his young son on his first raid. The boy is now a slave in my household and sleeps by the fire with my hounds and fights them fiercely for any tossed scraps. I am not an unreasonable man."

"The clothes have been thoroughly cleaned here by our monks," reassured the abbot. "And Jarl Arne has looked over the weapons, sharpened them and made any repairs that were necessary."

"Will the ship be in position at the appointed time?" continued Amergen, offering a nod of thanks to Abbot Ultan.

"It will," said the Dane simply.

"And you are content to make the journey afterwards?"

"Content is perhaps too strong a word," countered Jarl Arne politely. "But the risk will be reflected in the final price."

"Has Abbot Ultan spoken to you about the other matter?"

"Yes, he has indeed. And I will deliver your message as you have requested. I only hope that this Sami tribe are as hospitable as you seem to think they are. You do know how the Sami treat trespassers on their land?"

"I believe that they bend down two spruce trees and fix them to the ground. Bind the prisoner's hands to the treetops and then cut the ropes, thus releasing the trees," explained Amergen in graphic detail. "A most horrible way to die, I would imagine."

"Very nasty indeed," said the elderly cleric with a small shudder.

"For sure," agreed the big Dane with a shake of his head. "And if they really don't like you, they use four trees — one for each of your limbs!"

"That is why you must find the Sami shaman named Saras, and quickly. Once you have given him my message, he will ensure your safe passage. Besides, the Sami revile the Norse far more than they hate the Danes."

"I think that maybe you plan much mischief for our Norse friends?" said the Danish leader speculatively. "The details of which are, of course, no concerns of mine," he quickly added. "But if you do, then let us drink to your success," declared Jarl Arne, raising his cup. "Then we will haggle over the final payment. A 'tame Dane' is surely a rare commodity in these turbulent times, and as such, a very valuable thing."

*

Wolf walked up to the rugged headland that overlooked the ruined remains of the Fort of the Two Ravens as evening began to settle in. He was glad to have a little solitude and thankful for the silence. Once again, it felt good to simply listen to the sounds of nature: the rhythmic beat of the waves against the shore, the raucous screeching of the gulls as they hung upon the stiff breeze. The past few weeks had been hectic with planning and preparations, and while it had been great to catch up with some old comrades and meet a few new ones, Wolf was content to have a moment alone.

Before they had ridden out of Dublin, they had divided the squad of twenty Rangers into four units of five — Blade would follow later. Each section had left the town on a different day so as to arouse no suspicions. At a glance, the men simply looked like groups of hunters dressed in drab green buckskins, lightly armed with longbows, small side-axes, daggers and back-slung swords.

Under the command of Lieutenant Godfridsson, one detachment now lay hidden in the woods to the south of the old fort. Sergeant O'Neill's unit likewise watched the north as Corporal Hakon's group took cover in the forest and guarded the east. Wolf positioned his four men in a small ravine overlooking the shore to the west (Blade would make up the fifth whenever she arrived). Then they all simply hunkered down and patiently awaited Amergen's imminent arrival.

Wolf sensed that the men were on edge, which was understandable, given that the ambush seemed like an assignment better suited to a platoon of regular soldiers and not a task for shadow warriors such as the Rangers, who specialised in stealth, subterfuge and sabotage. Wolf also suspected that Commander Sten had quietly spoken to Lieutenant Godfridsson and Sergeant O'Neill, expressing his misgivings about the mission. They in turn had ensured that every man had been handpicked and well prepared for whatever might lay ahead.

Wolf felt uneasy about this location. Why, he couldn't really say, and yet there seemed to be something vaguely familiar about this place. Something sinister, something dark, as if an unholy deed still stained the tumbledown remains of the Fort of the Two Ravens. Then a soft footfall instantly broke Wolf's peculiar trance.

"I thought that you had given up this line of work?" said a woman's voice behind him.

"So did I," answered Wolf, turning to greet Blade.

"What brought you back?"

“Them,” said Wolf enigmatically, looking off towards the trees.

Blade followed his gaze, unsure of what he meant. But then Wolf always did seem a little strange when he was near the forest, thought Blade. As if he became some other person. Men — who on earth could understand such creatures?

“You look well.” Wolf softened his voice. “When did you arrive?”

“Just now,” answered Blade, casually accepting the compliment as an obvious fact. “They told me that you had wandered up here.”

“Did you have any problems on your way here to Thomond?”

“Nothing that we couldn’t handle,” replied Blade with a wry smile, tapping the handle of the sword strapped across her back.

“As usual. How have you been?”

“Busy. There’s no shortage of sword-work in this war-torn country for a girl with my exceptional talents.”

“I thought that you would have been married to a rich jarl by now and have suckled a clutch of even more lethal children?”

“Wolf! How could you say such a hurtful thing?” retorted Blade with feigned emotion. “When you know that I’m totally devoted to Sergeant O’Neill.”

A raven’s call, an alarm from a nearby sentry, abruptly ended their customary banter. Wolf threw back his head and mimicked the call in response, and then they both hurried down the hill to the remains of the fort.

They heard it before they could see it, rattling and clanking its way up what remained of the broken stone track that climbed up towards the ruins of the old fort.

"Hell's bells! The Vikings in Limerick could hear that bloody contraption," fumed Sergeant O'Neill. The wagon drew to a halt at the ruins and Amergen climbed stiffly down, leaving a nervous Brother Kevin to hold the reins.

"Could you not have made a quieter arrival?" asked Wolf, irritated by the unwanted attention such a commotion would surely attract.

"Some men hide in the forest, while others hide in plain sight," answered Amergen sagely, as Wolf's men emerged from the trees to investigate the disturbance. "Besides, who has any interest in an old wagon full of hay?"

"Is this our man?" asked Lieutenant Godfridsson with thinly veiled disbelief.

Wolf simply nodded, astonished by Amergen's reckless behaviour.

"What is this all about, Amergen?" asked Wolf impatiently. He and his men had worked hard to draw no attention to themselves and now Amergen had completely blown their cover.

"A word, Captain, if I may?" replied Amergen calmly, leading Wolf away from the wagon, beyond the earshot of his men. "Take a look at your men, at yourself."

"What is your point?" responded Wolf, with little patience for Amergen's riddles.

"My point is this: that you and your men appear to be exactly what you are: shadow warriors, Rangers. In short, mercenaries: men who can be hired by anyone who happens to be rich enough or powerful enough," stressed Amergen. "We have got to cast the blame for this abduction as far away from the kingdom of Thomond as possible. The very last thing that we need is King Mahon suspecting his Irish enemies, or worse, his Irish allies.

That would simply benefit our Viking enemies, and that's the very last thing that we want. In fact, we have to achieve the exact opposite and sow doubt and discord among the various Viking factions entrenched around the coastline of this beleaguered country. That way, we can keep Jarl Ivar guessing as to who really is behind all this for as long as we possibly can."

"Then what do you propose that we do now, at this late stage?" asked Wolf, seeing that he couldn't fault Amergen's logic but still a little perplexed as to why the little man hadn't mentioned all of this a damned sight sooner.

"That, Captain Wolf, is where my unruly wagon comes in," smiled Amergen, and then he called to Brother Kevin to begin removing the hay.

The hay was quickly unloaded and piled to one side, revealing the neatly stacked sacks of washed Norse clothing which Amergen had purchased from Jarl Arne at Saint Finbarr's monastery in Cork. Wedged between the bulging bags were shields, chain mail, axes and an assortment of other Norse equipment.

"We'll hardly be expected to wear those flea-ridden clothes?" muttered Ranger Campbell, a Scotsman who was always quick to complain.

"In my considerable experience, Irish fleas have always been well able to handle Norse fleas," expounded Sergeant O'Neill, eliciting a few laughs. "But if you're saying that Scottish fleas just aren't up to the task, well then, that's a different matter!"

Ranger Campbell had nothing further to say on the subject, nor did anyone else, so the Rangers quickly got on with donning their new Norse disguises, finding a great deal of hilarity in the whole affair.

“This one is for you, Wolf,” said Amergen, hauling out a sack from under the wagon seat. “This gear belonged to the ship’s captain.”

“And the rest of the payment?” pressed Wolf.

“It awaits you in a secure place, after the task is completed.”

“What’s in that other sack?” asked Wolf, mildly curious, pointing at the second smaller bag still tucked under the wagon seat.

“Something of no concern right now,” dismissed Amergen, hastily climbing up into the back of the wagon to rearrange the sacks which now held the Rangers gear as Brother Kevin began firing up the hay. Wolf began to wonder just how many steps ahead of him this cunning little man was — too many by far, he didn’t doubt. “Quickly now, Captain,” said Amergen with some urgency, glancing at the sack that still lay at Wolf’s feet. “We don’t have very much time.”

Chapter Five

VANOMON

Vanomon's stronghold stood on the opposite side of the Nordic fjord, well away from the sprawling shipyards with their acrid smells and continuous noise. The drum of such industry was in itself music to Vanomon's ears, but the endless moaning and wailing of the slaves was utterly tiresome. Through the arrow slit, Vanomon surveyed the bustling shipyards, which lay beyond the narrow inlet, with a great deal of personal pride. The jarls had been reluctant at first, but King Algar had seen the potential of Vanomon's expansive plan immediately.

The extensive shipyards, which stretched down the gravel beach as far as the eye could see in the evening light, had been a massive undertaking. One section of the northern shore contained a long row of hauled-out ships, their hulls being scrapped down and recaulked with a messy mix of sheep's wool dipped in pine resin. Such work was best suited to the small nimble fingers of the younger boy slaves. Another area of beach held a large number of new ships with their keels already laid and the planking well advanced up either side of each boat. Further along the waterfront stood the timber yards where the wood was cut, shaped and prepared for the ships already under construction. In the midst of this flurry of timber work stood several forges that were never idle, spitting out an endless supply of ships' nails, the essential component of these clinker-built ships.

This lethal mix of fire, dried timber, resin and pitch was of course a constant source of worry for Vanomon and the sentries who patrolled the torchlit shipyards at night. The possibility of a sudden attack by Danes or rival Norse kings was of much less concern to the guards, as the sheer high mountains flanking the fjord made the possibility of a swift attack by land most unlikely. Likewise, it would be next to impossible to enter the long, narrow inlet that led to the shipyards without being spotted by the sentries dotted along the mountaintops on either side of the fjord, their signal fires ever at the ready.

In any case, even if an enemy naval force did press up the inlet, the enormous ring fort in the valley beyond the mountains that backed onto the shipyards held over a thousand highly trained men. That military complex was further away than Vanomon would have liked, but because of the mountains, it was the nearest suitable location that they could find to build Algar's huge fort. Still, the small garrison stationed at the crook of Svartrfjord would be able to offer some immediate protection, if the need arose, until reinforcements could be rushed from the fort — a hard day's march over the mountains or a half-day's sail by sea. When the work on the longships was completed, they would have a naval force of sixty dragon ships ready for war. The Great Heathen Army of the Danes which had wreaked such havoc on England only a half a century earlier had amounted to a little more than thirty ships and a thousand men. This Norse army would be twice that number, concluded Vanomon with satisfaction. And it would be large enough to smash the smaller neighbouring island of Ireland into submission, routing any Danes who had managed to gain a tenuous foothold in this coveted land.

Vanomon withdrew from the draughty opening as the light began to fade and walked back towards the fireplace, caressing his bald head, as was his habit whenever he was deep in thought. Vanomon had shaved off the thinning remains of his hair years before, when he had come to realise that what was really important was that which was within his head, not that which grew upon it. Likewise, he now dressed in simple black robes, not just because he was a warlock, but because he could not abide the vanity involved in selecting what colours to dress in each and every day. The stone keep in which he lived also reflected Vanomon's austere approach to life. And besides some essential furniture, an abundance of books and scrolls was all that decorated his large living quarters.

The warlock shivered as he threw another log on the fire. Perhaps autumn was coming early, or maybe it was just the cold emanating from the walls of the stone fortress. Building the squat tower in stone was a novel idea in these northern parts, and it had cost the lives of a great many slaves during its construction, due to exposure and exhaustion. Still, Vanomon was content to suffer this loss of manpower, as the stronghold ensured that he could remain near the all-important ships while not running the risk of being trapped by his enemies and burned alive in his timber longhouse —a favourite tactic of the harsh Norse.

The feared warlock had also kept defence in mind when he had chosen the rocky outcrop that jutted into the fjord as the location for his citadel. On the face of it, the sea-gate just above the waterline provided the only access into the stronghold's interior; the existence of a secret tunnel was known only to Vanomon. All the slaves who had worked on the tunnel's excavation had been promptly executed upon its completion.

Vanomon's bodyguard Hugin tapped lightly on the

door of his chamber and announced the arrival of Ragner Ragnersson, then he led the tall Norse warrior into the room before going to stand discreetly nearby. Ragner was considered to be a skilled fighter and a charismatic captain who was popular among his men. He was also tremendously proud of his golden-haired good looks; he was arrogant too, and clearly an ambitious man.

"Thor's balls! It's colder than Niflheim in here," complained Ragner, casting a disapproving look at the stone walls as he went to sit by the fire. "Got anything hot to eat in this place?"

"Girl!" called Vanomon. "Bring us some food." The girl quickly complied, bringing in two steaming bowls of stew and placing them on a table near the fire.

"She got a name?" asked Ragner, looking her up and down, a little taken by the slave girl's slender figure, refined features and peculiar almond-shaped eyes.

"Not that I know of; she doesn't speak," answered Vanomon, showing little interest in the matter. "You can roll your tongue back in now, Ragner. That one is not for you."

"Old enough to bleed, old enough to butcher, I say," countered Ragner, continuing to leer at the young girl.

"Have a care with that one, Ragner, or it's you who could be butchered," cautioned Vanomon.

"What do you mean?" demanded Ragner.

"All that I can tell you is this," said Vanomon reluctantly as he set his bowl aside. "She was taken on a raid in Ireland, the details of which are unclear. On their return sailing to Norway, one of the ship's crew tried to rape the girl. Before he got a chance to mount her, a rogue wave broadsided the ship, and the man cracked his head on the gunwale as he was tossed overboard with his trousers still down around his ankles and a bemused look on his face. The trousers and boots swiftly filled with water, dragging the man to the bottom of the sea. The captain wanted to toss the young woman overboard. But the crew were terrified that this was the work of the Norns — those female deities who rule the sea —who in turn might have vented their anger on them if they were to harm the girl in any way."

"Is that all?" Ragner dismissed this. "Seamen and their foolish tales."

"Well, no, that's not quite the entire tale," continued Vanomon. "The crew were keen to off-load the girl as quickly as possible and sold her cheaply to a farmer from up north who was unlikely to have heard any disturbing rumours about the slave…"

"And?" interrupted Ragner impatiently.

"And it seems that the farmer's son tried to hump the girl in the hayloft. And when he had his trousers down about his ankles as he struggled to ride her, a cornered rat bit him on the arse as it tried to escape."

"Hilarious!" barked Ragner.

"Well, yes, or it might have been, except the boy's head instantly swelled up and turned black. The boy died a most agonising death. The farmer buried his son and killed every rat in the barn he could get a hold of, and then he brought the girl to me, pleading with me to take the female and whatever accursed hex went with her.

"Maybe I will wait until she has put a little more meat on those bones before I break her in," said Ragner thoughtfully while eyeing the girl suspiciously.

"Perhaps that would be wise, Ragner," agreed Vanomon, dismissing the girl with a quick flick of his head. The welfare of the female slave did not necessarily concern the warlock, but there was something strange about the Irish girl which intrigued him. Could she have some sort of latent power within her or about her which protected the girl, wondered Vanomon. If she did, then he was determined to discover what it was and to possess that magic himself. "What news from Algar's Fort?" asked Vanomon, keen to have no further talk about the girl.

"The jarls complain about the cost of all this, the warriors' whinge about the endless drills, and the whores complain about being overworked. In short, nothing new," reported Ragner, tossing his empty bowl onto the table.

"Any of the jarls complaining more than usual?" asked Vanomon casually.

"Jarl Gunn has plenty to say. He never stops whining," answered Ragner distractedly as he wrestled with a piece of meat that was stuck between his teeth.

"About what, exactly?" continued Vanomon affably, casting a secret glance towards his black clad enforcer, Hugin, which told him to pay close attention to the details of Ragner's report.

"About you, mostly," answered Ragner, flicking the offending piece of meat into the fire.

"How so?" probed Vanomon.

"He reckons that you're too close to King Algar. And that a warlock shouldn't have so much input into military matters; that is the business of jarls."

"I see," reflected Vanomon.

It was no more than he had expected. The jarls had been resistant to the whole idea from the start, unlike the king, who saw the merit of the massive fort, where a large army could be centralised and trained for one common purpose. For too long, each jarl had conducted his own hit-and-run raids, snatching a handful of wealth and considering it a success while not seeing the greater prize.

"Anything else?" pressed Vanomon.

"Well," began Ragner reluctantly, as he scratched his beard. "A lot of the jarls are threatening to take their slaves out of the shipyards and back to their farmsteads to get essential work done before the winter sets in."

"But then the ships wouldn't be ready for the invasion in spring!" snapped Vanomon angrily. Vanomon had already suspected that with King Algar off fighting rebels in the north, some of the jarls would seize the opportunity to slip back into their old ways.

"I know," appeased Ragner.

"Is Jarl Gunn behind this too?" persisted Vanomon.

"Look, I don't share pillow talk with the man, Vanomon," answered Ragner peevishly, becoming irritated with all the questioning.

"Of course not, Ragner," placated Vanomon, smoothing Ragner's ruffled feathers. Ragner might be vain, selfish and an incorrigible womaniser, but he and Vanomon had forged an unlikely alliance over the years. Both men were also convinced that whatever their futures might hold, the very things that they sought lay in Ireland. And while Ragner had made no secret of craving all those things that most warriors usually sought — gold, glory, women and land — Vanomon kept his own dark purpose for wanting to conquer Ireland very much to himself.

"I believe that Jarl Gunn has a son?" asked Vanomon indifferently.

"Yeah, just the one, I think," answered Ragner,

belching as he stood to leave. "A little less jawing and a little more humping might suit the jarl better, I'm thinking," added Ragner sagely.

"Excellent advice," commended Vanomon as he walked Ragner to the door and bade the warrior goodnight. Then Vanomon called his bodyguard, Hugin, to him as he resumed his seat by the fire.

"What do you need me to do, lord?" asked Hugin as he stood obediently by Vanomon's chair. Hugin was a young man who had come up the hard way through the ranks of 'Odin's Raven's', a secret cult dedicated to serving the warlock. Like all the other captured boys, Hugin had started in the shipyards. The stronger boys fought their way out and into Vanomon's elite band of assassins. The weaker boys had other uses, and the dead ones littered the floor of the fjord, providing good pickings for the crabs.

"Blind the boy," said Vanomon coldly.

"In both eyes?" asked Hugin clinically.

"Yes, I believe so," said Vanomon after a moment's thought. "Perhaps the son's loss of sight might illuminate the father's foresight and quell his unruly tongue. But be discreet," cautioned the warlock. "We need to keep the other jarls on side. Make it look like a tavern brawl or some such thing," concluded Vanomon, dismissing his bodyguard with a languid wave of his hand. Hugin made a curt nod and quickly left.

Vanomon watched Hugin leave, and he wondered about the Irish boy. But then, it was long since Hugin was a boy. Long since he had taken the child and his mother from an obscure fort on a desolate Irish shore — the Fort of the Two Ravens, the mother had called it. The Irish witch was still seething in some dark corner of his fortress, dabbling in her lotions and potions and torturing any stray Christian priest foolhardy enough to try and spread his putrid message in the wild north. She had been outraged when Vanomon had told her that her son would start in the shipyards, like every other foreign boy. The boy would earn his position, or he would not, Vanomon had told her simply. As for the prophecy about her son, if it were indeed true, it would run its own course.

Still, the Irish boy had proved himself to be both tough and resilient, and he was now the leader of Vanomon's own personal guard, the feared 'Odin's Ravens'. The warlock had renamed the boy after one of Odin's favoured ravens, Huginn, although he had been careful not to use the bird's exact name so as not to offend Odin, the dark god to whom he was devoted. Gods, if slighted, can prove to be such capricious creatures, delighting in dabbling in the affairs of men, thwarting their schemes, and turning their battle plans on their head. Odin was, of course, the greatest trickster of them all, especially when it came to battle craft. And Vanomon desperately needed Odin's blessings for the conflict of the 'dragons' that lay ahead in that age-old rivalry between the tribes of the Norse and the people of the Celts.

As to whether 'a boy from the Fort of the Two Ravens would sway the war between the White Dragon and Red Dragon', well, that remained to be seen. Vanomon thought it unlikely, but he would keep Hugin close by him, just in case.

Chapter Six

TRAPPED

Wolf tethered Balor with the other horses in the hollow behind the hill, their warm breaths pluming in the cool morning air. Then he strung his longbow and weaved his way through the congestion of heather and gorse to meet with Sergeant O'Neill at the foot of the hill.

"Jaysus! You certainly look the part in that get up," complimented O'Neill, admiring Wolf's Norse outfit of black leather, a polished-steel helmet complete with protective eye guards, and a chunk of chainmail draped over the nape of his neck. "I'm sure glad that you're on our side."

"Any sign of them?"

"No, not yet, but we do have a clear view of the mountain trail right back down to the valley, now that the mist has burned off."

This had been one of the reasons why they had chosen Eagle's Pass to set the ambush. That and the fact that the wagon track had to squeeze through the narrow cleft hemmed in by sheer cliff walls on either side, providing them with a natural chokepoint, coupled with the strategic high ground overlooking the isolated pass. A sharp-eyed sentry gave the raven's call alarm, and the men quickly gathered their gear and crawled swiftly up to the cliff's edge as Sergeant O'Neill growled at them to keep low and take off their shiny bloody helmets! They had counted eight riders in total. This meant that the escort for Princess Aoife would be trapped and completely outnumbered, which should allow for the girl's easy abduction and a relatively bloodless affair.

Wolf had hidden his eight men along the crest of the ridge on the near side, overlooking the pass, and positioned Lieutenant Godfridsson with his section on the far rim. To satisfy Amergen's desire to cast the blame for the kidnapping onto a rogue Viking force, Wolf had selected Corporal Hakon and Private Orme to parley with the column; both men had Norse origins with thick accents to match, as did the two other Rangers who would close off the track at the rear of the escort, thus sealing the trap.

The princess, arrayed in a long green dress and a dark hooded cloak, rode at the front of the small company alongside the guard commander, who chatted away to her amiably, their voices quite clear in the still morning air. The troop escort showed no reason for concern as their weary horses plodded up the stony track and into the narrow pass until Hakon and Orme ambled out on horseback from a hidden cleft in the cliff face and squarely blocked their path.

"We just want the girl," said Hakon bluntly, pointing to the two rows of Norse archers on either ridge, arrows nocked and at the ready. There was a strained silence. And then there was a sudden flurry of movement as one of the lead guards whipped out a readied horse bow that was concealed beneath his cloak. The twang of a loosed arrow broke the quiet, and the missile thumped through Orme's eye and pierced the back of his head, knocking him backwards out of the saddle; the Ranger was dead before he hit the ground. The commander of the guard seized his moment and grabbed hold of the reins of the girl's mare, dug in his spurs and barrelled headlong into Hakon's horse, forcing the animal to stumble sideways into a steep gully and fall heavily, pinning its rider beneath it.

In an instant, the two leading guards sprang from their horses, one throwing himself down on the neck of the felled horse and preventing it from getting up while his comrade snatched an axe from his belt, raised it with both hands above his head and prepared to cleave Hakon's skull in two. Wolf's arrow drove deeply into the man's armpit, halting him with the axe still poised above his head, and his last words caught in his throat, and then he slumped down dead upon Hakon's horse. Clearly angry at the death of his friend, the man draped across the horse's neck drew his dagger and prepared to launch himself at Hakon, but three arrows struck the guard simultaneously, killing him outright. The other two mounted Rangers were now pinned against the cliff wall by the four remaining guards, who appeared clearly intent on the pair's destruction, and ultimately, their own. Wolf rushed to the crest of the ridge and raised his arm for an instant, then dropped it decisively, ending the assault on the two Rangers with a devastating hail of arrows.

Blade had reacted quickly when she saw the guard commander bolt with the girl's horse in tow, and in a flurry of mucky clods, she had emerged from behind the hill and galloped down the mountain track after the man. Blade's horse, unburdened by weight, quickly gained on the pair and as she drew alongside the girl's horse, she stood up in her stirrups, drew her sword from the scabbard strapped across her back, and sliced down hard on the towed reins. The commander looked down at the severed straps in his hands with disgust, flung them back and savagely spurred on his horse and fled. Blade brought Princess Aoife's panicked horse under control, soothing the animal with soft words, and then she turned her attention to the frightened young woman. "Don't look so worried, honey, you're with me now," said Blade with an engaging smile, "so let's play nice."

"Damn it all! This is a right mess," said O'Neill, shaking his head. The sergeant, like the other Rangers, found it hard to comprehend the guards' obstinate refusal to yield; their utter recklessness had cost the six soldiers dearly.

The Rangers moved quickly through the carnage, collecting their arrows and their dead. Corporal Hakon, meanwhile, was dusting himself down and appeared to be none the worse for wear, suffering from little more than a dose of wounded pride.

"This one's alive!" a voice called out, the Ranger pointing towards a man propped against the cliff with an arrow buried in his chest.

"Why did you not yield?" demanded Wolf, angry at the senseless loss of life.

"Orders are orders, Jarl," said the wounded man simply.

"You were ordered to die?" asked Wolf.

"We were ordered to protect the princess, with our lives if necessary," said the man with some passion, wincing at the effort.

"Even if you were surrounded and outnumbered?"

"We were ordered to defend the girl with our lives or not to bother coming back home with them," answered the man with a hint of bitterness.

"Who would give such an order?" pressed Wolf.

"Why Brian Boru, of course. He's a hard taskmaster and not a man to be crossed. And who are you, mighty Jarl, a Dublin Viking maybe?" asked the dying man, keen to know who had wrought such swift carnage on this fresh autumnal morning.

"Maybe," answered Wolf vaguely, distracted by the sound of horses entering the pass and relieved to see Blade's horse coming towards him, Princess Aoife's unrestrained pony trotting happily at Blade's side. "Bring this man some water and find him a cloak," commanded Wolf, "Then let's get out of here, and quickly!"

*

The mood in the camp was sombre. They had wasted little time at Eagle's Pass, quickly gathering up their belongings and securing Private Orme across the back of his horse with as much dignity as time would allow. At the scene of the ambush, they had also scattered a few stray Norse arrows to mislead any pursuers as to the true identity of the attackers, then they had ridden hard back to the Fort of the Two Ravens. Here, they had gladly ditched their Norse disguises, changing swiftly back into their familiar green buckskins as Brother Kevin gathered up the discarded clothes, sorting and storing each outfit carefully back on his rickety wagon.

Sergeant O'Neill had thought that it would be dishonourable to bury Private Orme in his Viking disguise, so they had hastily dressed him in his Rangers greens too, before taking him into the woods to bid him a quiet farewell. Lieutenant Godfridsson was out doing his inspection of the sentries, while Blade was off somewhere taking care of the girl, leaving Wolf and Amergen to nurse a small fire and mull over their blood-soaked day.

"So much for a little light resistance," chided Wolf softly, but Amergen remained silent. "Amergen, what is this really about?" pressed Wolf, suspecting that there was far more to all this than first met the eye.

"I had some idea that Boru would instruct the guards to put up some stiff resistance, just for show, but nothing like this," admitted Amergen, staring vacantly into the fire. "Six dead..."

"Seven," corrected Wolf, glancing towards the trees, where Ranger Orme was being laid to rest with little ceremony. "All to what end, Amergen? Why has Brian Boru done this?"

"To trap you," confessed Amergen. "To corner you and your men."

"But why? I thought that this was all about his sister?"

"Brian cares little about what happens to the girl," said Amergen frankly. "The truth of the matter is that Boru needed you and your men for something far more important, so he wanted to back you into a corner to be sure that you would comply."

Static seemed to crackle about them in the silence as Wolf struggled to absorb the depth and complexity of Amergen's betrayal, straining to keep a straight face.

"So now we are to be outlawed, fair game for every blade in the country?" said Wolf as calmly as his smouldering anger would allow.

"You have killed six of King Mahon's household guard and abducted his sister, a princess who is betrothed to Jarl Ivar in a crucial peace pact; I would say that it is most likely that you and all these Rangers will indeed be outlawed, with a large bounty placed upon your heads. I dare say that the Limerick Vikings will have a bone to pick with you too," said Amergen, not in the least bit perturbed about the part that he had played in this whole underhanded affair. "But I do believe that all is not lost."

"Of course you do, and no doubt you have another twisted scheme up your sleeve which will set all this right?" snapped Wolf, suppressing his deep desire to strangle the little man.

"Do not be angry at me. This plan isn't all of my making," protested Amergen, tossing another branch on the fire.

"I'm sure that you played your part well, Counsellor," answered Wolf testily.

"I make no apology for my role in all of this, Captain. We are at war with these Vikings, and Brian Boru urgently needed you and the Rangers for a particularly daring raid that very few other men could do," responded Amergen with conviction.

"Could he not have simply asked?"

"You, perhaps, he could have reasoned with, using your precious wolves as leverage," said Amergen, gesturing towards the trees. But your Commander Sten is a businessman who is not in the habit of hiring out Rangers for missions that are, well, how shall I put it...?"

"Suicide?" offered Wolf.

"Maybe it will prove to be so," conceded Amergen, "but if anyone can get in unseen, get this job done and get out alive, it's the Rangers."

"Enough of your honeyed words, Amergen. What is this task?"

"I cannot give you the exact details at this time, but I do have the authority to tell you now that every Ranger who survives this mission will receive a full pardon and be very handsomely rewarded for their heroism."

"More of your secrets," said Wolf sourly.

"This is a secret that I must guard for now as our enemy has spies everywhere, and the fate of Ireland may well depend upon my discretion at this point in time. Believe me when I tell you that there are too many men in this country who would sell their soul for a purse of silver, even a bellyful of ale and a warm woman on a cold night. I cannot run the risk of loose tongues costing us the element of surprise, which is perhaps the only real weapon that we have," replied Amergen firmly.

"You have a dim view of my men, Amergen."

"Not just your men, Captain Wolf. Look, all that I can tell you for now is that a ship awaits us in the northeast, which might be no bad thing, as I feel that we had best soon leave this country. King Mahon has a very long reach."

"We?"

"We cannot simply abandon Princess Aoife alone in the wilderness," reasoned Amergen.

"There you go with that word again. We?"

"You don't expect me to just simply leave her in the tender care of you and your men? Besides, I too have a part to play in the task that lies ahead."

"Look it's bad enough having you hampering our stride, Amergen, but this is no place for a princess. I did what you asked of me, what Boru paid me for. I abducted the girl unharmed; it's not also my job to mind her," argued Wolf.

"Tread carefully, Captain. Yes, you have done as you were hired to do, but should anything now happen to Princess Aoife, you can be assured that her brothers will hunt down every wolf in the kingdom of Thomond, skin them, and sell their pelts to the traders in England. Then they will hunt for you, Captain, you and all of your men. I say these things to you as a friend," Amergen said more softly. "Brian Boru is a man who will not be thwarted, and he is not the kind of man you would want for an enemy. But he could be a very powerful friend, Captain Wolf."

"Very well," relented Wolf after a moment. "We will take the girl with us, but she will be your responsibility from this point on, Amergen."

"Agreed, Captain."

"Furthermore, she cannot travel with us dressed like that; it would attract too much unwanted attention. She must blend in with the rest of us. And she may need to wield a weapon if we find ourselves in a tight corner."

"Leave that to me; I have made some provisions. You will not find her lacking."

"And one more thing. I will not have the men fussing over the girl; a distracted Ranger makes mistakes. And errors in our profession usually cost lives," said Wolf sternly.

"Perhaps another more experienced woman might be better suited to help the girl along the way and keep the men focused on their business?" suggested Amergen slyly.

"So be it, Amergen. You and Blade will watch over the girl and make sure she keeps up and causes no trouble. There can be no princesses on this trip, and she will have to follow orders just like everyone else," warned Wolf.

"You have my word, Captain Wolf," assured Amergen.

But Wolf put little store in the man's promises, for Amergen had proved to be as slippery as a freshwater eel right from the very start. That morning, Wolf and his men had set out to lay a trap. By nightfall, it was the Rangers who now appeared to be well and truly trapped.

“This much I can tell you, Wolf,” offered Amergen, rising stiffly from the fire. “Your past is in some way connected to this place. That’s why I brought you here to begin with, to see if it might spark any memories for you?”

“The Fort of the Two Ravens?”

“Yes, this sorry place.”

“I can’t say it means anything to me,” said Wolf, casting a speculative glance around the moonlit ruins.

“Perhaps the answer doesn’t lie in the past entirely — maybe it belongs to the future too,” reflected Amergen enigmatically, and then he disappeared off into the darkness to find Brother Kevin and the two women.

Chapter Seven

FLIGHT

A dank morning mist clung to the headland as Wolf stole away to bid a quiet farewell to Balor. They had corralled the horses within the tumbledown remains of the old fort to break their outline from a distance, the crumbling walls offering a little shelter from the persistent breeze that whipped in from the sea. Wolf fished out an apple for the big black horse, leaving it nestled in the hollow of his open hand as the powerful stallion deftly bit the apple in two, chewed and swallowed, then nimbly removed the other half, leaving a mouthful of saliva in its place. Wolf placed his dry hand on Balor's forehead as the soft footfall behind him came ever closer, and then he closed his eyes and wished his trusted friend a silent farewell.

"You killed my men," said the stern voice of a young woman behind him.

Wolf opened his eyes and paused for a moment, then turned to face his accuser.

"That was not my intention," answered Wolf, and it was the truth, but then he found himself slightly taken aback by Princess Aoife's beauty and the complete transformation in her appearance. When they had abducted the woman yesterday, she had been wearing a long green linen dress beneath a dark velvet cloak. Today she was clad in black leather trousers and a matching tunic. Although smaller, the clothes were strikingly similar to the captured Norse outfit that Amergen had given to Wolf, which would explain the purpose of the mysterious sack that had been left stowed under the wagon seat.

"I doubt that fact will be of any consolation to my dead guards," said Aoife archly, briskly drawing back her long auburn hair into a ponytail and tying it off with a strip of dark velvet.

"No, I'm sure it will not. Nor will it be of much comfort to my man," conceded Wolf, seeing little point in arguing over the matter; she was, of course, right. In any case, he had no desire to antagonise her further. The situation was difficult enough as it was. "I see Amergen's been busy," Wolf said more gently, trying to change the subject matter. "Black suits you."

"Oh," said Aoife, a little thrown, looking down at her unusual leather clothing and not entirely displeased by what she saw. "He said something about it belonging to the son of a Norse sea captain. It seems that Amergen was well prepared."

"That's one thing you can say about the little man," responded Wolf. The crafty fox, he thought to himself. "Do you know how to use those?" asked Wolf, pointing to the Viking boy's slender sword strapped across Aoife's back and the neat dagger clipped to the black leather belt at her hip.

"A little," replied Aoife evasively, "but Blade has promised to teach me some of the finer points."

"I'm sure she has. Are you two going to get along?"

"I think so."

"Good," answered Wolf. "Look, for what it's worth, I am sorry about your men," he added with some sincerity as Balor nuzzled at his back for more apples.

"Yesterday didn't go as either of us had planned, Captain." The princess thawed. "It seems that we both must play some part in Brian's elaborate scheme. Amergen has told me a little of my brother's double-dealing; Brian was always a clever strategist. Did your man have family?"

"They will be provided for."

"That is something, I suppose," concluded Aoife. Content to be done with the thorny business, she then turned to leave.

"And what are we to call you now?" asked Wolf.

"What do you mean?"

"Well, it's most likely that the half of Munster and the Limerick Vikings are looking for you as we speak," speculated Wolf. "We can hardly continue calling you Princess, or even Aoife for that matter."

"I see what you mean," reflected Aoife briefly, then she noticed Wolf's longbow and quiver of arrows resting against a clump of moss-covered stones. "May I?" she asked. Wolf gestured towards the weapon and Aoife brushed past him, leaving the light scent of lavender lacing the air. The young woman took up the bow, selected an arrow, and then placed her feet perfectly. Aoife threw an expert eye down the shaft, and then nocked the arrow on the string. She drew back the bow with surprising ease and rested the taut string against her pursed lips, took a deep breath, held it, and then gently loosed the arrow. The arrow thumped into the side of the wagon in the near distance, causing Brother Kevin to leap out of the cart in a flurry of hay. Aoife raised her hand apologetically to the frazzled priest and handed back the bow to Wolf.

"Arrow: the name suits you," said Wolf with a slight tilt of his head, impressed by the woman's practised skill.

"A princess must learn a great many things, Captain," said Aoife cryptically, then turned to walk away but paused and added, "I never asked for any of this."

"That makes two of us, Arrow," confessed Wolf, which was just about the only thing that they both had in common.

"Am I your prisoner, Captain Wolf?"

"On the contrary, I am your protector," countered Wolf smoothly. "And for now, you are an honorary Ranger, so I would ask that you follow orders just like everyone else; all our lives could depend upon it."

Arrow seemed content enough with Wolf's answer but remained silent, made a curt bow, turned, and swiftly walked away.

"I see that Amergen has been up to his tricks again," said Lieutenant Godfridsson as he approached Wolf at the ruins, casting an admiring eye at Arrow as she hurried down the hill.

"You don't know the half of it," said Wolf caustically.

"Dare I ask?"

"The ambush was simply a manoeuvre designed to catch us."

"Designed by whom?"

"Boru and that fox Amergen of course."

"A pretty elaborate trap," said the lieutenant, "but why go to such lengths?"

"It seems that they are in desperate need of our particular skills. This gambit with the ambush was to ensure that we would comply with their demands; as outlaws, they now have us where they want us," explained Wolf coldly. "And if we do not undertake this next task, we will remain outlawed — legitimate targets for every cut-throat, bounty hunter and mercenary that this dangerous land has to offer."

"Could they not have gone through the usual channels, like everyone else?" asked Godfridsson after a moment, managing to keep his cool Danish exterior.

"I very much doubt that Commander Sten would have sanctioned this action, whatever it is. From what I can gather, it looks like a one-way trip to me," said Wolf bluntly. "All that I can wring out of the little man at this point is that a ship awaits us on the northeast coast in a large inlet called Carlingford Lough."

Amergen had been reluctant to even part with that piece of information that morning, but when Wolf had told him of his proposed plan to get them all out of there, the little man knew that he had little choice but to relent. Only on the condition, however, that Wolf provided him with an escort for Brother Kevin on his journey back to the monastery. In fairness to Private Campbell, he had accepted the onerous detail of accompanying the monk with feigned good grace when Wolf had approached him earlier. Perhaps the man had been glad of the opportunity to rectify his earlier lament about the suspect Norse clothing. As to why the priest needed an escort was beyond him, but Wolf knew better than to ask Amergen for a straightforward answer.

"The location of the waiting ship is for your ears only, Lieutenant," cautioned Wolf. "Amergen is a very cautious man who greatly fears loose tongues."

"It seems a little ironic that our cunning counsellor has concerns over the trustworthiness of our men, but I will do as you say, Captain. My lips are sealed," said his second-in-command.

"It may be that the little man does have the right idea," reasoned Wolf. "From what I can glean from him, the element of surprise seems to be the only real weapon that we may have on this mission. And I would rather not lose that edge and my head to a tongue well loosened by ale."

"A fair point. We will keep a tight grip on the flow of information, so, but the men will need to be told something."

"Yes, they will, but this is neither the time nor the place for that," said Wolf firmly, noting that the mist was lifting and the morning was now well established.

"How do you want to play this?" asked the lieutenant.

"From what I can figure out from talking to Amergen, we are little more than a half day's ride in front of Mahon's troops and maybe a day or so ahead of the Limerick Vikings. Should they decide to enter the chase too..."

"And they all have fresh horses."

"Exactly, so if all of us try and make a run for Dublin, I don't fancy our chances of getting there before we are intercepted by our pursuers, and then all of this will have been for nothing."

"Are you thinking of dividing our force?" asked Godfridsson, looking as though he doubted that he was going to like the answer.

"Yes. It's far from ideal, I know," admitted Wolf, "but 'a good plan today is better than a perfect plan tomorrow', Lieutenant. So I want you to take half the men and all of the horses and ride hard for Dublin. Each man will have a spare horse, so you should make good time that way. Weigh down the riderless horses with any extra gear, and that might fool them into thinking that we have all fled to Dublin with the girl; only an experienced tracker might spot the ploy. As you near Dublin, break into smaller groups and stable the horses in our safe houses, then filter back into the town and plan your journey north to Carlingford Lough from there. Best apprise Commander Sten of the situation and inform him that the rest of the payment awaits us at Carlingford Lough upon the safe delivery of the girl."

"And what do you intend to do, Captain?" asked Godfrid, uncomfortable at the thought of splitting the platoon and sending its leader off on foot through the wild heartland of Ireland. There again, Wolf always did seem to have a peculiar edge when he was in the wilderness.

"I will take the remaining Rangers along with Amergen and Arrow, and we will strike out northeast through the midlands. We will keep to the woods, bogs and wilderness, land ill-suited to horses. And should your ruse with the horses not fool them and they do double back and try to track us on foot, hopefully our trail will have gone cold."

"Captain, why not just leave the girl here with Amergen and make a run for it with us? It's not as if this Amergen character has done us any favours."

"If the girl is not kept safe, Boru and King Mahon will not hesitate to destroy all those that I care for. And then they will hunt for us."

"I see," answered the lieutenant quietly, not pressing Wolf for any more details.

"Look, Lieutenant, I know that you didn't sign up for all of this, so you can step down when you get the men back to Dublin if you wish. I will understand," offered Wolf.

"I started this thing with you, Captain, so I will finish it, or it will finish me," answered Godfridsson without hesitation. "And I'm sure that the men will feel the same way too."

"Thanks, Godfrid," replied Wolf with genuine relief; he would need every good Ranger he could get, and

Lieutenant Godfridsson was one of the best.

"Besides, with great risk usually comes great reward. It's not like any of us expect to die peacefully in our beds, in any case. And if these Christians are to be believed, then 'those who live by the sword, will die by the sword', and I've got no problem with that," reasoned Godfrid pragmatically.

"Perhaps there is a little truth in what they say," agreed Wolf. "But let's make it bloody hard for these bastards to kill us. Assemble the men, Lieutenant."

Stony-faced and silent, the officers and men formed in a circle in the centre of the ruined fort as a weak morning sun hung low in a watery sky.

"Despite our best efforts, men, the ambush did not go as well as we would have liked," began Wolf, his voice clear within the closed circle of Rangers.

"Crazy Munster men," muttered someone, probably a rival Leinster man.

"But brave ones all the same," qualified another, most likely a Munster man himself.

Wolf let the men mumble their thoughts out loud for a minute, and then he interceded.

"Men, Rangers deal with reality, not with things that might have been," said Wolf forcibly, casting a hard glance around the circle and putting a swift end to the grumbling. "Right now, we are too many and not enough. And if we take flight without thinking, we will most likely fly straight into trouble and find our ugly heads on the end of sharpened poles before the week is out."

"Too true, Captain," said someone after a few of the men gave a little dry laughter, "so what should we do now?"

"Rangers, there is a time for talking, and there is a

time for action, and right now we need to move, and move damned quickly," said Wolf decisively. "Lieutenant Godfridsson's section will take all the horses, pick up the Great Road that stretches towards the east, and ride hard for Dublin. Our unit will strike out northeast on foot through the midlands, and with a little luck, we will all regroup on the other side of this. The lieutenant and I will explain as best we can the predicament we now find ourselves in when the time allows, but this is neither the time nor the place for such talk."

It was clear from the mood of the men that they would be happy to be on the move again, glad to put this eerie place and the spoiled mission very far behind them.

"Ranger on the trail!" spoke out Wolf strongly, placing his clenched right fist over his heart in salute — a tribute reserved for fallen comrades.

"Ranger on the trail," echoed Sergeant O'Neill as he and the rest of the men replicated the salute in memory of Private Orme. With hand on heart, they showed that they honoured the dead Ranger while they called out to his god and to other fallen Rangers to watch out for another 'Ranger on the trail'. But the salute also meant much more than that. A clenched fist also signalled their strength and their defiance towards their enemies. Those few simple words likewise reminded each man that they were still Rangers on the trail of life, and if they did not put their loss squarely behind them and focus on the task at hand, then they too would soon become Rangers on the trail of death.

The men were steely-eyed now, and an air of determination surged through the band of Rangers. Nothing energised a man more than a struggle for his own survival, especially when the outcome of that fight still hung perilously in the balance.

“Prepare to move out,” ordered Wolf, and then beckoned to Sergeant O’Neill.

Chapter Eight

JOURNEYS

The camp was a hive of activity on that crisp autumnal morning, with everyone keen to be gone from the unsettling ruins of The Fort of the Two Ravens. Eight of Wolf's Rangers had taken themselves off to one side and were busy reconfiguring their equipment for the long trek ahead.

"Leave whatever gear you don't need on your horses, lads. Remember, 'ounces equal pounds and pounds equal pain'!" stressed O'Neill. They had of course heard all of this before, but there was always a certain comfort in hearing the sergeant's well-worn mantras repeated before each mission. "Travel light, you travel fast. And be sure to grease those blades, men. There'll be rain before the day is out." The Rangers took it all in their usual methodical stride and stayed focused on rearranging their kit. In addition to their regular weapons — sword, dagger, a longbow and a short axe — they would also carry their dark green cloaks, tightly rolling them into a bolt of cloth and slinging them across their backs. "And make sure that nothing rattles..."

"Or that nothing shines," finished off someone laconically. Fewer things were more lethal to a stealth warrior than an ill-timed rattle from metal equipment or an inadvertent reflection off their gear.

"Didn't I train them well?" quipped O'Neill to no one in particular, getting a few wry smiles from the men.

Blade, Wolf's ninth Ranger, was over at the wagon with Arrow, riffling through the Viking gear stored beneath the hay for a shoulder strap which would also allow Arrow to carry her dark cloak on the journey. The thick velvet cape might keep the girl warm at nights, but it could seriously hamper her during the long arduous march that lay ahead if it wasn't properly stowed.

"There, that's it," said Blade with satisfaction as she took a step back to admire her handy work, having adjusted the strap on Arrow's shoulder. Then she frowned. "Honey, you have a face as white as a full moon on a clear night, and at a distance you'll be just as easy to spot. We'll have to break up that outline somehow," declared Blade. Then she stooped down and dipped her fingers into the cart's axle grease and spread several black streaks across each of Arrow's cheeks. "Perfect!" exclaimed Blade, then noticed the smouldering look of anger on Arrow's face. "Look! Now we're sisters," added Blade hastily after quickly applying similar markings to her own face. Arrow, silent and stern-faced, bent down and daintily dipped her forefinger in the messy grease and then dabbed the tip of her finger on the end of Blade's nose.

"Now we're sisters," said Arrow with complete seriousness, and then the two women erupted into laughter, lifting the mood of the camp in an instant.

"Hey, what about me?" called over O'Neill.

"You're dirty enough, Sergeant," jested Blade.

"Aye, but you do say it so beautifully!"

Corporal Hakon, on the other hand, was not having quite so much fun. In a manly effort to put his equine embarrassment at the ambush firmly behind him, Hakon had adopted a no-nonsense approach to organising the horses for Lieutenant Godfridsson's patrol. Balor was having none of it; sensing the man's heavy hand, the powerful stallion was giving the corporal a torrid time until another horse handler with more soothing skills took charge of the agitated horse. Lieutenant Godfridsson heard the commotion and left them to it, continuing with his thorough check of the other horses — tightening cinches, securing straps, and ensuring that the long halters that they had rigged to the riderless saddles for the trailing horses were properly tied off.

Amergen was deep in private conversation with Brother Kevin at the back of the wagon, slipping the monk a purse of coins when he thought that no one was looking. Private Campbell, not quite sure where he should be, took himself up to the front of the cart and began harnessing the docile workhorse, suffering the good-natured hazing from his fellow Rangers with stoic acceptance and informing them all that the next time they met him, they should all address him as Brother Campbell. Furthermore, given his new calling in life as a protector of monks, if he ever did manage to have a say in such things, he would ensure that not one of their hairy arses would ever sit in heaven, Valhalla, or any other bloody paradise for that matter.

Alone with his thoughts, Wolf drifted up towards the ruins one last time, determined to wrench out some vestige of a forgotten memory from this brooding place. It was of no use; he could recall nothing of his past here. Not that he could remember much about his childhood, in any case. And yet Amergen had said that Wolf's past was in some way connected to the fort, but then the little man had said a lot of things. Still, what could Amergen have meant when he said that the answer to Wolf's past could well belong to the future? Could it somehow be involved in what lay ahead? Was the answer to be found at the other end of Wolf's quest? A faint movement at the tree line caught the corner of his eye. It was Willow and Shadow. His wolf siblings had sensed that the time had come for the Rangers to move out. Wolf pointed towards the northeast, and the two wolves silently withdrew back into the woods.

"Prepare to mount up!" called Lieutenant Godfridsson below, prompting Wolf to abandon his fruitless search at the ruined fort and make his way back down the slope.

"Mount up!" ordered the young officer and then swung lithely up into the saddle.

"Good speed, Lieutenant," offered Wolf.

"See you on the other side, Captain," answered Godfridsson with an easy smile and a curt nod, then tucked his spurs into his horse's flanks and led the whole noisy cavalcade down the shattered stone track until the small column finally disappeared out of sight. The absence of their friends, their horses and half of their force now fell heavily upon the men, giving them a powerful urge to be gone from this peculiar place. With little more to be said, Wolf nodded to O'Neill to lead out their diminished band. Wolf was glad to be finally turning his back on the ruined remains on the crest of the headland, content to let The Fort of the Two Ravens hold onto its sorry secrets, whatever they were.

"Move out," said the sergeant without fanfare, and they all filed silently into the forest.

The first signs of autumn were everywhere now. Having sensed the cooler nights and shorter days, some trees were already partly stripped in preparation for winter, others a little less so, while many appeared reluctant to relinquish the first of their russet leaves. But the forthcoming winds would soon take care of that. The seasonal harvest of seeds, acorns and berries for the forest's hard-pressed residents had also begun to appear, luxuriant red holly berries starting to add a dash of colour to the drab surroundings as rich clusters of deep purple elderberries hung heavy from their branches. Wolf's unit instinctively veered towards the higher ground and the cover of the evergreen pines and spruce trees, picking out deer trails and fox runs to follow as they struck out towards the northeast.

Wolf had selected the two O'Donnell brothers from the wild hinterland of Tirconnell in the northwest of Ireland to serve as scouts. The two young men were natural hunters and uncanny trackers who could probably track a duck across a lake on a winter's day. Cormac, the elder of the two, Wolf deployed as an outlying scout, posting him well forward of the main party. He then stationed Conall, the younger brother, well behind the group so that they would have some advance warning of anyone following closely on their tails. Conall would also sweep their trail clear of the more obvious signs of their passing.

O'Neill, Wolf placed at the head of their single-file formation, while he took up a defensive position at the rear — a likely point of attack. His rearguard overview also allowed Wolf to better assess the dynamics of their small band as they moved rapidly forward and to determine its strengths and its weaknesses. The seven Rangers at the core of the group were eager to cover ground, but they checked their pace a little to allow Arrow to catch her breath. All the while, they softly encouraged the girl, offering their support when it was needed and quietly pointing out any hidden hazards on the trail as they silently forged ahead. Amergen displayed his usual wiry strength and agility despite his white hair, and not for the first time, Wolf found himself wondering what age the man really was. The little man stayed close to Arrow and Blade and appeared to share a good rapport with them both. Amergen also seemed keen to promote the friendship between the two women; perhaps he thought a strong bond between the pair would greatly benefit Arrow on the hard two-week hike that lay ahead.

They came to the other side of the forest at noon and paused to stare at the strangeness of the barren land which stretched out before them, called the Burren. The Burren, or 'Great Rock', was an expansive plateau of limestone rock that had split into large, irregular squares in between which had gathered a unique array of stunted plants, which had gained a tenuous foothold in each trench's meagre layer of soil.

"Hardly ideal," said O'Neill disparagingly, not much liking the lack of cover.

"Hardly," agreed Wolf, but the area of bare terrain was far too great to skirt around. "The rocky ground will help to hide our tracks," he offered hopefully.

"True, but let's be careful where we put those traceless tracks," cautioned the sergeant, eyeing the hazardous cracks with suspicion. They moved out cautiously onto the peculiar table of rock as the uninhibited wind swept freely in from the nearby Atlantic, doing nothing to ease their sense of exposure. It was a truly wild place with little evidence of human habitation. Wildlife was sparse too, but it was there to be found when they looked closely. Stunted ash and hazel peppered the bleak landscape, while dwarfed hawthorns also clung tenaciously to life, providing a little cover for the resilient wrens and skylarks that had made this place their home. The wide splits in the rock sheltered all types of plant life too, with fescue grass, maidenhair fern and an assortment of unusual herbs all finding nourishment there. They in turn provided excellent grazing for the abundant mountain hares that darted nervously about the upland, trying to avoid the ravenous attentions of the energetic stoats.

"We should cross Thomond's border into Connaught by evening," said Amergen with optimism, having stalled so that he could walk alongside Wolf.

"That would be a start," answered Wolf, not sharing Amergen's sense of relief. If they got caught out in the open like this, it wouldn't matter whose territory they were in. Out here, they could easily be mistaken for cattle raiders or a rival tribe on the hunt for women and slaves. Besides that, Thomond and Connaught were allies, albeit uneasy ones, so they could expect little mercy from either. In short, they needed to get to cover, and quickly, or their situation could go badly wrong in more ways than one.

"The Shannon is going to be a major obstacle, Captain," continued Amergen with the air of a man who was out for a country stroll. "Have you given the matter much thought?"

Wolf looked at the counsellor incredulously for a moment and then he remembered where he was walking and refocused on his footing. Wolf had, in fact, done little else but think about the predicament; crossing Ireland's longest river, which was in effect Connaught's ancient border with Leinster, was going to be a serious problem, as the powerful waterway was both wide and deep. On their way to the old fort prior to the ambush, they had forded the mighty river on horseback further south, and not without some difficulty. Now they would need to find another crossing well away from Thomond, one that they could make on foot.

"The footbridge at Clonmacnoise monastery near the centre of the country is our best bet. We should get there in four to five days depending on what kind of pace we can set," said Wolf, looking pointedly at Arrow.

"Don't worry about the girl. She's tougher than she looks," reassured Amergen, catching on to Wolf's meaning. "She has the blood of kings in her veins."

"It's the blood that's seeping into her footwear right now that concerns me," answered Wolf, gesturing towards Arrow, who was now struggling to walk in the high, unfamiliar boots.

"Can we stop soon?" asked Amergen, rightly concerned by what he saw.

"Can you do something about it? We still have a long way to go."

"Yes, I'm sure I can find some herbs here to make a lotion that will ease the pain and help to heal her feet."

"When we clear the border, we can rest for the night," said Wolf, assessing the faltering light as Amergen hurried off to gather his herbs.

At dusk, they gladly left the Burren's surreal landscape behind them and quietly slipped across Connaught's porous border with Thomond. Cormac returned with the fading light and told them of a deserted cottage just over the brow of the next hill, nestled in the lee of a secluded glen which was fed by a freshwater stream. As if in strange synchrony with his brother's movements, Conall came into view with a brace of plump hares proudly draped over each shoulder.

At least they would eat and drink well tonight, thought Wolf. They had certainly earned it, Arrow most of all.

Tomorrow they would press deep into the heart of Connaught territory, where there was no shortage of wilderness, and for the green-clad Rangers, that all important cover of trees and scrub. Wolf hoped that tomorrow would bring them just as much luck as they had enjoyed this day when they had crossed the wide-open Burren undetected and unchallenged. But then luck did seem to have the perverse habit of giving with one hand and quickly taking back with the other, he reasoned cynically. In life, it was considered wise to seek the favour of the gods and not to incur their wrath, if such things were possible. Still, a man must also strive to create his own luck in this world and not leave too much resting in the lap of the gods, as these reserved gods might not always be listening, concluded Wolf as the night closed swiftly in. Then it began to rain softly, just as the wily O'Neill had predicted.

Chapter Nine

PURSUIT

The torches guttered in the wall sconces of the great timber hall as a chill autumnal wind darted in over the nearby River Shannon. In expectation of trouble, the king's hall at Beal Boru had emptied out with unusual swiftness that evening, leaving only King Mahon, his brother Brian, two slumbering wolfhounds and the ashen-faced guard commander who had somehow managed to escape from the disastrous ambush at Eagle's Pass.

"How can you stand there and tell me that?" asked King Mahon with stunned disbelief.

"My lord, we were outnumbered and..."

"How can you dare to stand there and tell me that!" roared Mahon, jumping to his feet to deliver his verbal assault. The two sleeping wolfhounds by Mahon's throne sprang up, looking angrily about them and then they growled at the guard, who was the obvious cause of this unwanted alarm.

"Steady, boys," soothed Brian, who was standing by the throne. "Go to the fire," he commanded, and the two lanky hounds trotted over to the warm flames and flopped down in a tangled heap upon the floor.

"Gone?! How could she be gone?" asked the king incredulously. "And my men?" The pained look on the guard commander's face said it all. "Lord God! All killed, my household guard. Those men were like family to me," sighed Mahon as he slumped down into his throne. "Norse, you say?" asked the king with a harsh edge to his voice, the cold thought of revenge slowly clearing his senses.

"By all appearances, my lord," answered Captain Mac Namara eagerly, glad to still be able to contribute to the conversation.

"Wait outside, Sergeant Mac Namara, I'm not finished with you yet," ordered the king. The demoted captain stalled for a moment, unsure if he had heard correctly, realised that he had, and then quickly left the hall.

"Who's behind this, Brian?" asked the king tiredly. A peaceable man by nature, sometimes Mahon found the weight of the crown a very heavy burden.

"It's hard to say, Lord King. The question is who has the most to gain by this kidnapping? Or it could simply have been a chance raiding party. It's still not too late in the year for Norse sea pirates to strike," offered Brian, trying to tease out all the possibilities.

"Could the O'Mahonys have planned this?" The long-standing enmity between the O'Kennedys in the kingdom of Thomond and the O'Mahonys in the neighbouring kingdom of Tipperary had been bitter and it had been bloody. That age-old feud between the two clans for the kingship of Munster had cost them their father, Kennedy, and two of their older brothers. It was a rivalry that the Danish leader Ivar had been keen to exploit, allowing the jarl time to fortify his river island stronghold before going on to establish the adjacent Viking town of Limerick — strategically positioned at the mouth of the River Shannon, a mere thirteen miles downriver from the O'Kennedys' fortress of Beal Boru.

"It's unlikely," answered Brian after a moment. "They're Ivar's staunch allies, and God's curse on them for it. So why would they want to snatch a bride already destined for Ivar's bed? That wouldn't make much sense."

"True," agreed Mahon, relieved for a brief moment that their sister hadn't fallen into the hands of their oldest enemy. "You were ever the thinker, Brian, a man for intricate strategy. That education with the monks at Clonmacnoise has served you well, Brother. How about the Dublin Norse then, or their Viking allies along the east coast? Could they be tempted to raid this far west?"

"It's a possibility," answered Brian, "but they don't normally fancy crossing the Shannon on land raids at this time of year; it makes for a tricky retreat. Still, they might make an exception to deliver a well-aimed strike at their old enemy, the Danes. Snatching Aoife could yield them a rich ransom while also humiliating Ivar on his own doorstep," he suggested.

"The truth of it is, we don't really have any idea who is behind this," concluded Mahon after a long pause. "For now, we had better tread carefully; our enemy could be closer than we think."

"I think that would be wise, Lord King."

"How do you suggest that we go forward from here, Commander?"

"I think that a compact force is all that is required for now. Best not go trampling all over our neighbours' territory with a small army; it might send out the wrong signal," cautioned Brian.

"God knows we have enough to deal with as it is," agreed Mahon.

"I will send out a war band at first light, my lord. We will soon pick up Aoife's trail and unearth the truth of this matter," assured Brian.

King Mahon nodded his assent as he rose stiffly to leave.

"You had better send an emissary to sooth Ivar's anger

and dampen his ardour. His nuptials will have to wait a little while longer."

"I will send an envoy at dawn."

"Bring her back to us, Brian," said Mahon as he paused at the hall doors, "and when you find the outlaws who took her, I want you to take them down, hard!"

"As you command, my lord."

"One more thing, Commander," added the king as he opened the door. "Send Sergeant Mac Namara with that patrol. If he proves himself worthy, he may well regain his rank. The prospect of redemption can provide a man with some powerful motivation."

Brian went to the fire and sat near the drowsy hounds, all three content to share in each other's silence. As he gazed thoughtfully into the glowing embers, Brian felt no sense of satisfaction in deceiving his brother about the ambush and the truth about Aoife's abduction. Mahon believed that the conflict between the O'Kennedys and the Danes of Limerick could be resolved by treaties, trade and a marriage alliance between the hoary Ivar and their younger sister Aoife. From bitter experience gained from fighting these Vikings, Brian knew otherwise. But Brian could not, nor would not openly defy King Mahon over this proposed union, as their division would simply play into the hands of their enemies. Yet neither could he stand idly by and watch Mahon make this futile offer of Aoife to their arch enemy — to the very man who had murdered their mother eleven years ago. In many ways, Ivar was little more than a cunning animal, hungry for territory, greedy for power and lecherous for women; he would simply abuse Aoife and use her as a political pawn to keep Mahon in check. If Mahon dared to attack his Limerick stronghold, Ivar would happily cut Aoife's throat without a moment's hesitation and toss her over the palisade right before their very eyes, if he thought that it might demoralise the Irish troops.

As children, the world had seemed like a very harsh place for Brian and Aoife when their parents and brothers had been murdered in a sudden attack by the O'Mahonys and their Danish allies, recalled Brian bitterly. On that dark day, they had clung to one another as bewildered youngsters, trying to console each other as they struggled to make sense of that harsh lesson. Anger soon replaced tears as plans formed to supplant sadness, and Aoife and Brian had vowed from that black day forth that they would always be there to protect each other. Moreover, they would also learn well how best to defend themselves and never be that helpless again. In time, they would exact their revenge on all of their enemies.

Until Brian had made his next dangerous move, he needed Aoife well away from Mahon's ill-conceived marital manoeuvres. For now, at least, he must entrust his sister to Amergen's care, the guise of anonymity and the protection of these elusive Rangers. A 'sheep among wolves' she might well appear, but Aoife had prepared well for a day such as this. Still, skill at arms alone would not be enough to defend her in these dangerous times, when the difference between friend and foe was far from certain. Wherever her journey with Amergen might take her, Aoife would also need to be 'as wise as serpents' too.

*

It was a cold day, a grey midmorning, dark banks of low-lying clouds rolling in from the southwest, drifting up over the Shannon Estuary and shedding steady sheets of rain over Limerick's huddled buildings. Most of the town's residents had reluctantly retreated indoors, while barefooted male slaves in ragged clothes laboured to unload the merchants' big-bellied knarrs tied up along the river-wharf under the cold gaze of hawk-eyed overseers, who were wrapped in warm furs with quick whips that were ever at the ready. On such wet days as these, the female slaves were put to other uses indoors.

There was a heavy silence in Jarl Ivar's hall as he digested the messenger's unsavoury news while gnawing on a meaty rib, the quiet only broken by the muffled sounds of resistance from a new female slave who was being broken in by Cuallaidh in a dark corner of the hall.

"Will you shut that bitch up!" yelled Ivar. "I can hardly hear myself think."

A low snarl from Cuallaidh and a stifled thud resulted in a whimper of pain and the faintest sound of sobbing from the compliant slave.

"Who could have done this, O'Mahony?" asked the Danish leader.

"Are you sure that they were Norse?" questioned the Irish king, stepping out from the shadows along the wall, having listened intently to the man's report. "What makes you so certain?"

"I am just relaying King Mahon's message," clarified the envoy. "We sent out a search party at dawn," he added, deftly masking his deep unease at being in the heart of his enemy's hall. It took a brave man or a fool to walk into the fort of a Danish jarl and tell him that Vikings had just abducted a young bride that was destined for his bed. "Their clothes, weapons and accents seemed to suggest so," elaborated the messenger in an attempt to ease the tension. "But then, we are no experts on your countrymen."

"The Norse are no countrymen of ours," snarled Ivar with menacing undertones.

"Perhaps we are done with this emissary?" interjected O'Mahony before the jarl's temper got the better of him. Besides, it would be unwise to discuss this business while Mahon's man was still in the hall.

"Get something to eat in the kitchens on your way out," said Ivar, remembering his royal manners.

"Have you pissed off the Norse in Wexford again?" asked the king of Munster when the envoy had left the hall. The proximity of their stronghold on the southeast coast of Ireland made them one of the more likely culprits.

"Not that I know of. Our Danish allies in Waterford keep a tight leash on them anyway," reasoned Limerick's Danish leader.

"So that leaves the Dublin Norse. What are your spies telling you? Are they in the mood for raiding these days?"

"Those lazy bastards are making way too much silver shipping slaves in and out of Ireland. What would they want with one scrawny princess — a ransom, maybe? The O'Kennedy brothers have quickly rebuilt their wealth this past ten years. Many have even been calling the younger one Brian Boru, Brian of the 'cattle-tributes'. Bloody upstart!"

"There is no doubt that the O'Kennedys are starting to regain their power. And perhaps the answer to all this might lie closer to home than we think?" suggested O'Mahony.

"What do you mean?" demanded Ivar, tossing the

stripped bone into the smouldering fire pit.

"As we well know, Mahon is a shrewd diplomat, and so he offers his sister in a marriage pact between the O'Kennedys and their near neighbours, the Danes in order to promote peace. At the same time, they quietly continue to rebuild their strength in order to challenge me for the Munster throne," explained O'Mahony. "Think about it, Ivar. It only stands to reason that the O'Kennedys secretly have little desire to wed their sister to a Danish jarl, the very person who brutally killed their mother and slaughtered half their clan."

"What you say may be true," conceded Ivar, "but if Mahon challenges you for the Munster throne, it would also mean confronting me."

"Perhaps the O'Kennedys plan to rid Munster of us both," speculated the Munster king.

What O'Mahony said made sense, but then maybe that's exactly what the king of Munster wanted him to think, considered Ivar carefully. These Irish kings could weave a trap just as easily as a spider could spin a web. Ivar kept his own counsel for a long moment, as he needed to make certain that this particular snare wasn't being laid for him.

"To find out who planned this ambush, we need to find the girl and the men who took her, and then we can pry the truth out of these thieves with sharp knives," said Ivar with resolve.

"And how do you propose that we do that?"

"The only way that we can now: to pick up Aoife's scent and follow it wherever it leads. And I have just the hound to sniff her out, Cuallaidh!"

Cuallaidh was Ivar's youngest son, and he was trouble, but then a weed does not consider itself to be a weed and thrives accordingly. Some men's sons strive to outdo their father's successes, while others are content to use and abuse their father's power; Cuallaidh happened to be the latter. Cuallaidh had always been quick to maim, rape and kill, secure in the knowledge that he was Ivar's son. Lately, though, he had become a liability, seeing little difference in killing one Irish man or the next just as Ivar was struggling to gain new Irish allies to add to his O'Mahony and O'Donovan coalition. Now, thankfully, Ivar had a task well suited to Cuallaidh's nasty skills, one that would take him and his cohort of cutthroats well clear of Limerick, for a while at least.

"Find these bastards, Son, and bring me back my bride, and you and your men will be richly rewarded," offered Ivar. "And when I'm done with the O'Kennedy bitch, I'll give her to you to play with."

Cuallaidh's answer to this added incentive was to give a slow, chilling smile. Cuallaidh certainly had his flaws, but he also had a tenacious streak, and once he was set on his quarry, he was relentless and well suited to the name that the Irish had given him in recognition of his cruelty: Cuallaidh, which meant 'wild dog'.

"And if you cannot bring back any prisoners, make sure that you cut every ounce of truth out of these raiders. I want to know who really is behind this abduction and why. Take Rasende with you too," ordered the jarl. "That berserker can find anyone's trail, no matter how cold it is."

Rasende's reputation as a fearsome warrior and an unnatural tracker was well deserved. Draped in animal pelts and invoking the savage power of the bear in his secret berserker rituals, most considered Rasende to be some sort of mystical Wild Man who was best avoided.

Very few were surprised that someone, somewhere, had fittingly named him Rasende, the Danish term for 'furious savage'.

Chapter Ten

EVASION

The weather was crisp, the skies bright and clear, while the wind was barely a whisper. They had left the stark lands of the Burren far behind them and pressed on deep into the heartland of east Connaught. They had moved silently and as swiftly as Arrow's grazed feet would allow. Amergen had done his best with the few herbs he had been able to gather in the Burren, but he would need to find some proper medicine soon to prevent Arrow's feet from becoming infected.

Wolf had posted Farrell out front as lead scout. The tough Connaught man knew this rugged terrain well, and the Rangers always utilized that type of local knowledge whenever possible. Alert and effective, Wolf had opted to leave Conall O'Donnell to take up the rear and 'dust' their tracks as best he could. Willow and Shadow ranged far out on their flanks, although Wolf suspected that the two wolves were spending a lot more time with another pack these days, which was only to be expected, as wolves will be wolves.

The going underfoot had been heavy, soggy and tiresome, but it would have been a whole lot worse if not for their skilled guide. Farrell had led them deftly through the congested pine forests, weaving trails across the expansive wetlands and picking firm paths across the treacherous bogs. He was a quiet, reserved and intelligent man, a very experienced Ranger who seldom spoke, but whenever Farrell did proffer one of his astute opinions, everybody duly listened.

They had arrived at the still shores of Lough Rea as a

lurid sun sat low in a magenta sky. Gratefully, they had slaked their thirst as they watched several large flocks of starlings weave intricate flight patterns above the lake before they eventually settled down to roost. The large lake was almost halfway to the Clonmacnoise monastery and that vital bridge over the River Shannon. And as the surrounding woodland could provide them with good cover for the night, Wolf had thought it best to call it a day.

Wolf's decision to camp for the night seemed to please everyone. Blade and Arrow had rapidly disappeared off down the shoreline to wash away the grime of the hard trek. The men retrieved coiled fishing lines and hooks from their gear and set them quickly to work. Amergen was particularly happy at their choice of location, as he knew of a small monastery called Saint Brendan's on the opposite shore where he was fairly sure that he could obtain some medicine for Arrow's ailing feet come the following morning.

They had encountered very little human life on their journey to the lake that day although they had occasionally glimpsed two horsemen on high ground in the distance. If the pair of outriders were searching for them, it was hard to say. Feeling relatively secure, they had risked a small fire to cook their fish, screening the worst of the flames with their cloaks and then dousing the fire straightaway. Well fed, refreshed and briefly warmed by the fire, Wolf had posted sentries as the autumn night swiftly fell, and they all quietly settled down to rest for the night.

At first light, Amergen had set off for the nearby monastery with O'Neill as backup. Wolf was ill at ease at this unwanted exposure, but he also recognised the importance of a potion for Arrow's feet. They were making slow enough progress as it was, and if her feet became infected, they would be going nowhere at all. Ostensibly, O'Neill had gone with Amergen to keep him out of trouble and to pick up some welcome supplies. But more importantly, he had gone to glean any useful information that might have drifted up from the south about their daring abduction and escape.

The early morning sunshine was a welcome gift at this time of the year, so they had gathered to wait in a small clearing in the woods where they could soak up the tepid heat. Farrell had gone off to reconnoitre the route up ahead, while the O'Donnell brothers took their turn on sentry duty, so Wolf allowed the remaining Rangers to rest and tend to their equipment. A bow that is left strung for too long can lose its effectiveness. Arrow went to pass by Wolf on her way to meet Blade, who was preparing two sword-length sticks of willow at the other side of the clearing, but then she paused and turned towards him.

"I may have been a little hard on you, Captain," said Arrow evenly. "Amergen has told me that you were simply carrying out Brian's instructions. It seems that you are in fact my protector, and not my captor."

"I'm glad that you see it that way, Arrow," answered Wolf. "How are your feet?" he asked, avoiding any further talk of the ambush.

"I'll survive," she said, looking down at her high calfskin boots. "They're not quite what I'm used to."

"I'm sorry I couldn't give you a horse. Too many tracks," explained Wolf.

"Not to mention a trail of easily followed dung! I do understand, Captain Wolf. It's hardly ideal horse country anyway," added Arrow, as she surveyed the wild country that surrounded her.

"She gives tough lessons," said Wolf, looking over towards Blade, who was trimming two hefty looking sticks for Arrow's first fencing class.

"So do I, Captain," replied Arrow enigmatically and then went off to meet her instructor.

Wolf thought it best to stay to one side to allow the rest of the men to relax and be themselves, so he sat against a nearby fallen tree where he could mull over his plans while idly listening to their barrack-room banter.

"Of course, the O'Byrnes are not just the kings of the Wicklow Mountains; my ancestors were once the kings of Dublin too," crowed O'Byrne. "That was until you lot came along." This last barb was aimed at Bergman, the only Norseman in the group. O'Byrne was a stocky bull of a man with a temper to match, and he had an endless capacity for stirring up trouble.

"Our clan can trace its ancestry all the way back to a chieftain who had wed a princess of the 'Sea-People'. She had left the sea to live on land," boasted O'Sullivan, a broad, hardened fighter from a craggy peninsula in the far southwest of Ireland.

"That's impossible," rejected O'Byrne bluntly. "Sure, mermaids are supposed to be good-looking!"

The others saw the humour in that slight, but O'Sullivan did not, mumbling something under his breath as he vigorously continued to sharpen his dagger.

"What I do not understand is why every second Irishman seems to be descended from a king or a mermaid or some other such fanciful thing," said Bergman mischievously. The big Norwegian was a skilled warrior and a natural seafarer who had a vast knowledge of the seas around the Western Isles and the jagged Scandinavian coast. They called him Berg for short, which was apt, considering that berg was the Norse word for 'mountain'.

"Ha! That's good coming from you, Berg," flung O'Byrne. "Don't all you Vikings claim to be descended from Odin? He must have been one bored god or one horny bastard to want to spawn you horde of heathens," reasoned the Irishman.

That got a laugh from O'Sullivan and Ferret, but Bergman scowled at this unholy comment. It was a bad business to be making fun of the gods.

"You big oafs and your outrageous claims," mocked Ferret. "The only thing that you were ever king of, O'Byrne, was a tavern." They all enjoyed that image, even O'Byrne. "I am the only one here who has ever been a king, Waterford's very own 'King of the Thieves'!"

The other three laughed heartily at that. There were very few men who could get away with calling that lethal trio 'big oafs', but they all had a soft spot for the little man and cut him more slack than most on account of his harsh childhood alone on the streets. Growing up as an orphan on the mean streets of Waterford was a hard life and a dangerous place for a fatherless boy.

"Laugh all you like, but I had to work hard to earn that title," continued Ferret undeterred. "There was no lock that I couldn't pick, no gap that I couldn't squeeze through and no purse that I couldn't snatch. The guards always wanted to beat me, the soldiers tried often to kill me and the priests — well, let's just say that they had other ideas, but I soon cured them of that," said Ferret with a malicious grin as he whipped out a wicked-looking knife.

Whoever had named the young man Ferret had done

well, thought Wolf. For this ‘King of Thieves’ could get in almost anywhere and steal just about anything. Still, to his credit, Ferret never stole from his friends. But like that little weasel, the young man had a wiry strength and could easily dispatch prey much larger than himself. And perhaps as a result of his brutal upbringing on Waterford’s Danish streets, he also resembled his namesake in a more chilling way, as this human ferret was a stone-cold killer too.

Wolf had worked with all of these men before, and they were all highly experienced Rangers who were no strangers to the boiling cauldron of battle. Whatever mission Amergen had in store for them, Wolf was certain that he could completely depend on every single one of them and that each of them would bring their own unique skill set to the challenge ahead. Some tasks would require the strength of a bear, others the skill of a wolf, but sometimes the expertise of a fox just might prove crucial. Regardless of their seeming differences, they were all Rangers to the core, loyal to each other and bound together by their utter determination to succeed, no matter how great the odds stacked against them. For they had all learned through many hard trials that ‘it wasn’t the size of the dog in the fight, but the size of the fight in the dog’ which could ultimately sway the day.

The men suddenly noticed that the sharp crack of the willow ‘swords’ had increased dramatically, as had the vocal exertions of the two women. The men were speechless. A skilled swordfight, even one with practice sticks, could be an enthralling contest to watch; between two capable women, it was truly captivating. Blade and Arrow both moved with speed, grace and precision, and it was obvious that the pair had been well drilled in swordplay. What shocked the men most, they couldn't really say. Was it seeing the consummate Blade being made to work so hard by her new student, or the fact that the unassuming Arrow had possessed such astounding ability all along? Arrow's stick broke in the ferocity of Blade's assault, and both women took a quick step back, heaving for breath, their eyes intently locked upon each other. Then they seemed to snap out of the white heat of the moment, gave each other a curt nod, and without another word, went their separate ways.

Blade went to walk past Wolf, sucking an angry-looking welt on the back of her hand. Wolf opened his mouth to say something, but Blade raised a menacing eyebrow and blasted him with a dark look, so Wolf thought better of it.

"Here ended the lesson," said Blade without further elaboration as she stomped past. As to what the actual lesson was and who exactly got it, was very hard to say.

Amergen and O'Neill re-entered the clearing and walked briskly towards them. There was something urgent about O'Neill's demeanour which made Wolf spring to his feet and give the two standard raven calls to summon back the sentries. Amergen was wearing a triumphant smile as he approached, holding aloft what looked to be some sort of unction wrapped in a ball of muslin. When he saw Arrow, he veered off towards her to get to work on her feet. O'Neill's stolid face told another story.

"Ferret!" called O'Neill, and then he tossed the small sack of supplies over to the young man, who acted as their unofficial quartermaster. Ferret needed no further instruction and got quickly to work dividing the stash of small oatcakes, apples and dried fish as the wiry figure of

Farrell emerged from the tree line.

"Trouble?" asked Wolf.

"Horsemen," answered O'Neill simply.

"Those two outriders that were shadowing us?"

"It's most likely them," agreed O'Neill. "They showed a lot of interest in us at a discreet distance. Then made a deliberate show of mounting up and departing from the monastery grounds at an easy pace, but a little later we saw them galloping off to the west."

Wolf considered all this for a moment while making a mental note of the return of the two O'Donnells, who had arrived back at the clearing.

"Get everyone ready to move, Sergeant," ordered Wolf. "No need for alarm just yet, but let's make it fast."

"Prepare to move out, lads, and smartly now!" called O'Neill sharply. "We might soon be having company."

"Farrell!" summoned Wolf, and the Connaught man left his food and was before him in an instant. "What way does the land lay ahead?"

"There's a good track heading northeast from the lake. It probably connects the monastery to the next village, Captain," explained Farrell, looking off in the direction of the trail and making a pointing gesture with his hand.

"Solid enough for horses?" asked Wolf.

"It is," replied Farrell slowly and then swiftly guessed Wolf's reason for asking.

"Is there another way northeast, perhaps a little less suitable for horses?"

"The Black Bog, maybe, but it's a dangerous place, Captain Wolf."

"Though not for you, Farrell?" ventured Wolf.

"No, not for me, Captain. I hunted there often in my youth; game was plentiful, as most people tended to stay out of it. I'm fairly sure that I can still remember the layout of the place. But they are bad lands for a horse or anyone weighed down by any armour or chainmail — swamps and sinkholes everywhere."

"Even so, you could guide us safely through?"

"I can if you all stay close and match my steps," responded Farrell earnestly. "And if they do try to follow us across the bog, we could pick them off one by one and dump the bastards down a sinkhole; they would never be found again."

"Good report, Ranger Farrell," commended Wolf. "Grab some food and get your gear. It's high time that we were out of here."

Suddenly, Willow's long, doleful howl of alarm echoed from the west, and Wolf knew with a terrible certainty that the warning was meant for them.

"Everyone, after Farrell to the Black Bog," commanded Wolf. "Now!"

Chapter Eleven

TRACKERS

The men were sullen as they gathered before the fresh barrow which had been heaped to one side of Eagle's Pass. The brooding sky and persistent wind that forced its way through the narrow gap did little to lift the mood of the platoon as they looked upon the cold cairn which now covered their slaughtered comrades.

"We thought it best to cover them up before the wolves and ravens came back for another feed, Captain," explained a local chieftain named McKenna.

"What of their weapons and war gear?" asked Captain O'Halloran.

"We buried all that with them; they will need them in the next life."

Captain O'Halloran thought the part about the wolves and ravens was probably true, but he very much doubted the rest. The chieftain was gambling that no one would have a mind to dig up these sorry souls for reburial, and even if someone did, McKenna would no doubt blame grave robbers for the missing weapons.

"Rest assured, McKenna, that King Mahon will hear of the honourable way that you have treated his men, and no doubt he will want to repay you accordingly," said O'Halloran evenly. The chieftain was unsure how to interpret that statement, so he simply grunted and went off to find his horse.

"Captain, I found this down between the rocks," said a scout and handed O'Halloran a stray arrow. "It looks like the Raiders had picketed their horses beyond the ridge, and their tracks seem to be heading off to the northwest."

"Black fletching with a birch shaft, most likely Norse," offered Sergeant Mac Namara. "And there," he pointed, "that appears to be a runic symbol etched on the haft of the iron head, possibly the maker's mark, but more likely a curse."

"You know your arrows, Sergeant," commended O'Halloran.

"Should we follow them, Captain?" The former officer was still finding it hard to get his mouth around calling someone else captain, but Mac Namara was hopeful that his demotion could be swiftly reversed.

King Mahon had secretly instructed him to get to the bottom of this whole ambush business; the king seemed to be sensing something peculiar about the entire affair. "You are to be my eyes and ears out there, Sergeant," the king had ordered. "Most commanders admire Brian as a warrior and tend to report directly to him, but you will answer to me alone on this matter. Do well on this assignment, Sergeant Mac Namara, and you will find that your fall from grace will be very short-lived."

"We have several possibilities to consider here, Sergeant," answered Captain O'Halloran thoughtfully as he tapped the arrow against the side of his leg. "If it was a Norse sea-raiding party making for a hasty retreat to a waiting ship on the west coast, then we are already too late. If, on the other hand, they were the Dublin Norse or perchance those based at Wexford, then it would seem that they would both want to take the fastest route east to make good their escape."

"By the Great Road?" suggested Mac Namara.

"Exactly, Sergeant," replied O'Halloran with a hint of satisfaction. "That is why we must head northeast directly and pick up the Great Road, striking east for Dublin.

Once we have found the road, if I am correct, we will also find their trail."

"Should we not determine where their trail from here leads to, Captain?"

"Indeed we must, Sergeant," replied Captain O'Halloran with enthusiasm, and Mac Namara could almost hear the trap snap shut. "You will follow their tracks in case they did make a break for the west coast, but if they did not, don't be one bit surprised if they change direction and veer northeast to pick up the Great Road. And if that is the case, you will soon be on their tails," concluded the captain. To be fair to him, O'Halloran wasn't the worst of them, but Mac Namara sensed that he hadn't really wanted a disgraced officer tagging along with his platoon, so now he had the perfect opportunity to offload him. "Sergeant Brady!" called the captain. "Give the order to mount up and move out. You had best get going too, Sergeant. Time is of the essence. Here, take this," said O'Halloran without malice, handing him the arrow. "I'm sure that you will want to return this curse personally."

*

Sergeant Mac Namara had had no difficulty in following the Raiders trail from Eagle's Pass. In their haste to escape, they had cut a wide swath through the wilderness with little regard to their pursuers. Whoever these men were, they seemed to possess an intimate knowledge of the terrain and had pieced together a descent route northwest, using hidden trails to reach a less well-known ford across the River Shannon. Mac Namara had a sense that they were long gone, and so followed their trail swiftly with little concern of encountering them.

As the light began to fade, Mac Namara drew close to the western coast and found what appeared to be the remains of an old fort perched on an isolated headland. The sergeant hobbled his horse to graze on a small patch of green and then went up to examine the tumbledown ruins in the failing light. Despite a cursory effort to remove any trace of their presence there, it was obvious that the Raiders had used the crumbling fort as some sort of staging post, the rutted wagon tracks and tell-tale signs of mustered horses nearby only confirming his suspicion. Even now, in the poor light, Mac Namara could clearly see that the Raider's trail had not continued west to the nearby coast and a meeting with a waiting ship. They had instead turned sharply off towards the northeast, heading in the direction of the Great Road, just as Captain O'Halloran had predicted.

At last, Mac Namara could dare to hope. If Princess Aoife had indeed been taken to the ships, then she would have been lost forever, taking with her any chance of redemption for them both. But if she was still to be found somewhere on this land, come first light, he would press on hard and he would find her and rescue her, no matter how many obstacles stood in his way. In so doing, he prayed that he could finally restore his shattered honour and regain his lost rank. Perhaps, secretly, Mac Namara also dreamed of other things too.

*

Their departure from Limerick had been muted. No one had bothered to venture out of their warm beds on that cool morning to see off the fourteen horsemen. Some whores might miss them, and a few tavern keepers might briefly lament their absence, but very few others would be sorry to see them leave. Ivar had also declined the pretence of a farewell salute to his son, Cuallaidh, a slight which had not gone unnoticed by his men. As you wish, thought Cuallaidh — Ivar would pay for that insult along with all the others he had heaped upon him over the years — then he dug in his spurs and led out his squad towards Eagle's Pass.

Cuallaidh had expected a company of men. He would have settled for a platoon, but to be given only a squad of soldiers was a glaring insult. Ivar had insisted that he take Rasende as his tracker. Cuallaidh had no issue with that, as the man was a ferocious warrior and a cunning scout, even if he was a law unto himself. But he did resent being lumbered with Hersir Gunnar. Gunnar, an experienced commander, was being sent along with the squad as an advisor to the younger Cuallaidh.

Gunnar didn't think much of this new role, as a 'hersir' would normally command between fifty and a hundred men and he considered this posting by Ivar to be beneath his rank and a serious waste of his abilities. Everyone knew that Hersir Gunnar was really there to keep a leash on Cuallaidh, the 'wild dog', and his deadly pack, as they had a bad reputation of leaving a trail of destruction in their wake. The permanent scowl etched upon Gunnar's face was there to let them all know just what he thought of this particular task. Sooner rather than later, Cuallaidh intended to cut Gunner loose and relieve the hersir of his onerous burden, regardless of Ivar's plans.

Gunner aside, Cuallaidh was well satisfied with the rest of his squad, as they had all fought and caroused together many times before. He was particularly pleased that Erik had been keen to come along. Besides being a lethal warrior with a shrewd mind, Erik was the nearest thing to a friend that Cuallaidh had ever had, and he was also popular with the rest of his men.

Scarface, as his name suggested, was Cuallaidh's most seasoned campaigner and readily commanded the respect of the other nine warriors who had all truly earned their fearsome reputations. One way or another, they were all outcasts and misfits, as he himself was. Secretly, they had all sworn their allegiance to Cuallaidh on the understanding that 'a rising tide lifts all ships'. In return, Cuallaidh had pledged to be their leader and improve their lot in life in any way that he could. And whatever this mission held in store for them, they would try and find a way to turn this cynical assignment to their own best advantage.

Ivar could give him no more troops, as he suspected that the O'Kennedys were planning some sort of trouble for him, or so he had said. But behind it all, they both knew the real truth: Ivar disliked Cuallaidh, always had. Of course, such things were easy to perceive and so much harder to prove. Perhaps Ivar blamed him for the death of his wife, who had died giving birth to Cuallaidh. Or maybe Ivar saw something in Cuallaidh that reminded him of his own more ruthless side, sensing some trait in him that he secretly loathed or privately feared.

Whatever the reason, Ivar wanted rid of Cuallaidh, and if his youngest son never came back, he still had two other sons, Aralt and Dubhcenn, who were more to his liking. Ivar had also used the opportunity that the girl's abduction had provided to weed out some of Limerick's worst rabble-rousers. That they also happened to be counted among Cuallaidh's friends had made the pruning job all the easier. Ivar had let Cuallaidh have his pick of the troublesome pack. That way, it would give him the impression that he actually had some choice in all of this.

Cuallaidh had been wise to all of Ivar's tricks, but he had carefully played along nonetheless, acting the part of a dutiful son who was willing to follow his jarl's orders. Ivar might be his father, but he was a Danish jarl first and foremost, and a wise king uproots a perceived threat long before that plant ever gets a chance to flourish. At Ivar's behest, he had selected his squad from his father's list of undesirables, just as he had been instructed. The eleven men that Cuallaidh had chosen had all been pushed to the outer margins of Viking society, and it had given them all an unholy alliance over the years.

Cuallaidh had of course protested that such a paltry complement of troops was not befitting for a jarl's son. But Ivar had simply proffered one of his tiresome sayings by way of compensation: 'Better weight than wisdom a traveller cannot carry — the poor man's strength in a strange place, worth more than wealth'. Cuallaidh had sensed that he could be straying onto dangerous ground if he had pushed the matter much further, so he had held his tongue and consoled himself with venomous thoughts of revenge. For he had been left in no doubt that his father cared little for him and probably did not expect him to return, one way or another.

So be it, thought Cuallaidh coldly as they cantered towards the mountain pass. Regardless of the odds, he would find the O'Kennedy girl with the meagre troops that he had been given, just as he had been ordered to do. And he would destroy anyone or anything that stood in his way. Then perhaps Cuallaidh might just defy Ivar and keep the female for himself and start a dynasty of his own. Maybe Cuallaidh could even find some way to make this princess love him. If she would not, that mattered little, for the woman could still provide him with many royal sons without the need for such elusive affections.

Chapter Twelve

BADLANDS

The Black Bog was a bleak place, an expansive wetland pockmarked by stagnant pools and wind-scoured peat hags. There were some pockets of dry ground: elevated enclaves of rolling heath land draped in dry heather and rust-coloured bracken. Ravens and red kites ruled over this upland bog, while bog cotton and glossy black slugs thrived in the marshy stretches. The fluctuating mists of autumn did little to improve the pensive aspect of the landscape, but they did provide excellent cover for Wolf and his men as they fled across the desolate land.

The Rangers had bolted into the mist-covered bog without delay, as the drum of horses' hooves pressed ever nearer. Conall O'Donnell had remained behind as a rearguard scout to spy on the progress of their pursuers as he lay well hidden on a heather-covered hummock, his view partly hampered by the sporadic fog. Their nettle-green cloaks and the uniformity of their dress and weapons marked them out as Connaught troops, and there was little doubt that the fifteen riders were after them. They had milled around the rugged road which bordered on the verge of the bog in search of their trail and then had barged into the bog on horseback the moment they had found the Rangers' mucky tracks.

The first horse had become bogged down almost immediately, and a second animal swiftly followed its fate, the horses whinnying in wide-eyed terror as the men dragged and cajoled the shivering creatures to somewhat firmer ground. It was a rash move to take horses into this quagmire, thought Conall, but the melee did buy Wolf and his men more badly needed time.

Some sense then seemed to prevail among the Connaught men, and five of the men returned to the road with all but one of the horses. This seemed to be an excessive guard for the picketed animals, but then again, maybe they feared that the Raiders might double back and make an attempt to seize the horses, reasoned Conall. The officer in charge had retained his horse as befitted his rank, and he had driven his struggling mount forward to demonstrate his superior horsemanship. His arrogance had been short-lived. For now, the unfortunate creature was firmly stuck in a hungry bog hole, which sucked it down with every flailing effort that it made to free itself. The officer was now screaming ineffectual orders at his men, who were ill-equipped to haul out the sinking horse. Whether the officer was outraged at the loss of his ornate saddle, his horse, or both was very hard to say.

Command of the Connaught patrol then seemed to shift to someone else, possibly a more experienced sergeant, who took decisive control of the chaotic situation. Even at a distance, Conall could easily see that the grey-haired man was now issuing clear instructions to the other eight soldiers. Following his directions, they quickly removed their cloaks, armour and anything else that might impede their progress across the marshy ground. They placed their gear beside the officer, who sat on a lonely rock, staring blankly into the bog hole that had just swallowed his horse, the occasional bubble of air escaping to the surface to remind him of his folly.

Suitably prepared, the Connaught men moved out swiftly, needing to waste little time trying to find firm ground, as the Rangers' well-chosen tracks were still clearly visible and easy to follow. Conall gauged the rapid pace of the patrol and knew that Wolf and his men could not stay ahead of the Connaught soldiers for much longer. The Rangers were hampered by their ongoing efforts to determine solid footing, and besides that, Arrow's feet had become considerably worse. Having seen enough to worry him, Conall carefully crawled away from his vantage point and slipped back down into the hollow which lay behind it. From here, he struck out to the northeast. Keeping low, he utilised the folds and creases of the land to conceal his urgent lope back towards the ever-advancing Rangers.

Wolf listened to Conall's grim assessment with deep concern. The Connaught patrol and their own force were evenly matched, but a pitched battle could prove more costly for the Rangers, who had no prospect of reinforcements or replacements and so could ill afford to lose anyone needlessly. Besides that, any walking wounded could slow them even further and end up becoming a serious liability to the group. One thing was certain: they could not simply wait until the Connaught men were snapping at their heels. "Incisive report, Ranger O'Donnell," commended Wolf. "You had better gather everyone in, and sharply."

Sergeant Kavanagh was no fresh-faced recruit and thought that the pursuit into the bog was pure folly — on horses, it was sheer madness. He had advised his young leader to circle around the bog and wait for the Raiders on the other side, but Lieutenant O'Connor had been keen to prove himself and wouldn't heed his counsel, stupid boy. Now Kavanagh was left with this fool's errand, chasing these sorry bastards on foot across this damned slob land. Still, Kavanagh did reckon that his Connaught men had an edge over the fugitives. Having ridden here, his men had fresh legs, whereas the Raiders had obviously trekked here from some distance away. As well as that, Kavanagh's men could easily follow the mucky trail across the treacherous ground without having to explore every tentative step themselves, whereas the Raiders would have little choice but to go cautiously as they searched for firm footing.

The wavering mist was suddenly swept aside for a brief moment, just in time for Kavanagh to spot the tail end of the escaping party slip over the next heather-covered hillock. Better still, it was clearly obvious that one of the fugitives was limping badly. Sensing an easy victory, Kavanagh urged his men up the slope for the final kill. When two archers suddenly reappeared on the crest of the rise, he realised in an instant that he had just blundered straight into their trap. For while Sergeant Kavanagh had been focused on pursuing the quarry ahead of him, the Raiders had used the intermittent mist and the contours of the land to covertly manoeuvre their men into position around him. Cunning bastards, thought Kavanagh bitterly, before a lethal hail of arrows rained down mercilessly upon the unprotected Connaught men, felling them where they stood.

Wolf walked slowly out of the mist towards the wounded sergeant and rested his hand upon the hilt of his dagger while the other Rangers went among the injured Connaught soldiers, dispatching the dying without triumph or pity, collecting their own arrows as they went and pilfering any others that they could find.

"Leave me be, young man," said Kavanagh, raising his hand in a feeble defensive gesture as his punctured abdomen seeped warm blood into the cold, hungry ground. "I'm done for."

"You should have let us be, Grey-Beard," said Wolf, not unkindly, removing his hand from his dagger and placing the bottom of his bow on the ground, leaning lightly on the other end.

"Who are you people?" demanded Kavanagh, having expected Vikings and now unsure what to make of Wolf's dark green buckskin clothes.

"Rangers," answered Wolf simply.

"Shadow warriors," spat Kavanagh, with an equal measure of scorn and respect. "I knew it; regular soldiers would have no business heading into this godforsaken place."

"We're not overly fussy about such things."

"So it would seem," answered Kavanagh warily, trying to get a measure of the man who stood before him. "Well, do you have the girl, or did I die for nothing?" he ventured. Wolf considered his response for a moment and then decided to offer 'a trout to catch a salmon'.

"Yes, we have the girl. Now, tell me soldier, who was the man who led you here?"

"Lieutenant O'Connor," said Kavanagh sourly, "the king of Connaught's son, out to earn his spurs. It was only a matter of time before the damned fool got us all killed."

"And who are you?"

"Sergeant Kavanagh," he responded with pride, drawing himself up and grimacing with the effort.

"What exactly have you heard about the ambush at Eagle's Pass?" pressed Wolf, trying to glean any useful information.

"That you lot are bad bastards is what I heard!" retorted Kavanagh angrily. "They say that you gouged out those men's eyes, cut off their balls and smeared their dead bodies with horse dung."

"Ridiculous," answered Wolf calmly. The sergeant eyed him hard for a long moment and seemed persuaded that Wolf was indeed telling the truth.

"Aye, I thought it was all bullshit when I heard it. Who could be arsed with all that nonsense? The Norse, maybe?" said the sergeant through ragged breaths. "They're after your blood all the same, young man."

"I don't doubt it," answered Wolf, turning and walking away. Then he paused, nocked an arrow and turned back towards the mortally wounded man.

"See you in hell, Ranger," said Kavanagh defiantly.

"Until then, Sergeant," replied Wolf, then swiftly drew back his bow and loosed the arrow in one fluid movement, ending Kavanagh's suffering in an instant.

*

The mood among the group since the killing of the Connaught men had been sombre, their low spirits only compounded by the dismal rainswept landscape which surrounded them. For almost two days, they had slogged their way across the sodden upland, sorely testing Farrell's knowledge of the featureless terrain. They knew that they had been left with little option but to deal with their pursuers in the way that they had, but that didn't mean that they had to like it. Now they would have both Connaught and Munster forces clamouring for their blood.

They finally escaped the cloying clutches of the Black Bog late on the afternoon of the second day. And although the ground in the pine forest was not altogether dry, it was a welcome relief from the spongy morass of the bog. They had made their way to the edge of the forest by dusk and now had a clear view of the footbridge over the River Shannon. Here, they remained quietly hidden at the tree line as Wolf considered their next move.

There was only one token sentry posted at the bridge, which likely meant that news of the dead Connaught soldiers had not yet reached this far northeast. But that could all change very quickly, and they needed to cross the bridge that night before a large Connaught force was deployed along the Shannon to block their escape. They could, of course, kill the sentry, even restrain him, but either action would only confirm to their pursuers that they had indeed fled this way. Dead or alive, this one guard was proving to be an obstacle that was going to be hard to get around.

"Maybe I could handle this one?" suggested Arrow beside him as Wolf pondered his options. "I think there have already been enough Connaught men killed on my account."

Wolf opened his mouth to persuade her that that had not been the case, but he could see that the death of the men in the badlands still clearly pained her. Perhaps if she could save the life of this young Connaught soldier, it might go some way towards easing that hurt.

"Just be careful," said Wolf gently, then he watched her limp off towards Amergen and Blade who were standing nearby.

As darkness fell, Amergen and Blade emerged from the trees, supporting Arrow between them as she limped along as best she could. They had left their weapons behind them, and the two women had cleaned their faces and donned their cloaks to obscure their military attire.

Blade and Arrow had also unbound their hair to soften their appearance, while Arrow had drawn up her hood to partly conceal her face. The sentry appeared startled and alarmed to see these people approach him from the woods at this dark hour. Amergen raised his arm and hailed the soldier, pointing towards the injured Arrow.

Unsure of what to do, the sentry grasped his spear in both hands, barring their access to the bridge as the unlikely trio hobbled ever forward amidst an endless stream of talk. Blade was jabbering away all the while, relieved to have finally found a strapping young soldier as she continued to console her injured friend. Meanwhile, a distraught Amergen earnestly pleaded with the man for his help. Seeing that the youth was static with indecision, Arrow collapsed in a heap, sending Blade into hysterics as Amergen became even more animated. The sentry's resolve finally crumbled, and Blade helpfully took the soldier's spear to allow him to carry the injured Arrow to the nearby monastery at Clonmacnoise, just beyond the river.

Wolf and his men wasted little time in silently crossing the footbridge over the turgid river, glad to be leaving Connaught as they furtively slipped into the neighbouring kingdom of West Meath. They were content that the young sentry had been spared; enough Connaught blood had been spilled already. As things stood, the unintended casualties of circumstance were piling up all around this mission. What was supposed to have been a simple kidnapping and a 'minor action' was now turning into a very real struggle for their own survival. Wolf wondered how much more blood would be spilled before they finally got this girl to safety. Instinctively, they kept clear of any human habitation near the monastery, darting quickly into the cover of the nearby trees as the soft autumnal moonlight offered to light their way.

Having crossed over the mighty Shannon, they were at last done with the province of Connaught. But the Rangers very much doubted that the men of Connaught were in any way finished with them.

Chapter Thirteen

SEARCHERS

Huddled in his red cloak, Sergeant Mac Namara had spent an uncomfortable night at the Fort of the Two Ravens as a gusting breeze scattered wizened leaves across the headland. He had risked a meagre fire in the crook of a crumbled corner of the ruin, but the weak flames did little to banish the autumn cold. What little sleep he did snatch had been fitful, the unsettled sound of the nearby sea echoing his own troubled thoughts.

How could the Raiders have known the exact time that the escort for Princess Aoife would travel through the remote Eagle's Pass? How could they have been so familiar with the Thomond terrain? Did they have local help? Was someone close to home deeply involved in all of this, hence King Mahon's suspicions? Whatever the case was, Mac Namara could not presume to trust anyone until he got to the truth of the matter.

The congestion of horse tracks and the heavy-wagon trail had been easy to follow that morning, and the sergeant had arrived at the Great Road without incident after a solid day in the saddle. A timber causeway two spear lengths wide, the Great Road was a lot less taxing to traverse than the mucky track he had encountered earlier. But Mac Namara felt very exposed, travelling alone across these large swaths of windswept bog that stretched across the midlands. It was believed that the ancient Druids had envisaged these causeways across the country as a means to travel to their sacred sites and had duly badgered the High Kings of Ireland to build them. The maintenance of these highways was now the responsibility of each local king, and they had the good sense to position their own strongholds and settlements well away from these thoroughfares and any potential problems that they were likely to bring.

After another cold and frugal night camped in a pine forest beside Lough Ree, Mac Namara lost little time getting back onto the Great Road at first light, his stiff limbs glad of the warming movement. He munched slowly on another small oatcake that he had fished out of his saddlebag as he continuously scanned the treeless terrain for any hint of danger. Travelling alone was never ideal, especially here, as these badlands had the reputation of concealing outlaws and outcasts. Vikings also made frequent use of these roads in their endless raids for slaves or any other portable goods, and Mac Namara, his horse and his weapons would provide them with a very profitable catch.

By midday, Mac Namara was relieved to have finally reached the fresh tracks of a large band of horsemen heading east. He was fairly certain it was O'Halloran's troop by the obvious discipline of their formation. Captain O'Halloran was a shrewd officer, and like so many of the younger fighting men, he was strongly drawn to his charismatic commander, Brian Boru.

Mac Namara suddenly reined in his horse, the animal whinnying in protest. The light was fading, so he dismounted and tied the reins to a nearby gorse bush. On closer inspection, it was just as he thought: the wagon that they had been following had veered off the Great Road onto the lesser Northern Road heading towards the northeast, and without any escort. That was a puzzle in itself, but why the captain had not seen fit to send someone after the wagon was beyond him. Perhaps

O'Halloran was convinced that his quarry lay in Dublin, and he had little time or men to waste on a rickety wagon heading off into the woods. Or maybe the captain knew something that he did not, which was Mac Namara's suspicion all along. Whatever the case, the wagon had played some part in the ambush and could well yield vital clues as to who really was behind the well-planned raid.

If Aoife had been taken to Dublin, Captain O'Halloran and his men were fast approaching, and one more man-at-arms would make little difference in that wasps' nest, as force alone would be of little use in the Norse stronghold. O'Halloran would probably have little choice but to negotiate a hefty ransom for the Thomond princess, if she was there at all? There again, if Aoife was in some way linked to this mysterious wagon, then someone needed to follow it.

Mac Namara mounted his horse as dusk settled across the bog and paused at the junction of the two roads. The Great Road stretched east across the moorland, while the Northern Road disappeared off into a darkened forest. To the east lay an easy road, comrades, the promise of a soft bed and a warm meal. But instinct, perhaps even something deeper, drove Mac Namara towards the north. He nipped his spurs lightly into his horse's flanks and headed warily into the woods as a steady mizzle began to fall.

*

They had made good time from Eagle's Pass, helped by the fresh tracks of a lone horseman that ran before them — probably those of an Irish scout from Thomond. The ruined fort, shrouded in an autumnal mist, had obviously been the base used by the Raiders, who were now long gone. The clutter of horse tracks and the rutted wagon trail that they had left in their wake could still be clearly seen heading towards the northeast. But Rasende did not seem convinced by the tracks, for some inexplicable reason, and continued to stare at them silently.

"What is it, Rasende?" asked Cuallaidh quietly as the big tracker remained on his hunkers, studying a cluster of hoof marks.

"Thor's balls! What is it, man?" barked Gunnar. The hersir had been a pain in the arse ever since they had left Limerick. The men were sick of him, and Cuallaidh knew that he would have to deal with Gunnar sooner rather than later, or the hersir could well find his throat cut in the middle of one of his long, grating snores. Rasende ignored Gunnar and walked off slowly towards the trees, scrutinizing the dewy ground as he went and leaving them all gathered around the ruins in an uncomfortable silence filled only by the screeching of the nearby gulls. Eventually, Rasende returned, looking a lot more certain of his secret theory and beckoning for Cuallaidh alone to follow him back to the Raiders' tracks.

"See here? And over there?" said Rasende, pointing towards the ground, but he could see by the quizzical look on Cuallaidh's face that he would have to explain further. "Look at the size of those hooves, they're huge!" He placed his brawny outstretched hand within a hoof print for emphasis.

"A big horse, a stallion maybe?" offered Cuallaidh, trying to follow the shrewd tracker's train of thought.

"Yes, but no ordinary stallion. This animal is a prize beast, damned near seventeen hands high, I reckon, and a herd leader who is being led along like a lowly donkey and not much liking it, by the looks of it," reasoned Rasende, gesturing towards the scattered tracks of the big horse. "It's as if someone had been trying to lead him, bring him under control. Someone..."

"Who had not been his master," finished Cuallaidh quietly, looking off towards the trees and starting to get a sense of the web that Rasende was trying to spin. "How many?"

"Hard to say, Ivar's Son," answered Rasende, getting to his feet. He found it hard to get his mouth around Cuallaidh's strange-sounding Irish name, so he never really tried. "A section of ten, maybe more. They made some attempt to cover their tracks, but they were moving fast."

"Because they have the prize?" probed Cuallaidh.

Rasende shrugged his shoulders and spread his hands as if the answer was so obvious that it needed no answer.

"We will need to leave the horses behind if we are to follow them," stated Rasende.

"Is that really necessary?" said Cuallaidh warily, imagining the ire of his men at being reduced to common foot soldiers.

"They intend to use terrain ill-suited to horses. Why else would they split their force and march off into the wilderness?"

"Can we be sure that they have the girl?"

"Why this ruse if they don't? And why is a leader's horse being led off somewhere by someone else?"

"Because that leader has gone off in a different direction," concluded Cuallaidh, staring at the trees beyond the ruins. "Can you follow their trail?"

"If something touches the ground, I can track it. One more curious thing: there are wolves."

"Attacking them? Stalking them? What, damn it?"

"Shadowing them, maybe even with them," puzzled Rasende. "I don't know; it's hard to say. I've never seen anything like this before."

"You're not making much sense, Rasende. How can wolves be 'with them'?"

"I know it sounds crazy, but..."

"In Odin's name, will someone tell me what is going on here?" demanded the hersir, having ambled up on his horse, irritated at his exclusion from what was obviously a serious discussion to determine decisions that should be made only by leaders.

"Rasende reckons they have divided their force, and some have taken off on foot into the trees," answered Cuallaidh simply, pointing towards the forest.

Perplexed, Gunnar looked from one to the other, trying to unearth some underhanded trickery between the pair.

"But why would they do such a foolish thing? Split their force and put half their men on foot in a rugged place like this? Why?"

"It's most likely a ploy to spirit away the girl while we go chasing after these more obvious tracks," reasoned Cuallaidh, glancing down at the wagon ruts and the condensed animal tracks stamped into the hardened ground.

"We will have to leave the horses to follow them," said Rasende, which was just about the last straw for the hersir.

"What! Are you both completely mad? Abandon our horses and go off traipsing through enemy country just because you saw some peculiar tracks and a few broken twigs? It's out of the question. As senior man here, I will not allow it!" fumed Gunnar, glaring at them both.

Cuallaidh looked hard at Rasende and then gave a flick of his head towards the hersir. The powerful tracker understood and reacted fast. In a blur of movement, Rasende took two quick steps and then struck the jaw of Gunnar's horse a savage blow with his meaty fist, felling the horse in an instant. The hersir, to his credit, extracted himself from beneath the fallen animal with surprising speed, whipping out his dagger as he did so.

Erik, his empty hands raised in the air, swiftly placed himself between Rasende and Gunnar as the big tracker looked on impassively, his hand resting nonchalantly on the hilt of his knife, indifferent to Gunnar's murderous glare. The hersir then surveyed the dangerous band of warriors arrayed before him and saw only a wall of menace on the verge of attack, so he very slowly eased his dagger back into its sheath before it provided them with a feeble excuse to attack.

"So, that's the way of it," said the hersir calmly, regaining a semblance of composure. "This is far from over. We will settle this when you get back to Limerick," said Gunnar firmly, brazenly scanning the group before resting a cold, hard stare on Cuallaidh. Looking at Erik, he quietly added, "But I very much doubt that any of you crazy bastards are going to survive that long."

Then the startled horse instinctively struggled to his feet, dazed and staggering. The animal's valiant efforts distracted them all for a moment, easing the tension and breaking the dangerous impasse. When Hersir Gunnar turned back towards Cuallaidh's band, Rasende was already heading towards the trees, and the rest of the men had quickly moved off to take their gear from their horses. Truth be told, Gunnar was glad to be rid of them;

they were all trouble, always had been. And he knew with cold certainty as he watched them eagerly prepare for the hunt that only violence and mayhem lay in the path of these bloodthirsty renegades.

"I reckon you'll be taking the horses back to Limerick, so?"

"Aye, and if you had any sense, Erik, you'd be coming back with me."

"Yeah, maybe you're right, Hersir," said Erik pensively as he watched Cuallaidh's pack file silently into the woods, "but the dice have been cast. Let them fall where they will."

Chapter Fourteen

ESCAPE

The morning had begun badly. It was almost noon when the trio finally left the monastery at Clonmacnoise, setting off at a casual pace towards the woods where the Rangers lay in hiding from the night before. The late start was bad enough, but to make matters worse, Arrow was now perched on a small black pony.

"I know, I know," said Amergen with upraised hands, "tracks and all that, but the monks insisted. And it would have looked damned suspicious if we had refused their generous offer."

Wolf glared at the three of them, finally fixing his focus on the innocent animal.

"Arrow's feet are infected," said Blade simply and then ambled off towards O'Neill and the other Rangers, who had gathered around the unlikely scene.

"His name is Blackie," said Arrow helpfully.

"Of course it is," answered Wolf a tad peevishly, trying to keep his temper.

"We did get some provisions," offered Amergen, patting one of the bulging saddlebags draped behind the saddle.

"Thank Christ for that," barked Sergeant O'Neill, breaking the awkward moment. "I'm bloody starving. Ferret! Get to work."

"Can we keep him?" asked Arrow hopefully. "Just for a little while?"

Whether Arrow wanted to keep the pony because of her feet or simple affection for the sturdy little animal, Wolf couldn't say. In any case, they hadn't much choice but to keep it, thought Wolf, as Arrow, on foot, was slowing them down at the very time they needed to be swift.

"For now, anyway," softened Wolf, much to Arrow's relief, then he turned towards the gathered Rangers.

"Rangers, the element of surprise is gone. They're onto us. And they have horses. We can expect the soldiers of Connaught and Munster to soon be on our tails. There's no cover here worth talking about," continued Wolf, gesturing towards the open beech wood that stretched out before them, shafts of mist-fused sunlight probing through the thinning branches into every darkened corner. "Speed is all that's left to us now, men. It's time for us to make a run for it," he reasoned, sweeping the group with a hard look. "The men of Connaught will be keen for our blood and will waste little time trying to pick up our tracks. They will simply unleash their wolfhounds to sniff out our trail. We must find some way to shake them off, a ruse to buy ourselves some time."

They pushed on through the sprawling woodland, running at a steady lope across the crisp leaf-strewn ground. The Rangers ate little and drank sparingly as they went to avoid any risk of stomach cramps. Blackie was tireless, and the Rangers were glad to be able to press on because of the hardy little animal. Arrow was a proficient rider, and the pair worked together seamlessly. From time to time, Amergen took hold of the pony's tail in order to keep up and catch his breath, but he was still well able to hold his own.

They avoided the areas where plumes of smoke rose above woodland settlements and hoped that secret eyes did not see their hurried passing. The Rangers might be in

Meath now, but that did not mean they were safe; the men of West Meath kept a close eye on their borders for Connaught troops invading from the west and Viking raiders striking from the east. The Rangers could easily be mistaken for either and treated accordingly.

Towards dusk, the forward scout trotted back to the main party. Wolf knew by the look on Cormac O'Donnell's face that he wasn't going to like what he was about to hear.

"There's a big lough up ahead," gasped O'Donnell, trying to catch his breath. "It's blocking our route, Captain."

"How large?" asked Wolf.

"Take a day, maybe more, to go around it. Hard to tell in this light," said the scout, taking a canteen of water from Farrell.

Wolf told the unit to take a breather as he quietly digested the unwelcome news.

"Most likely Lough Owel," offered Sergeant O'Neill, for this was his homeland, the territory of the southern O'Neills.

"Anything else?" asked Wolf.

"There's a sizable settlement by the shore. Hard to get near it because of the dogs, twitchy bastards!"

"What has them so jumpy? What are they protecting?" considered Wolf aloud.

"Could be the livestock pens beyond the fish racks at the far end of the village," ventured O'Donnell.

"They're fishermen too?"

"Aye, they've got a string of dugout canoes tied up along the shore on this side of the village."

"How many?" probed Wolf.

"Enough, Captain," answered Cormac with a rueful

grin. "If we can get anywhere near them without rousing those damned dogs."

Wolf walked off alone into the moonlit woods, cupped his hands about his mouth, tilted back his head and sent out a long, lonesome howl into the clear night sky. Then he waited. Before long, his call for help was answered by the welcome sound of Willow in the near distance, quickly followed by the low, familiar howl of his wolf-brother, Shadow. Soon, the surrounding woods filled with the continuous howling of a large wolf pack that had been silently hunting nearby. Then Willow came forward out of the trees as the packs' moonlit eyes watched them both from the woods. Shadow kept his distance, as was his way, but Wolf could clearly see by his positioning in the group, front and centre, with tail held high, that he was now one of the new leaders of this pack.

"It's good to see you, Willow," said Wolf with a warm smile. "Sorry for interrupting the hunt, but I need your pack to hunt for me tonight, Sister." Then Wolf stretched his arm towards the settlement, pointed down low and stabbed a fanglike thump towards his neck. Willow had seen her human brother make that sign before and knew full well what it meant. Wolf and Willow silently held each other's gaze for a moment, no words necessary to explain the strange and powerful bond that existed between them, and then she trotted back into the trees to gather up her pack for a very different kind of hunt.

O'Byrne and O'Sullivan had quickly taken the saddle off Blackie, stripped him of his bit and bridle and chased the confused pony off into the night. The Rangers hastily hid the trappings beneath a holly bush and then quietly rejoined the rest of the unit, who were hidden on the outskirts of the settlement, waiting. Wolf had simply told them to 'be ready', offering no further explanation. No one thought to question him. The Rangers had long suspected that Wolf had his own strange ways. Even so, they trusted him completely.

The first of the village dogs began to bark, urgent and angry, then a second and third joined in, their barking growing louder and more insistent as the sound of agitated animals drifted towards the settlement. Any guard dog worth his salt was barking furiously now as the sound of breaking fences and panicked livestock filled the still night. Men began shouting, running towards their precious pigs and goats with torches held high as wolves darted in and out of the holding pens, driving the terrified animals through the flimsy wattle fences and out into the dark dangers of the night.

Now the Rangers made their move. Staying low and silent, they slipped down to the lake shore. The quick nimble fingers of Blade, Arrow and Ferret softly began loosening the mooring lines that held the long dugouts, while Amergen and Farrell ensured that there were four paddles for each canoe. Keeping down, Wolf, O'Neill and the two O'Donnell brothers took up a defensive position along the shore as Bergman, O'Sullivan and O'Byrne shoved the remaining canoes out into deeper water, eliminating any risk of pursuit.

The Rangers were adept at using such stealthy craft. Amergen and Arrow, on the other hand, were ill at ease, so Wolf put each of them into a separate dugout. The first three into each boat settled themselves on the flat of their shins and balanced the narrow canoe as the fourth person shoved the craft out and gingerly hopped in at the back. They eased the paddles gently into the dark water and brought them out again just as softly, trying to keep any noise to a minimum.

Hearing only the village dogs and no shouts of alarm from the shore, Wolf risked a backward glance at the settlement but saw only a string of frantic torches moving about the other end of the village. He offered a silent thanks to Willow, Shadow and their new pack for the mayhem they had unleashed on the village that night. No doubt the wolves would claim their reward and feast well into the night.

Crossing this broad lough would buy them valuable time and put some welcome distance between them and their pursuers, who would now most likely have to travel around the expansive lake. Best of all, this body of water would break their ground scent, shaking off any wolfhounds that had latched on to their trail, thought Wolf with satisfaction. Then he set his sights forward, took his direction of travel from the stars, and started to paddle in earnest across the dark moon-dappled lake.

*

The chase to Dublin had been a close-run thing. Towards the end of the gruelling journey, Lieutenant Godfridsson and his Rangers had been sorely pressed to stay one step ahead of the Munster troops, who had the fresher horses and seemed well motivated by bloodthirsty notions of revenge. As they drew ever nearer to the sprawling Norse enclave, the lieutenant dispersed both Rangers and horses at every opportunity, using the natural contours of the land to shield their movements.

"What are they waiting for?" asked Corporal Hakon as the two men sat astride their tired horses, concealed in a pine grove on high ground near the town.

"Their leader is no fool," answered Godfridsson. "Dublin is happy to do business with just about anyone, but they can slam their gates shut and go onto a war footing in a moment, if needs be. He can't risk getting any closer with a troop of surly Munster men in tow."

"But surely the Norse already know that they are here?"

"You can be damn sure their scouts are watching them as we speak — us too, for that matter. They're just waiting with fast horses to see what the Munster men intend to do."

"Movement," piped Hakon.

"Clever boy," said the lieutenant with a wry smile as they watched the Munster leader and two other horsemen break away from the column and trot slowly towards the town.

"Wise move," commended Godfridsson. Then they wheeled away their horses and drove the weary animals on towards Dublin.

Corporal Hakon had taken the exhausted horses to be stabled, while the lieutenant blended in with the boisterous townsfolk, discreetly awaiting the arrival of the Munster leader.

"What are the festivities for, friend?" asked Godfridsson of a passerby, sensing a heightened air of exuberance about the place.

"Where have you been stranger? It's been the talk of Leinster. Jarl Kanarvan is to marry a royal princess today from a ruling Irish clan — a pretty young thing, and feisty too."

"Horny old bastard!"

"Clever old bastard, more like. With powerful Irish allies, it won't be so easy for our Irish enemies to push us back into the sea, eh? At last, a proper foothold on this land!"

"What's the girl's name?"

"Gormlaith or some such thing," answered the passerby. "Who can pronounce these tongue-twisting Irish names?"

They both laughed, and the man hurried off to join in the street celebrations, which were sure to hold the promise of some free ale.

The three Munster soldiers slipped quietly into town, their red cloaks tactfully tucked behind their saddles. After a brief discussion, one man led away the horses to be stabled, while the leader and his hefty companion headed off down a busy thoroughfare, most likely towards Jarl Kanarvan's elevated stronghold in the heart of the fortified town to announce their presence. Godfridsson followed at a discreet distance, blending in with the throngs of busy people.

Suddenly, the two Munster men veered off the main street and slipped into a rougher section of town which led down towards the docks. Godfrid was surprised by the detour and the obvious fact that the pair seemed to know these sordid backstreets very well. Certain that he had not been spotted, the lieutenant kept close, intrigued as to where they might be going. When they finally stopped at the Dirty Dog tavern, he was completely stunned.

Seeing little else for it, Godfridsson waited a brief moment and then slipped unobtrusively into the dingy tavern after them. Instinctively, he headed towards a table in the shadows and signalled to a passing serving girl. The harried-looking wench gave the table a cursory wipe and placed a horn beaker on the table with little fuss, then poured out a cup of frothy ale from her jug.

"Food?" she asked. Godfrid just shook his head.

"Two bits," said the girl.

He tossed three coins onto the table, and she muttered something that sounded like thanks and then went off about her duties, trying to avoid the grasping hands of the more lecherous patrons.

The big soldier at the bar was obviously the muscle and exuded the required air of protective menace. The leader chatted away amiably to the innkeeper, casually glancing about the tavern for any signs of curious onlookers. When the Munster leader discreetly placed a gold coin standing on its edge for the barman's attention, Godfridsson very nearly choked on his beer.

Well, well, thought the lieutenant. 'Life on the edge' was just full of surprises. Then he drained his beer and slipped softly out of the tavern.

Chapter Fifteen

MIDIR

They reached the far side of the lough in the dead of night and ran the three canoes up onto a sandy gravel shore. To reduce their time out in the open, Wolf had earlier assigned each member a particular role for when they made landfall so that the team would act quickly and decisively, thus limiting their exposure.

Arrow and Amergen jumped out of the boats without delay and ran up either side of the small beach, took cover at the tree line, and kept a sharp watch towards the lough. The O'Donnell brothers set off swiftly to scout along the shoreline on either side of the strand; they would also take care of any tracks left on the beach on their return. Ferret, Blade and Farrell spread out and pressed deep into woods to set up a silent perimeter and three essential listening posts. Wolf and O'Neill stayed low and took up a central defensive position at the tree line, with one watching the woods while the other scanned the shore.

Berg, O'Sullivan and O'Byrne set to work on sinking the long canoes. They dared not risk the noise of hacking through their wooden hulls to hole them, so they leaned them over to coax the brackish water into them. The Rangers took no pleasure in destroying the fishermen's precious craft, but they could not simply leave the boats hauled out on the strand for all to see where they had secretly put ashore. Content with their work, they shoved the sinking boats out into deeper water and then took to the trees. The lake would take care of the rest and swallow up the hollowed-out canoes.

The O'Donnell brothers made a swift return to the beach, each carrying a lush pine branch. With the shoreline now empty, they swept the sandy ground clear of any footprints, working their way back towards the tree line. On reaching firmer ground, they carefully discarded the branches and went off to join the others hunkered down amongst the beech trees.

Sensing no immediate danger, Wolf stood and gave the short yelping bark of a fox to recall the sentries. The Rangers seldom used raven calls at night, as they could sound suspiciously out of place. Foxes, on the other hand, were highly nocturnal, and pairs kept in regular vocal contact with a wide range of far-reaching barks, yelps and screams. On landing, the unit had worked well together, considered Wolf. They had moved rapidly and with real purpose. Now all they could do was hope that their efforts to remain concealed would prove to be successful. One thing was certain: time would quickly reveal if they had indeed been spotted by the secret eyes of an outlying sentry. Even the chance passing of a sharp-eyed night hunter or just the curious gazes of a couple courting by the shore could easily lead to their swift downfall.

Stiff-legged and sore after several long hours hunkered down in the canoes, they were all glad to get their limbs moving again. Several of the party were visibly tired, and Arrow was struggling with her grazed feet, but Wolf dare not let them rest near the shore. The signal set, Wolf sent Cormac O'Donnell up ahead as a forward scout and then positioned Conall to the rear, well clear of the main party. The Rangers then silently slipped into single-file formation with Wolf leading out the squad. O'Neill was to act as a rearguard, while Arrow, Amergen and Blade were positioned in the centre of the column. Then they pushed on stealthily towards the northeast, heading deeper into the moonlit woods.

Undergrowth was sparse beneath the congested beech canopy, so Wolf had to settle for a leaf-littered hollow for a little cover for the night. Wolf gave two yelping fox barks in either direction to let the O'Donnell brothers know that the Rangers had stopped for the night and that the scouts now had the first watch.

The weary party slid gratefully down into the leaf-strewn dip, and O'Neill moved quietly among them, selecting Rangers for sentry duty for the remainder of the night. Arrow's feet had suffered badly on their last hard march, and to her credit, she voiced no complaint but simply curled up in her cloak on a bed of crisp dry leaves and instantly fell asleep. Others hungrily delved into their diminished stores of food and water, then quickly wrapped themselves in their cloaks and bedded down for an uneasy night.

With sentries posted and the camp settled, Wolf took a moment to collect his thoughts. He pulled his cloak about him and leaned back against the slope, thankful for a dry night and a clear sky. Blackie's track straight from the monastery to the lake was unavoidable but regrettable, reflected Wolf, and it would make for an easy trail to follow. The three canoes had been vital, and they had had little option but to cut loose the rest, but no one would believe that all the dugouts had simply worked themselves free.

As for the risky dash through the woodland in broad daylight, that didn't even bear thinking about. Their situation was getting more desperate with each passing day, their list of enemies growing with every step of this haphazard journey. Arrow was tough, but she was in trouble, and her feet could give out at any moment. They needed horses, enough for all of them, but finding horses was not so easy in this sparsely inhabited terrain. In truth, they needed a piece of luck from somewhere, anywhere, but they needed it now.

A wolf is running hard through the moonlit woods, his lolling tongue flecked with saliva, his lungs bellowing. He is tired, near his end, but still he must run, for the wolfhounds are gaining on him, thirsty for his blood. Angry men with lurid orange torches that hold the dreaded fire are not far behind them, so he must run, or he will die.

'The wolf that kills the shepherd's sheep is wise to run,' came a familiar voice through Wolf's disturbing dream.

'Midir, is that you?' he asked.

'Your fight does not lay here, Wolf. Rise up, gather your men and follow me. Quickly now!'

"Halt! Who goes there?" challenged O'Neill.

Wolf awoke with a start, unaware that he had drifted off into a fitful sleep and glad to escape from his unsettling vision. He sprang to his feet as O'Neill drew his sword and called out again.

"Who goes there?" he demanded with menace in his voice.

"It's just an old friend," placated Wolf, seeing the familiar shadow of Midir standing near a tree. "Put away your sword."

"An old friend, you say?" accepted O'Neill, warily, giving Wolf a quizzical look but knowing better than to ask his captain any awkward questions.

"Gather up the men, Sergeant. We need to move, quickly."

“It looks like all of them are here,” answered O’Neill as the two scouts pounded simultaneously into either side of the camp.

“Riders combing the woods to the east!” reported Cormac O’Donnell and then grabbed a breath.

“How many?” asked Wolf.

“Way too many for us, I reckon, Captain.”

“And there is a line of men with torches sweeping through the trees from the west. I’m pretty sure I heard wolfhounds too,” added Conall.

“Numbers?”

“I didn’t hang around to count them, but thirty at least, Captain.”

Follow me! said Midir to Wolf with the mind-speech, then he took off swiftly into the woods.

“Everyone with me, now!” called Wolf as the sound of barking wolfhounds began to reach them, then he set off after Midir into the night. Wolf would have preferred to have been further back in the group to ensure that everyone was keeping up, especially Arrow. But he doubted that any of the others would have been keen to take point in pursuit of this fleet-footed stranger as they fled for their lives through the trees.

Midir suddenly stopped at a large outcrop of rock and waited for the Rangers to gather up. Satisfied that they were all there, he walked up to the rock, placed his hands on a smooth section of stone and said a string of strange words, then stood back. Nothing happened, and the Rangers looked at each other with deep concern; not only were they surrounded and outnumbered, they were now also relying on a madman who talked to rocks. But then the slab of stone appeared to slowly and silently dissolve, releasing a luminous green glow from the entrance of the cave. Some instinctively shuffled back as others touched amulets or crosses, whispered of witchcraft and mumbled quiet prayers to their respective gods.

"Steady, men," cautioned O'Neill. "Beggars can't be choosers."

"Sorcery!" muttered Berg.

"Not everything in your world is as it seems," answered Midir. Still seeing only suspicious faces, he flatly added, "Come with me if you want to live."

Wolf knew that words were useless at a time like this, so he simply followed Midir into the cave and trusted that the baying of the nearby hounds coupled with the sound of fast approaching horses would prove motivation enough for his men.

Midir placed his hands on the rock near the mouth of the cave and spoke a few words in the same mysterious dialect, and a screen of stone magically solidified behind them, closing off the outside world and plunging them all into silence.

"Stay close," said Midir without preamble and quickly headed off down the roomy tunnel. He touched the walls of the cave as he went, in some arcane way igniting the dormant particles of peculiar green stone embedded in the rock, forcing them to give off their ephemeral light.

"Take up the rear, Sergeant. And everyone stay alert!" ordered Wolf, then set off after their fast-moving guide. The cave was damp and cool at first, but it became wetter the deeper they got. The steep, slick ground caused the occasional slip and mumbled curse as weapons clattered noisily off the rocks. As they went, the eerie green light faded behind them, forcing them ever onwards.

They felt the mild heat at first, but then they began to see the glowing light below. Eventually, the ground levelled out as the tunnel went towards a large well-lit cavern clearly visible up ahead. Whatever illuminated this vaulted space at this depth, they still could not see until they finally rounded the last bend. There at the back of the cavern was an opening twice the height of Wolf and just as wide, filled with a thick white mist, behind which emanated a wall of dazzling light. Some balked and took a step back, shielding their eyes. More stood with mouths agape, lost for words. Others were simply mesmerised.

"It is a portal, a gateway, nothing more," calmed Midir. "It cannot harm you, but do not linger as you pass through." Then he walked towards the slow-moving mist and paused. "But know this: you will not survive what lies ahead if you do not trust me. If we wanted you dead, it would be done already," said Midir starkly and then disappeared into the portal.

Wolf gave O'Neill a meaningful look and gave a quick flick of his head towards the portal. The sergeant knew full well what that meant. The captain didn't want to order O'Neill and would have preferred to lead the way himself, but if Wolf went through first, he could not be sure that everyone would follow him. In most worldly things, the Rangers would not hesitate to follow their captain, but this was something altogether different, and Wolf did not want to run the risk of leaving anyone behind; a return through the portal might not be possible.

"Alright then, let's be having you!" barked O'Neill good-naturedly. "Couldn't be any worse than this dingy hole," he joked. Then he fired Wolf a wink and went boldly into the vapour.

Blade took a quick look around her and went swiftly towards the portal, then stopped. "Well, what are you all waiting for? It's not like we can go back," she reasoned, glancing towards the darkening tunnel. Then she followed O'Neill into the mist. Not wanting to display any further reticence, the rest of the group wasted little time and smartly followed after Blade, leaving Wolf alone in the cavern.

Wolf took a moment to look around him as the last of the weird green light faded on the cave walls. There was something strangely familiar about all of this, some latent memory, a fleeting thought that remained tantalisingly out of reach. Perhaps the answers lay on the other side of this gateway, or maybe there would just be more troubling questions. Then he took a deep breath and quickly followed his Rangers through the portal.

Chapter Sixteen

NORTH

Rasende had been right. A small group of Raiders had taken off by foot through the forest, heading north and veering east. They had taken some care to cover their tracks, but they appeared to have been moving fast and had still left some signs, though not enough for Rasende to determine their numbers. The big tracker had been right about the horses too. The ragged terrain chosen by the fleeing ambushers was no place for their animals.

The Raiders' tracks had been harder to follow across the stone-paved Burren. But Rasende had found a disused hut where a small party had stopped for the night and cooked some small game over a meagre fire. Scarface was pretty sure it had been used by their quarry, as the camp was in keeping with the Raiders' line of travel.

Following these kidnappers through the wild patchwork of scrub, forest and wetlands that covered east Connaught had proved challenging for Cuallaidh and his reluctant foot soldiers. Whoever had led these Raiders through this rugged rainswept land seemed to know this wilderness very well.

Cuallaidh's men had been irritable since relinquishing their horses, and the long slog through the wetlands of Ireland's most westerly province had done little to improve their dour mood. The sweet-sounding chime of a nearby monastery bell had come at a fortuitous time for Cuallaidh, as he could sense that the men's lust for the hunt was beginning to wane.

Cuallaidh, Erik and Scarface had moved cautiously forward through the trees to get a closer look at the small lakeside monastery as the last of the evening light began to fade.

"We need supplies," said Erik pragmatically.

"More importantly, we need information," stressed Cuallaidh, as it was highly likely that some or all of the Raiders had stopped at the monastic settlement for the very same thing.

"And I think that the men could do with a little sport?" suggested Scarface with a crooked grin. "I saw some pretty nuns," he explained. Cuallaidh knew better than to try and come between a dog and its meat; he also knew that it would be wise to let his hounds slip the leash for a while, or he could end up with no pack at all.

"Tell them to make it quick," allowed Cuallaidh. "We have little time to spare."

"We had better not torch the place. Smoke could be seen halfway across the country on a clear day," warned Erik. "We don't want a troop of Connaught horsemen bearing down on top of us."

"That's the last thing we need," agreed Cuallaidh. "Neither can we let these people report how few in number we really are."

"And how do you propose that we prevent that happening?" asked Erik, sounding as though he was not going to like what Cuallaidh had to say.

"Simple: we leave no survivors."

Cuallaidh's pack waited in the trees until the church bell rang for morning prayers. When they were certain that the mass had started, they made their way quickly and quietly to the church, sending two men around the back of the small chapel to seal off the building. Rasende loped off towards the few outbuildings that there were to dispatch any stragglers and silence the dogs.

Cuallaidh opened the church door softly and took a few slow steps into the chapel as the rest of his men filed in wordlessly behind him and fanned out around the walls. The congregation, mostly monks and a small number of nuns, stopped praying and watched in silence, transfixed with fear.

"All are welcome here," said the old priest hesitantly, unsure of what to make of this unexpected interruption. When the Viking leader slowly closed the creaking door behind him and rammed the bolt home, the elderly monk finally accepted that these men had not come here to pray.

After the slaughter, Cuallaidh pulled the church door after him as he left, shielding his eyes from the bright autumnal sun.

"I doubt that place will ever be considered sacred again," said Erik to no one in particular, visibly shaken by the savage brutality he had just witnessed.

"The abbot said that there had only been two of them," stated Cuallaidh as he casually wiped the monks' blood off his knife onto his trousers. "They gave them some provisions and a little medicine to treat grazed feet."

"There's bound to be a reckoning for this," thought Erik aloud.

"Since when did you become so bloody squeamish?" snapped Cuallaidh.

"Here, have some of this piss," said Scarface, tossing Erik a skin of altar wine. "It's better than nothing," he joked, then went off to gather up Cuallaidh's blood-spattered pack.

*

Lieutenant Godfridsson stood in the shadows of the darkened warehouse, just beyond the tepid candlelight, silently listening to the man who had just chased him halfway across Ireland.

"The death of the Thomond Guards was regrettable," continued Captain O'Halloran, "but perhaps they were a little over-zealous in their performance."

"Which is to their great credit," responded Commander Sten with due respect.

"Indeed. Still, contracts must be honoured," he went on and held up one finger. The big man standing behind him duly responded and tossed a large bag of coins onto the makeshift table, sending up a plume of dust.

"Final payment for the ambush. You will also find a little compensation in there for your dead Ranger. Use it as you see fit." And then the captain held up two fingers. Once again, his bodyguard fished out two more heavy bags and tossed them onto the table with no finesse, the jarring sound filling the empty building.

"Consider this a down payment for your next assignment, Commander," explained O'Halloran.

"Which is what, exactly?" asked Sten irritably. He'd listened earlier to Lieutenant Godfridsson's troubling report and was not one bit pleased with this type of coercive persuasion.

"I myself do not know the exact nature of the mission, but I do know that a great deal of planning has gone into it."

"Not by me," countered the commander.

"That may well be," conceded the captain. "I am simply a messenger here. Amergen alone knows all the details. What I can tell you is that the Rangers' next target lies in the far north."

"And should we refuse?"

"That would be most calamitous," sighed O'Halloran. "Those Rangers who were involved in the killings would of course remain outlawed, as indeed would their families. And make no mistake, Commander, we know exactly who they are."

"I don't doubt it, Captain."

"Believe me when I tell you that Brian Boru has a long reach, and it may soon become even longer. He would be a bad enemy to have, Commander Sten. On the other hand, he could be a good friend to the Rangers, as he values their skills much more than most."

"And what are we supposed to do with the girl?" questioned Sten, starting to see the lie of the land.

"Put her in a convent somewhere," answered the captain dismissively as he rose to leave. "Brian will send for her when the time is right. This task is something of great importance to Boru. Renege at your peril, Commander Sten," warned O'Halloran as he paused at the warehouse door. "That being said, if your men do indeed succeed, rest assured that Brian will reveal his hand in this scheme to King Mahon, and all will be well for these Rangers," stressed the captain, deliberately glancing towards the darkness where Godfridsson stood concealed. Then Boru's messenger and his henchman stepped out into the night.

"He's a smooth one," said Godfrid, walking out of the shadows and securing the warehouse door.

"Aye, he's all of that. And this Boru is a clever bastard. He has us rightly cornered," answered Sten thoughtfully as he strummed his fingers on the table.

"What do you want us to do, Commander?"

"I reckon the only thing that you can do, Lieutenant,"

responded Sten eventually. "You must meet it head-on, as you would any other assignment. And whatever it is, Captain Wolf will have to use all of his skills and cunning to lead the Rangers through it. He will also need all the support that you can give him, Lieutenant."

"I started this mission with Captain Wolf. I fully intend to finish it with him."

"I would expect nothing less from you, Godfrid. Have you given any thought as to how you are going to get your men to Carlingford Lough, Lieutenant?"

"The quickest way that I know how, Commander, but I may need a little help with that."

*

The servant boy sauntered down the moonlit wharf, watched closely by Godfridsson and his men, who lay hidden in the dark shadows, ready to move. The young lad whistled a jaunty tune as he went, a wine skin over one shoulder and a small sack of food over the other. Peppered with wind-harried torches, the mooring area was quiet, as most people were off celebrating Jarl Kanarvan's marriage to the young Irish princess, Gormlaith. All the landing docks were congested with boats of all sizes, a forest of masts bobbing gently on the water. The boy was enthralled. He had never seen so many ships in one place, even in Dublin. Every notable jarl and chieftain from the Isle of Man to the Western Isles and beyond were here for this momentous alliance between the most powerful Irish clan in Leinster and the Dublin Norse, all of them eager for a share of any future lucrative trade.

"Who goes there?" called an alert sentry, jumping up

from his warm seat by a glowing brazier.

"I was sent down from the Great Hall," answered the boy amiably as he continued to approach.

"By who?" demanded the soldier, suspiciously.

"By Jarl Jorgensson, sir. He said that he would enjoy the wedding feast all the better if he knew that his boat was being well watched. So he thought to send the sentry on duty some extra rations so that he might watch his ship more closely than all the others."

"Jarl Jorgensson, you say?" questioned the sentry, rummaging through his memory for any reference to the name as he warily took the wine skin and bag of food. "From where?"

"He is a great jarl from the far north, sir."

"Which boat is his?" asked the sentry, scanning the rows of ships tied up along the torchlit wharf.

"When I asked him that, he simply said, 'Why it's the best one of course,'" repeated the boy, innocently looking out upon the mass of ships to see if he could behold this floating wonder.

The sentry tossed the boy a penny and sent him on his way. "Tell Jarl Jorgensson that I will take good care of his boat," called the guard through a mouthful of bread. "Whatever bloody one it is," he muttered, settling himself back down on his comfortable seat as he eagerly yanked the stopper out of the wine skin.

*

The wine had been laced with the herb valerian, a powerful sedative that had rapidly produced the desired effect. The sentry was snoring now, slumped in his chair by the fire. Sten's boy, Toke, had done well.

Godfridsson and his men emerged from the shadows and slipped down along the docks past the sleeping sentry, as silent as wharf rats. The lieutenant was glad he didn't have to kill the soldier. A slain guard and a missing boat spelt thieves, and that would have brought the promise of a swift pursuit, whereas a 'drunken' sentry and the curious loss of an inexpensive craft might suggest poorly secured lines and shoddy seamanship, with the boat having simply drifted off with the outgoing tide. Hopefully, it would be that initial uncertainty which would buy the Rangers the head start they so badly needed.

They chose their boat carefully: a small skiff that could be quickly and easily manoeuvred by the nine men. Hakon hopped in and took the precious longbows and quivers from the Rangers. He stowed them safely at the front of the boat and covered them over with a spare piece of lanolin-smeared sailcloth. Godfrid took the tiller and appointed a lookout to the bow as others quietly broke out the oars, three for each side. The last man loosed the lines fore and aft, pushed the boat off and jumped gingerly in. They eased the boat out into the dark-flowing waters of the River Liffey, and the outgoing tide swiftly picked up the light craft and swept it along.

The Rangers needed to be strong swimmers and proficient seafarers for their nefarious trade, so they were just as comfortable at sea as they were on land. Oars fitted, they set them rhythmically to work: Dip, pull and pause. Dip, pull and pause. A short spell of steady rowing soon brought them out into the lively waters of Dublin Bay as a clear moon filled the broad inlet with its soft luminous light.

"That sentry will be having a flogging for breakfast!"

joked one of the men in a hushed voice.

"Damned fool. Whoever heard of a jarl giving a rat's arse about the likes of us?" whispered another, probably Sven; the skinny Norseman seldom had a good word to say about anything.

"If a thing looks too good to be true, men, it usually is," cautioned the corporal as he prepared to raise the sail. And wasn't that the truth of it, thought Godfridsson. So much for the simple ambush and a 'minor action' in Thomond, he concluded wryly, then ordered the men to ship their oars and set the sail as the seaworthy skiff finally cleared land.

A fresh southwesterly breeze quickly filled the sail, and the lieutenant swung the boat towards the north, heading up the Irish Sea. If the wind stayed with them and the sea remained calm, they could be at Carlingford Lough by morning. And although nobody cared to say it, they all secretly hoped that Captain Wolf and the other Rangers would find a way to make it there too.

Chapter Seventeen

EIRU

Wolf finally emerged from the mist. He felt nauseous and disorientated and had lost all track of time. The walk through the portal might have only been a few short steps, but Wolf had absolutely no recollection of his feet ever having touched firm ground.

"Not to worry, Captain — we all felt the same," offered O'Neill cheerily. "A few of them even threw up!"

"What is this place?" asked Blade, trying to make sense of the luminous sky: a slow swirling mist of pale blues and soft pinks with no obvious sign of a sun.

"Your world and ours are but two sides of the same coin, joined by the slimmest of edges. You have just crossed over that short bridge," explained Midir.

"Who rules here?" asked the sergeant suspiciously, having already set up a defensive perimeter around the cave entrance which led back to the portal.

"This is the realm of the Tuatha De Danann, the abode of the People of the Goddess Danu. But other things dwell here too, dangerous things. And not all the Tuatha are well disposed towards mankind," warned Midir. "Remember, not everything is as it seems in our world either."

"And how are we to leave this peculiar place?" asked Wolf.

"With the upmost care, Captain. Listen well, Rangers," continued Midir earnestly. "You must not step off this track; for you it is the 'Path of Life'. Never draw your weapons here, no matter how great the provocation," stressed Midir. "Do not eat or drink anything while you are in the 'Land of the Ever-Living Ones', or you will never leave this place again; such sustenance is not meant for mortals."

"Time moves differently here, Rangers, so we dare not delay," warned Midir, then headed off swiftly on the grassy track. The Rangers fell quickly into formation behind him. Wolf took point and O'Byrne took up the rear, while everyone else slipped into single file.

At first, it was a strange, open land with blue-green meadows of tall grass sweeping out on either side of the trail. A warm waft of air swept over them from time to time, but the dry scented breeze did not feel like any earthly wind that they had ever known. It was bright here too, though not uncomfortably so, despite the curious absence of any sun.

Soon, they entered into a darkened wood of gnarled, stunted trees, where unseen creatures skittered through the undergrowth and dim indistinct shapes darted across the twisted branches. They could sense hungry stares boring into them with every step that they took into this forbidding place. Leering eyes seemed to keenly watch them too, patiently waiting for the trespassers to make one fatal mistake.

They heard the laughter at first. Then they came upon a small clearing in the woods where a group of young women in translucent shifts played and frolicked, chasing after an innocent fawn. On seeing the Rangers, they stopped. One nubile nymph ran excitedly over to the track and began making seductive gestures towards O'Byrne; the big man stalled to drink in her sensual curves, lust dripping from his pores. Forgetting himself, O'Byrne went to step off 'The Path of Life'.

"O'Byrne!" shouted O'Sullivan, snapping his friend

out of his amorous trance, and halting him in his tracks.

The woman rounded on O'Sullivan in an instant, her face hideously transformed into that of a snarling beast. She then resumed her normal appearance and turned back to O'Byrne, giving him a sweet smile and then bounded off to rejoin the game. Startled and shaken, the two men hurried to catch up to the group as the pitiful sounds of the tortured fawn began to fill their ears.

The Rangers were glad to have cleared the eerie forest and were once again traversing the blue-green plains. Here, the rolling landscape was peppered with groves of oddly coloured trees, vibrant oranges and vivid reds mostly, but there were lighter shades too, such as lilac, saffron and little hints of silver. Occasionally, there stood alone a gold-coloured tree shimmering in the surreal breeze, shrivelled leaves scattered beneath its boughs. It was hard to tell if these bright colours belonged to a summer or an autumn in this unusual place, but the black leaves which dotted some of the trees certainly appeared to be completely rotten and seemed somewhat out of place.

Suddenly, the ground began to rumble with the rhythmic pounding of two separate sets of heavy hooves. The Rangers scanned the plains in alarm but could see nothing even though the frightful sound grew ever louder as the invisible creatures charged towards them.

"Hold!" commanded Midir. "Hold your ground!"

The Rangers now saw the imprint of the long bounding strides made by the two invisible beasts, their enormous feet trampling the grass in their wake as they thundered towards them.

"Do not draw your weapons, men!" ordered Wolf, seeing several of the Rangers already reaching for their swords. “Heed Midir’s words; our lives may depend upon it.”

The beasts came to a shuddering stop at the very edge of the grassy track and sniffed deeply at the men beneath them, like so much ready meat, the putrid stink of the creatures’ breath filling the air. It was clear now that the invisible animals could not touch them while they remained firmly on ‘The Path of Life’. Indeed, it seemed as though the beasts’ headlong charge had been a ploy to use fear to drive the Rangers away from the protection of the path.

“Steady, lads!” called O’Neill. “Steady now.”

A frightened deer suddenly broke cover from a nearby grove and went to make a run for it. The rash movement caught the attention of one of the creatures, and they could sense its massive head swing around to home in on its new prey. Then the invisible duo bounded off again. One of them quickly caught the hapless deer and violently shook it in its jaws, snapping the animal’s neck in an instant. It then flung the carcass to its companion as they ran, who tossed it up in the air and caught it again within its mouth. They tussled over the dead animal after that until they finally ripped it apart, sending a spray of blood and entrails flying through the air.

“Horses!” called Midir, to Wolf. “And they’re moving fast.”

“Take up your positions, men!” ordered Wolf. “Horsemen approaching.”

A troop of dark horsemen were riding hard towards them, and everything about their demeanour spelt menace. Their horses were sleek and black, matching the dark attire of the riders, who held lethal-looking lances at the ready as they approached. Only their leader was adorned with any colour; a velvet cloak of crimson red billowed about him as he hard-hauled his fearsome mount to a bone-shuddering stop.

"Who dares to trespass on my land?" he demanded as his boisterous mount snarled at them with carnivorous teeth.

"These people are under my protection," said Midir forcefully. "And we have the right to safe passage across these lands, Lord Dearg."

"I decide who has the right to cross my territory, Prince Midir. And I decide who will not," pronounced Lord Dearg. Then he stood up in his stirrups and sniffed the air. "You have human women with you — leave the females and be on your way."

On hearing the threat to Blade and Arrow, the Rangers braced themselves and began reaching for their weapons.

"Do not take up arms, Rangers!" shouted Midir above the growling anger. "That's exactly what they want you to do. Draw your swords, and they will surely cut you down where you stand!"

The loud, piercing sound of a screeching eagle suddenly filled the air, the clarion call cutting right through them all and halting any further movement.

Three distorted pillars of shimmering light then appeared on the plain and quickly coalesced into the outline of three slender women, who boldly walked towards them. All three were regally dressed in gowns of green, their refined features, pale skin and almond-shaped eyes clearly setting them apart from the race of men. The golden-haired woman in the centre with the silver circlet was obviously the leader of the trio, and it was she who spoke first.

"Would you impede my champions on their quest,

Lord Dearg?"

"Queen Eiru," answered Dearg with a respectful nod, then went on to explain himself, but paused when he saw the withering look on Folda's face.

"The question was a rhetorical one," said Folda caustically.

"Be on your way, Lord Dearg," added Banba evenly. "There is nothing for you here."

"My lady," conceded the 'Red Lord', then savagely wheeled around his powerful horse and angrily led his men away.

"Time is against us, Prince Midir. You must not linger here," continued Eiru.

"So I can see, my lady. The signs of decay are everywhere," answered Midir sombrely, scanning the landscape around him.

"My lady, my sword is yours," said Berg for some bizarre reason. He went down on one knee, bowed his head and offered up his clenched fist clasped within his other hand.

"Berg, my rock," said Eiru gently as she softly rested her hand on his fist. "All of your swords do indeed belong to me," added the queen warmly as she scanned the group. "And I have been closely watching each and every one of you," she went on, and then focused her attention on O'Neill.

"Sergeant O'Neill, a king's son without a kingdom." O'Neill seemed a little stunned by Eiru's cryptic remark, but the grizzled campaigner hid it well.

"O'Byrne, you must learn to direct that temper of yours to where it can do most good," advised the queen. Abashed, O'Byrne mumbled something and stared down at the ground.

"O'Sullivan, one of your female ancestors did indeed come from the Sea-People. But you would do well to remember that our sea-cousins are not always our allies," cautioned Eiru. O'Sullivan puffed up like a strutting pigeon and threw O'Byrne a triumphant look.

"Fearless Ferret, you will need all of your cunning and bravery for what lies ahead of you, my tough little man."

"The deadly Blade," said Eiru with an appreciative smile. "Remember that a good sword is made up from many layers of steel, one soft, the next hard. Too hard, the blade will snap. Too soft, the weapon is useless." Wolf wasn't quite sure what Eiru meant, but Blade seemed to understand the message and gave a little tilt of her head.

"You have suffered much, Aoife, my sharp little Arrow. Be healed," said Eiru tenderly as she rested her hand on the girl's shoulder. Arrow simply looked at the ground as the warm tears escaped down her face.

"Tenacious Farrell: hardy, shrewd and dependable," complimented the queen. The tall Ranger looked well pleased with the assessment.

The queen then surveyed the O'Donnell brothers and seemed well pleased by what she saw. "The Hounds of Tirconnell," she announced. "You must continue to be vigilant; you are their eyes and their ears." The brothers bowed in unison.

"Well, have you found the girl, Amergen?" asked Eiru bluntly.

"I believe so, my lady," responded Amergen, appearing a little subdued.

"Time is running out, wizard."

"I will succeed, Queen Eiru."

"If you do not, you will lose much more than the

colour in your hair the next time," threatened Eiru, and then she turned her attention to Wolf.

"And of course you, my wild Wolf, the leader of our quest," began the queen and then switched her communication to the mind-speech.

Born of woman, nurtured by wolves and reared in the Land of the Ever-Living Ones — little wonder you ponder where you belong.

Where do I belong? asked Wolf. It was a question that troubled him.

You belong in all three worlds, Wolf. Above all, you truly belong with yourself. But know this, 'Wolf-Man': should you happen to survive in your hazardous profession, your rearing in this place will come at a cost. Time will move a little differently for you than it will for other mortals. It is an inevitable consequence of a childhood spent amongst the Ever-Living Ones, finished Eiru enigmatically. Then the queen addressed the group:

"Time is against us all in this fight. Our enemy grows stronger with each passing day. You must not delay on your journey to the far north; Odin's viper is already coiled for the strike," warned Eiru. "Do not dally in this land, my fine champions. It is no place for mortals," stressed the queen as she turned to walk away, inadvertently revealing her talon-like foot for a fleeting moment as it slipped out from beneath her long flowing dress.

Eiru may rule here, Wolf, but the creatures of the world answer to me, said Banba with the mind-speech. Then she held out her arm and a hooded crow flew from a nearby tree to land on this soft perch. *I cannot interfere with the laws of nature in your world, and the contest between the Red Dragon and the White Dragon must run its course. But your enemy seeks aid from beyond the veil of your world; in desperate times, you must do the same, Captain,* counselled Banba. *Only the hooded crow and the raven have the intelligence to travel between our world and yours,* Banba explained. *When you are in dire need, Wolf, send a hooded crow to me and I will do what I can. Do not use the raven, for that trickster is Odin's bird, and so cannot always be trusted, as that dark god is in league with our enemy.*

The hooded crow gave Wolf a long, hard look, committing his face to the collective memory of those of his kind, and then the bird went off about his business.

"Do not tarry here, Wolf; the Land of the Ever-Living Ones is a perilous place for humans, even for you," warned Banba as she went to rejoin her sisters. Then all three walked off across the plain and simply disappeared.

Chapter Eighteen

CONCLUSIONS

It hadn't taken Sergeant Mac Namara long to catch up to the slow-moving wagon. He had been able to hear the creaking cart well before he could see it.

What he did eventually observe surprised him. Mac Namara wasn't quite sure what it was that he had been expecting to see. But a simple monk and his helper driving a wagon of hay certainly hadn't been it.

In fact, the entire scene appeared somewhat odd. Why haul a cart of fodder from one end of the country to the other? Another thing that the sergeant found a little puzzling was the depth of the wagon tracks, which seemed way too deep for just a load of hay. And the creaks and the groans that the rickety cart made suggested that it contained a lot more than harmless forage.

Mac Namara had shadowed the trundling cart for several days now, weaving his horse carefully through the wizened woodland that overlooked the Northern Road. He was fairly certain that they didn't have Princess Aoife secretly hidden beneath the hay, as the pair showed scant interest in the contents of the wagon at any time. Still, he was sure that the cart had in some way been involved in the ambush at Eagle's Pass. Perhaps the two men were on their way now to meet up with the rest of the Raiders? And maybe there was something of value buried under the hay? When the wagon stopped for a midday break, the sergeant decided it was an opportune time to have a closer look.

Mac Namara found a small grassy clearing in the

woods and hobbled his horse there to graze. Then he hid his saddle and any other cumbersome gear and slipped off his distinctive red cloak as an added precaution. Most of the autumn leaves and a few weary branches had already surrendered and lay defeated on the forest floor, leaving the woodland bare and good cover very hard to find.

Using a sprawling holly bush to shield his stealthy approach, Mac Namara got down on his belly and slithered quietly down the slope, using the bed of dry leaves to propel him gently along. Peering through the holly's lush foliage, the sergeant silently scrutinized the unlikely pair below.

The monk was prattling away, obviously content to let his God watch over him and his companion protect him. The escort looked far more alert and had the hard look of a fighting man about him. Yielding to Mac Namara's weight, a rotten branch under the leaves beneath him suddenly broke, shooting a muffled snap out into the still forest air. Mac Namara cringed at the sound of the sharp crack and silently cursed his ill luck. He continued to remain perfectly still, watching, waiting and hoping that the unnatural sound hadn't been heard by the men below.

The escort held up his hand to stop the monk talking while his other hand went instinctively to the dagger hidden beneath his dark green cloak. The man swivelled his head from side to side, his mouth slightly ajar, attempting to pick up any more unusual sounds as he walked slowly towards the wagon. He slipped off his cloak and tossed it carelessly onto the seat of the cart, revealing a buckskin outfit of forest green. Then he slowly reached beneath the wagon seat and retrieved a longbow and a quiver of arrows, all the while scanning the woods around him. Casually, he nocked an arrow as he walked around the cart, then he suddenly swung around to face Mac Namara's position and let the arrow fly. The arrow thumped into an oak tree right beside the sergeant, quivering with the force of the strike. Mac Namara stayed stock still as the archer stared hard at the holly bush for a long moment. Then the escort turned away and spoke briefly to the monk, who quickly gathered up his belongings and got back up on the wagon.

Was the man guessing? Was it a lucky strike? Or did the skilled archer know exactly where Mac Namara was? Whatever the case, it was a shrewd move by the escort, and the sergeant got the message loud and clear: stay well away or you'll get the next one! Whoever this man was, he certainly was no acolyte, concluded the sergeant as the cart trundled off down the Northern Road.

From now on, Mac Namara would need to be far more careful and follow the suspicious wagon at a much safer distance, or he could easily find himself on the wrong end of well-aimed arrow. Not only that, one more mistake could jeopardise the only tangible connection to Princess Aoife which the sergeant had left.

*

After the slaughter, Cuallaidh had ordered his men to ransack the small monastery for any portable wealth. Valuable chalices, silver crosses, candlesticks and coins were all gathered up. Ornate clasps and hinges were ripped from holy books, and the gold and silver leaf was torn from the tabernacle door. Cuallaidh's pack had then rifled through the butchered corpses that lay strewn about the church, hacking off a couple of swollen fingers to remove a few stubborn rings. The bloody spoils collected, the killers had grabbed whatever provisions they could quickly find, and then they had fled into the nearby bog.

Keen to put plenty of distance between themselves and their atrocities, Cuallaidh's men had moved quickly over the open bog land, greatly helped by the Raiders' mucky tracks that went before them. Halfway across the rain-swept marsh, Rasende had paused to point out the scattered bloodstains of a possible ambush. The big tracker reckoned that someone who had been poorly prepared had gotten way too close to these deadly Raiders and had paid the ultimate price for their folly.

"These Raiders know their business," Rasende had said: a sober warning to them all.

The bridge across the Shannon at Clonmacnoise had been guarded. Cuallaidh had been in no mood for delay and was for killing the two sentries until Erik had pointed out that someone might make the connection between the unexplained massacre at the small monastery and the murder of the two Connaught guards on the bridge, which would surely bring a host of angry Connaught troops down upon their heads.

"Too much of a coincidence," Erik had cautioned.

Cuallaidh had heeded his friend's concerns, and they had spared the two sentries. Instead, they had used the cover of darkness to steal a boat and had paddled softly across the wide river, abandoning the craft to the mercy of the current. Rasende had been confident that he could pick up the Raiders' trail beyond Clonmacnoise, so they had given the monastic grounds a wide berth and headed for the cover of the trees north of the settlement.

The Raiders had obviously picked up a pony at

Clonmacnoise, which had left them much easier to track as they fled into the kingdom of West Meath. Rasende had speculated that someone could have been injured at the ambush in the bog. But Cuallaidh had been of the opinion that the foot medicine that the Raiders had been given at the small monastery and the pony were both in some way connected.

"Perhaps the princess is struggling to keep up with the tough pace being set by these fast-moving Raiders?" he had ventured.

The big lake had stalled their rapid pursuit towards the northeast. With the curious absence of any boats to steal, Cuallaidh's men had been forced to tramp around the soggy fringes of the lough in order to pick up the Raiders' trail again on the other side of the lake. At first, Rasende had found it difficult to detect any signs of the Raiders along the far shore, but when he pressed a little further into the beech wood, he soon found their trail.

Sensing that the Raiders were now struggling to keep ahead of them, Cuallaidh's pack redoubled their efforts and pushed hard all that day. The Raiders' scuffed tracks through the dry leaves had been easy to follow and had led Rasende straight to a leafy hollow where their quarry had obviously spent the night. But now there were other tracks too, those of different men. Horses and hounds had also been here.

Bloodshed in the bog, hurried horsemen and eager hounds combing through the woods: it seemed that Cuallaidh's pack were not the only ones that were hunting these elusive Raiders.

*

Eventually, Rasende made some sense of the profusion of tracks and picked out a hasty trail that veered off into forest. They quickly followed the tracks to the base of a rocky outcrop, where the Raiders' trail seemed to just simply disappear.

Perplexed, they scoured the woods in every direction but were still none the wiser. Rasende pushed on alone towards the northeast to see if he could pick up their trail again a little further on, but the look on the tracker's face when he returned seemed to say it all.

"Nothing," he said simply, clearly trying to process the vexing riddle.

"Nothing?" asked Cuallaidh incredulously.

"How can there be nothing, Rasende?"

"I don't know what kind of witchcraft this is, Ivarsson, but their tracks stop here," stated Rasende flatly as he stared at the base of the rock. Then he placed his hands softly on the slab of stone to see if it was in fact real.

"Maybe it's some kind of trap?" said Scarface, scanning the woods around him as Rasende poked about at the base of the outcrop, looking for something.

"What's that he's drawing?" asked Nielsen, as Rasende began scrawling some sort of shape on the face of the rock with a stone he had found at the base of the outcrop.

"It looks like that old nun that you humped back at the monastery," poked Gorm, generating a few raucous chuckles.

"Any fjord in a storm," growled Nielsen, not appreciating a joke at his expense.

"That looks like a map of Ireland," suggested Larsen.

Rasende ignored them all and went on with the drawing. His outline of Ireland completed, he etched several marks down across the centre of the map and then scraped a diagonal line northeast, right through them all.

"We may not know where they are, but we do know where they've been," explained Rasende, pointing to the symbols marked on the map and the connecting line he had drawn through them all. "So we do have a fair idea what direction they're heading," reasoned the tracker as he scrawled one final X at the top end of his angled line where it met Ireland's vertical east coast.

"And is there anything of note between here and the sea?" quizzed Cuallaidh.

"Even if there is, Ivarsson, we can still continue to search for these Raiders on our way to the east coast," reasoned Rasende.

"And what's at that last X where your line meets the east coast?" asked Scarface.

"A waiting boat, maybe?" speculated Rasende.

"There is a fjord there, alright," offered Larsen. "I think it's called Strangfjord."

"Aye, it's Norse for 'rough fjord', and it's aptly named," stated Scarface. "A narrow inlet with a savage run, shallow waters and small islands scattered all over the place."

"Who controls it?" asked Cuallaidh.

"The Ulstermen still hold it, I think. Defend it like angry wasps, they do. It's hard to get a foothold on the shore there," answered Scarface.

"There is another fjord up there named Carlinfjord. I sailed up it once. I think it's Norse for 'steep-sided fjord', which is accurate enough. Good deep water all the way in," described Larsen.

"And it's a lot nearer than Strangfjord," added Rasende.

"Anyone, any idea who rules there?" asked Cuallaidh.

"It's not that straightforward," began Scarface. "The Danes have a fort at the head of the lough. The Irish have a coastal settlement at the centre of the inlet and are happy enough to trade with both the Norse and the Danes when they're not busy fighting against them. And then the Norse have a large stronghold at Annagassan, which is near the mouth of the lough. All three tribes claim ownership of the fjord. So far, nobody has managed to take outright control of it."

"Sounds like an ideal place to anchor a waiting ship," suggested Rasende.

"Does this Irish settlement have a name?" asked Cuallaidh.

"I think they just call it Carlingford, after the Irish fashion," said Larsen.

Cuallaidh carefully considered everything that his men had said. And it seemed a reasonable theory that these Raiders could indeed be fleeing to a waiting ship. If the Raiders got the girl out of the country, then they might never find her again. Maybe there had been some sort of strange witchcraft here, as Rasende had said. Still, there was no denying that these cunning Raiders had consistently travelled northeast, whatever their motivation. So there was no reason to suppose that that one fact was about to change, just because they had somehow managed to mysteriously disappear. In any case, it wasn't like they had very much choice at this point anyway, reflected Cuallaidh.

"We will continue northeast and try to pick up their trail again. If we do not find them, we will see what answers this Carlinfjord may have to offer. Who knows? We might even find some new allies there too," concluded Cuallaidh thoughtfully, then he ordered his men to move out.

Chapter Nineteen

CARLINGFORD

A wan dawn seeped into the eastern sky, the feeble light obscured by grey banks of low-lying clouds. Seagulls had begun to rouse themselves and hovered above the skiff for a while in hopes of an easy meal, then noisily wheeled away when they saw that the boat had nothing to offer.

Columns of smoke began to rise from the small settlements scattered along Ireland's east coast as people roused themselves from their slumber in need of warmth and food. The large Norse stronghold at Annagassan was clearly visible in the distance as they passed, easily identified by the congestion of sooty plumes amassed in one place.

The wind had remained fresh from the southwest ever since they had slipped stealthily out of Dublin in the dead of night. An occasional gust pushed hard against the flooding tide which swept down from the north, heaping the surface of the slate-grey sea into small white wavelets.

The mainsail alone had been ample to propel the small craft steadily northwards, so most of the men wrapped themselves in their dark green cloaks and took their turn to sleep while others manned the watch. The rigging had needed little tending, as the direction of the wind suited the square sail. But the low freeboard allowed the odd rogue wave to slosh some water over the gunwale from time to time, which meant regular bailing was inevitable.

Sensing the breaking day, the men began to stir themselves. Refreshed by a little sleep and well pleased at their cunning theft of the Viking boat, they awoke in good spirits, content to wrestle with another day.

"Are you not going to wave goodbye to your cousins, Thorsten?" asked McMahon mischievously as Annagassan faded into the background on their port quarter. The brawny Ulsterman from the rugged heart of the Mourne Mountains had a real knack for stoking up trouble, especially when things were quiet.

"Those Norse scum are no cousins of mine, you Irish sheep-shagger," growled the big Swede, a stoical man at the best of times.

"Have you been bragging about your sex life again, McMahon?" chided O'Carroll. The canny Leinster man and McMahon were usually thick as thieves, but that was no reason for O'Carroll to miss out on a little fun.

"And would you look at who's talking? You must have humped half the whores in Dublin at this stage. God only knows what state your tackle is in!" countered McMahon sourly.

"Why, that's terrible talk, McMahon, even if there is a little truth in some of what you say. Still, that's no reason to be maligning a man's gear like that. It just isn't Christian," retorted O'Carroll with mock indignation. "Am I right, Ferguson?"

"I think that you are all animals," said the former monk dryly. Ferguson had been a novice on one of the isolated islands off the Scottish coast when his monastery had been attacked by the Norse. Whoever had survived the initial onslaught on Iona had been carried off into slavery. Ferguson had only escaped because he had been halfway down a cliff face collecting fulmar eggs at the time of the raid. The young Scot had decided on a change of profession after that, but he still secretly said his prayers.

"Hansen knows I'm right; he seems like a reasonable man," persisted O'Carroll. He knew full well that he was playing with fire, poking at the brooding Dane, but he just couldn't resist it. "What do you say, Hansen?"

"I say that you two talk enough bullshit for all of us," said Hansen flatly.

"Amen to that," added Ferguson sardonically.

Well pleased with themselves, McMahon and O'Carroll laughed heartily.

"Does anyone know these waters?" called out the lieutenant as they neared the mouth of Carlingford Lough, veering the skiff northwest as Hakon adjusted the sail. It was of course a legitimate question, but Godfrid's tone let the men know that playtime was over and it was high time to focus on the seafaring business at hand.

"I do, Lieutenant," answered Kelly cheerily. Then the fresh-faced Irishman made his way astern to Godfridsson at the tiller. "I used to fish around here with my grandfather when I was a nipper. The lough itself is wide enough, but you do need to be careful here at the mouth; the entrance is narrow and pretty shallow in places."

"Farming not the life for you, Kelly?"

Kelly suddenly went very quiet, and Godfrid knew he had inadvertently said something wrong.

"I liked it well enough, Lieutenant," answered Kelly after a heavy silence. "But the Norse came one day and burned the whole place to the ground. Killed my parents and abducted my sister. I had been up there in the Cooley hills, tending the sheep." He pointed towards the low mountain range along the southern shore as they headed up the calmer waters of the lough.

"Sorry, Kelly, I didn't know."

"That's alright, Lieutenant. It's not something I tend to

talk about. I haven't been back here in a long while."

"And what of your sister?"

"I went to the slave pens in Dublin to see if I could find her, but it was already too late. Someone told me that the Dublin Norse had just shipped out several boatloads of Irish women to the east. I'm pretty sure that she was one of them. Doubt I'll ever see her again. I didn't see much point in farming again after that."

"You will have another family one day, Kelly," said Godfridsson earnestly. "And you will be a farmer once again. The world is never short of soldiers who are good at destroying everything that they touch, but it takes real farmers like you, Kelly, to grow things."

Kelly seemed to take some comfort from Godfrid's words, and then a shout rang out from the port bow:

"Carlingford Village, up ahead! Over there, Lieutenant," called the lookout from the bow, pointing left towards the bristling Irish fort perched atop a natural rocky outcrop, a sprawling village huddled about it.

"Best reef that sail, Corporal Hakon!" called out Godfridsson as they drew nearer to the long, congested wharf. "Break out a couple of oars. And ready those lines! Steady as she goes, men."

They had made it this far, anyway. And if Godfrid knew Wolf, he was fairly certain that the captain would also find a way to get his Rangers to Carlingford Village, whatever that might entail.

*

Later that day, Midir led Wolf and his Rangers to another of the mysterious portals, which opened out into a large cavern beneath a complex of damp caves.

The remainder of their journey through the land of the Ever-living Ones had not been without further incident. And the Rangers had seen many more strange wonders but other things too, disturbing sights and sounds that they would much prefer to forget.

The Rangers followed Midir closely as he climbed quickly through the labyrinth of dank tunnels. He touched the wet rock as he passed, activating the smatterings of embedded green stone and forcing them to give off their soft light. All of them kept up with the brisk pace, eager to leave the surreal netherworld behind them — keen, too, not to be left alone in the utter darkness when the last of the eerie green light finally faded away.

At the end of the tunnel, Midir placed his hands gently on the rock face and spoke in a strange lilting language which none of them could understand, then he took a step back. A section of the hard rock seemed to shimmer and warp at first, then the stone slowly began to dissolve as if it were nothing more than a mere veil of sand.

The Rangers spilled quickly out of the cave entrance, which was set at the foot of a craggy mountain ridge, and they were thankful for the natural moonlight. Gratefully, they gulped down the cool, salty air as they drank in the familiar starry sky that stretched above them.

"They will soon forget this place," said Midir as he remained in the entrance of the cave. "But a few dark traces of their time here may forever haunt their dreams."

"Where are we?" asked Wolf, scanning the mountainous terrain about him as the O'Donnell brothers instinctively set out to scout the rocky slopes.

"These are the Cooley Mountains. A low range of hills nestled in the northeast of the country," explained Midir as someone began to vomit loudly behind a nearby boulder.

"The sickness will soon pass, as will the other things," reassured Midir, seeing the look of concern on Wolf's face as he looked about his men. Most of the Rangers seemed a little shaken by their weird experiences, one way or another.

One half of O'Byrne's face appeared badly sunburned after his close encounter with the sirens in the twisted forest. O'Sullivan was rambling on about the Sea-People. Berg had a beatific smile on his face and looked like a man who had just had some sort of spiritual experience. And to make matters worse, O'Neill, Blade and Amergen all seemed unusually subdued. Arrow, on the other hand, kept repeating with a mixture of delight and disbelief that her feet had been magically healed, while some of the others were off discreetly getting sick.

"You must not delay here, Wolf," warned Midir. "The men of Munster and Connaught still clamour for your blood. And Ivar's hounds search high and low for you and the jarl's stolen bride. All the while, our greatest enemy is rapidly gathering his forces in the far north, growing stronger with each passing day."

"What can you tell me of this target that we must strike?" asked Wolf, trying to glean any vital information.

"All that I can tell you for now is that you must gather up your men swiftly, Captain, and go quickly northwards towards the Cold Country. Once there, you will need to go deep into the viper's lair and rip out his fangs. Amergen will show you the way. Heed the wizard's words well, as he serves us too in this quest."

"Thanks, Midir," said Wolf simply; there was little else he could say.

"Perhaps you and your Rangers might do some small

service for me one day," suggested Midir as he turned to walk away.

"Captain!" called Cormac O'Donnell from the ridge above. "You might want to come up and see this."

Wolf turned back to answer Midir, but the cave entrance had already closed, sealed off once more with a shield of solid rock.

Thank you, for everything, Midir, said Wolf solemnly with the mind-speech as he rested his hands softly on the cold stone.

Memories of the land of the Ever-Living Ones are fleeting, and that's for good reason. But you would do well to hold fast to Banba's counsel. Hurry, Wolf! You have much to do and time is against us, came Midir's words drifting back.

Wolf hauled himself up onto the ridge beside O'Donnell and was not disappointed at what the scout had to show him.

"Well worth a look, Captain?" said O'Donnell with satisfaction.

"A very welcome sight indeed, Cormac," answered Wolf, sensing a rare moment of relief as they admired the view that lay before them. Hemmed in by the Mourne Mountains on its northern coastline and the Cooley Hills along its southern shore, Carlingford Lough stretched out before them as far as the Irish Sea, its calm waters glittering beneath the light of a full moon. At the very foot of the Cooley Mountains lay the Irish stronghold of Carlingford, village torchlights twinkling by the shore.

Wolf and his Rangers had made it despite all the dangers and obstacles that had been stacked against them. Now all that they could do was hope that Lieutenant Godfridsson and his men had somehow made it to

Carlingford too and that Amergen's promised ship lay ready and waiting somewhere down below. Whatever perils lay ahead for Wolf and his men, the abduction of Princess Aoife had brought the Rangers far too many enemies in Ireland for their limited numbers to contend with. Amergen's ship was crucial to them right now if they were to have any hope of putting distance between themselves and their pursuers.

"That's odd, a full moon," puzzled Wolf.

"And what's so strange about that?"

"The night we fled with Midir into the cave in the woods, the moon was barely into its first quarter," explained Wolf.

"So?"

"That was well over a week ago."

"But how can that possibly be, Captain? We were only with Midir for a single day!"

"My point exactly, O'Donnell," answered Wolf simply.

Unable to fathom the perplexing matter, they silently admired the lough for another brief moment, and then they both hurried down from the ridge.

Chapter Twenty

REUNIONS

Preparations had been hectic, but the banter among the men had been good. They were all glad to be back in each other's company, though none of them would care to admit it. Still, they were all keen to hear of each other's embellished stories of escape and eager to learn of any new ruse that might give them an edge in the future.

Wolf's men thought that the lieutenant's Rangers had done very well to stay ahead of the Munster men all the way to Dublin. And they admired the stealth that they had shown in stealing a boat from under the Norsemen's noses. The drugging of the guard, they considered to be a right piece of low cunning indeed, and they had all laughed heartily at the sentry's misfortune.

Godfridsson's section reckoned that the attack by the wolves on the lakeside settlement had been a canny piece of good luck, allowing for the theft of the canoes. Most of Wolf's men tended to agree. A few others thought that it had been a bit more than good fortune alone, but they kept their opinions to themselves. Wolf's men also seemed to have been a little vague about the final section of their journey, saying only that they had fled into strange caves near the midlands and then emerged again in the Cooley Mountains. Some of the men had appeared utterly confused about their subterranean journey, while a few refused to talk about the caves at all.

Wolf's section, Godfridsson's squad, and Amergen's ship, the Sea Eagle, had all made it safely to Carlingford. And they had spent the previous day stocking the vessel with additional stores of dried fish, salted meat, water and ale. They had also scoured the village for additional arrows and left Amergen to deal with the customary visit to the local Irish chieftain, Conn O'Hanlon, who held the high fort in the heart of the settlement. Ostensibly, Amergen had gone to pay his respects and settle their account for the use of the wharf, but he had also gone there to glean any useful information. And it seemed that the Norse and the Danes were gearing up for an all-out battle against each other for control of the lough. All that it would take at this point was something, or somebody, to set the whole thing off.

The Sea Eagle had been remarkably well equipped to begin with. The hold of the Norse longship had already held everything from spare clothing to basic weapons, shields, and grappling hooks with long coils of walrus rope attached. There were large vats for fresh water too, even cauldrons, spits and salt so that hot meals could be prepared on the shore. And there were ample sea chests for all of them to keep their belongings dry; the heavy timber boxes could also serve as oar benches if the need arose. Already stored inside each sea chest was an essential sleeping bag lined with sheep's wool, the outer part sealed with a layer of waterproofed linen. Someone had even thought to pack a chest full of fresh bandages, clean linen, small pots of healing lotions, potions, and other strange instruments used in the curing craft. Also secured in the hold were two large earthen jars. Amergen had said that all the men needed to know for now was to keep flame well away from the curious containers and that he would explain all to the Rangers in due course.

The wharf had been bustling since early that morning with ships busy taking on cargo, keen to catch the noonday tide. Pelts, hides and bales of wool were all being hoisted into holds, while a handful of Irish wolfhounds, housed in separate cages for shipping, launched at each other with noisy regularity, much to the amusement of their handlers, who clattered their cages from time to time to shut the dogs up. Noisy hucksters also peddled their wares to the pestered sailors as a couple of bawdy women lewdly offered to provide more intimate services before the crewmen returned to the cold comforts of the sea.

In a bid to find a little quiet, the small group had moved off towards the end of the wide wharf. Wolf had been keen to be gone from the tight confines of Carlingford Village, but Amergen had wanted to wait, saying only that he was still short one piece for his Tafl board. Wolf had known better than to press him for answers, as the little man always seemed to have one more trick up his sleeve. When Brother Kevin's rickety wagon came creaking down the congested wharf, Wolf wasn't in the least bit surprised. And he very much doubted that the monk had come all this way just to deliver his load of fodder. Most likely, the Norse outfits that they had used in the ambush at Eagle's Pass were exactly where they had left them, stacked neatly beneath the hay.

"At last, the final gaming piece for our board, Captain Wolf," said Amergen with satisfaction, directing Brother Kevin towards the moored Sea Eagle.

"A sight for sore eyes," announced Ranger Campbell as he approached the small party at the end of the wharf, leaving the monk to organise the unloading of his own wagon.

"Problems, Campbell?" asked Wolf, scanning the horizon behind the Ranger for any signs of trouble.

"No problems, Captain. It seems that nobody is the least bit interested in a creaky old wagon full of hay," answered Campbell in his droll Scottish accent. "But... and maybe it's nothing..."

"Let me be the judge of that," pressed Wolf. "What is it?"

"It's just that I had the damndest feeling that we were being followed, Captain. I might have scared them off with a warning arrow back in the woods, or maybe they just hung back after that."

"Any idea of numbers, Ranger?"

"No. As I say, Captain, could be nothing at all; just thought I should mention it."

"Thanks, Campbell. You were right to mention it."

"Just one more thing, Captain. I didn't know anything about this little diversion. I thought that we were going to some monastery in Cork. Next thing I know, we're heading north," explained Campbell.

"Our Amergen is just full of surprises," answered Wolf dryly, firing the little man a sharp look.

"Did everyone else make it, Captain?"

"They're up in the village. I gave them a pass until noon, and then we ship out on high water. Go grab yourself something to eat, Campbell, and take Brother Kevin with you; he'll need something too before he gets back on the road," said Wolf. "The crew can unload the wagon."

*

Godfridsson was again giving them the gist of what Captain O'Halloran had said: the threats, the pardons and the part about the convent. "Put her in a convent; that's all he said," concluded the lieutenant.

"Saint Bridget's convent is just beyond the Cooley Hills. Brother Kevin could take her on his way back," suggested Amergen as the coxswain of the Sea Eagle bawled abrasive orders at his harassed crew to unload the wagon, driving on a male slave mercilessly as he struggled up the gangplank under the weight of the heavy sacks. Wolf thought that it would have been better if the Rangers served as crew from here themselves, but Amergen had simply said that they would need the skilled coxswain and his deckhands at a later stage in the journey.

"Alone and with no protection?" asked Wolf, returning his attention to the matter at hand. "When we already know from what Midir has told us that Ivar's men are still combing the country for the princess. Is that really wise?"

"Well, don't look at me," said Blade stiffly, then gave a little shudder at the very thought of being stuck in a convent on protection duty.

"We can't just abandon her alone in a convent after all that we have done just to get her here," reasoned Wolf, vaguely watching a hooded beggar in a ragged cloak as he made his way slowly down the crowded wharf, rattling a dirty bowl as he went. Something seemed odd about the stooped man, but Amergen's insistent argument brought Wolf directly back to the question at hand: what were they going to do with Princess Aoife?

"It's what Brian wants," continued Amergen.

"But does Brian know that Ivar's men are still hot on our tails?" argued O'Neill. "If we just stick her in a convent, then we might as well just hand her over to the bastards now, save a lot of trouble."

"Sorry, Arrow," apologised O'Neill for his angry outburst. "You know what I was trying to say."

Arrow gave the sergeant a thin smile. The crouched beggar hobbled slowly towards them, and then he suddenly reared up and seized Blade from behind, pressing the edge of a dagger tight against her bare throat.

"Let the princess go or I'll kill your woman," said the beggar coldly as his ragged cloak fell to the ground behind him.

"Harm a hair on her head, and you will never make it off this wharf alive," said O'Neill with surprising vehemence.

"Everybody, hold!" called Wolf, showing the beggar his empty hands to try and keep the man calm.

"Is that you, Captain Mac Namara?" asked Amergen slowly.

"It's Sergeant these days," said the beggar with a hint of bitterness.

"You know this man?" asked Wolf.

"He had been the captain of the Thomond Guard at Eagle's Pass."

"Release Princess Aoife now or I swear this bitch gets it!" growled the beggar as he tightened his grip, appearing a little thrown by the presence of King Mahon's counsellor.

"Enough of this!" shouted Arrow, stepping forward. "Captain Mac Namara, release her now," ordered the princess. Mac Namara slowly eased his grip, and Blade whirled out of his deadly embrace and drew her sword in a trice.

"Blade, please," asked Princess Aoife, holding up a placating hand.

Blade relented, putting away her sword with a flourish

and sending Mac Namara a scalding look.

"You can put away your dagger too, Captain. None of this is what it seems," said Aoife sternly. Mac Namara looked foolish standing there now with his puny dagger. Even the noisy gulls that hovered above the wharf seemed to mock his discomfort with their raucous calls, so he sheepishly put his knife away.

"Strange as it may seem, Mac Namara, these people have been my protectors. Although it appears as if all that is about to change," said the princess coldly, firing Amergen a withering look.

"I am just following Brian's instructions, my lady," offered Amergen feebly.

"You consider yourself to be a counsellor to both my brothers?"

"I would hope so."

"Then by extension, that would make you my advisor too, would it not?"

"I suppose it would, my lady."

"Well then, I think that your advice is wayward in this matter, Counsellor. Perhaps you should reconsider it, Amergen, and provide me with better," said Aoife archly. Then she turned her attention towards Wolf, leaving Amergen to respond with a small nod of his head.

"Captain Wolf, you told me once to consider myself an honorary Ranger and I have at all times tried to conduct myself as one, have I not?"

"You have, my lady," answered Wolf carefully, having been forcibly reminded that their Arrow was first and foremost a Thomond princess and a powerful woman in her own right.

"And you have used all of your cunning and ability to keep me safe until now?"

"I have."

"But now you do not think that placing me in a convent will keep me safe?"

"I do not, my lady," answered Wolf honestly. "But what would you have me do, Princess? We must leave on the next tide, and I cannot spare the men to guard you; we are few enough as it is."

"Then let me remain where I feel safest, with you and your men, Captain," said Aoife simply.

"I will not allow it!" spurted out Mac Namara. "King Mahon has tasked me with finding you, and I dare not return home without you again."

"Mac Namara, you are a soldier in King Mahon's army, which is commanded by my other brother Brian, which means that you serve my family. Do not presume to bark orders at me, Sergeant," said the Princess icily, and then turned her attention back to Wolf.

"If this task that lies ahead is of such great importance to Brian, I can assure you that it is of equal importance to me," reasoned Aoife. "Well, what do you say, Captain Wolf? Will you take me with you, or will you leave me here to the tender mercies of these Danish dogs?"

"I'm not sure that any of us are going to be safe where we are going," said Wolf soberly.

"He's right, Princess," interjected Amergen, and Aoife rounded on him in an instant.

"My dear brother Mahon contrived to have me placed in the bed of the man who killed my mother, while you and Brian conspired to use me as bait in your elaborate trap to ensnare Captain Wolf and his men, so do not dare preach to me about safety, Amergen. Spare me your hollow words of concern."

"How about it, Captain? Will you allow me to

continue to serve as an honorary Ranger?"

"I cannot guarantee your safety, Aoife. We are going to a very dangerous land, and many of us may never return."

"I would ask nothing more of you than would any other Ranger."

Wolf glanced over at Amergen, who remained remarkably quiet on the matter, the little man simply giving a barely perceptible shrug of his shoulders.

"Very well, Princess Aoife," answered Wolf after a long moment. "But hear me well on this: I have two conditions which are not negotiable.

"Firstly, I have no need of a princess on this trip, I need Rangers. If you step on board that ship, you will do so as Arrow, and you will do a Ranger's work and follow orders like the rest of the unit."

"I would have it no other way."

"Secondly, you will take Sergeant Mac Namara as your personal bodyguard, as befits a person of your rank. I need to know that someone is watching your back at all times, as I cannot. And I will need to use all of my Rangers for what lies ahead."

"Agreed, Captain," responded Aoife reluctantly, appearing a little peeved at Wolf's second stipulation.

"How about it, Munster man? Will you join our little venture? Will you guard your princess?" asked Wolf. He had of course his own good reasons for wanting to bring Mac Namara along; a blind fool could see that he was in love with the girl, which made him the ideal man to protect her. Such misplaced infatuation was most likely doomed, as a princess was usually destined for another royal bed.

Besides all of that, Wolf could not allow Mac Namara

to return to King Mahon and reveal Brian's complicity in the abduction of Aoife; the resulting rift between the two brothers could bring about the abrupt end of any hope of a royal pardon for Wolf, his men, and the wolves of Thomond.

"Aye, Captain, I will do as you ask," answered Mac Namara evenly. Yes, he was suspicious of Wolf and these so-called Rangers, but it wasn't like he had very much choice.

"So be it," concluded Wolf. "You may retain your rank, Sergeant Mac Namara, but remember that you have no authority over my men, and I will expect you to follow orders, just like everyone else."

"I understand, Captain."

"Amergen, I reckon that you have some explaining to do to our newest recruit?" said Wolf a little pointedly and then turned his attention towards more pressing concerns.

"Sergeant O'Neill, round up the sentries. We may have to move quicker than we had planned," ordered Wolf. "If this man had the wit to follow the wagon tracks, it's quite possible that someone else may have thought of it too."

"Lieutenant, will you gather up the rest of the men from the village? We may not be able to wait for the high tide," concluded Wolf, then he headed towards the Sea Eagle, but paused and looked back.

"Sergeant Mac Namara, do not blame my men for what happened at Eagle's Pass. They were only following my orders, and none of us took any pleasure in that day's work. It seems that we were all being played on that sorry day," said Wolf accusingly, casting Amergen a cold look. Then he hurried off to the ship.

Chapter Twenty-One

FAREWELLS

It was almost noon, a bright autumnal day crowned with a crisp blue sky dotted with small wispy clouds. There was no wind, and little rafts of well-fed seabirds bobbed contentedly on a peaceful sea. Despite the picture of calm, Wolf felt uneasy about the wagon having been so easily tracked to the waiting ship and kept a wary eye towards the approaches to Carlingford as he stepped up their preparations.

Amergen, Arrow and MacNamara were still deep in conversation at the end of the wharf. Blade had gone with Sergeant O'Neill to recall the sentries, while the lieutenant was rounding up the remaining men from Carlingford Village. Wolf took advantage of the quiet to walk about the deck of the Sea Eagle before the Rangers piled back onto the ship.

The small crew were busy with chores and studiously ignored him. One man was mending a spare section of sail, another was lashing down a small rowboat in preparation for their journey on the open sea, while a youth was high in the rigging repairing a shroud and being closely watched by a curious hooded crow perched on top of the mast. The slave noisily laboured below deck, securing the heavy sacks of Norse weapons and clothing in the hold in readiness for the voyage ahead.

Wolf stopped from time to time to study some small detail of the vessel, acutely aware of the coxswain's glare from the stern, which bore into him with every step that he took.

"You keep a tidy ship, Coxswain," announced Wolf as

he approached the stern. "My compliments, Otto, and indeed, my thanks for delivering the ship here on time. Brother Kevin will take you back to Cork."

Lost for words, Otto seemed to smoulder with anger.

"Jarl Arne would want me to remain with the ship," answered Otto with thinly veiled defiance, having finally found his tongue.

"A ship has no need of two captains. I will take command of the ship now. Your work here is done, Coxswain."

An awkward silence followed as Wolf idly examined the clever caps used to close the openings for the oars. "I had thought to appoint you as my helmsman," he added eventually, "but I would greatly fear for your safety."

"My safety?" asked Otto suspiciously.

"The men that are about to board this ship have been highly trained to kill, quickly and quietly," explained Wolf. "I very much doubt that they will long suffer your harsh ways, Otto. I cannot watch them at every moment of the night, and it's quite likely that one of them will cut your throat in the dark hours and toss you overboard before we have even left the Irish Sea."

"I can reef my tongue," answered Otto after a long moment, a little rattled but far from cowed.

"Then again, maybe the position of helmsman is beneath you?" asked Wolf indifferently, checking the tension on several of the shrouds.

"It is not beneath me."

"It is not beneath me, Captain," casually corrected Wolf.

"I can curb my rough ways, Captain. But I dare not return to Jarl Arne and tell him I have simply handed over his prize ship to strangers."

"No, I don't suppose that you can," conceded Wolf. Having made his point, he saw no need to labour it. "Tell me about the ship, Helmsman."

"She is Norse, Captain, but I wouldn't hold that against her. She's well-built all the same. Jarl Arne found her skulking along the east coast up to no good, so he soon put an end to their plans. We took the sea-eagle emblem off the sail in case we met any of the former captain's kin; they might ask some awkward questions. Held onto the ship's name, though — bad luck to change the name of a boat. We stowed the sea-eagle figurehead below before we entered the lough. It's best not to offend the spirits of the land."

"She seems somewhat short?"

"Aye, she's a Karvi, Captain, part raider and part trader. It's certainly a little shorter than some other warships, only sixteen pair of oars. But she's fast, manoeuvrable and not too hard to push through the water when you have to break out the oars, which can't be said of the long dragon ships: heavy beasts to move when you haven't got any wind," explained Otto with a sliver of pride, and then he seemed to pause.

"Well, what is it, Helmsman?" pressed Wolf, sensing Otto's hesitation to speak on some matter.

"I don't know what you're planning, Captain, and I don't need to know, but I'd like to take her back home with me again, if I could?"

"I am open-handed when it comes to most things, Otto, but I am tight-fisted when it comes to squandering possessions of real value such as good men, fast horses and fine ships. I can make no promises, but I'll do what I can."

"That's good enough for me, Captain," answered Otto,

appearing to be content with what he had heard. Perhaps he had met too many men who would put their own greed and vainglory above everything else, but he seemed satisfied that Wolf was not such a man.

"Now tell me about your crew — do you trust them?"

"I trust them well enough, Captain."

"Are they Danes?"

"Karl, the one who's mending the sail and Magnus are. No idea about the boy, Snorri. We picked him up as a stray on a wharf somewhere along the way. We call him Snorri the Squirrel by times. You can see why," added Otto, looking up at the rigging. "That's about the height of it, Captain."

"Aren't you forgetting someone?"

"You mean the slave?"

"Does he have a name?"

"None that we ever learned of, so Jarl Arne just named him Hund."

"Dog?"

"Aye, Captain, the jarl reckoned that he didn't need to know the man's real name if he didn't want to part with it," answered Otto. "Said the name Hund would do well enough, as all that an obedient slave had to do was come quickly when he was called, like any good dog."

"Call him up here, Helmsman."

"Hund!"

The slave appeared from the hold and quickly ran up the deck, his bare feet slapping on the planks. Then he stood before them submissively, his head lowered, staring down at the deck.

"I will have no slaves on this ship," said Wolf bluntly. The slave looked fearful, his eyes scanning from side to side as if he was contemplating making a run for it.

"Will you serve here as a freeman?" asked Wolf. The slave looked up slowly to see if the pair were playing some cruel joke on him, then he looked fearfully towards Otto.

"Do not look at him. I command here," said Wolf forcefully.

"And if I will not?" asked the slave nervously.

"Then Brother Kevin can take you back to Cork and whatever kind of life awaits you there."

The slave seemed uncertain of what to make of all of this, unsure if he could trust this tall man who was simply handing him his freedom. Wolf sensed the slave's hesitation and added, "If you wish to serve here voluntarily, then you may do so, and if you survive what lies ahead, then you may walk away a free man, just like the rest of us. Well, what do you say?"

"Aye, Captain, I will serve as a free man," answered the slave with fervour, firing Otto a nasty look, which did not go unnoticed.

"What is your real name?"

"My name is MacLeod," said the man after a moment, growing in stature as he spoke out his name with pride.

"You are Scottish-Norse?"

"Aye, Captain."

"Can you handle a weapon?"

"I can handle many weapons, Captain," responded MacLeod with a crooked grin.

"Good, and you may need to. But know this, MacLeod," continued Wolf sternly, "if Otto or any of the crew should suddenly find their throat cut, I will only be looking for one person on this ship, and I will show you no mercy. Are we clear?"

"Yes, lord. I will give you no cause to regret your

decision here this day."

"There are no lords here, MacLeod. When it's required, Captain will do. Other than that, you can call me Wolf."

"See our quartermaster, Ferret, when he returns. He will give you some clean clothing and something for your feet. You may also use some fresh water to wash away that filth. And shave your head no more, MacLeod; you are a free man now."

MacLeod looked down at the deck to hide his unruly tears.

"You can resume your duties, MacLeod, and see to it that you follow orders, just like everyone else," added Wolf, sensing that the man needed to be alone with his thoughts for a moment.

"Aye, Captain," replied, MacLeod, appearing glad to be able to tear himself away, but first he dragged a dirty arm across his face and looked Wolf boldly in the eye. "I don't know why you have done this deed, Captain, but you have done a good thing this day, and I will never forget it," said MacLeod fiercely, and then he walked away with his head held high.

"Why would you do such a thing, Captain?" asked Otto with genuine disbelief.

Wolf would let the scholars and monks argue over the rights and the wrongs of such matters, but even a blind fool could see that slavery was a vile thing. Still, Wolf had his own reasons for freeing the slave.

"Given half a chance, any slave worth his salt is bound to make a run for it at some point," explained Wolf. "The problem for us is that he may do so at the worst possible time. And that could seriously jeopardise our mission and put all our lives at risk. This way, MacLeod had the choice to serve here freely, like the rest of us, or return with the monk and remain a slave."

*

They had bid a staid farewell to Brother Kevin at Carlingford wharf and a soft breeze slowly pushed the Sea Eagle down the still waters of the lough as Wolf made his way towards Arrow, who stood alone at the bow.

"You seem displeased with our agreement," said Wolf, getting straight to the point.

"I have no need of a minder, Captain," answered Arrow a tad sorely.

"The bodyguard is not for you, Arrow. I know that you can handle yourself," placated Wolf. "He is for the princess; a wise Tafl player guards his queen well."

"Not everything in life comes down to the simple rules of a board game, Captain," responded Arrow tersely.

Wolf suspected that there was a little more to all of this than met the eye, and he did have some inkling of the problem, but some reefs were best avoided altogether.

"Perhaps you're right," conceded Wolf, "but then again, it does appear that your brother Brian has managed to corner me with such tactical games, so I am here. And it also seems to me that you too have outfoxed me, so you are here, and now you need to make the best of it, Arrow. A distracted Ranger can quickly become a dead one and also put the lives of his fellow Rangers at grave risk. Whatever it is that ails you, Ranger, best stow it in your sea chest for now. I need all of my Rangers fully focused for whatever lies ahead."

"Of course, Captain," responded Arrow smartly,

having been sharply reminded of the terms of their agreement.

"That's something you don't see every day," called out someone behind Wolf, and he turned to find his men staring up at a headland at the mouth of the lough.

"Peculiar, wolves don't normally come out in daylight like that," added another.

"What would they be hunting up there in broad daylight?"

"Seals, maybe?" offered someone.

"They would be mighty bloody seals that could climb all the way up there," scoffed another, eliciting a few half-hearted laughs.

Then a wolf gave out a long doleful howl. It was Willow, and the rest of the large pack loudly joined in, silencing the men in an instant.

Wolf wanted to call back, but he knew that some of the men already thought him strange enough as it was and that his name already said a lot about his nature, so he showed no reaction at all.

It appeared that Willow, Shadow and their new pack had picked up the Rangers' trail again after their strange subterranean journey; only time would tell if the Rangers' enemies had managed to do the same. Then the howling petered out and the pack drifted away from the crest of the headland, leaving one grey wolf to silently watch the Sea Eagle as the ship slipped out into the Irish Sea.

The men muttered about bad omens. It was as if the wolves had gathered to bid a final farewell to one of their own, some said in hushed tones. Others looked knowingly at each other and held their tongues on the matter. The natural high spirits that came at the start of every sea journey rapidly began to seep away from the

Rangers, and Wolf could sense it.

"A fine ship, wouldn't you say, Lieutenant?" said Wolf loudly as he strode boldly down the deck towards the stern.

"A fine ship indeed, Captain."

"Let's see what she can do, Lieutenant Godfridsson," ordered Wolf, stealing a secret glance up at Willow, who still stood silently on the bluff.

"Very well, Captain."

"Oars if you please, Sergeant O'Neill," called out Godfridsson.

"Oars!" bawled O'Neill. "And lively now! About time you lot did a bit of light exercise. Remember..."

"You're all crew," interjected someone.

"And if you don't work, you don't eat!" finished off another.

"Didn't I train them well?" said O'Neill with satisfaction to no one in particular, as he marched proudly up the deck.

"Take us north, Helmsman," ordered Wolf as the Sea Eagle began to slice through the water.

"Aye, Captain, north it is."

Chapter Twenty-Two

SHIPS

Having mysteriously lost all trace of their quarry at the rocky outcrop deep in the beech wood, Cuallaidh's pack had been left with little choice but to press on towards the northeast. Cuallaidh had posted his tracker, Rasende, up front and deployed his best hunters out on his flanks. But all to no avail: it was as if the Raiders had simply disappeared. The men muttered about the nefarious use of witchcraft, grumbling about the strong taint of magic that seemed to seep through this brooding land.

Not knowing what to expect, they had approached the Cooley Mountains cautiously from the southwest as a dusky pink glow filled the evening sky. Staying low, they had crept up from behind a treeless saddle to observe Carlingford Village down below. Carlinfjord Lough itself was a long natural inlet well suited to shelter ships, and the sizeable harbour near the village was still bustling with activity in the fading light.

Cuallaidh had thought that it would be foolhardy for them all to simply stroll down into the village, as they had no idea of what to expect. So he had sent Eric, who was a smooth talker and a shrewd listener, armed with a purse full of silver, to ferret out any useful information. Meanwhile, Rasende and the other scouts had continued to comb the surrounding hills for any sign of the Raiders' tracks, while the rest of them had made camp in a nearby pine forest, risking a small fire to keep out the damp autumnal cold.

Erik returned at dawn, puffing and panting after his steep climb up the mountain, laden with two sacks of provisions.

"Well?" asked Cuallaidh impatiently.

"They were there alright," answered Erik, dropping the stores to the ground and trying to catch his breath.

"When?"

"About a week ago," said Erik as he sat against a tree and wiped the sweat from his brow.

"How many?"

"A dozen or so, but they met with others."

"Others?"

"One party came down from the mountains about a week ago and were joined by another band of men who were already there," explained Erik, then he took a drink from a water skin.

"How can you be sure that they all belonged to the same outfit?" probed Cuallaidh.

"They were all dressed the same for a start, dark green buckskins, as if they were all part of the same military unit or maybe a troop of mercenaries."

"And how did you learn all this?"

"Silver loosens most tongues," smiled Erik, firing a depleted purse back to Cuallaidh. "A tavern whore who serviced some of them asked if they were all hunters or something, on account of their green clothes, and one of them mumbled something about being a Ranger."

"A Ranger?"

"Aye, she wasn't really sure what he meant by it either."

"Anyone here know anything about these Rangers?" asked Cuallaidh, scanning the group of men who had gathered to hear Erik's report. Most of them seemed mystified, but not all.

"I do, Jarl," spoke up Larsen. "They're stealth

warriors, assassins and raiders who mostly operate in the shadows, well away from any shield wall. They're cunning bastards and ruthless too. They can slip ghostlike into any stronghold and slit a jarl's throat while he's still humping his slaves, then torch the place and disappear back into the night before anyone knows they were even there."

"There's more," continued Erik. "A party of these Rangers recently sailed into the harbour in a small skiff."

"What of it?" pressed Cuallaidh.

"The boat had been stolen from the Norse in Dublin."

"And how could you possibly know that?"

"A whore who works the docks told me. She said a Norse ship came in from Dublin a few days later looking for the skiff. They said it had been stolen during Jarl Kanarvan's wedding celebrations."

"How could she know all this?"

"She humped the sentry who had been left to guard the Norse ship while the captain and the rest of his crew went off to find some answers. He told her that several ships were scouring the east coast in search of the stolen boat. It seems that the jarl was incensed by the brazen theft of the craft during his nuptials and intended to make a nasty example of the culprits."

"Your point being?" asked Nielsen, who tended to rely on his brawn more than his brain to solve most things.

"His point being that it looks as though Rasende was right all along, that these Raiders did indeed split their force in two soon after the ambush, and that the group who stole the boat most likely took all the horses back to Dublin, while the other band set off on foot through the midlands," explained Cuallaidh.

"Having made it to Dublin, why would they risk stealing a boat from the Dublin Norse to come all the way back up here?" puzzled Scarface.

"Because they have some unfinished business?" ventured Cuallaidh.

"Or they still have to deliver the girl?" suggested Scarface with a twisted grin.

"That would explain the ship," offered Erik.

"What ship?"

"The one that they all left in: it had been waiting for them for several days."

"Damn it! We were right," blurted Scarface.

"Did you learn anything about the ship?" pressed Cuallaidh.

"That particular piece of information cost me the most," said Erik ruefully. "She's called the Sea Eagle. The whore thought that it looked like a Norse longship, but it seemed a little shorter than most. Still, she reckoned it had carried away up to thirty men."

"A Karvi, most likely," suggested Larsen.

"Did she know if there was a woman with them?" asked Cuallaidh eagerly.

"She was fairly sure that there were two. She reckoned one looked like a fighter, but the prettier one looked a little bit more refined."

"She sure seems to have been well informed for a common whore. Can we trust her?" asked Scarface.

"Good information is a very valuable commodity in Carlingford these days, so it pays to keep your eyes open. There are spies everywhere; the Irish watch the Norse and the Danes, while they both scrutinise each other for any sign of weakness. It seems that a war is brewing for outright control of the lough. The Norse at Annagassan grow stronger by the day while the Danish jarl, Burgeson, continues to become weaker and more isolated in his stronghold at the head of the lough up near the village of Omeath. The Irish chieftain O'Hanlon has very few fighting ships, so all that he can do is watch and wait. Then he'll make his peace with the victor and try to negotiate a bearable tribute."

"Did the whore see what direction the Sea Eagle went?" quizzed Cuallaidh.

"No, but I did get talking to a couple of fishermen who reckoned that they saw her heading north. They couldn't be sure as they were out fishing in the Irish Sea at the time and could only see the ship in the distance."

"What would take them north?" asked Larsen. "All the lands north of Ireland and west of Scotland as far up as the Shetland Isles are infested with Norse."

"It's a shrewd move," said Cuallaidh. "They can't risk running south, as the Norse control the Irish east coast. They will most likely head west when they clear the mainland and then slip back down along Ireland's west coast, then secretly stash the girl somewhere close to home."

"How can we be sure that they'll eventually veer west?" asked Erik.

"What could possibly take them north into enemy territory at this time of the year? There would be no safe haven for them anywhere up there," Cuallaidh reasoned. "Our purse might be a whole lot lighter, Erik, but you have done well," commended Cuallaidh, thoughtfully hefting the depleted purse as the seeds of a plan began to grow in his thought-box.

"Maybe you paid those whores for a little more than information?" poked Gorm, getting a few raucous sniggers.

"No need to — your sister was there and she was giving it out for free," replied Erik casually. Gorm bristled at the barbed retort, but the rest of the men enjoyed the jibe, especially Nielsen.

"We don't have time for this," snapped Cuallaidh, putting an end to the laughter. "They already have a week's head start on us. Still, with favourable winds and good seamanship, we could soon whittle that down."

"Aren't you forgetting something?" asked Erik.

"So we need a ship and a few more men," answered Cuallaidh simply.

"And how do you propose that we get them?"

"Like most things in this life, with a lot of guile and a little silver," smiled Cuallaidh enigmatically, and then he went off to meet Rasende, who was the last scout to return to the camp.

"Any luck, Rasende?" asked Cuallaidh, but it was clear that the big tracker was reluctant to speak. "Rasende?"

"Promise me that you will not speak to the others of what I am about to tell you," said Rasende earnestly.

"But why?

"Just promise me, Ivarsson."

"Very well, you have my word. Now get on with it."

"I found tracks. I'm fairly sure that they belonged to the Raiders, the right number, same shape footprints, exact same footwear."

"That's good, isn't it?"

Rasende seemed to be struggling to find the right words, and Cuallaidh finally lost his patience.

"Thor's balls, Rasende! Will you just spit it out?"

"Their tracks came from the side of the mountain,"

spluttered Rasende.

"From a cave?"

"There was no cave."

"What are you trying to tell me, Rasende?"

"I'm telling you that their tracks began at the foot of a stone slab on the side of the mountain, the same way that they disappeared at the base of the rocky outcrop in the beech wood."

"But that doesn't make any sense."

"None of this makes any sense," answered Rasende irritably. "That's why I don't want you telling the rest of the men. They'll think that I'm mad."

"What does all this witchcraft mean, Rasende?"

"I don't know, Ivarsson. I've never seen anything like this before."

"Do these Raiders possess some sort of magic, or do they have a mighty wizard with them?"

"Maybe, or perhaps they have some strange allies?"

"Or very powerful friends?"

"The tracks lead down towards the village," gestured Rasende.

"You were right all along, Rasende; they did have a ship waiting at Carlingford. We're very close."

"You intend to follow them?"

"Do we have much choice? We can hardly go back to Limerick empty-handed."

"I guess not," answered Rasende, but it was clear that he had his reservations.

"Have you got something to say, Rasende?"

"Is this girl becoming an obsession for you, Ivarsson?" asked the big tracker bluntly.

Cuallaidh bridled at the suggestion, but he kept his temper.

“If we can catch this girl, she will give us leverage, which in turn can get us wealth and power. Isn’t that what we’re truly after?”

Rasende chewed over Cuallaidh’s words for a brief moment and seemed content with what he had heard.

“Where are we to get a hold of a ship around here, Ivarsson?”

“I think Omeath will be our best chance.”

“What’s in Omeath?”

“A cornered Dane,” replied Cuallaidh cryptically.

*

Jarl Burgeson’s hall in Omeath was not an inviting place. The men seemed belligerent, the women sullen and the slaves appeared utterly broken. Lean mongrels circled Cuallaidh and Rasende menacingly as unkempt children glared at them from the shadows. The jarl, perched on a low dais and flanked by two advisors, had a perpetual scowl on his face and seemed determined to grant these strangers little satisfaction.

Having briefly introduced himself and staying as near to the truth as was prudent, Cuallaidh, outlined the circumstances which had brought him to the jarl’s stronghold on that day.

“So, as you can see, Jarl Burgeson, now we are in dire need of a ship if we are to pursue these thieves.”

“And what makes you think that I will help you?” replied Burgeson, unmoved by Cuallaidh’s plight.

“I had thought that perhaps as fellow countrymen, we might help each other. And besides, I do not come here empty-handed,” added Cuallaidh and held out a heavy sack.

The jarl shot a serving boy a sharp look, and the lad quickly darted forward and snatched the bag from Cuallaidh's hand and quickly took it to Burgeson, who simply gestured with an impatient hand to turn the contents of the sack out at his feet. There were some gasps and a few purrs of satisfaction from the shadows as the glittering objects of silver and gold glittered in the torchlight, but the jarl kept a straight face.

"Hardly enough here to buy a ship, young man," grumbled Burgeson as he poked with his foot through the monastery's stolen treasures. Then he pointed at a ring, and the serving boy swiftly retrieved it and handed it to the jarl, who scrutinized the precious object with the dried blood of its previous owner still caked about its edges.

"Certainly not, Jarl Burgeson," agreed Cuallaidh, "These trinkets are simply a token of our friendship. As I said, perhaps we could help each other?"

"And how could you and your twelve men possibly help me?"

There was a snigger from one of the jarl's advisors at the mention of Cuallaidh's meagre numbers, but it quickly died in the man's throat when Rasende stabbed him with an icy stare.

"My father, Jarl Ivar of Limerick, has long sought a powerful ally on the east coast," lied Cuallaidh smoothly, "a strong jarl with a well-protected fjord which would allow him to raid and trade with the north of England and even Scotland. You are the only Danish jarl who still boldly commands along this part of the Irish coast, but for how long?"

There was a low rumble of anger from the onlookers at Cuallaidh's last remark; there might be a grain of truth in his words, but some thoughts were best left unspoken. The jarl held up his hand and the chatter soon died away.

"Jarl Ivar has many ships?" asked Burgeson keenly. It was obvious that Cuallaidh had finally piqued the jarl's interest.

"And many men too," added Cuallaidh.

"And you could forge such a pact?"

"I could," answered Cuallaidh with the utmost conviction, even though he secretly thought that such an alliance would be highly unlikely.

"But you do not have enough men to protect a ship," pointed out the jarl. "The first pirate that you meet could snatch it out of your hands just as easily as a mother takes a toy away from an unruly child."

"What you say may well be true, wise jarl, but this is the predicament that we find ourselves in. Perhaps you could offer some solution?"

Burgeson considered the matter for a long moment and then consulted with his advisors. And it seemed clear from their muffled tones, and given their precarious situation, that they were all of the opinion that they had much to gain and very little to lose by granting Cuallaidh the use of a single ship.

"I admire your grit, young man," said the jarl loudly, firing a sour look around the hall. "I will lend you a ship and a dozen of my young men. Perhaps they might learn a thing or two," he added rather pointedly. "You are right, Cuallaidh; we Danes must stick together. How else are we to defeat these Norse scum? Enough of this talk. Come, let us eat and drink. All this flapping makes me thirsty," announced the jarl as he shoved the bloodstained ring onto his finger. "And later, you must tell me all about your father's fleet of ships."

Chapter Twenty-Three

SEAWAYS

Their journey north had started well despite their hasty departure from the village. Having cleared Carlingford Lough, they had pulled out into the Irish Sea and swung northwards, a fresh southwesterly breeze and an ebbing tide helping them on their way. The weather was crisp but bright, and the men were in high spirits. Even Mac Namara appeared to blend in with the buoyant mood of the Rangers; it seemed that barrack-room banter was the same the world over. And if the sergeant still held onto any ill will towards the men who had killed his troops at Eagle's Pass, then he hid it well. What was a little harder to conceal was the silent strain that seemed to exist between Mac Namara and Arrow. It was as if the sergeant had been on a quest to rescue a princess and instead found a woman who had no desire to be saved. And while the pair remained courteous to one another, the easy interaction that they had shared at Eagle's Pass was no longer there to be seen.

As they slipped into the North Channel, a narrow seaway squeezed between Ireland and Scotland, Otto needed to work the tiller hard to keep the Sea Eagle on course through the powerful currents. Weary of the chaffing and the constant strain, the rudder strap suddenly snapped. They managed to fashion a temporary tie, but the damaged tiller forced them to veer west towards Rathlin Island, just north of the Irish coast, in order to make some swift repairs.

At Rathlin, they ran the ship up onto a sandy shore in the lee of the island, and Otto and Karl set quickly to work. Wolf sensed the concerned eyes of the hidden islanders as they secretly watched their every move, so he swiftly dispatched Sergeant O'Neill to speak to the local chieftain. He also sent Ferguson, a former monk, to reassure the nearby monastery that they were in fact Irish, regardless of their Norse ship, and that they meant the islanders no harm.

Taking advantage of the lull, Wolf instructed Magnus and Snorri to mount the stern-faced Sea Eagle figurehead on the stem post at the bow of the ship and to secure their Viking war shields along the top of the gunwale on either side of the boat. He also ordered his men to change into the Norse clothing which had been stowed below deck, as everything north of Rathlin Island, either on land or on sea, could well be considered Norse.

Amergen also made the most of the unexpected landfall, lighting a small fire well away from the ship and placing a bucket of water nearby. Having dipped the head of an arrow into the sticky solution contained in one of the curious earthen jars secured in the ship's hold, he then called Wolf and his men over to the fire.

"This substance is known as Greek fire," announced Amergen, holding the arrow by the feathered fletch. None of them had heard of it, so they took him at his word.

"And this is what it does," added the little man as he dipped the head of the arrow into the fire. The iron arrowhead instantly erupted into a lurid flame and continued to burn intently when he withdrew it from the fire.

"Now, if one of you will take that bucket of water and douse the flame, gently if you please, Lieutenant," asked Amergen as Godfridsson ever so slowly coaxed a little water from the bucket. Instinctively, they jolted back as the water touched the flame, causing the fire to react angrily and burn even more fiercely. The Rangers were mightily impressed at Amergen's demonstration and needed no further instruction, and they quickly set about dipping their own arrows in the highly flammable gel.

The rudder strap repaired, they struck out northwards once more, navigating by the sun during the day and the Pole Star by night. They kept to deep blue waters, well clear of any reefs or settlements, for while they might pass as Norse at a distance, closer inspection might prove to be a different matter. They quickly found their sea legs, and the journey soon fell into a familiar pattern of manning the watch, cold meals and snatched sleep. Off duty, the men mended their weapons and tended to their gear while speculating about the names of the low slivers of grey-green land tinged with the shades of autumn that lay off in the distance.

Some of the Rangers knew these sea routes fairly well, but McLeod seemed to possess an intimate knowledge of these particular waters. With favourable winds and calm seas, the broad islands of Islay and then Mull soon passed them by on their starboard side. McLeod advised Wolf to keep to the west of the Inner Hebrides and avoid the string of treacherous channels that lay between the Scottish mainland and the clutch of scattered islands — places where a ship could be suddenly holed or easily trapped. Wolf thought that McLeod's advice seemed reasonable, so they kept to the west of the tiny island of Tiree, staying in the pristine waters that ran between the Inner and Outer Hebrides.

Norse shipping had been thankfully scarce, as many men were most likely busy on their farmsteads, preparing them for the long winter siege that lay ahead. In the narrow channel of Little Minch, which ran between the islands of Skye to the east and Harris towards the west, they encountered one Norse ship laden down with female slaves which was heading towards the south. The ship had been busy tacking into a brisk southwesterly breeze and would no doubt have welcomed a break and an exchange of news. But the Sea Eagle was on a dead run and appeared to have no desire to stall, so the Norse Captain steered his ship towards the Sea Eagle as close as he dared.

"Late in the year to be heading north?" he called out over the breeze as the ships neared each other, and he closely scrutinized the Sea Eagle and her wary crew.

"The king's business is never late!" replied Berg cheerfully. Wolf had warned the big Norseman to be ready to converse a little with his fellow countryman should the need arise. Berg could sense the man's unease as the ships began to pass; no man wanted to be accused of delaying the king's messenger. "It looks like your pockets will be full of silver this winter," shouted Berg jovially, and the man seemed happy to change the subject.

"Aye, and our beds will be warm too!" he hollered as the ships passed beyond each other, much to the amusement of many men on both ships.

The waters of Little Minch soon opened out into the broad expanse of the North Minch, which stretched from the western Isle of Lewis to the Scottish mainland. This prompted a sullen response from some of the men who knew these waters well, and they became subdued and watchful. A few Rangers told hushed tales of peculiar Sea-People who inhabited the caves beneath this stretch of the sea. They also related disturbing stories of how these strange creatures could control the weather and the sea and that they would sink a ship out of sheer spite or simply to get their hands on some precious cargo within. Corporal Hakon got wind of their wild tales and laughed heartily at their outlandish nonsense, teasing them without mercy.

"Mermaids, you daft beggars!" scoffed Hakon, much to the hilarity of some. But others scowled at his irreverence, almost fearful that he might somehow incur the wrath of these vindictive Sea-People, who were reputed to have long memories and even sharper hearing.

At Cape Wrath, at the northwest corner of the Scottish mainland, Wolf decided to keep west of the Orkneys. He didn't want to run the risk of being trapped by sea pirates in the narrow stretch of the Pentland Firth, which ran between the Scottish coast and the cluster of northern islands. The Orkney Isles were known to be a lawless place, and the jarls of Orkney reluctantly bent the knee to any king and were, essentially, a law unto themselves and best avoided altogether. Besides that, the primary sea route between Norway and Scotland ran down along the Orkney's eastern coast all the way back up to the Shetland Isles and beyond, making it no place for Wolf and his men to tarry.

A week of clement weather had been much more than the Rangers could have expected at this time of the year, but they all knew that it couldn't last, and they were right. Their passage from beyond the Orkney Isles to the small island of Fair Isle proved to be a very rough crossing, with the agitated Atlantic throwing powerful rolling waves at them while tempestuous autumn winds battered them from the west, the harried breeze sorely lamenting as it raced through the rigging. All about them, the grey sea was flecked with foam. It was menacing and it was angry. Dark clouds matched its surly mood and hurled bursts of stinging rain at them without remorse. They reefed the mainsail and kept the ship's bow pointing into the big swells, fearful of getting turned broadside in such an unforgiving sea. And then they took death's grip of anything that felt remotely secure and bailed for their very lives.

Weary and sodden, the Rangers slowly rowed the Sea Eagle into the cove of North Haven, a sheltered harbour on the northeast corner of Fair Isle. The small island appeared to be little more than an elevated fortress of grass-covered rock in the middle of nowhere, but it was a welcome sight indeed. Strategically positioned halfway between the Orkneys and the Shetland Isles and a good day's sailing from Norway in the east, Fair Isle had long served as an isolated outpost for harassed mariners. The island wasn't very large, but still, it held up to twenty Norse farmsteads. While they never turned away a sailor in distress, they had long learned to be wary of strangers until they determined the true purpose of their visit, be it to trade or to raid.

Wolf sent two of his Norsemen, Berg and Sven, to reassure the islanders that they were only passing through and that they would be leaving as soon as the weather had cleared. Berg's friendly manner quickly put them at their ease, and as there were no inns to be had on the island, they were happy to sell the strangers some of their precious winter stores and allow them the use of a nearby hay barn so that they might have some shelter out of the unrelenting wind.

The following morning, Wolf took himself up a breezy headland on the east of the island to get a better look at the state of the unsettled sea. The big swells were calming down now, and the dark clouds were starting to break up, revealing promising pockets of bright blue as the wind began to ease. Wolf stared hard out across the grey sea-road and wondered what trials lay ahead for the Rangers and if many of his men would survive the raid on the fjord.

Amergen had finally revealed their ultimate destination and the true nature of the Rangers' mission: the destruction of the shipyard at Svartrfjord in Norway. Amergen's plan was bold, it was difficult, and it was dangerous, but with the element of surprise, it was possible. Escape was another matter entirely. Wolf had fully briefed his men on the details of the audacious attack, and then he quietly hammered out the finer points of the raid with his other leaders, secretly hoping that Amergen's information would prove to be reliable. Even at this late hour, Wolf had the nagging suspicion that Amergen was still holding something back, some crucial part to all of this. But he knew better than to try and pin the little man down, as he was as slippery as a freshwater eel.

"How can you be so certain about the inner workings of this Svartrfjord?" Wolf had asked when Amergen had first laid out his plan.

"A king's counsellor has need of many spies," Amergen had answered with a sly grin.

Wolf didn't doubt that for a moment.

*

Wolf heard footsteps climb the headland behind him and waited for a voice to speak.

“It looks like the geese have more sense than us,” said O’Neill laconically as they watched the large flights of barnacle geese migrate south for the winter.

“Trouble?” asked Wolf, getting straight to the point, as he doubted that the sergeant had climbed up the headland just to watch the birds.

“McLeod is gone.”

“Gone? Have you searched the island?” quizzed Wolf, disappointed but seldom surprised by the vagaries of human nature.

“Aye, Captain, such as it is. Still, he could be hiding anywhere.”

“Have any weapons been taken?”

“Ferret says we’re down a good sword and a scabbard too.”

“Have any of the fishing vessels put back out to sea yet?” questioned Wolf.

“A few. You think he could have stowed away on one of them?”

“Maybe.”

“Can we trust him?” probed O’Neill, voicing their silent concern.

“Probably — he doesn’t know the details of our plan anyway, not unless he managed to pick up some loose talk on the ship.”

“Nothing reached my ears on the ship, Captain. I’m pretty sure that the men would have kept a tight hold of their tongues around the crew of the Sea Eagle.”

“I’m sure you’re right,” agreed Wolf, “but we just can’t take that chance.”

“Get the men ready to move, Sergeant. We sail for Svartrfjord at first light.”

Chapter Twenty-Four

DECISIONS

Cuallaidh was well aware that approaching Rathlin through the morning mist was a considerable risk, but it meant that the islanders wouldn't see them coming. Larson had taken part in a raid on Rathlin three summers past and so he knew the island and its surrounding waters well. And besides the monastery, there was also a sizeable settlement on the island, which was large enough to cause them real trouble and was best avoided altogether, or so reckoned Larson. So stealth was essential.

With its square sail lowered, the Storm Raven eased its way tentatively towards Rathlin's sheer northern shoreline as the still wind held its breath. They needed to avoid the main harbour in the lee of the crooked island to the south, so Cuallaidh selected a sheltered cove surrounded by steep headlands, and they slowly rowed their way in.

Softly, Larsen coaxed the oarsmen forward from his vantage point at the bow of the ship, carefully guiding them through the hull-gouging pinnacles of rock which pierced the calm waters all about them. Finally, the timber keel gave out a satisfied sigh as it slid smoothly up onto the shingle shore, spurring the men to quickly rack their oars and secure the ship to a nearby boulder. They left their shields onboard and strapped their swords to their backs in readiness for the difficult ascent.

Rasende picked up a steep goat trail at the foot of one headland and they slowly set off, struggling to follow the precipitous path as it picked its way up to the top. They grabbed hold of tufts of rough grass and shrubs as they climbed and grappled with slick ledges peppered with loose rock, startling resting seabirds who noisily took to flight. Eventually, they hauled themselves up onto to the crest of the headland, where they paused to catch their breath, wiping the bird shit off their hands on the dew-drenched grass.

Cuallaidh took a moment to admire his new ship bobbing contentedly on the sea down below; the Storm Raven was certainly a much better craft than he could have possibly hoped for. A typical Danish Karvi with a sleek, dark hull and a black mast, its distinctive stripped sail of red and white furled neatly on the yard. Why Jarl Burgeson had seen fit to give Cuallaidh such a fine vessel, he couldn't rightly say. Perhaps the ageing jarl had felt the need to impress a potential new ally? Or maybe Burgeson had simply been lured by the promise of riches and the thoughts of renewed glory? Whatever his motivation, Cuallaidh couldn't care less. He had little interest in the faded dreams of old men.

Leaving a handful of capable men to guard the ship, they pressed south across the rock-strewn terrain, the vaporous fog screening their advance and muffling their approach. The dull chime of a nearby bell fortuitously guided them to the monastery's boundary wall, where they hunkered down to survey the cluster of stone buildings that were spread about the grey church. Perhaps it was the thick mist, but there was a pensive air of quiet about the place now that the bell had finally stopped ringing. Cuallaidh signalled to Rasende to move cautiously forward to determine if anyone was praying in the chapel.

It had been the big tracker's suggestion that they

secretly put in at Rathlin to try and glean some information about the Sea Eagle, speculating that if the Raiders had indeed veered west, then it was quite possible that they might have anchored at the island for the night and perhaps sought provisions from the monastery. Rasende swept his palm downwards to indicate that the church was empty.

"Maybe the bell was to call them to their noonday meal?" reasoned Erik.

"That's possible," agreed Cuallaidh, and directed Rasende towards the next largest building which stood nearby.

Rasende darted over to the refectory and quietly listened at the door for a moment, and then he beckoned Cuallaidh over.

"Larsen, do you remember where they hang that bell?" asked Cuallaidh.

"I think so."

"Then go quickly now and cut the rope to it before we are discovered, and then join us at their eating house."

The refectory door creaked open and Cuallaidh stepped in from the cold. Some monks threw him a surly look as the unwelcome draft cooled their broth, but that look soon changed to fear when Cuallaidh's men silently lined the walls of their dining hall.

"There is no need for alarm," called out Cuallaidh, graciously closing the door behind him.

"We will not detain you from your meal for long," reassured Cuallaidh as he slowly walked between the long tables. "We simply require some information, and then we will be on our way."

The monks and the field hands looked to each other for solace but only found worried faces.

"We are in search of a ship, a Norse craft named the Sea Eagle. Perhaps you know of such a vessel?" asked Cuallaidh politely. "It may have put in here a week ago?"

There was complete silence, but Cuallaidh's insistent footfall left the monks in no doubt that answers would be forthcoming, one way or another.

"I am the abbot here," said an elderly man a little waspishly from an elevated table positioned crossways at the head of the hall. "And what is this vessel to you?"

Cuallaidh sensed by the way the abbot had phrased his response that he had indeed seen the ship.

"They have stolen from me. I simply wish to retrieve what is rightfully mine," replied Cuallaidh quite reasonably.

"The ship of which you speak did put ashore here a week ago. They came in peace and left the same way," replied the abbot tetchily. "The ship might have been Norse, but the crew were Irish," he added in an attempt to pacify the unwelcome intruders and send them quickly on their way.

"And how could you be sure that they were Irish?"

"Because they sent a messenger here who was a former monk on Iona. And they also dispatched another Irish envoy to the local chieftain, assuring us both that they had only put in for needful repairs and nothing more."

"In what direction did they leave?"

"Young man, I do not spend my days idly observing the comings and goings of ships," answered the abbot primly. "We have important work to do here, the Lord's work."

"They went north, Jarl," said a voice from the back of the room.

"Are you certain?" pressed Cuallaidh, turning his attention towards the person who spoke; the big man was either a servant or a slave, and he had the uncanny look of a Norseman about him.

"Yes, Jarl, I am certain that it was north."

"How could you know this?" continued Cuallaidh, signalling the man to come forward.

"I was tending sheep on the southern ridge when I saw them run their ship up onto the strand. I think they needed to repair their rudder, but it's hard to see well when you're lying on your belly trying not to be spotted," explained the shepherd.

"And you're sure it was Norse?"

"She was Norse alright. Her strakes were stained a natural brown, not like that black stuff they smear on Danish hulls. They fixed on the figurehead too while they had her beached, some sort of eagle, I think. And they mounted their round shields along the gunwale before they left, overlapping, Norse-style. They must have been expecting trouble."

"You seem to know a lot about ships for a shepherd?"

"I wasn't always a shepherd. Got washed up here after our ship went down in a sudden storm two summers past. The monks took me in, asked me no awkward questions, and I've been here ever since. I tend to their sheep to earn my keep, that is all. My name is Alrick, and while I may not look it now, I was a Viking once, just like you."

"And you're certain that it went north?"

"I watched it closely in case it was some sort of low 'Loki trick', but it kept on heading north until it disappeared out of sight."

"Would you recognise this ship if you saw it again?" asked Cuallaidh, mulling over his options.

"I would. But there's more, Captain."

"Go on."

"When they landed here, they were wearing some sort of green clothes, buckskins maybe. They looked like hunters."

"What of it?"

"Perhaps it's nothing, but when they left, they had all changed into Norse clothing."

"Were there any women with them — and I don't mean whores — someone who might have looked highborn?"

"I thought that one or two of them looked light on their feet, Captain, but it was hard to tell at that distance. Maybe there was."

"What kind of twisted cunning is this?" growled Rasende. "Irish mercenaries disguised as Norsemen sailing a Viking ship into northern territory? Who are these people? Who could they be working for?"

"When we find the girl, we will also find them. Only then will we get the answers that we seek," responded Cuallaidh simply.

"Surely you do not intend to head into the north on the word of this shepherd?" asked Erik incredulously.

"And why not?"

"I would have thought that that was obvious, Cuallaidh. Because it would mean taking what is clearly a Danish ship with a paltry crew of twenty men into the heart of Norse territory, and for what, exactly? Is this princess really worth risking all our lives for?"

"If you wanted a life without risk, Erik, you should have stayed latched onto your mother's teat," mocked Cuallaidh, getting a few sniggers from some of the younger men, but most of the seasoned warriors knew that Erik was right.

"Heading into the north was not part of our agreement, Son of Ivar," stated Balder icily. Burgeson had sent along the grizzled veteran to guard his ship and guide his own men, but Cuallaidh still held command.

"We were to go west after these raiders and then strike south for Limerick to secure men and ships," reminded Balder. "That was the arrangement for the use of the Storm Raven and the allegiance of Jarl Burgeson's men."

"Do you honestly think that I can simply show up empty-handed at Limerick and demand ships and troops for an unknown jarl who got his sorry arse trapped in some Irish backwater?" answered Cuallaidh sharply.

Balder fairly bristled at the insult to Jarl Burgeson but appeared to have the good sense to realise that Cuallaidh had a point, so he reefed his tongue for now.

"But what would possibly take these raiders north with this Irish princess? Are they after a ransom or are they seeking out some sort of refuge for the girl?" persisted Erik, not dissuaded by Cuallaidh's barbed words.

"Perhaps there is some safe place not too far to the north where they can stash the girl," replied Cuallaidh. "Somewhere near but just far enough beyond Irish waters to avoid prying eyes."

"I know of such a place," offered Alrick hesitantly.

"Where is it? Spit it out, man!" demanded Cuallaidh.

"The island of Iona, off the Scottish coast. There is a nunnery there where they educate the daughters of royalty and keep them out of trouble until their families can safely marry them off."

"How do you know of this place?"

"I hear them drool about it at night when they think that no one is listening," explained Alrick, nodding his head towards some of the younger monks, who looked on in wide-eyed wonder as the intruders openly discussed their plans. The older clerics appeared to suspect the reason for the Danes' indifference to the presence of the monks and fervently mumbled their prayers, somewhat resigned to their inevitable fate.

"I know of this island, and it's a fairly exposed piece of land with clear water to the west and a broad channel to the east. It's no size at all, ideal for raiding," said Larsen. "I'd say it's no more than a good day's sailing to the north."

"And if this girl that you seek is not there?" asked Balder coldly.

"Then we will hump these nuns at our leisure, steal their silver and set sail for Limerick, for we will have chased this O'Kennedy bitch for long enough," answered Cuallaidh with a sliver of truth. "And who knows, maybe the very answers that we seek lie much closer to home than we think?"

Balder grunted his begrudging approval and asked, "So how are we to recognise this ship?"

"We have an eyewitness here, do we not?" answered Cuallaidh, gesturing towards Alrick. The big Norseman seemed to shift uncomfortably as Cuallaidh moved his final Tafl piece into place. "But perhaps this particular Viking has spent too long in the company of placid monks and docile sheep?"

"I have not!" retorted Alrick angrily.

"Show me," countered Cuallaidh smoothly and handed Alrick the haft of his axe.

Chapter Twenty-Five

SVARTRFJORD

Sullen clouds drifted across the high mountains that overshadowed Svartrfjord as a chill wind swept over the 'dark fjord', harrying its grey waters before racing off towards the sea.

King Algar seemed somewhat displeased, concluded Vanomon as he stared at the back of the monarch's broad shoulders, which appeared tight with tension, his feet braced as if for battle, while his overlapped hands tapped together impatiently behind him.

"You said that there would be sixty ships?" continued Algar irritably as he peered through an arrow slit in Vanomon's rooms, unhappy at the number of finished ships that were hauled up on the far shore of the fjord.

"The other ten will be ready by the spring, my lord," placated Vanomon. "We must go further afield these days for suitable timber. And many of the craftsmen have returned to their farmsteads to make them ready for the winter; without them, I can do very little."

The king's sour grunt told Vanomon exactly what Algar thought of those two excuses.

"We could still use those trees that line the entrance to Svartrfjord?"

"Who owns that longship moored at the wharf near the guardhouse?" asked the king, finding a more pleasing topic to discuss and ignoring Vanomon's question.

"It belongs to Ragner Ragnersson. He is the Captain of the Guard at the shipyard this week."

"A fine warship, even if she sits a little low in the water for my liking, but a sleek craft nonetheless."

“Indeed, my lord. That smaller skiff below by the Seagate belongs to me,” added Vanomon with some little pride. “It’s quite adequate for the few coastal journeys that I might make.”

“It hardly has any place out on the open sea,” noted Algar with a trace of sarcasm.

The king certainly had a burr up his arse about something, thought Vanomon, not appreciating the slight to his vessel, modest though it was, and he decided that it was high time to steer Algar towards the cause of his aggravation.

“Some wine, my lord?” offered Vanomon, pouring the drink quickly before the king decided to decline. “Rest assured that the remainder of the ships will be ready come the spring,” continued the warlock smoothly, directing the king to the other seat by the fire.

“They need to be, Vanomon,” responded Algar as he sat. “Your grand plan might be a good one, but this venture is costing me a fortune. And the jarls grumble endlessly, like so many unruly children.”

“You are weary after your travels, my lord. Will I have my cook prepare a midday meal for you?”

“No, I must catch the tide at noon,” responded the king vaguely, tapping his finger on the rim of his goblet.

“Another time then, my lord?”

“Perhaps your cook will be fully mended by then?”

“My cook?”

“Come, come, Vanomon. You may have your personal network of spies, but I still have a few informants of my own,” chided Algar. “Will the woman recover?”

“In time, maybe, but she will never be anything to look at,” admitted Vanomon, seeing that there was little point in denial.

"The men are uneasy about this Irish girl, Vanomon. I hear disturbing talk of witchcraft, and it seems that there have already been a handful of these odd events."

"There have only been three such incidents that I know of."

"And what do you know of the girl?"

"Very little, my lord. She is a slip of a girl from Ireland who can't or perhaps won't speak. It's hard to tell."

"That much I already know, but does she actually have some sort of secret powers?"

Vanomon shrugged his shoulders.

"Honestly, my lord, I don't really know. I have her closely watched day and night, and nobody has seen her chanting rituals or casting spells. She seems quite ordinary in most ways, even a little innocent. Granted, her appearance is a tad different to most girls; she's slender and her facial features are more refined, while her eyes are a peculiar almond shape. But she tends to her chores and keeps to herself."

"Innocent or not, trouble seems to follow in her wake," countered Algar. "What happened with the cook?"

"It seems that she went to beat the girl and then simply burst into flames."

"Which is hardly all that surprising in a kitchen?"

"And I would be inclined to agree with you, my lord, but a kitchen maid told me that the cook was nowhere near the fire when it happened."

"Perhaps there was a spark trapped within the folds of her greasy clothes?"

"That is possible."

"But you suspect otherwise?" suggested Algar

shrewdly.

"It's very hard to say, sire."

"Well, do you believe that the girl herself could have some magical abilities or that she may be protected by some other power?"

"The truth of the matter is that I just don't know, my lord. Perhaps the incident with the cook, the dead boy in the barn and the drowned sailor were all just a strange sequence of events," ventured Vanomon, trying to play down their importance, for now he was wary of the king's sudden interest in the girl. Secretly, Vanomon had little doubt that there were powerful forces at play here, but just what they were, he couldn't really say. But Vanomon was determined to possess that power if he could. Algar's sudden curiosity in the girl now meant that he would have to move much faster than he had intended.

"And did the girl warrant this beating?" pressed the king, determined to make rational sense of it all.

"I think that you had better be the judge of that yourself, my lord," began Vanomon and then paused to choose his words. "It seems that the girl had been playing with a rat that had crept into the kitchen in search of scraps. That's when the cook went mad with her broom and tried to clatter them both."

"Playing with a rat?"

"I know, it sounds a little far-fetched. But it appears that the girl has an uncanny way with nature, wild creatures, plants and such."

"She seems to be a very strange girl indeed. Still, I didn't think that you would be having problems with rats within these stone walls," observed the king, stealing a furtive glance at the floor around him.

"On the contrary, my lord: it seems that they find

these human fortifications very much to their liking and dig their burrows where they will and pilfer our stores, safe from most predators. The dungeons are infested with the pests. My gaolers reckon that there is quite a contest going on down there between the prisoners and the rats to see who will eat who first!"

"An absorbing battle, no doubt," said the king with a small shudder. "But these troublesome rats are your problem, Vanomon. The girl has regrettably become mine."

"How so?" asked Vanomon cautiously, for it seemed that they had finally arrived at the true source of Algar's irritation.

"The men are unsettled by the presence of this Irish girl. They fear that she might put a Hex on the spring campaign against her homeland."

"I think that their imagination has got the better of them, my lord," suggested Vanomon.

"Well, of course it bloody has. But fighting men can be a superstitious lot, as well you know. And I need their minds fully focused on the upcoming war in Ireland, not ruminating on this strange girl. These Irish are tough bastards who will not give up without a hard fight."

"What would you have me do, my lord?" asked Vanomon evenly, although he was fairly certain that he already knew what Algar had in mind.

"I will leave the precise details up to you, Vanomon," answered Algar briskly as he stood to leave. "You are the sorcerer here, after all. But I want it done soon. We need to stamp out these whispers of witchcraft, and quickly. So do whatever rituals must be done and then sacrifice this girl for all to see. Better still, you can say that she is an offering for the success of our campaign in Ireland. That way, they will all see that she is just a skinny Irish girl and nothing more."

"As you wish, my lord, and what of the remaining trees that line the entrance to the fjord? Are we to use them to build the last ten ships?" asked Vanomon again as the king swung a travel cloak about his shoulders.

"No, best leave them where they are for now," replied Algar as he paused at the door. "Removing those last tracts of forest might only attract unwanted attention from ships prowling along the coast," he concluded thoughtfully, then stooped out the door and was gone.

*

Through an arrow slit in his rooms, Vanomon watched King Algar's ship sail down the narrow fjord. Like most monarchs that he had known, Algar was puffed up with his own self-importance and had no concept of real power: the very strength of the gods themselves. And not just some abstract aspiration muttered by a deluded monk, but the actual power of Odin himself, right here on earth.

Vanomon had searched for many years throughout the wild pagan lands to the north. He had endured many hardships on his quest for knowledge, just as his dark god Odin had done. On his dangerous journey through these savage countries, Vanomon had seduced powerful witches and beguiled great magi. Some he had stolen from, others he had tortured to extract their arcane arts. In time, he had acquired a wealth of powerful lore, and he had ruthlessly wielded that dark magic in his rapid rise to power. And now he was finally ready to entice his cruel Lord Odin back to walk upon the earth once more, but first he would need to make an offering fit for a god.

Ireland would provide him with the opportunity to amass such an oblation. King Algar and his jarls could carve up this choice land among them and squabble over its silver, but Vanomon would have his share of the spoils too. For after their victory in Ireland, Odin's ravens would secretly gather up many of Ireland's highborn kings and queens. They would select from among its fair women and fine champions, its comely children too, and all would be sacrificed on Odin's bloody altar to make their dark god incarnate once more. On that fateful day, Vanomon would stand at Odin's right hand and serve as his high priest. Then the kings of the world would know the meaning of true power.

Caressing his bald head, Vanomon returned to the fire, deep in thought. The arrival of the Irish girl had posed him some troubling questions, for in all of his travels, he had never seen this type of subtle sorcery before. Did the magic emanate from the girl herself? Or did it come from those who protected her? And could those very same spirits also shield Ireland itself?

The Irish witch who wandered the bowels of his stronghold was deeply disturbed by the Irish girl, believing that the slave was being guarded by the old gods of Ireland: ancient demigods who still somehow dwelt beneath the land in some parallel netherworld. The witch was adamant that she would play no part in harming the girl and had warned Vanomon to steer well clear of the unusual female, which was all good and well, but he dare not defy his king. Not when his ultimate goal to restore Odin to this earth was so very close at hand. But how could he safely kill the girl without bringing those powerful forces down upon himself? Vanomon's arcane arts had given the warlock a great deal of protection against his mortal adversaries, but he very much doubted that mere witchcraft would prove effective against such a potent supernatural threat. First and foremost, Vanomon would need to know more about this strange girl.

"Hugin!" called Vanomon.

"Yes, my lord," answered his ever-present bodyguard, stepping out from the shadows.

"Find me the men who snatched this girl from Ireland, and quickly. We must learn all that we can about this female slave," ordered Vanomon.

"As you wish, my lord," responded Hugin and dutifully turned to leave.

"But first, bring this Irish girl to me. And do it quietly."

Chapter Twenty-Six

INCURSION

The unsettled sea was still brooding after the storm, and the westerly wind had continued to blow petulant gusts, but Otto and his crew knew their trade well, and they had trimmed the sail instinctively with every whim of the wind, pushing the Sea Eagle ever eastwards across the grey expanse of the North Sea. They had reached the Norwegian coastline at dusk. Mindful of hidden sentries posted along the mountains on either side of the fjord, they had sailed on northwards past the entrance to Svartrfjord, paying it no heed at all. Then they had doubled back in the darkness and held off near the entrance to the fjord.

"There!" rasped Amergen, keeping his voice low as he pointed towards a single torchlight on the shore, which then quickly disappeared.

"There's a small cove there with navigable waters, well hidden from the sentries," said Amergen. "We can beach the ship there."

"You're sure that's our man?" asked Wolf, wary of walking into a trap.

"Certain — that was the signal," answered Amergen as the Rangers carefully rowed the Sea Eagle towards the shore. "He's been expecting us for some time; everything has been arranged."

The ship's bow slipped softly up onto the sandy shore and the Rangers sprang quietly out, grateful for a dry night and the sullen clouds which masked a full moon. They had changed back into their familiar green buckskins and had darkened their faces in readiness for the raid, arming themselves with their usual weapons: back-slung swords, daggers, axes and longbows, along with quivers of arrows dipped in Amergen's Greek fire. They also checked their gear to ensure that nothing would rattle or glitter in the darkness and give away their position. Stealth and surprise would be their greatest weapons, while speed would probably be their only hope of escape.

A small, brown-skinned man with a weather-beaten face stepped out from the tree line and waited without a word.

"He's our man," spoke Amergen softly, raising his hand to steady the men as some of the Rangers instinctively reached for their weapons.

The little man, dressed in deerskins, beckoned them to quickly move towards the cover of the trees, and the Rangers gladly darted into the forest, alert to danger and wary of every sound.

"Saras, my old friend," said Amergen with warmth as he hugged the strange little man, who continued to remain silent. Then Amergen stood back and began making signs and gestures with his hands.

Saras responded in kind, strongly gesturing towards Wolf and the Rangers.

"What's he saying?" asked Wolf, puzzled by the exchange.

"He says that you are all too big!" answered Amergen with a grin.

"Too big for what?"

"You'll see, but he had better be wrong!"

"Can't he speak?"

"No." Amergen looked at Saras and pointed to his neck. "A parting gift from the slavers who captured him and many of his Sami tribe," explained Amergen. "It was meant to be a killing blow, but luckily for us, he survived. That's why Saras is helping us. These are the very Norse who robbed him of his voice and wiped out half of his family. The Sami are normally a peaceful people who live to follow their reindeer herds across the northern lands, but they have long suffered at the hands of the Norse, Saras more than most. And although he might not look it, Captain, he is considered to be a great leader among his people and a very powerful shaman."

Saras signalled towards them and then went further into the forest, beckoning them to follow as he went. Finally, he stopped at a small clearing in the woods which was dotted with long low-growing bushes. Then he began pulling back the foliage near one of the shrubs, revealing a strange looking shape as the full moon found a break in the clouds. The object revealed, Saras swept his hands towards the clearing and then indicated the figure twenty with his fingers.

"Twenty canoes?" asked Wolf.

"Twenty kayaks," corrected Amergen. "But Saras thinks that you are all too big to fit into them. I understand his concern, but the cockpit looks big enough to me," reckoned Amergen, looking down at the sea kayak. "I requested that they be purpose-built for big men," he explained. "The Inuit, who have no love for the Norse, use them in the frozen north for hunting and travel; they cost the Sami people a small fortune in reindeer meat as payment."

"They're light," said Wolf, lifting one end, having closely examined the long craft, which was skillfully constructed from driftwood, whalebone and sealskins smeared with some sort of grease.

"And strong," added Amergen. "That's what makes them ideal for the task at hand. Each man can easily haul it out of the water and hide during the day, and then travel up the fjord by night."

"How many nights?" asked Wolf.

"You should reach the shipyard tomorrow night," estimated Amergen, "as long as you are not spotted by the sentries on the mountains."

"Could we not simply approach this shipyard using the forest for cover?" enquired Wolf.

"There are random patrols through the forest at night," explained Amergen. "A pitched battle with a handful of Norse soldiers would only alert our enemy to our presence here and scuttle our real objective: the destruction of this fleet. If you travel silently on the water, well clear of the shore, not even a night patrol will know that you are there."

"It seems that you have thought of everything," commended Wolf, impressed at Amergen's planning. "How did you manage to place the kayaks here under their noses?"

"I had a lot of help from Saras and his people, for a price, of course. And let's just say that a 'tame Dane' from Cork played a crucial role in getting the kayaks here," added Amergen cryptically.

Wolf knew better than to ask Amergen for any more details, as the little man was frugal with the truth. So he switched his focus to more pressing matters and wordlessly ordered his men to get the kayaks to the water's edge.

The Rangers wasted little time in carrying the kayaks through the forest and down to the shore. Forming into pairs, they made good use of the bone toggles fitted on either end of each sea kayak, carrying two boats between them with relative ease. They only needed seventeen kayaks in total, so Wolf was for leaving the remaining three hidden as a last resort for any escaping Rangers who got separated from the main party. But Amergen thought that it might be useful to keep one kayak on board, so they carefully lifted one of the spare craft onto the Sea Eagle before shoving the ship off the sandy shore.

Working quickly and quietly, the Rangers gently coaxed their longbows up into the bows of their elongated kayaks. Every man had two full quivers of arrows which he also stored in the light craft, ensuring to spread the weight evenly. Reluctantly, they removed their axes and daggers from their belts and stowed them too, as the opening in the kayak appeared to be a very snug fit indeed. To leave them with some ready means of defence, the Rangers retained their back-slung swords, adjusting the angle of the weapon to avoid the scabbard clattering off the stern of the craft.

Silently, Wolf gave the signal, and each man clambered into their kayak as best they could. The Rangers were no strangers to canoes and soon found their balance, quickly coming to terms with the clever double-bladed paddles. Fairly content that each man was reasonably stable, Wolf slowly moved off out of the cove. They gave the headland at the entrance of the fjord a wide berth, as there were sure to be hidden reefs and back eddies that could drag them in and pin them up against the ragged rocks.

Wolf's kayak rocked alarmingly as he cleared the headland and was met by powerful unseen currents which lurked around the entrance of the fjord. He focused on his balance and adjusted his stroke to contend with the dark swirling waters, breathing a sigh of relief when his flimsy craft finally slipped into the calmer waters of Svartrfjord.

Clouds were now sparse, and the full moon glared at them as it hung above the head of the fjord. In open water, they felt very exposed in the luminous light. But if they strayed too near to the shore, they ran the risk of encountering a night patrol, or worse, keel-gouging rocks. As for the sentries posted along the mountain ridges, all that the Rangers could hope for was that they were too busy warming themselves by a fire to notice any small movements on the water. And even if they did spot some disturbance on the surface of the inlet, hopefully they would put it down to hunting dolphins or a pod of orcas following a shoal of herring into the fjord.

Softly, they made each stroke as they pushed their way up through the dark waters of the fjord, the steady rhythmic paddling allowing Wolf a quiet moment to consider his thoughts. His battle plan was a simple one: Wolf, Sergeant O'Neill and another six of his men would eliminate the shipyard sentries on duty before they had a chance to raise the alarm, and then they would raze the shipyard to the ground. Lieutenant Godfridsson, Corporal Hakon and seven more Rangers would neutralise the remainder of the garrison housed in the guardhouse, by fair means or foul. Should the Rangers survive the raid, each man would make good his escape by paddling out to the waiting Sea Eagle, which should have cautiously moved up the fjord on the night of the raid, having safely spent the daylight hours well offshore.

Each man knew that after the attack, the Sea Eagle would need to quickly leave the fjord at the first glimpse of dawn or run the risk of being trapped by reinforcements from King Algar's fort, which lay just beyond the mountains. Wolf had drummed it into the men that the Sea Eagle was to wait for no one, not even him if that happened to be the case, or the ship and everyone on it would needlessly fall into enemy hands. As timing was crucial, neither indeed could the raiding party wait for any stragglers prior to the attack; if any man got into trouble on the water, he was to make his way to shore as best he could and lie low until after they had struck, or run the risk of jeopardising the entire mission. Any individual who was left behind after the raid would need to fashion their own escape, perhaps making use of one of the two hidden kayaks. Or if their numbers allowed, they could try and steal an enemy ship.

They rounded a slight bend in the fjord and saw the shipyard's torchlights twinkling in the distance as the first sign of dawn light slowly began seeping into the sky above the mountains towards the east. With the cover of darkness slipping away, they began to search for somewhere to lie low during the daylight hours.

Wolf pointed towards a small island that lay ahead which was positioned at a welcome distance from the fjord's shoreline. Senses alert, they paddled slowly towards the tiny spit of land, mindful of jagged rocks that might lurk beneath the shallow waters. There was no sign of any human presence upon the island. A rugged piece of rock-strewn land with a congestion of shrubs and stunted trees concentrated at its centre, it was ideal for their needs.

Cautiously, they hauled their kayaks out of the water, muttering stifled curses as they slipped and skidded across the rocky foreshore. Careful not to damage the stretched skin on their precious craft, they quickly concealed their kayaks beneath the thick foliage at the heart of the island, startling way too many noisy birds for their liking. Having retrieved their weapons and some scant supplies, the Rangers took cover and settled down, wrapping themselves in their dark green cloaks and melding in with their natural surrounds.

Wolf took the first watch as dawn broke in earnest, grateful that they had made it through the first night. His thoughts swiftly turned to the Sea Eagle, and he hoped that the ship had made it to safety too. Picking the guard detail for the Sea Eagle had not been easy. Every Ranger wanted to be part of the raid, but someone needed to protect the ship if they were to have any hope of escape. O'Sullivan had hidden his disappointment well, but Wolf needed someone who was both a natural seaman and a skilled Ranger to stay with the ship. Wolf's reasoning seemed to appease O'Sullivan somewhat. Arrow was way too valuable to risk on the raid, and while Mac Namara might prove useful, Wolf needed Rangers that he knew and could depend upon completely. In fairness to Blade, she hadn't made a fuss about being left behind to guard Arrow, but her displeasure was clear for all to see.

It had actually been Amergen who had suggested that Ferret should be the final Ranger to make up the ship's guard, for some reason. Wolf had thought little of it at the time and so let Amergen have his way on the matter, but now Wolf wasn't so sure that it had just been a casual suggestion. Amergen always seemed to have some hidden agenda, and even now, on the very eve of the raid, Wolf still couldn't be sure that the little man didn't have another trick up his sleeve. And there had been something peculiar about Amergen's eagerness to have one of the spare kayaks onboard the Sea Eagle, too, that raised Wolf's suspicions. And why had Amergen seen the need to take Saras with him when they left after the Sami shaman had handed over the kayaks?

A hooded crow landed on the nearby branch of a stunted hawthorn and scrutinised Wolf for a moment. Then it looked down at the men huddled in their green cloaks, tilting its head inquisitively before returning its gaze to Wolf.

"You're right, hooded crow, some things are simply imponderable," whispered Wolf with a wry smile.

The bird gave him an intelligent look and then flew off to find its breakfast.

Chapter Twenty-Seven

AMERGEN

Otto and his crew deftly held the Sea Eagle steady in the small cove as wavelets lapped impatiently at the ship's hull. The sheltered inlet beside the entrance to Svartrfjord did afford them some cover, but they still felt fairly exposed, awash in the luminous light. Their strategy had been to leave quickly, wait well offshore and then return the following night, but Amergen's duplicitous plan had quickly scuttled all that.

"If you want our help, Amergen, you could try being forthright for once," suggested Arrow evenly, barely concealing the smouldering anger that they were all surely feeling at the sudden change of plans.

Amergen remained silent for a long moment, his face thoughtful in the moonlight. Then he went and sat on a nearby sea chest with a heavy sigh and rested his hands upon his knees.

"What is it that you want to know?"

"Why is this girl so important to you?" continued Arrow. Amergen appeared uncomfortable with the question, then he simply spat out the truth of the matter.

"If I return to Ireland without her, my life is forfeit," answered Amergen bluntly.

"You would lose your life over this slave girl?" quizzed Blade.

"I know it sounds far-fetched. But that outcome alone would hardly be the worst of it," added Amergen cryptically. "The girl is no ordinary child; she belongs to Eiru and has no place in our world."

"How did she end up in a backwater like this?" asked

Ferret, glancing around him at their unlikely setting.

"The fault is mine," said Amergen with a heavy heart. "I had been using sorcery to spy on Vanomon's plans, and he detected my presence and suddenly reversed the spell, causing a rent in the thin veil that screens our world from the Land of the Ever-Living Ones. The girl innocently wandered through the temporary portal into a nearby forest and was snatched up by a Norse raiding party."

The Rangers remained silent, trying to make some sense of Amergen's peculiar story while the Sea Eagle bobbed gently by a lee shore.

"Surely the fault is not yours entirely?" offered O'Sullivan.

"Eiru didn't quite see it that way," answered Amergen ruefully. "In a fit of anger, she turned my hair white." He gestured towards his head," 'Let that serve as a constant reminder of your folly', she snapped, and ordered me to find the girl before the coming spring or suffer the harsh consequences."

"Seems like a lot of fuss over one girl," said Blade.

"Except that she's no ordinary girl," replied Amergen solemnly. "She is what the Ever-Living Ones call a Child of Summer." Amergen could see that they had no understanding of what he had just said, so he went on to explain the nature of things as best he could.

"There is no sun in the Land of the Ever-Living Ones, existing as it does in a shadowy realm of its own. A Child of Summer is born to them every thousand years or so; sometimes it's a girl, other times a boy. The child wanders freely through their otherworld, effortlessly bringing rebirth to nature there just as the sun does in our own world. Without such a child, their realm would wither. As a consequence, our own lands will suffer badly too until harmony in their shadow world is restored."

The Rangers were stunned by Amergen's dire words and shifted uneasily as a damp chill began to seep into their bones. It seemed that the loss of this girl could seriously affect them all, one way or another.

"Does the captain know about any of this?" asked Arrow.

"No. I thought that Captain Wolf and his men had enough to deal with— best that they remain focused on their own role in all of this. Still, the destruction of the shipyard would provide an ideal diversion to allow a small team to slip into Vanomon's stronghold and rescue the girl," suggested Amergen with a sly smile.

"And the escape plan for the captain and his men, is that now to be altered too?" demanded O'Sullivan.

"No, that will remain the same. The ship must be clear of the coastline by dawn and then return tomorrow night as planned. But know this, all of you: the same deadline will apply to anyone who might decide to leave this ship in order to help Saras and me. The Sea Eagle must sail at the first sign of dawn after the night of the attack with whoever has made it back to the ship. Or every single one of us will be lost for nothing," stressed Amergen, staring hard at Otto, who stood stoically by the tiller.

"I will see to it," responded Otto, having followed the discussion closely.

"And how do you expect to enter Vanomon's fortress unnoticed?" questioned Mac Namara.

"Saras knows of a secret tunnel," responded Amergen.

"How could a reindeer herder know what is sure to be a closely guarded secret?" pressed Mac Namara, looking towards Saras, who keenly watched from the shadows.

"Because he was one of the slaves who had been forced to dig that tunnel," answered Amergen simply. "To keep the existence of the tunnel secret, Vanomon ordered the execution of all the slaves who had worked on it. Saras and a great many of his Sami tribe were taken out to sea, and once there, these Norsemen cut their throats and cast them overboard. His executioners got sloppy at their blood work, and Saras survived the slash to his throat and somehow managed to get ashore." Amergen pointed at his neck as he looked at Saras; the little man stepped forward and pulled back his collar, revealing the ragged scar. "I have come for the girl, and I will take any assistance from anyone who cares to help me. Saras, on the other hand, has come for revenge and will not be thwarted, so maybe we could all find a way to help each other here?"

"With the use of the tunnel, it sounds like a straightforward extraction to me," ventured Blade.

"If things go smoothly, it could be," agreed Amergen, "but there's one small problem: the other end of the tunnel is closed off by a door."

"So?"

"It's bolted on the far side."

"Ah, that could be a slight problem, alright," agreed Blade.

"Not if we had someone who was well versed in sneaking into places that he wasn't supposed to be in," suggested Amergen. All eyes went to Ferret, and the young man shifted uncomfortably, uneasy at the sudden scrutiny.

"I will do nothing that could jeopardise the captain's mission," said Ferret fiercely.

"Nor would I ask you to do such a thing," placated Amergen, "but maybe there is a way that both objectives could be achieved together?"

"Maybe," conceded Ferret, "but I still don't understand this sudden urgency. Is this girl in some sort of danger?"

"The simple answer to that is yes, Ferret," answered Amergen sombrely. "Eiru has tasked Banba with the protection of the girl, which she has done admirably up until now by the subtle use of her powers over nature. But Vanomon has been ordered by King Algar to execute the girl, and he must do it very soon."

"How could you possibly know all of this?" demanded Mac Namara.

"I may have made my mistakes in the past, Sergeant, but I am not without some craft," countered Amergen tetchily. "The old gods still speak to me in the old ways, through signs, dreams and other ways beyond your understanding."

"That may be," allowed Mac Namara. "So it's these gods that have told you about the planned execution of the girl?"

"No, it was Saras who told me that part," clarified Amergen. "He has a spy in the shipyard, and the guards talk freely. It seems that many have heard strange rumours about this girl, and King Algar wants no loose talk of witchcraft tainting his fleet, so the girl is to be a blood offering for the success of his ships."

"I will do it," piped Ferret. Amergen sprang to his feet and squeezed the young man's arm in appreciation.

"Can you handle a kayak?" asked Amergen eagerly.

"I am a Ranger. I can do whatever is required," answered Ferret simply.

"Of course you can. That is the way of the Rangers, as I have come to learn and admire," commended Amergen.

"I will help also," offered Arrow. "Eiru lifted me up in my hour of need, and it is only right that I help her now."

Mac Namara instinctively went to object but caught the steely glint in Arrow's eyes and thought better of it, so he changed tack instead.

"As will I," echoed the Sergeant, at which Blade groaned softly.

Mac Namara might be a solid soldier, but she very much doubted that he would be well suited for the subtle work of the shadow warrior, making her task to protect Arrow even more difficult. But wherever Arrow went, Blade was to go also. That was the last order that Wolf had quietly given her before he had left, more or less: 'Guard Arrow with your life, Blade; all our lives may depend upon it.'

"Count me in too," said Blade casually. She might have to shadow Arrow every step of the way, but Blade would welcome the action. She had been bitterly disappointed not to be a part of the raid on the shipyard, but the rescue of the girl would be some consolation.

O'Sullivan was conflicted. The safety of the ship was paramount for Wolf and his men, but Amergen's tiny band would need all the help that it could get. O'Sullivan looked to Otto for answers, and the coxswain could sense his dilemma.

"Have no fear, O'Sullivan. We will still have enough men to handle the ship," said Otto, but he could clearly see that this was not the assurance that O'Sullivan was seeking. "The ship will be there tomorrow night, just as we agreed. You have my word, Ranger," added Otto firmly.

O'Sullivan nodded, seemingly content that the coxswain would honour his word, and then he turned his attention to Amergen.

"Whatever you have in mind, Amergen, we had best be getting on with it," urged O'Sullivan. "The night is moving on, and Otto must be well clear of the coast by dawn."

"We need to get the Sea Eagle to the other side of the fjord unseen," answered Amergen.

"And how exactly are we to do that without being spotted by the sentries posted along the mountains?" asked Mac Namara, starting to get a little exasperated with Amergen's ill-conceived plan.

"It seems that Banba might have a say in that," suggested Amergen with some satisfaction, pointing towards the open sea and the rolling bank of sea fog that was fast approaching the entrance to the fjord.

"Can you weave your way through this mist to the other side of the fjord, Otto?" asked Amergen.

"With care and complete quiet, I can."

"Good, you shall have it," promised Amergen, then he left his coxswain to ready the ship and gathered in his small band.

"We have very little time to go through our plan, but then we need very little time, as our plan is both brief and simple," began Amergen, and then he laid out the bare bones of his scheme to snatch Eiru's girl from Vanomon's stronghold.

"After we have rescued the girl, we will need to find some way of getting ourselves out to the Sea Eagle before it sails," stressed Amergen, "so we must waste no time in finding a boat."

"One last thing," concluded Amergen. "Remember,

we must make our final move only after the captain and his men have set the shipyard ablaze. The resulting chaos should provide ample diversion for our stealthy friend here to gain access to the fortress and unbolt the tunnel door."

They nodded silently, and some patted Ferret's shoulder to wish him good luck. Then they all hurried off to ready their gear and prepare a sackful of torches.

*

Saras guided them to an abandoned jetty some distance up the far side of the fjord. No one cared to ask him how he knew of its existence, but they could all venture a guess. Drifts of sporadic sea fog laden with moisture screened their approach to what remained of the weather-beaten platform, the thick mist muffling the sound of the Sea Eagle as it thudded softly against the wizened wharf.

The small Sami sternly signalled for them to maintain complete silence, not that the Rangers needed telling. But Mac Namara had a heavy touch despite his best efforts, and they had all cringed more than once since landing. The ship swiftly unloaded, they pushed the Sea Eagle away from the wharf and gave it a silent wave. With a little luck, Otto and his crew would get the vessel far offshore before the approaching dawn crept into the eastern sky.

They quickly gathered up their gear and placed the kayak on the gravelled beach. Saras led the main party off into the cover of the nearby trees and waited as Ferret and Amergen carried the light craft down to the shoreline and placed the bow in water. Ferret slid carefully into the sea kayak and took up his paddle as Amergen held the stern steady and then he shoved the small boat out into the fjord.

"Until tomorrow night, my stealthy friend," whispered Amergen with the trace of a smile, and then he hurried back towards the trees as Ferret and his kayak silently disappeared into the mist.

Chapter Twenty-Eight

RAID

Wolf and his men had spent a cold night on the Island of the Hooded Crow. A damp mist had moved up Svartrfjord in the darkness and drenched everything that it touched, chilling the Rangers to the bone. As dawn approached, the mist lingered, reluctant to leave the sanctuary of the fjord and offering only temporary pockets of clearance by way of compensation.

At first light, the sound of two longships heading up the fjord came to them across the water, a steady dip of oars accompanied by the occasional crack of a whip and a muffled outcry of pain. Wolf thought that it was probably the slaves being brought to the shipyard for their day's work. When the faint sounds of hammering began drifting back towards the Island of the Hooded Crow, Wolf reckoned that he had been right about the dark nature of the ships.

The nearby forest which hemmed in the fjord seemed unusually quiet, devoid of the usual sounds of wildlife, which was hardly surprising as most of the woodland animals had most likely been hunted out in order to feed the many hungry mouths at the shipyard. Still, there seemed to be a strange sullenness about this forest too, thought Wolf, as if the trees sensed that their days were numbered and that they too would soon suffer the fate of their felled brethren in yards nearby.

When the mist briefly parted, they soon saw the real reason for the eerie silence: strung from the trees that fringed the fjord were the gruesome remains of men and women, judging by the tattered remnants of their clothing. There were children there too. Their brutal end no doubt meant to serve as a harsh reminder to the other slaves to obey and dare not resist. A plump raven that had been feasting on what remained of the latest victim sensed eyes upon him and stared boldly back at the hidden Rangers, gave a defiant caw, then carried on with his macabre work.

No one had said a word, but Wolf had sensed a cold rage settling in the heart of the Rangers at such wanton cruelty; night couldn't come soon enough for them or for their brooding blades. Wolf and his men had settled down as best they could beneath the cover of their dark green cloaks, quietly eating their meagre rations as the day had gone on steadily about them.

At dusk, the slave ships retraced their route back down through the misty fjord, most likely to secure the slaves for the night. The fog had been useful, but it could well prove to be a double-edged sword, reasoned Wolf, for while the damp mist would help to screen their approach and muffle any sound, it could also make things tricky for the Rangers. Still, each man felt that he already knew the shipyard very well, even though he hadn't yet set foot in it, for every Ranger had quizzed Amergen time and time again for every morsel of information that the king's counsellor had gleaned from his spies. Now they had a complete picture of the layout of the shipyard etched upon their mind's eye.

They slipped quietly off the Island of the Hooded Crow as soon as darkness had settled, Wolf quietly reminding them all to keep a short space between each kayak or run the risk of getting separated in the fog. Wolf had taken point in their arrow formation, and if not for the rhythmic hammering of a metal object on what was possibly an anvil coming from the shipyard, he could have easily become disorientated in the dimness and the shifting mist.

After several hours of hard paddling, they finally saw a long row of elevated torchlights stretched out all along the shore, the flames appearing and disappearing in the swirling vapour. Stationed further back and set wider apart were the bright braziers that served to keep the sentries warm in between patrols. Wolf paused a short distance from the shore to allow those behind to move up and fan out on either side of him. No words were necessary now, for every Ranger already knew what was expected of him. Satisfied that everyone was in place, Wolf simply pointed towards the shore.

The line of kayaks went stealthily through the mist, making their way towards the gently sloping shore. The Rangers slid their craft quietly up onto the sand and gravel beach and sprang out of their kayaks without delay. Dividing into teams of two, they grabbed hold of the bone toggles on either end of each boat and carried the kayaks swiftly up the beach, hiding them in the shadows of the timber stacks that lined the foreshore. Their swords already strapped across their backs, each man set about carefully retrieving his longbow, quivers, axe and dagger, quietly securing the small arms to their waist belts before quickly getting into position.

The mist had thinned considerably in the freshening breeze, allowing the full moon to briefly flood their surrounds with its lucent light. Wolf took the opportunity to peer along the Rangers' skirmish line which had spread out along the foreshore, each man huddled down in the darkness as he waited for the signal. Wolf took a brief moment to scan the shipyard ahead for any immediate signs or sounds of danger. All appeared remarkably still, and even the camp dogs seemed to be slumbering at their posts, which was to be expected; only a madman or a fool would contemplate attacking a place like this with such a paltry force of men. Wolf raised his arm for all his men to see and then slowly brought it down until it pointed towards the shipyard — madmen or fools, there was no turning back now. Lieutenant Godfridsson and his section went directly to the guardhouse, while the captain and his men dispersed and filtered cautiously through the shipyard.

The strong scent of raw timber and other sharp odours assailed Wolf's nostrils as he stalked through the newly constructed ships. An arrow nocked and two more tucked down the side of his waist belt, Wolf went stealthily towards a small open-sided lean-to with the glowing embers of a forge reflecting off a well-worn anvil which was mounted in the centre of the floor. There appeared to be no sign of life in the darkened shack, but then a young boy who had been sleeping on the floor suddenly sat up half-awake, the whites of his eyes the only thing which distinguished him from his gloomy surrounds. Wolf placed a forefinger against his lips, and the slave boy looked at him with dulled eyes and then glanced possessively at the small pile of ship's nails stacked neatly by the forge; content that his quota of nails was still safe, the boy closed his eyes and lay back down upon the earthen floor. Wolf eased the tension on the bowstring and stepped softly back into the night. Little did the sorry urchin realise that it had been the regular clanging of his unerring industry which had guided the Rangers safely through the mist, reflected Wolf sombrely. Then he moved on steadily towards the sentry's brazier which burned brightly in the near distance.

The fog was fleeting now, so Wolf advanced with greater care through the rows of propped-up ships. He paused when he heard the sound of snarling being directed towards him as he stalked softly through the shadows. Swivelling his head to pinpoint the source of the growls, Wolf sensed that the guard dog was tethered, as the location and the distance of the threat never seemed to waver.

"Wolves in the woods again, eh?" soothed the sentry who was seated near the glowing fire.

When an arrow buried itself in the dog's chest, the sentry stared at it for a moment, then he made a scramble to grab his spear, which was propped up against a nearby ship, but the second arrow caught him in the armpit as he reached for his weapon, knocking him onto his back with a sharp bark of pain.

"You should have listened to the dog," said Wolf as he stood over the guard with the sentry's own spear now levelled at the man's throat.

"Who are you?" snarled the guard, sensing that his death was very close at hand.

"We are the wolves," replied Wolf simply, then he drove the spear quickly into the sentry's throat.

Wolf heard the sound of two men in casual conversation heading towards him through the high rows of longships, and he quickly snatched the remaining arrow from behind his belt and fitted the notch to the bowstring.

The two guards, who seemed to have been heading towards the burning brazier, finally emerged from between the long lines of standing ships. They stopped suddenly and looked about them in confusion, trying to make some sense of the strange scene that confronted them in the pale moonlight. They stared with disbelief at the dead sentry, who had a spear rammed into his throat, while their guard dog lay motionless, an arrow driven into its chest. The two guards then seemed to simultaneously switch their attention to the tall archer who stood calmly before them. One soldier finally began fumbling for his axe, and Wolf loosed his arrow, driving it into the man's throat, felling him in an instant. His companion looked on in horror as his friend gasped and gurgled, desperately trying to draw down his final breaths as blood flooded into his airway. Aghast at the sudden turn of events, the remaining guard looked back at Wolf as if searching for an answer to all this nocturnal mayhem.

"Well, are you just going to stand there all night?" asked Wolf casually.

The guard bristled at the taunt and angrily drew his axe, which was exactly what Wolf had wanted; an enraged axe man was usually a predictable opponent. The man charged at Wolf, appearing a little perplexed as to why the archer just stood there instead of trying to string another arrow or even grab a different weapon. The sentry hollered a guttural war cry, hoisted the axe above his head and brought the weapon down with savage strength. Wolf deftly sidestepped the burly man and brought up his bow stave in an outward arc, deflecting the blow of the axe and forcing the guard's own momentum to propel him onwards. The sentry's flank now exposed, Wolf whipped out his dagger with his free hand and plunged it deep into the man's side. The guard shrieked in pain and his legs buckled, then he collapsed down onto his knees, grabbing his punctured side.

“At least you will die with a weapon in your hand, as your dark god demands,” said Wolf with no hint of scorn, then he stepped up behind the guard and dispassionately dragged his dagger across the man’s throat. The sentry remained upright for a moment, his hand clasped about his throat as he tried in vain to stop his lifeblood from seeping through his fingers, then he fell forward and landed heavily upon the ground. Wolf sheathed his dagger and quickly nocked another arrow in readiness. He steadied his breathing and scanned his surrounds for any other signs of imminent attack, but all that he could hear were the muffled sounds of muted scuffles drifting towards him from other parts of the shipyard.

With his senses on high alert, Wolf took up a position beside the burning brazier and perched his two quivers of arrows nearby, mindful of the highly flammable nature of the arrowheads, which were dipped in Amergen’s Greek fire. Wolf touched the readied arrow to the fire and then instinctively took a step back, keeping the angry flame that engulfed the arrowhead, well away from the bow stave. Wolf hoped that the lieutenant and his section had succeeded in their primary mission to neutralise the guardhouse — the very last thing that the Rangers needed now was a running battle against superior numbers. In any case, Wolf knew that he could delay no longer; the Rangers’ first priority was to destroy these ships. Wolf sent his first flaming arrow high up into the night sky. It was the signal that his men had been waiting for. Flights of fiery arrows soon shot up into the air in response, raining down destruction from every corner of the shipyard. Fires quickly sprang up everywhere, hungrily devouring the dried timber as tars, resins and sailcloth further fed the greedy flames. Here and there, it sounded as though a foolhardy few tried to douse the gorging fire, only to flee the blaze with screams of fear and pain as the flames snapped back at them in anger and only grew bigger.

The cool breeze had strengthened, sweeping aside whatever lingering mist had remained, further fanning the fire into a furious rage. Timber planks began to split loudly, and heated ship's nails sundered, fragments flying dangerously off in all directions. Plumes of acrid smoke billowed up into the night sky, accompanied by hordes of gleeful sparks. The full moon was unhindered now and able to illuminate the glaring destruction of the shipyard. A diligent sentry posted atop a far mountain was quick to spot the horrendous fire below him and quickly lit his warning beacon. Soon a string of readied bonfires was ablaze all along the mountain ridges on each side of the fjord, urgently summoning troops from Algar's Fort.

Wolf had watched with a sort of vague detachment as the signal fires began to erupt all across the darkened heights, continuing to rain his fiery arrows down upon the burning shipyard. His quivers all but spent, Wolf looked about him with a sense of grim satisfaction. There would be no stopping this voracious beast now, he thought. The heat was growing oppressive, and the pungent smoke had begun to burn his eyes, so Wolf slipped his few remaining arrows behind his waist belt and swiftly left the burning shipyard.

With the ships now firmly ablaze, Wolf's thoughts quickly turned to Godfridsson and his men. Their plan to deal with the guardhouse had been a cold-blooded piece of low cunning — a dark deed which was not uncommon in these savage lands. If the lieutenant did not succeed with the strategy, it would force the Rangers into a pitched battle that they could ill afford, as it would scuttle any chance of a swift escape. And speed was the very thing that they needed, concluded Wolf, as he hurried towards the guardhouse. Time was their enemy now.

Chapter Twenty-Nine

COMPLICATIONS

After separating from the other Rangers, the lieutenant and his men had moved swiftly towards the guardhouse, making their way methodically through a sprawling yard of scattered sheds and timber stacks and darting through the shadows whenever the mist melted away to allow the moonlight to flood the deserted yard. Upon reaching the guardhouse, a long, squat building with log walls and a thatched roof of dried rushes, they quickly surrounded it with the silence of wharf rats, then they readied their bows and waited.

Using a length of tough walrus rope he had taken for the task, Godfridsson quietly slipped the lashing around the front door handle of the guardroom, securing it with a round turn and two half-hitches. Finding a solid pole close by, he tied off the other end of the rope with a similar knot. Then he slipped back into the darkness and waited until Kelly had time to secure the rear door, which led off to the latrines.

Kelly moved towards the backdoor cautiously, grateful for the sudden bank of mist that screened his approach. He stepped softly onto the timber steps that led up to the door, cringing when the last step creaked in protest. Kelly stood stock-still, listening for any sounds of alarm, but all that he could hear were the faint sounds of snoring. He pressed on, deftly fastening the door handle and wrapping the other end of walrus rope around a porch post, then he hurried back into the shadows.

When a flaming arrow buried itself softly into the rush roof of the guardhouse, Kelly went to light his own arrow at a burning torch close by but froze when a sudden movement caught the corner of his eye. He dropped to one knee, laid his bow gently on the ground and slowly drew his dagger. It was possible that someone had left the guardroom to use the latrines and was now returning. It mattered little; Kelly could not allow the man to reach the fastened door and raise a commotion. An arrow in the darkness might miss its mark, but a close-up blade would be certain.

The mist was fragmenting now, so Kelly stayed low and kept to the shadows, circling around behind the hooded man. Breathing lightly, he placed each foot carefully before him as he closed the distance between them, and then he silently pounced. With one hand clamped around his victim's mouth and his dagger pressed tightly against the man's throat, Kelly dragged the guard back towards the cover of the shadows to finish him off, but straightaway he knew that something was wrong. The body felt far too slender, and the hairless face was soft. Neither was the person's scent unpleasant, and the muffled sounds that came from beneath Kelly's clasped hand seemed far from manly.

"Silence!" hissed Kelly, staying his knife hand as he tried to gather his thoughts. But the lithe frame continued to struggle in his grip, and somehow Kelly's captive managed to wrench his mouth free.

"Irish, you are Irish?" whispered a woman frantically as she wriggled around to face Kelly. "I am Irish too!"

"Jesus! You're a woman! Get down and be quiet," growled Kelly, grabbing her arms and hauling her down into a crouch as flights of flaming arrows began falling on the guardhouse roof.

"Take me with you. Don't leave me here with these

dirty animals," pleaded the woman as she seized Kelly's buckskin tunic, but then she noticed that his attention had been drawn towards a movement in the shadows. The woman followed Kelly's gaze, and when she saw a drunken soldier staggering towards the guardhouse as he fumbled with the front of his trousers, she snatched the axe from Kelly's belt in an instant and bolted towards the guard.

"You filthy pig!" shrieked the hysterical woman as she threw herself at the bewildered man, knocking him onto his back and then laying into him with the axe, screaming obscenities with every swift and savage blow. With an effort, Kelly finally wrestled the frenzied woman off the butchered man, quickly wrenching the bloody axe from her hands before she decided to turn the weapon on him.

"If you don't shut up, you are going to get us all killed!" snarled Kelly as he shook the woman's shoulders. The intensity of Kelly's words seemed to bring her slowly back to her senses, and she looked down at her reddened hands and blood-drenched dress in dismay. And then she suddenly broke down in tears. Kelly ushered the female into the shadows and held her close to him in the darkness, trying his awkward best to console the shattered woman and silently praying that her uncontrolled sobbing might be somewhat muffled by the cradle of his chest.

*

Wolf and his men hurried from the blazing shipyard and made their way swiftly towards the burning guardhouse.

"Numbers, Sergeant?" asked Wolf as O'Neill fell into a trot beside him.

"A few cuts and bruises, some singed hair, but no casualties, Captain," replied O'Neill with much satisfaction.

"That's way better than we could have hoped for, Sergeant."

"So far, so good, and I see that the Sea Eagle has made it too, Captain."

"A sight for sore eyes," said Wolf with relief as they glanced out towards the ship holding steady in the moonlit fjord.

"You doubted Otto, I think?" asked O'Neill.

"And you didn't?"

"I'm happy to be wrong," admitted the sergeant.

"As am I," confessed Wolf, slowing his pace as they drew near to the blazing guardhouse. "I don't think that our men need to see this," said Wolf, sensing the sombre mood of Godfridsson's section as they silently gathered to witness the murderous result of their 'hall-burning'. "Best get our men back to the ship, Sergeant."

"I will never forget those screams," said Godfridsson, acknowledging Wolf's arrival beside him as he continued to stare at the raging flames.

"War is a brutal business, Lieutenant," replied Wolf tersely; there was little else that he could say.

"Some tried to break out through the roof, and every time that we cut one guard down, another man would rush to take his place, even though it meant certain death."

"Better a quick death by a fast arrow than a slow one by a torturous flame," reasoned Wolf, deriving no satisfaction from the harsh death of the Norse soldiers.

"There's not much honour in this, Captain, is there?" said Godfridsson a little bitterly as the sickly stench of seared flesh hung heavy on the air.

"We didn't come here for honour, Godfrid," answered Wolf calmly, "or for glory, or for any of those things that shield-wall warriors put such high store in. And like it or not, we are ill-prepared to simply do battle with a larger force who have the added advantage of shields, chainmail and reinforcements. We are shadow warriors, and such is the nature of our trade."

"Perhaps," conceded Godfridsson reluctantly.

"We were tricked into completing this mission, by fair means or by foul. And we have succeeded where very few others could have. The odds might be stacked against us now, but we must try and lead our men back home, Lieutenant," concluded Wolf firmly. "We owe them that much."

"Indeed, Captain," responded Godfridsson smartly, finally tearing his eyes and his thoughts away from the smoky flames. "And I thank you for that reminder."

"Any losses, Lieutenant?" asked Wolf, forcing Godfrid's attention back to the task at hand.

"Not that I can see," answered Godfridsson, casting a quick glance over his men, who had gathered up behind him in the lurid light. "But I don't see Kelly. I sent him around the back to secure the rear door. Perhaps he didn't hear the recall?"

"That's possible with all this noise," agreed Wolf, gesturing towards the creaks, cracks and groans of destruction emanating from the dying building.

"I will find him, Captain," offered Godfridsson and turned to leave.

"No, I will search for our lost sheep, Lieutenant," responded Wolf. "It would be better if you got the rest of your men back to the ship. We will soon follow."

Godfridsson stalled for a moment and seemed unhappy to let the captain go in his stead but looked uncertain how to phrase his concerns.

"There is no time to lose, Godfrid," encouraged Wolf. "The warning beacons are ablaze across the mountain peaks, and you can be damn sure that King Algar is making ready his warships as we speak. If we do not clear Svartrfjord by dawn, we will surely be trapped and certainly outnumbered."

The lieutenant gave Wolf a parting look and a knowing nod, and then he waved his men towards the shore.

*

Wolf nocked an arrow and moved cautiously towards the far end of the burning building, feeling very exposed in the glaring blaze, his hearing hampered by the sounds of the gorging flames, his vision blurred by the stinging smoke. He stopped and gave the soft trill of a curlew call, the signal for recall, and then he waited. The same birdcall came swiftly back to him, and he turned towards its source in readiness. Expecting only one, Wolf hauled back on the bowstring in suspicion when two people clasped closely together came out of the shadows into the firelight.

"Captain, it's me, Kelly!" said a hushed voice.

"Who's that with you?" asked Wolf suspiciously, slowly easing his bow as he peered at the approaching pair.

"I can explain everything, Captain," beamed Kelly, a supporting arm gently draped around a woman's shoulders.

"Then do so, Ranger, and quickly."

"She's Irish!" beamed Kelly, as if that explained everything.

"This is not a rescue mission, Kelly."

"I know, Captain, but she's just killed a guard," replied Kelly with concern.

"So I can see," answered Wolf, observing her bloodstained appearance.

"They'll string her up for sure, Captain," fretted Kelly. "We can't just leave her here, can we?"

Wolf looked the woman up and down. Her bloody clothes and guilty red hands could not be easily explained away to her captors, that was certain. And Kelly was right: they would hang her for sure. When a slave wielded arms against their master, it was considered one of the very worst crimes in Norse society. A slave who murdered their owner was sure to receive a sorry end.

"Have you got a name?" asked Wolf.

"Niamh," answered the woman sullenly, staring at Wolf with surly eyes, which was understandable, as most fighting men surely looked the same to her.

"We all carry our own weight in this outfit, no exceptions," said Wolf, addressing them both.

Kelly quickly withdrew his protective arm from around the woman and straightened up, while Niamh glared at Wolf with hostility.

"She's your problem now, Kelly," stated Wolf briskly. "But if she causes any trouble or impedes this mission in any way, you are to deal with her immediately. Do we understand each other, Ranger?"

"Yes, Captain," responded Kelly soberly as he stared at the ground, for that instruction meant only one thing.

"You will go with Kelly, you will do everything that

he tells you to do, and you will do it smartly and you will do it quietly," stressed Wolf. "Have I made myself clear?" Niamh nodded her head slowly and stared at Wolf with cold eyes.

"Take her down to the shore and put her into my kayak and get her out to the Sea Eagle, Kelly," ordered Wolf after pondering the problem for a moment. "And do it without any further delay."

"But we cannot take your kayak, Captain!" protested Kelly.

"Ranger, the only thing that separates us from this rabble is discipline. Without discipline, there is no control, and without that, we are nothing," chastised Wolf.

"Sorry, Captain, I didn't mean to question your orders. It's just..."

"Don't worry, Kelly, I'll soon find another boat to ferry me out to the Sea Eagle. This place used to be a shipyard, so there's bound to be something still lying about," joked Wolf, getting a weak smile from Kelly. "Now you two get going."

Wolf watched the pair as they hurried off into the night and wondered if Kelly had by chance found himself a wife. He needed to be hard on them both in order to keep them alive, for this was neither the time nor the place for soft sentiments. Then Wolf thought he heard a faint whirring noise behind him being drowned out by the dying spasms of the burning guardhouse — sling! — He realised a fraction too late then a sharp pain erupted in the back of his head, as the speeding stone crashed into his skull. Stars burst before his eyes, his head spun wildly as his stomach heaved, then his legs suddenly buckled beneath him, and he fell heavily to the ground.

"Don't kill him," growled someone behind Wolf, and the voice sounded as though it was laced with pain. "That bastard belongs to me."

"What are we do with him?" replied another.

"Vanomon will want to question him. Bring the assassin to his stronghold," replied the first, and then he paused as stifled sounds of agony escaped from his body. "But remember this," he eventually gasped, "no one is to kill that murdering bastard but me."

Angry hands hauled Wolf up off the ground as his eyelids finally surrendered to the sudden blow. Warm blood oozed down the back of his head, and his body went limp as he drifted off into a stupor. Then all at once, Wolf's world went black.

Chapter Thirty

BANBA

Ferret paddled carefully towards the looming stronghold, his senses taut with apprehension. The mist had become more sporadic, and the full moon flooded the fjord with its soft light whenever the bright orb held sway. The vivid glare from the blazing shipyard along the far shore filled the night sky with its violent throes. And while the spectacle was sure to provide Amergen with the diversion he so badly needed, it was certain to put the warlock's guards on high alert.

Vanomon's fortress was an imposing edifice of sheer stone that appeared to grow up out of the rocky outcrop upon which it was firmly rooted. Arrow slits peered out at the world with hostility and seemed to give the great grey beast the illusion of life. Ferret studied the apertures closely as he quietly guided his kayak towards the small slipway that served the sea-gate. He noticed that the openings were at their most narrow at the lower levels — mere slits near the ground floor, but gradually widening with each successive floor.

Giving a final thrust of his paddle, Ferret allowed his kayak to drift into a sheltered cleft between the starboard bow of a tied-up skiff and the slipway. He used his hand to fend off the boat strakes as his craft glided in, avoiding any hint of a sound. Hearing no challenge, Ferret eased himself out of his kayak and hunkered down on the slipway, scanning his surrounds for any sign of a threat. Satisfied that he had not been observed approaching, Ferret carefully retrieved his sword and dagger. His axe, bow and quiver of arrows would only prove to be a hindrance as he scaled the walls, so he left them where they were. Instinctively, Ferret made a dash for the cover of the shadows that gathered beneath the high walls. Once there, he quickly made his way around to an internal corner in the structure, where he searched along the soft joints between the stones for the slightest hint of a purchase on the smooth walls.

The loud scraping of a metal bolt being drawn back suddenly filled the quiet night. Ferret pressed his back hard into his dark corner and hoped that the grey stone would absorb his outline. A nearby door creaked slowly open, throwing a little orange light onto a short flight of stone steps that led down to the shoreline. A guard poked his head out of the doorway, and he briefly checked the area, then he hurried down the steps to the shore. Ferret didn't know what to make of the sentry's odd behaviour until he heard the sound of the man being violently sick.

It was an opportunity that was too good to miss. The distance between Ferret and the open door was short, but it was exposed except for the shadows. Ferret could certainly do with a little luck, but he would also need to use all of his customary stealth and speed. He nipped across the slick rocks, listening closely to the sounds of the sick sentry, who loudly heaved his supper out onto the shore. Detecting no sounds beyond the doorway, Ferret took a chance and darted in, dagger at the ready. He was met with no immediate sounds of alarm and found himself in a winding passageway that was dimly lit by a torch mounted in a wall sconce. Beneath the flickering light stood a chair, a small table and the remains of the man's supper left sitting at the bottom of a bowl. Faint sounds occasionally drifted down the passageway from the rooms above, and the stale smells of cooking that had wafted down from the kitchens still clung heavily in the air. Ferret heard the groaning guard make his way laboriously back towards the doorway, so he scampered on up the corridor, reckoning that the kitchen was as good a place as any to start his search for the girl.

The kitchen had remained warm after its day's work, the amber glow of the raised fire pit taking the edge off the darkness. Ferret stepped cautiously into the kitchen, the scent of burnt meat nipping at his nostrils.

"Banba told me that you would come," said a soft voice from the shadows. Ferret spun to face the female's voice, his dagger poised uncertainly.

"She did?"

"She came to me in a dream last night and told me to be ready. She also told me to sprinkle a little hemlock in the sentry's supper. Was this of help to you?"

"The guard went out the sea door to be sick, and I slipped in," answered Ferret.

"He will be dead by morning," said the girl simply.

"They call me Ferret," he responded after a heavy silence, unsure of how to comment on the poisoning of the sentry.

"Ferret!" exclaimed the girl with mirth. "I do like ferrets. They are so stealthy and courageous, cunning little creatures too. Are you all of these things, Ferret?"

"I hope so."

"You will need to be, my brave champion," replied the young woman, stepping out of the shadows. "I am Riona."

"We have come to take you home," said Ferret a little awkwardly, strangely unsettled by the girl's bewitching beauty.

"We?"

"My friends await us in the secret tunnel. Do you have any idea where that might be?" asked Ferret hopefully.

"Banba has told me where to find it. The rats tell her everything," replied Riona with certainty. "The entrance is hidden in plain sight down in the dungeons."

"Can you take me there?"

"I can, but we will need to be very careful; there is trouble in the dungeons tonight."

*

His hands bound tightly together, Wolf hung from a timber beam, his feet barely touching the dungeon floor. He appeared delirious, his head was slumped forward, and drool dripped from his mouth as he mumbled incoherent words.

"Well, well, if it isn't the Green Man," said a cold voice from the shadows of the dimly lit cell. The man stepped forward, scattering a handful of rats that were reluctant to move from the dirty straw that was strewn across the floor.

"I knew that you were trouble when you walked into the Dirty Dog tavern that day in Dublin," continued the big man as he stood before Wolf. He grabbed hold of Wolf's bloodied hair and yanked his head back, thrusting the stump of a severed finger before Wolf's face. "Remember this? Remember me?" asked Bjorn, his voice dripping with hatred.

Wolf's eyes floated in their sockets and his tongue lolled about his mouth as he moaned and babbled. Bjorn dropped Wolf's head in disgust and looked towards a sword and dagger hanging on the damp wall near the cell door.

"It looks like I got your sword in the end, Green Man. That nasty dagger too," said Bjorn casually, then he suddenly drove his hefty fist into Wolf's exposed side. Then he watched closely for his prisoner's reaction, but Wolf barely responded. "That's for getting me sent to this shit-hole," said Bjorn. "Still, being a prison guard at Svartrfjord does have certain advantages: Vanomon keeps us well supplied with Irish whores." He laughed, then hammered his fist into Wolf's other side. "And that's for cutting off my finger, you Irish bastard," added Bjorn with venom, peering hard into Wolf's eyes for any sign of lucidity, but he saw absolutely nothing.

"They must have hit you pretty hard, Irishman. Perhaps you will have those head staggers for the rest of your miserable days. Maybe I should keep you as my dog, chain you up outside my longhouse, feed you scraps and let my children beat you daily?" suggested Bjorn. "But I do not think that you will live that long, Green Man. Vanomon is keen to torture you for honest answers, and the Irish witch sorely wants to carve your heart out and shove it down your throat. But Ragner has claimed the right to execute you, slowly. And he has sworn to kill anyone who deprives him of that pleasure."

Wolf continued to babble nonsense, broken sentences and slurred words.

"Ragner might have been cunning enough to break out through the roof of the burning guardhouse, but you have robbed him of his golden locks and ruined his pretty looks. He squeals like a pig in pain now when they smear that putrid stuff on his ravaged skin. And he prays for the day that he can come down here and hack you into tiny pieces," related Bjorn with satisfaction as he headed for the door.

Wolf went on rambling.

"Your men slipped up, Green Man," continued Bjorn as he slotted the key in the door. "Instead of keeping watch on the guardhouse for anyone trying to flee the flames, your man was busy wrestling with one of our whores, which was lucky for Ragner, but not so good for you, Irishman."

"Hide...quickly! Gold," muttered Wolf under his breath.

Bjorn paused and relocked the door.

"Did you say gold, Green Man?" probed Bjorn quietly as he walked across the floor.

"Must hide... gold!" mumbled Wolf.

"Yes, you must hide it. But where?" coaxed Bjorn softly, leaning in close to Wolf's lips in hopes of catching the whispered answer.

Suddenly, Wolf locked his legs around Bjorn's waist and bit down hard on the side of his neck, digging in deep with his teeth, tearing into flesh and ripping apart vital blood vessels just as the wolves had taught him.

Bjorn struggled free from Wolf's savage grip, protectively clamping a hand over the ragged wound at the side of his neck as dark red blood pumped rhythmically out of his jugular vein.

"You bastard!" gasped Bjorn in disbelief, staring at Wolf in astonishment. Wolf spat a morsel of bloody flesh at him in response and glared at Bjorn with defiance.

"You filthy animal," rasped Bjorn as warm blood flowed freely through his fingers. Sensing that he was done for, he staggered towards the weapons that hung near the door and snatched the dagger from its scabbard. Bjorn turned and gave Wolf a malicious grin and took two faltering steps towards him, but his legs would go no further.

"Bastard!" said Bjorn weakly as his eyelids began to flutter, then his legs buckled and he dropped down hard at Wolf's feet, his face buried in the mouldy straw.

Wolf looked quickly about him for any means of escape. He tested the resolve of the rope that held him, but his pummelled sides sang out in agony with the effort. A faint movement caught the corner of his eye, and he turned to find a hooded crow perched on the ledge of the arrow slit in his cell.

"Have you come to mock me, grey-crow?" asked Wolf as he dangled from his rope. The brazen bird cawed back boldly and continued to look at him as if trying to communicate some meaningful message. Wolf stared into the crow's intense eyes, struggling to understand the bird's intent and then slowly starting to recall the faded words of an old promise that had been buried deep in his dusty memory.

"Go quickly and tell Banba that I am in dire need of her help," urged Wolf. The hooded crow replied with a sharp caw and then flew off into the night.

The rat slept comfortably in its nest of straw buried deep within the stone wall. He had fed well in the man's kitchen, where food was always plentiful.

'You have done well for yourself, King Rat,' said a pleasant voice in his dreams. He had heard the voice of the 'Shining-One' before. And he had greatly feared it.

'I have,' he responded respectfully.

'Do you remember when I found you huddled in your wet burrow, cold, starving and afraid of the soaring hawks who strike without warning?'

'I remember,' answered the rat cautiously.

'And do you recall when I led you to this place, and I told you that I might require a small service from you one day?'

'Yes, I remember that too.'

'Well rise up, King Rat. For I have a task for you this night: a rope to chew, nothing more.'

'But I am full and warm, and I do not like ropes. Stringy things,' lamented the rat.

'Rouse yourself, rat, or I will send a feisty stoat to chase you from your nest!'

'I am yours to command, Shining-One.'

'As a reward for your labour, I will leave a little something beneath the rope,' softened the voice as it went on to give the rat his task.

The rat awoke with a start, stretched himself, and then slipped from his nest. He hurried through a familiar labyrinth of slick tunnels, scaring lesser rats out of his way. After a little searching, the rat found an opening high up in the cell wall, and he dropped down onto the timber beam. The rat had no fear of heights and crept confidently across the rafter until he found the rope that held the dangling man. He set quickly to work, biting through the leather rope with his sharp incisors.

Helped by the man's weight, the rope soon snapped, and the prisoner collapsed in a heap on the floor. His task completed, the rat looked down to claim his reward and saw the dead man sprawled upon the floor. Using the carcass to break his fall, the rat jumped off the beam, bounced off the dead body and landed unharmed upon the straw floor. Sensing their presence, the big rat bared his frightful teeth at the horde of rats that had gathered in the shadows for the feast. They would all have to wait until their king had eaten his fill.

Wolf swiftly gathered his senses, retrieved the dagger from Bjorn's lifeless hand, and quickly set about slicing through his binds. Seeing the enormous rat greedily lap up Bjorn's blood reminded Wolf to wipe his own bloody mouth, so he dragged his buckskin sleeve across his face.

"My thanks to you!" whispered Wolf to the indifferent rat as he went to leave. "At least you have been well rewarded, my friend."

Wolf quietly lifted his sword from the wall hook and slowly cranked the cell door open. The torchlit corridor seemed surprisingly absent of guards. It was possible that they had been redeployed to fight the blaze in the shipyard, speculated Wolf as he made his way cautiously up the stone steps until a sudden movement on the stairs above caught his attention. Dagger in hand, Wolf pressed himself into the shadows as the two figures furtively descended the stairs. He readied himself to strike as they grew nearer but then balked at the final moment.

"Ferret?"

"Captain!" exclaimed Ferret as he leapt back instinctively poised to defend himself. "You're the last person that I expected to meet down here," he gasped, then saw Wolf's blood-matted hair. "Are you injured?"

"It looks worse than it is," answered Wolf, checking the congealed mess at the back of his head. "Who is this? And why are you in the fortress?"

"It's a long story, Captain," answered Ferret, anxious to get moving again.

"And probably not one that can be told here?" deduced Wolf.

"Not really."

"But why are you down here in the dungeons?"

pressed Wolf, glancing up the stairs for any sign of the guards.

"There's a secret tunnel, Captain."

"In the dungeons?"

"Riona is going to show us," replied Ferret with confidence.

"I see," mused Wolf as he studied the enigmatic girl. "It must be a very long story indeed."

"I can explain everything as soon as we find a little cover."

"Has Amergen got anything to do with this?" ventured Wolf.

"Aye, Captain," sighed Ferret, looking a little sheepish.

"I might have known," answered Wolf, appearing not the least bit surprised. "In any case, we don't have time for all that now. Best get to this tunnel before we are discovered," he urged, sensing that the night was fast slipping away and the first light of dawn would soon be upon them.

Chapter Thirty-One

BREAKOUT

"This is the one," said Riona, stopping at a cell door at the end of the dimly lit corridor.

"How can you be so sure?" asked Wolf.

"Banba has eyes everywhere."

"I don't suppose those eyes saw where they hid the key?" asked Ferret hopefully.

"There is no need for a key," answered Riona as she lifted a torch out of the wall sconce by the door and handed it to Ferret. "This is the handle that opens the door," she explained, then pulled down on the metal bracket, the cunning lever creaking in protest as the door popped ajar.

Wolf cautiously pushed open the heavy door and peered into the darkened tunnel as a breath of fresh air raced past him, harrying a few abandoned cobwebs that clung to the rough walls.

"They will be expecting you alone, Ferret. We will wait here and guard the door. But do not delay; time is against us," urged Wolf, sensing that dawn was upon them.

Ferret held his torch high as he moved carefully down the narrow tunnel but soon stopped when he suspected that there might be someone waiting around the next bend.

"Amergen, is that you?" hissed Ferret down the tunnel.

"Kill that bloody light!" growled Mac Namara's hushed voice, and Ferret quickly doused his torch in the dirt.

"You did it, Ferret!" beamed Amergen as he hurried around the corner, his outline barely visible in the faint light that seeped down from the open doorway.

"Of course he did, he's the Ferret!" whispered Blade, softly patting him on the back.

"We may have a patrol on our tail. We heard noises," explained O'Sullivan. "Hence the caution. Best be getting out of here. I reckon that they're not too far behind us."

"I found the girl!" said Ferret excitedly as he led them back to the door.

"Great, now all we have to do is find a way out of this hellhole," responded Mac Namara dryly.

"And that's not all I found," continued Ferret as he led them through the cell door.

"Captain!" gasped Amergen, both relieved and confused in equal measure.

"Are you injured, Wolf?" asked Blade anxiously as she rushed towards him, alarmed to see him propped up against the wall with blood caked around his neck.

"It looks worse than it is," reassured Wolf as he pushed himself upright. "I'll be fine."

"What are you doing here, Captain?" asked Arrow with concern.

"I might ask the same of you. Of all of you," said Wolf with little warmth. And each of them shifted a little awkwardly under his questioning glare.

"The fault is mine," placated Amergen quietly, his head slightly bent in contrition.

"It matters little whose fault it is now," dismissed Wolf. "We are trapped, and we need to get ourselves out of here, and fast. Can we go back through the tunnel?"

"Saras seems to think that someone is following us," explained O'Sullivan, glancing back towards the open door. "Perhaps a forest patrol picked up our trail?"

"Can he figure out how many?"

"Seven, maybe nine," provided Amergen.

"Too risky trying to tackle them in the tunnel," considered Wolf aloud. "Quickly, we need to close off this door before they're upon us."

"Any suggestions, Ferret?" asked Wolf after they had secured the door that led to Vanomon's secret tunnel.

"We could go back through the kitchen. It was pretty quiet when I passed through there earlier," answered Ferret. "From there, we should be able to use the passageway that leads down to the sea door."

"Sea door?"

"Aye, Captain. It opens onto the foreshore near a slipway."

"Were there any ships tied up?"

"There was one, a sizable skiff."

"Big enough to take all of us?" asked Wolf hopefully.

"It was no dragon ship, Captain, but I reckon she'll do," answered Ferret with a lopsided grin.

"Good. See if the kitchen is still clear and get back to me quickly," ordered Wolf, and Ferret hurried off down the corridor. Wolf then turned his attention to the rest of the party, but Saras suddenly jumped out in front of them with his arms raised, blocking their way.

Amergen hand-signed his confusion to Saras, and the little Sami responded with a flurry of intricate signs and movements with his agitated hands.

"What does he want?" snapped Mac Namara.

"In a nutshell, he wants Vanomon," explained Amergen. "That was our agreement: he would guide us through the tunnel to rescue the girl. But he was here for Vanomon."

“So?” asked Wolf, casting Mac Namara a cool glance.

“He fears that if you go charging up through the fortress, he will lose the element of surprise, which he desperately needs,” reasoned Amergen. “Vanomon is a powerful warlock, so Saras is going to need whatever edge he can get.”

“What would you have me do, Counsellor?”

“Let him get a head start, Captain. That’s all he asks.”

“I will give him the time it takes to sharpen a sword and no more,” responded Wolf after a moment.

Saras seemed content with what he had heard, and Wolf watched as the little man quickly disappeared into the shadows, and then he turned his attention to the waiting party.

“Capture is not an option,” said Wolf bluntly, sternly holding each steely eye that watched him. Then they formed up in readiness and waited in silence until Saras had slipped into position.

*

Vanomon stood at a window in his rooms and coldly watched his dreams of glory go up in flames on the far side of the fjord. He had sent every able-bodied man that he could find to fight the savage fire and to root out the arsonists; perhaps it was too late for the ships, but they might capture more of the raiders. And those prisoners would offer up many truths before Vanomon allowed death to release them. King Algar was sure to want answers. Algar would also want someone to blame, and Vanomon knew only too well where the blame would finally fall. But Vanomon would be long gone before the enraged King returned, for the warlock had kept his skiff well prepared for a day such as this.

*

Saras squeezed softly through the half-open door, wordlessly thanking the guiding spirit of his people for the absence of any guard as he slipped undetected into Vanomon's candlelit rooms. The warlock was transfixed by the conflagration that consumed the nearby shipyards and was oblivious to the little man as he moved stealthily across the floor. Saras paused in the shadows just beyond the firelight, and he quietly brought a small tube up to his mouth with practised precision. He quickly took aim and gave the hollow pipe a short sharp blast of breath, sending a silent dart flying through the air. The feathered barb buried itself deep in Vanomon's neck, and he staggered as the powerful toxins raced through his bloodstream. The warlock turned to face his attacker and seemed to recognise an old familiar foe — one that he thought had died a very long time ago. And then Vanomon slumped against the wall and slowly crumbled down into a heap upon the floor.

The shaman stood over Vanomon, who glared at him with baleful eyes while the rest of his body refused to obey. Having retrieved a small purse of blood-red powder from inside his tunic, Saras dipped his thumb in the thick dust and then pressed it hard into Vanomon's forehead, silently mouthing incantations all the while. His wordless curse uttered, Saras then tipped a portion of the crimson powder out onto his hand and then suddenly blew it into Vanomon's face, temporarily blinding the warlock. Content with his spell, Saras gave a crooked grin and then hurried from Vanomon's rooms.

*

"The guards are back!" said Ferret breathlessly, having hurried back down to Wolf's party, who were waiting on the dungeon stairs.

"Where?" demanded Wolf.

"They're gathered in the kitchen, getting food by the sounds of it."

"How many?"

"I couldn't get close enough to count. A dozen maybe, but that's not the worst of it."

"Spit it out, Ferret."

"The entrance to the passageway down to the sea door is at the far side of the kitchen," answered Ferret despondently.

"Surely there is another way?" pressed Wolf.

"Is there, Riona?" asked Ferret gently. The girl scanned the small party that was staggered along the dimly lit stairs, paying particular attention to the bigger men in the group, and then she turned towards Wolf.

"There is a small tunnel that could take us around the kitchen, down to the passageway that leads out to the fjord." Riona pointed. "It starts up there on the landing."

"How small?" probed Wolf.

"I think that these tunnels were built so that young boys could quickly take fresh arrows to any part of the fortress," explained Riona.

"Show me."

*

The tunnel was small, it was low, and it was narrow. Mac Namara muttered bitterly beneath his breath every time he clattered his head off the rounded ceiling or knocked his elbows off the tight walls. The sergeant's moaning had become more constant lately, and he had left them all in little doubt about his opinion regarding this type of 'sneaky warfare'. They had quickly snatched three torches from the wall sconces on the landing area. Wolf had taken one torch and gone out in front of the group, keeping Riona close by. O'Sullivan, he had positioned in the centre with another torch, well clear of those in front of him. Towards the rear, Wolf had placed Mac Namara with the third torch, where he could grumble away to his heart's content. They had all shuffled forward in a low ambling gait for what seemed like an eternity until Wolf stepped gratefully out into the passageway, painfully straightening his back as he checked the corridor for any signs of life.

"This is it!" whispered Ferret excitedly as he stepped out of the narrow tunnel. "The sea door is just around that corner. I can see the sentry's table."

"Sentry?"

"Not anymore. But I'll check it out, Captain," offered Ferret and hurried on down to the sea door as the rest of them waited for Mac Namara to exit.

"Damn it!" hissed the sergeant, clobbering his head one final time as he uncoiled himself from the tight tunnel.

"I doubt that these tunnels were designed with you in mind, dear Captain," said Arrow in a kindly way, having waited near the opening for Mac Namara to arrive.

"It does my heart good to hear you call me that," answered Mac Namara warmly, all his aches and pains magically melting away.

"But you will always be my captain," responded

Arrow affectionately.

"Nothing more?" probed the Sergeant tenderly.

"More?" responded Arrow in confusion, and Mac Namara's romantic dream evaporated in an instant.

"Halt! Who goes there?" bellowed an angry voice down the passageway as Saras came barrelling around the bend towards them, pointing frantically behind him.

"Tell your brothers..." began Mac Namara and seemed to struggle for the right words.

"Tell them what?" encouraged Arrow, utterly thrown by the sergeant's peculiar behaviour.

"Just tell them!" snapped the sergeant as he drew his sword and went to leave.

"Captain, I don't understand!"

"Go now, Princess Aoife. I will keep them at bay for as long as I can," softened Mac Namara with an enigmatic smile. Then he squared his shoulders, marched boldly up the passageway and was gone.

*

Mac Namara's brave sacrifice had bought them precious time, and the eight fugitives had raced across the rocky foreshore to the slipway at the sea-gate, not daring to look back. Darkness was lifting and the dawn light made them feel very exposed and completely alone, for the Sea Eagle was well and truly gone. Saras grabbed the kayak that Ferret had left behind him and swiftly set off down along the coastline, quickly disappearing from sight. They loosened the skiff in a trice and quickly edged the boat out into deeper water, where a fresh breeze blew the light craft straight down the fjord. Wolf worked the tiller while Amergen went off to look around the small ship.

O'Sullivan and Ferret swiftly set the main sail and adjusted the rigging, their movements and actions largely instinctual, their need for talk minimal. Mac Namara might not have been one of the Rangers, but his heroism had touched them all, Arrow more than most, and Blade and Riona were doing their best to console the young woman as she huddled in the thwarts.

"A good man, that Mac Namara," said O'Sullivan with deep respect as the skiff cleared the calmer waters of the fjord and started to settle into the rhythm of the open sea.

"Better than we gave him credit for," agreed Wolf as he studied the leaden grey clouds that were drifting down from the north on a strengthening wind. He was quietly troubled by the sergeant's loss, but now was not the time to consider such vexing matters.

"Best get everyone wrapped up, counsellor; there's a storm on the way," advised Wolf as he swung the skiff south, a concerned eye surveying the boat's low freeboard, which flirted way too close to the surface of the roiling sea.

"I saw a handful of cloaks packed into the hold, some provisions too," replied Amergen. "The boat is called the Osprey, by the way, Captain. I wouldn't be surprised if this had actually been Vanomon's own ship. It certainly seems to be well provisioned for a quick escape."

"Did Saras kill him?"

"It will take much more than a shaman or any ordinary blade to kill a warlock as powerful as Vanomon; he's too well protected by his arcane arts. Saras has bought us a little time, nothing more. I very much doubt that we have seen the last of Vanomon."

"And what of King Algar?"

"Ruined, I would imagine," speculated Amergen without a hint of sympathy and went off to break out the cloaks.

"Do you think that they made it, Captain? The Sea Eagle, I mean?" asked O'Sullivan as he tightened a shroud on the gunwale.

"Godfridsson is a canny officer. You would need to be pretty shrewd to get the better of him," replied Wolf optimistically as stray drops of rain started to find their mark.

"I hope so, Captain," responded O'Sullivan sourly. "That bastard McMahon still owes me three silver bits!"

Chapter Thirty-Two

ENCOUNTER

They had struck out west from Svartrfjord as dawn slowly seeped into the eastern sky behind them, and a fresh northerly wind whipped down across their starboard bow. The mood on the Sea Eagle had been sullen as they stowed the oars and hoisted the mainsail, the Rangers directing all their angst into the yard as they vigorously hoisted the horizontal pole up the high mast. The men knew that Lieutenant Godfridsson had his orders to follow, but they didn't have to like them. Leaving fellow Rangers behind simply went against the grain.

Some of the men had been for holding off near the coastline in case Captain Wolf and the others managed to make it to the shore. But the lieutenant had reasoned that while their sentiment was commendable, such a foolhardy action would most likely result in the seizure of the ship and slavery for the twenty men onboard. And if that wasn't bad enough, there was no telling what the Norse might do if they recaptured Niamh, for they were sure to learn that she had killed one of their own. Of course, no one onboard the Sea Eagle could argue against Godfridsson's sound logic, blunt though it was. And after a painful silence, the Rangers had reluctantly accepted the inevitable and set about readying the ship while Otto set a course across the North Sea as many anxious eyes kept a keen watch towards their wake.

O'Neill did his best to lift the men's spirits as he strode up and down the pitching deck suggesting that "If anyone can get out of a tight corner, it's the captain. And they all knew how crafty Amergen was and how lethal

Blade could be. Why, even Arrow is no slouch with a sword and gave Blade a run for her money with the practice sticks!" he reminded them fondly. A few of the men chuckled warmly at the memory and then told others the story of the mock fight in the woods. "And you couldn't have two better Rangers at your back than O'Sullivan and Ferret. Why, I bet you a silver bit that that big ox Mac Namara could also show you a trick or two!" exclaimed O'Neill, which got a handful of laughs. "You can be sure that Captain Wolf wouldn't thank you for getting yourselves killed worrying about him," he reasoned.

The Rangers murmured their approval at that.

"He would want you to focus on your duties and keep yourselves alive, men, because you can be damned sure that he will be doing just that!"

Having cleared the coast of Norway and seeing no immediate sign of threat on the grey horizon, the lieutenant sent Ferguson among the wounded to tend to their needs. The former monk was well versed in such things and soon made good use of the small jars of ointment and bandages stored in the sea chest in the hold, and having treated the usual assortment of burns, cuts, knocks and abrasions, Ferguson made his way towards Niamh, who was huddled in her cloak alone at the bow, quietly looking out to sea.

"Are you hurt?" he asked. Niamh looked at him with blank eyes and refused to answer. "Maybe this might help?" continued Ferguson, fishing out a small wooden cross and handing it to the girl. Niamh slowly took the crucifix and looked at it curiously but seemed determined not to speak, so Ferguson turned to leave.

"Where was God when I needed him?" she asked, a

tear of anger escaping down her cheek. Ferguson seemed at a loss for words, the rhythmic crash of the Sea Eagle cutting into the next swollen wave sounding oppressive in the silence.

"He's here now," he offered softly, gesturing towards the great expanse of sky and sea that surrounded them, hoping that his simple words of faith would somehow soothe her pain. Niamh stared hard at him for a long moment as if trying to gauge the sincerity in his eyes, and she seemed content with what she saw.

"Perhaps," she replied evenly and appeared to hold the small cross just a little closer.

Favourable winds had taken them swiftly southwest across the brooding North Sea towards the rowdy Isles of Orkney. Godfridsson told his helmsman to make good use of the gathering dusk to give the lawless islands a wide berth. Otto knew the straits between the Inner and Outer Hebrides well, as did most raiders and traders who plied these waters. But as darkness began to fall in earnest, the seasoned coxswain became a little more cautious as they slipped into the wide expanse of the North Minch, instinctively seeking the comfort of the North Star towards his stern and the distant glitter of scattered firelight as it twinkled along the inner and outer Isles. The night sky was clear, the stars appeared sharp, and the full moon bathed the seascape in its soft luminous glow. The waters were calm too, but Otto saw no reason for complacency, so he sent Snorri aloft to act as a lookout and posted Karl to be his keen-eyed pilot at the bow. Magnus, as ever, stood ready by the sail, working in quiet unison with Otto, deftly adjusting the billowing sheet with every wavering breath of the wind.

"Get some rest, Lieutenant. I can take the first watch,"

offered O'Neill, coming to stand by Godfridsson at the stern.

"A pretty speech earlier, Sergeant," complimented the lieutenant. "Do you think that the captain can make it?"

"It's not him that I'm worried about, Lieutenant; a wolf needs no lessons in survival," replied O'Neill quietly, pensively looking out to sea.

"So someone else burdens your thoughts?"

"Best get some rest, Lieutenant," answered the Sergeant evasively. "Morning comes quickly."

*

The dawn raid on Iona had gone badly. A sharp-eyed lookout had spotted the distinctive red and white sail of the Danish ship as it neared the monastic island and rang the warning bell as if his life depended on it. Cuallaidh had given strict orders not to torch the place and alert nearby troops. But one of Jarl Burgeson's young bloods had lost his temper. Incensed at finding no silver, he had kicked over a stand of burning candles in the empty chapel, and a dried-out tapestry had instantly gone up in flames, hungrily spreading up into the church rafters and sending a column of black smoke high up into the clear morning sky for every local warlord to see.

Pressed for time, Cuallaidh's pack ran frantically through the grounds of the monastic settlement, only to find deserted buildings which had been hastily vacated. Confused, they hurried on towards the sound of the insistent bell and found themselves confronted by a high round tower constructed of solid stone. Curiously, the only way into this narrow column seemed to be through a small door set at the height of a mast above the ground, with no obvious way of reaching it.

"What trickery is this?" growled Rasende.

"Clever bastards," said Erik, appearing to be impressed with the Christians' ingenuity. "That's where all your nuns and priests are probably huddled, with all their gold and silver too."

"And how did they get into such a stronghold?" asked Cuallaidh, having walked around the tower, closely examining the structure.

"A rope?" suggested Balder as he approached the trio.

"Too slow — a ladder most likely," reasoned Erik.

"And where is this ladder now?" asked Rasende irritably, the manic bell ringing at the top of the tower beginning to grate on all their ears.

"They pulled it up after them, and then they barred the door," explained Cuallaidh tersely, starting to feel as though he had ventured too far out on a limb with this raid and could now hear the branch creaking ominously behind him.

"Surely there's another ladder around here somewhere?" speculated Rasende as he looked about him.

"I very much doubt it," replied Erik with certainty. "I'd say a ladder is the very last thing that you'll find on this particular island."

"What are we to do now?" asked Balder, sounding almost satisfied; he had been against the raid on Iona right from the start.

"Because of your men's indiscipline, the only thing that we can do, flee!" snapped Cuallaidh.

"I will discipline the man who started the fire," offered Balder quietly, humiliated by the rash behaviour of his men.

"You can be damned sure that you will, Balder. But his punishment will be of my choosing, not yours," growled Cuallaidh, and then he ordered his men to hurry back to the ship.

*

The day had broken bright and sunny. High rolling banks of white clouds tinged with grey drifted across the blue sky, creating an ever-changing pattern of sunshine and shadow dappled across the blue-green water. The sea was settled for late autumn, a grey-bluish plain of low-rolling wavelets flecked with soft white crests that came and went at their ease. Otto had sent Snorri aloft once again as they hurried through the narrowing waters of the Little Minch; one way and another, channels always made the helmsman nervous. The men's spirits had begun to lift as they started to sense the approach of Irish waters, the crisp sea spray being hurled off the bow and into their faces doing much to wash away their troubled mood.

"Ship ahead, port side!" hollered Snorri from the rigging above, and the lieutenant and O'Neill hurried to the bow.

"There!" said Godfridsson, pointing south-southeast. "A red and white sail with a dark hull."

"Danish by the looks of it," answered O'Neill, having fixed his sights on the ship.

"And she seems to be on her own."

"What madness would take a party of Danes raiding deep into Norse waters?" asked the sergeant, gesturing towards the dark plume spiralling into the sky beyond the island of Tiree. "Judging by the location of that smoke, I'd say they've just attacked Iona."

"She's turning north, Lieutenant!" called out Snorri with concern, his sharp eyes and lofty perch giving him a distinct advantage.

"Perhaps they're really searching for Princess Aoife," pondered Godfrid, closely studying the craft as it turned into the wind. "What else would take a lone Danish ship all the way up here?"

"You think that they could be Ivar's men?"

"It's a possibility. How else could you explain such a brazen folly?"

"The O'Kennedy girl must be of great value to them to take such a risk."

"There is a fine line between daring and recklessness," said Godfridsson sagely. "Sometimes you only realise that it is the latter when it's way too late."

"But how could they have known where we had gone?" contended O'Neill.

"The hills have eyes, Sergeant," speculated the lieutenant, always sensing that the Rangers were being watched, especially when they least expected it.

"And tavern folk will talk," conceded O'Neill, for well he knew how quickly its patrons would trade information for a hefty purse of silver or even a bellyful of ale.

"She's coming towards us, Lieutenant!" shouted Snorri in alarm.

"The bastards mean to board us!" spat O'Neill in disbelief.

"I think that we are too evenly matched for that, Sergeant. I doubt that they'd risk it. I reckon they'll try to ram us," replied Godfridsson coldly. "They're tacking into the wind, so they will need to generate more speed if they are to intercept us and smash into us amidships."

"What do you want us to do, Lieutenant?" asked

O'Neill, intently watching the Danish Karve as it raced to intersect the Sea Eagle's line of travel. Godfridsson coolly considered their situation and then studied the wind for a moment. It was still with them and blowing steadily from the north.

"We need to let them get close," answered Godfrid finally, and it was clear that the lieutenant had hatched some sort of clever strategy.

"How close?"

"Don't worry, Sergeant, we'll be ready for them when they get here," said Godfridsson with a mischievous smile. And then he laid out his plan for O'Neill.

*

They had fled from Iona empty-handed. And now there was a smouldering resentment between Jarl Burgeson's men and Cuallaidh's pack over the burning of the church. With time, Scarface and some of the others were convinced that they could have reached the high door in the tower and smashed their way in, but with the church belching out black smoke for all to see, time was something that they no longer had.

"What now, Ivarsson?" asked Rasende as the crew worked quickly to take the Storm Raven westward, well clear of the mainland and the hostile Scottish and Norse warships that were sure to soon appear.

"A pity that you couldn't track across water, old friend," grumbled Cuallaidh at the tiller as the large island of Tiree passed them by on their starboard side.

"You can do no more," consoled Erik as he approached Cuallaidh at the stern. "There is no shame in returning to Limerick now. We have left no stone unturned. At least it's a clear run from here westward and then south down along the Irish seaboard. We could be home within the week."

"Sail off the starboard bow!" called out someone urgently. And they all turned their attention to the Norse ship in the near distance as they cleared the island of Tiree.

"What is it, Alrick?" yelled Cuallaidh, seeing the big Norseman hurrying to the bow for a closer look. When the warrior turned to him with a broad grin on his ruddy face, Cuallaidh already knew the answer.

"It's her!" hollered Alrick. "It's the Norse ship that beached at Rathlin. Odin is with you, Jarl," he laughed, having swiftly cast aside the tedious religion of the Christians.

"We don't have time for this," argued Balder as the Storm Raven altered its course and headed northwest towards the oncoming ship.

"We'll have to be quick, Ivarsson," encouraged Rasende, firing Balder a dangerous look. "There will be many ships here soon, all looking for our heads."

Cuallaidh paid them all little heed and focused his attention on the prey that had eluded him for so long.

"Cuallaidh, what do you propose to do?" asked Erik with concern, noting the dark brooding look on his friend's face.

"The only thing that we can do with so little time: ram the bastards!" snapped Cuallaidh angrily.

"But what of the girl, if she's with them, surely she could be injured?" reasoned Erik.

"That's a risk that we'll have to take. We'll hole the ship, pull back swiftly and let it sink, then wait to see what floats to the surface," coldly explained Cuallaidh.

"If the Irish bitch is there, then she's there. If not, well, at least we can say that we finally dealt with these thieving bastards."

"And...?"

"Break out the oars!" called out Cuallaidh, having lost patience with Erik's questions.

"And the survivors?" finished Erik quietly, although he already appeared to know the answer.

"The crabs need to feed too."

Chapter Thirty-Three

NEMER

The Osprey's passage across the North Sea had been a perilous one. To make matters worse, they had been dogged by a trailing longship since they had fled Svartrfjord, so could ill afford to make any mistakes. The Osprey had handled well for a small boat, but the little skiff was woefully ill-suited for the rigours of the open ocean. Amergen was no stranger to these grey turbulent waters and had kept them on course across the trackless expanse as Wolf worked the tiller and O'Sullivan skilfully trimmed the small square sail.

Designed for coastal travel, the Osprey's upper strake sat precariously close to the high rolling waves which constantly threatened to overwhelm the gunwale, tossing splurges of saltwater into the small craft with unnerving regularity. Setting her grief for Mac Namara aside, Arrow soon joined Blade in bailing out the shallow boat until tiredness overcame them. Then they handed over the onerous task to Riona and Ferret, who worked relentlessly to empty out the unwelcome seawater, the curious girl never straying too far from her new companion.

The northerly breeze had been reasonable all that day and the weather unusually kind for autumn, but the wind began to strengthen as night fell and they neared the northernmost outpost of the Orkney Isles. They looked longingly towards the glittering lights ashore and the promise of shelter and the comfort of solid land as it passed them by to port. But they knew that the Orkneys were no place for honest folk to tarry, as the islands were a dangerous place. The longship that followed in their wake appeared to be steadily gaining on them too, so they pushed on through the moonlit waters towards the broad strait of North Minch, an expansive seaway bound by the Scottish coast towards the east and the Outer Hebrides off to the west.

They entered the North Minch with a flooding tide in the dead of night, Amergen going quietly among the weary crew with a water skin and a small sack of dried stores. They kept towards the deep water in the centre of the wide strait, well clear of hidden rocks, back eddies and lurking rip currents, all of which were sure to be found nearer to the land and could only prove treacherous for their light craft. While they all had their misgivings about the Osprey's low freeboard and small sail, the sleek craft still fairly skimmed across the open water, giving them every reason to hope for an escape.

"I think we're going to make it," said Amergen optimistically, seeming to be impressed by the little boat's surprising speed through the fast-flowing strait. Wolf wanted to think that he was right, but he had learned all too often that fate could be a very fickle friend indeed.

"I wouldn't speak too soon, Counsellor," warned O'Sullivan, staring up at the flapping sail, perplexed by the dramatic drop in the wind.

"What strange work is this?" muttered Wolf, unsettled by the sudden calming of the moonlit sea and the swift disappearance of the breeze. And then something brushed against the keel of the boat, sending it into a gentle sway.

"What was that?" asked Arrow nervously.

"A dolphin, maybe?" suggested Blade, then the hull of the Osprey was struck again more forcefully, sending the little craft into a precarious rocking motion.

"There!" shouted O'Sullivan, pointing towards a strange dark grey outline which had fleetingly disturbed the surface of the water and submerged again just as quickly.

"Over here too!" called Ferret, peering down into the inky-black sea. "Whatever they are, they seem to be surrounding the ship."

And then one side of the Osprey was suddenly thrust high up into the air, tossing them all into the cold waters of the North Minch with startled cries and angry shouts. Wolf surfaced and treaded water to stay afloat, wheeling around as he tried to get a glimpse of their assailants in the murky darkness below. But he could see very little, only feel something occasionally brush against his legs, something very strong; whatever these creatures were, it was obvious that they were quite at home in the water.

And then Wolf was suddenly seized by the leg and hauled down under the surface. Saltwater stung his eyes, making it hard for him to see anything clearly in the murky water. As he was pulled ever deeper, the acrid seawater forced its way up into his nostrils, threatening to swamp the back of his throat. Instinctively, Wolf swallowed hard to relieve the increasing pressure deep within his ears, easing the intense pain a little. He struggled against the powerful grip which was dragging him down into the darkness, his lungs burning with the desperate effort until he realised that he was only wasting what precious little air that he had, so he stopped thrashing about and tried to make some sense of his desperate situation. Wolf peered down below him into the gloom to try and identify the nature of his attacker, but all that he could make out was a dark indistinct outline and some blurred flashes of silver. Then small, alarming bubbles began escaping through his compressed lips as he found himself becoming light-headed and seriously disorientated, uncertain now of where was up and what was down. And he had suddenly become dangerously chilled and extremely sleepy.

*

Wolf found himself vaguely listening to the slow, steady drip of water falling upon water. He pondered why this simple sound seemed unusually loud and why everything else seemed so incredibly quiet. Something warm and abrasive pressed against his cheek, but he was not unduly concerned, as there was something reassuring and familiar about the sensation. And then he slowly opened his eyes to the welcome sight of sand. Wolf drew down a great gulp of air and then began coughing violently, vomiting up small quantities of seawater as he struggled to get up onto his knees.

"Here, this will help," said a soft voice, and Wolf looked up to see a strange looking woman standing before him, handing him a goblet. "It's only fresh water," she added, seeing the suspicious look on Wolf's face. Wolf slowly took the metal cup and cautiously sipped the sweet water, using the time to study the dark-haired woman's pale face, refined features and peculiar almond-shaped eyes. Her clothing looked unusual too: the close-fitting trousers and tunic seemed to be made from some sort of silver mesh, and her long dark grey cloak and black calf-length boots also appeared to be crafted from the same distinctive material.

Wolf heard coughing and the sound of weak voices,

and he looked down along the short stretch of sand to see the rest of his party slowly coming to their senses as a second female in similar attire moved among them with water, while a third woman was deep in conversation with O'Sullivan. Wolf looked about him as he tried to get his bearings and found that he was in a large domed cave. Its limestone walls and roof appeared to be peppered with some sort of amber rocks which gave off a soft golden light. The sound of dripping water came from behind him, and Wolf turned to find a still pool which was disturbed occasionally by a drop of water falling from the cavern roof.

"Where are we?" asked Wolf, discreetly feeling about his drying clothes for his sword and dagger as he tried to make some sense of his unusual surroundings.

"You are in the 'Land beneath the Sea'," replied the woman without further explanation.

"Why have you taken our weapons?" demanded Wolf, having scrutinized the rest of his party and cast a glance along the short strand, with not a single weapon anywhere to be seen. It was highly unlikely that they had lost all of them to the sea.

"King Nemer wishes to meet you," said a male voice firmly in the background. And then a tall figure stepped from the shadows. "I am Styr," said the man, whose dark appearance and clothing clearly resembled that of the three women. "Your sickness will soon pass; it is to be expected. When you are all ready, I will take you to the king."

"And our weapons?" pressed Wolf.

"No human is allowed in the presence of the king while bearing arms," explained Styr flatly. "The others have taken your weapons with them, but they will soon be returned to you. Now come."

The three women left swiftly, disappearing off into the openings in the limestone rock that lined the sandy shore and leaving Styr to lead Wolf and his small party into a labyrinth of tunnels that seemed to fan out in all directions. Each spacious tunnel was also illuminated and warmed by the same amber coloured rock which had been embedded into the walls of the pooled cave. The ground beneath them was solid and relatively level, the stone floors worn by many years of use. And as they followed quickly behind their powerfully built guide, Wolf pondered what sort of race Styr and his people could possibly be.

Finally, they left the last tunnel and entered into an enormous limestone cavern that expanded out before them and reached high up above their heads. Dotted throughout this vast hall were rough-hewn pillars that reached from the polished stone floor up to the very dome itself as if they were supporting the weight of the great roof. Here too were hunks of amber rock set randomly into the rough limestone walls and vaulted ceiling, filling the subterranean grotto with a soft golden light and pleasant warmth. Curious dark-haired onlookers, all dressed in similar garb, had gathered in the wings near the raised dais to observe Styr lead the small party of 'Land-People' towards the king. A human in King Nemer's court was a rare event; seven all at once was a sight to behold.

"My lord, I have brought the Land-People as you requested," announced Styr with a small bow.

Unsure of what to make of their surreal surrounds and not knowing what was expected of them, Wolf's party also gave a modest bow but kept their mouths shut and their ears open and waited for the king to speak. Nemer was a big man and dressed more finely than most of those gathered in the hall, a plain silver circlet of rank resting upon his head. He studied them closely with dark piercing eyes, stroking his short black beard thoughtfully as he did so.

"Well, what did you expect, fishtails?" boomed the king in a powerful voice, and then laughed heartily at his humorous poke as a polite laugh rippled back from the wings. "Impractical things, really," he continued amiably. "But some of our young females have been known to misuse their shape shifting powers to sport such fishtails in order to tease gullible sailors," scolded Nemer, scowling towards one particular group that had gathered in the shadows.

"Why have you brought us here, great king?" ventured Wolf cautiously as he straightened up to face Nemer.

"I feared that Ragner's fast-moving warship would have hunted you down before another day had passed."

"And such things are of concern to you, mighty lord?"

"Not at all, Captain Wolf," replied Nemer with a small laugh. "But I promised our land-cousins, the Ever-Living Ones, that I would watch over you as you crossed over our sea. It seems that you are all of great value to Eiru," added the king as he cast an appraising eye over them all, his gaze lingering on the three women for a moment. "Indeed, it was our rogue wave that prevented Eiru's precious girl from being raped when she was being shipped off to Norway."

"We are in your debt, King Nemer," said Wolf with a gracious bow, but he was in no doubt that there was more to the king's intervention than met the eye.

"All that I would ask is that you and your people dine

with us tonight after our hunting party has returned. It is seldom that we get your kind down here. And then we will take you back up to where you belong," replied the king smoothly. "We have fine wines here, venison, cheeses and all manner of tasty food. Every good thing finds its way down to us in the end."

"It would be our pleasure, great lord," answered Wolf with as much enthusiasm as he could muster, for he suspected that the king's largesse was not all that it appeared.

"Excellent!" purred Nemer, well pleased. "But first, you must rest after your arduous experience. The journey down to our world can be very hard on the human body. Styr will take you and your party to a place where you can rest and recover," concluded the king and waved them away with a backward brush of his hand.

Unsure if they were guests or prisoners, the seven fugitives followed Styr back down through the tunnels, uncertain of where they were or how they were to escape from this otherworldly place.

"We are in grave danger here!" hissed O'Sullivan into Wolf's ear as they followed Styr deeper into the tunnels.

"How can you be so sure?" whispered Wolf.

"Surilia told me."

"Surilia?"

"It's a long story," said O'Sullivan quietly. "But it's a trap, Captain. They plan to lace the wine and drug us tonight and then toss us back into the sea to make it look like a drowning."

"Why would they want to do such a foul thing?"

"Nemer wants the girl. He wants to keep her powers here in their world," said O'Sullivan in a hushed voice. "His people weren't expecting three women in our boat last night and didn't know which female to take, so they took us all. Now he needs to get rid of us in a way that appears natural so he can keep Riona's capture a secret. Nemer doesn't want to risk an all-out conflict with Eiru. And it seems that Banba could make things very difficult for his hunters anywhere near the Irish coast."

"How can we trust this Surilia?" whispered Wolf. "How?!" he demanded, seeing O'Sullivan's reluctance to answer.

"Because we are related," muttered O'Sullivan meekly. "She could somehow sense it from me when we first met."

"And you believe her?"

"I do, Captain. Remember what Eiru told me. 'One of your female ancestors did indeed come from the Sea-People'. But Eiru also warned me when she said that 'you would do well to remember that our sea-cousins are not always our allies'," stressed O'Sullivan.

"Will Surilia help us to escape from this place?" asked Wolf in a hushed voice as he and O'Sullivan lingered a little further back, well away from Styr's hearing.

"I believe she will," whispered O'Sullivan with conviction. "She said that she would come to me after we had spoken to the king."

"Let's hope that you are right, O'Sullivan," said Wolf softly as he laid his hand on the Ranger's shoulder. "For we must be long gone before this Nemer lays out his crooked feast for us, or we could be heading to a watery grave," concluded Wolf soberly. And then they hurried to catch up to the rest.

Chapter Thirty-Four

RETRIBUTION

The morning breeze had remained steady from the north, a brisk wind that gently filled the sail but did little to trouble the surface of the blue-grey sea. The day had continued overcast, with glimpses of autumnal sunlight escaping through any gaps in the low-lying cloud and glittering off the rippled water. And although it was already late into the year, there was no real bite in the air.

Having cleared the Western Isles, a long line of hazy hills in the near distance, they could have banked away west towards the Atlantic Ocean and made a run for it. But the Sea Eagle was on a dead run with a fresh breeze sweeping in across its stern and pushing the ship steadily southwards, so the lieutenant had ordered Otto to maintain their course through the Sea of Hebrides and let the enemy ship come to them. The Danish Karve had cleared the small island of Tiree and was still struggling towards them into the wind, its square sail close-hauled and its rowers labouring hard against the flooding tide.

"The bastards will be tired by the time they reach us," said O'Neill with satisfaction, observing the Danish ship approach as he stood beside Godfridsson at the bow.

"That's the idea, Sergeant," answered Godfrid with a small smile, glancing down along the Sea Eagle to ensure that his plan was ready and everything was in place.

"It's going to be a close-run thing, Lieutenant," added O'Neill, the sergeant's tone holding a rare sliver of concern.

"It needs to be, Sergeant, if it's to work," answered Godfrid, appearing calm as he watched the enemy ship power towards them with surprising speed.

"It'll be a right piece of low cunning if it works, Lieutenant," said O'Neill with a rueful grin.

"Best take up your position, Sergeant," replied Godfrid, grabbing hold of a rope that was wrapped about the stem post as the enemy's faces grew ever clearer. "It looks like we're about to find out."

*

"Why aren't they changing course?" asked Cuallaidh suspiciously, having positioned himself at the bow of the Storm Raven to closely watch the enemy ship.

"They think that they can outrun you, Jarl," offered Alrick behind him. The big Norseman had taken a keen interest in the chase since they had fled from their bloody slaughter on Rathlin Island.

"Scarface, we need more speed!" called out Cuallaidh over his shoulder.

"You heard the jarl!" yelled Scarface as he prowled up and down the deck. "Pull harder, you lazy bastards!" he bellowed, earning himself a surly scowl from Balder, who had been busy brooding at the tiller.

"You have them now, Ivarsson," purred Rasende beside Cuallaidh as the distance between the two ships quickly closed to the length of a spear-throw. "It's time to send these Irish bastards to the deep."

"Prepare to ram!" hollered Cuallaidh and grabbed hold of the gunwale as Balder aimed the Storm Raven's solid bow for the long, thin strakes that ran along the portside of the enemy ship, now a mere axe-throw away.

*

“Turn!” roared Godfridsson, whipping down his raised arm. Otto swiftly shoved the tiller out, bringing the Sea Eagle around hard to port. The ship tilted precariously, sending anything that wasn’t secured skittering across the deck. Magnus and Karl hurried to readjust the rigging and reset the billowing sail, anxious to quickly harness the breeze on a broad reach. The sudden manoeuvre had slowed the Sea Eagle more than they would have liked, but it was a risk that they had to take. Godfridsson knew that they would still have the advantage of momentum, and the Sea Eagle quickly adapted to the sudden shift, swiftly picking up speed again as it headed towards the southeast.

They had given the Danish ship precious little time to react, so the Karve simply kept its course, its crew rushing to ready themselves for the enemy ship as it went to pass them by on their starboard side. As if sensing the brewing conflict, a mob of screeching gulls had gathered above the two ships, eager to dip their beaks. A volley of arrows, axes and throwing spears rained down upon the Sea Eagle as the ships passed by, less than the span of a mast apart. But most of the missiles thudded harmlessly into a row of interlocking shields set two rows high along the Sea Eagle’s starboard side, much to the annoyance of the snarling Danes.

“Now!” hollered Godfridsson. And the top row of shields was swiftly lowered, allowing a line of men to step forward and quickly hurl small earthenware jars which had previously contained the healing potions that had been stored in the hold. The delicate jars smashed asunder upon striking the Danish ship, spreading a strange sticky substance all across her deck and down along its strakes. The Danes hurled torrents of abuse at their Norse enemies as they quickly stepped behind their protective wall once again and raised their shields, sending across another barrage of lethal missiles laced with Danish contempt.

"Fire!" roared the lieutenant as the two ships hurried past each other. The upper row of shields was removed once more and a line of archers stepped forward and loosed a string of flaming arrows, which flew high and then fell with terrible accuracy upon the doused deck of the Danish ship. The sticky Greek fire which had been spread about the craft by the smashed jars instantly erupted into flames. Thick black smoke fed by the dark, oily substance that had been smeared upon the ship's timbers stung the men's eyes and badly clogged their throats.

The sea breeze freshened, further fuelling the flames. And then the sky suddenly darkened as if an angry god scowled down with pleasure at the plight of the stricken Danes. Fanned by the increasing wind, the fire raced up the mast with delight, attacking the sail and eagerly devouring the lanolin-rich cloth. A quick-thinking man tossed a bucket attached to a rope into the sea, hauled up a pail of water and hurled it towards the flames. But he leapt back in horror when the fire snarled back at him like a ferocious animal, snapping at his face and grabbing hold of his leg. The warrior screamed in pain and leapt overboard, his fellow Danes watching on with morbid fascination as the flame which had engulfed the sorry man grew even stronger in the water, consuming their fellow crewman entirely.

Seeing that water was of little use against such a malevolent flame, the Danes began beating at the fire with their cloaks, which only made a bad situation worse, breathing even more valuable air into the untameable beast. And although the men were loath to admit such a dreadful thought, the harsh reality was that the Storm Raven was well and truly lost. All that remained to Cuallaidh and his men now was for them to throw themselves upon the mercy of the sea.

"Why don't you try pissing on it!" yelled Sven triumphantly, grabbing hold of the rigging and hopping up onto the gunwale. A stray arrow swiftly found the side of his neck. Instinctively, he clasped his hands about his throat as he struggled to draw a breath and turned as if to say something. Then his eyes fluttered, and he toppled over the side and was gone.

"A lucky shot," spat O'Neill angrily, irritated at the needless loss of a man.

"Not so lucky for Sven," responded his friend Berg dourly.

"Damned idiot should have saved his crowing for the tavern!" growled O'Neill, in no mood to dispense sympathy.

"Three ships approaching us from the east!" called out Snorri urgently from above, pointing off towards the nearby Scottish coast. "And they're moving fast, Lieutenant!"

Godfridsson and O'Neill raced to the bow to gauge what faced them, the fate of the Danes now well and truly sealed.

"Have we any Greek fire left?" asked Godfrid hopefully.

"We just used the last of the stuff on the Danes, and to good effect, Lieutenant," commended O'Neill.

"Do we have many arrows?"

"We hardly have enough to tackle one ship, let alone

three."

"Any suggestions, Sergeant?"

"Let's make a run for it, Lieutenant."

Godfridsson gauged the distance between the Sea Eagle and the fast-approaching ships, then he looked longingly out towards the west and the wide-open sea.

"I think it's too late for that, Sergeant," answered the lieutenant after a moment's thought. "We'll hold our course for now and try to brazen it out. Tell the men to discreetly arm themselves, but nobody is to make a move unless I give the order."

"Norse or Scots?" asked O'Neill as the three ships drew near.

"Along the Scottish coast, it's hard to tell the difference these days," replied Godfrid, unsure of what to make of the three Norse-style vessels, which were strangely devoid of any figureheads.

"It looks like they want to parley," said O'Neill, pointing towards the man standing at the bow of the leading ship with a reversed shield held high.

"And it seems that we have little choice but to listen," concluded Godfrid. "Spill the sail, Sergeant, and quietly ready the men."

*

The helmsman on the approaching ship certainly knew his trade, and he quickly reduced his craft's speed as it came tight alongside the Sea Eagle without grazing a single strake. A warrior with his head and face concealed by an impressive helmet and draping chainmail deftly stepped from one gunwale to the other with the practised ease of a man who had spent a lifetime about ships. The warlord jumped lightly down onto the deck as his own ship smoothly pulled away, and it was clear from his bearing and attire that he was a man of considerable rank.

"Who commands here?" asked the warlord casually as he slowly peeled off his calfskin gloves.

"I command here," answered Lieutenant Godfridsson, stepping forward.

"Has Captain Wolf deserted you?" asked the warrior pleasantly as he undid the strap of his helmet and lifted the sweaty armour off his head.

"MacLeod?" asked Godfrid uncertainly.

"Yes, it is I, Lieutenant," answered MacLeod with a small smile. "But these days I am referred to as Chief MacLeod, Lord of the Western Isles," he clarified, stealing a cold glance towards Otto, who appeared a little nervous as he stood by the tiller. "And Captain Wolf?"

"He is to follow," explained Godfridsson curtly.

"I see," said MacLeod, running his fingers thoughtfully through his damp hair. "It seems that I owe the captain a sword, Lieutenant. And I am a man who likes to pay his debts. But I cannot return that bloodstained sword, as it hangs above the fireplace in my hall, a constant reminder to all would-be usurpers."

"I'm sure that the captain would be pleased that you have put the sword to such good use," responded Godfrid cautiously, far from certain of MacLeod's intentions.

"Of course, I do owe the captain a great deal more than a sword. I owe the man my life, Lieutenant," said MacLeod with obvious sincerity. "It was my duplicitous cousin who had me sold into slavery," spat MacLeod, "in order to seize my rightful throne. That's why I could never reveal my true identity: my captors would have bled my people dry for a hefty ransom."

"The captain will be glad to hear of your success, Chief MacLeod," responded Godfridsson respectfully.

"If he makes it," said MacLeod shrewdly, eyeing the green-clad men about him, who were bristling with arms. "I don't know what your business was in the north, but it's clear to me that you are hardly wine merchants."

"Captain Wolf is a resourceful man. He will find a way," answered the lieutenant evasively.

"Perhaps, but the true purpose of your visit to the north country will no doubt soon reach these shores, and you are sure to be hunted men," replied MacLeod, fixing Godfridsson with a knowing look. "I would prefer when that time comes that your Norse enemies do not find you in our waters; we do have certain ties with the north," added the chief cryptically.

"And we have no desire to linger in your waters, Chief MacLeod, and would have been long gone but for the delay," explained Godfrid, gesturing towards the burning wreckage of the Danish ship and the survivors clinging to the debris.

"I am glad to hear it, Lieutenant," softened Macleod. "And it seems that you have done us a great service here today, for we had been hunting these Danish dogs."

"They left us with little choice. Whoever they are, they seemed determined to destroy us," considered Godfridsson aloud.

"And now it is they who are utterly destroyed," said MacLeod without pity as he surveyed what was left of the Danish ship and what remained of her crew. "I will send a ship to escort you safely to the Irish coast in case there are any more of these marauders abroad," offered the chief, eager to move the Sea Eagle along.

"You have our thanks, Chief MacLeod," responded

Godfridsson politely, choosing to accept the shadowing ship as a courtesy and nothing more. "And what of them?" he asked, looking over towards the Danish survivors who were left dangling in the water.

"I wouldn't concern yourself about that rabble, Lieutenant," dismissed MacLeod, summoning his ship to come alongside. "From this day forth, they will be nothing more than slaves."

*

Cuallaidh and what remained of his crew were tiring as they struggled to stay afloat, finally ditching any armour or weapons that threatened to drag them down to the deep.

"What are they waiting for?" rasped Alrick, working hard to keep his head above water.

"They're waiting until all the fight has gone out of us," answered Erik bitterly, spitting out a mouthful of seawater. "And then they will simply haul us in like so many dead seals."

"You young fool, Cuallaidh," snarled Balder as MacLeod's ships slowly moved towards them. "Your arrogance has made slaves of us all."

"Stay strong, Ivarsson," whispered Rasende enigmatically as he floated close to Cuallaidh. Then the strange tracker slipped softly beneath the surface of the sea and was gone.

Chapter Thirty-Five

SURILIA

Styr had led them to a cold, sparse room, a large square space that appeared to have been hewn out of the limestone rock. There was no door in the door space and no furniture in the dimly lit room.

"If you wish to rest before we eat, there are rolled-up mats over there in the corner," said Styr formally. "They may not be what you're used to, but they are more comfortable than they look. You will also find a cloak for each of you there," he added as he went to leave. "It can be chilly down here for Land-People."

"And our weapons?" asked Wolf bluntly.

"They are there too," replied Styr, pausing at the doorway. "Just as you were promised," he concluded, then turned and briskly left.

"If they mean to harm us, why would they give us our weapons back?" puzzled Ferret aloud as the Rangers hurried to strap on their retrieved arms.

"They want to put you at your ease and make you feel safe," said a female voice from the doorway. "It makes little difference that you have them back now," explained Surilia as she walked casually into the room. "You still will not be allowed to carry weapons in the presence of the king."

"Why should we believe anything that you have to say?" replied Wolf flatly. "These are your people after all."

"These are not my people," snapped Surilia. "One of their hunting parties snatched me when I was just a child, and I have been a captive here ever since."

"And that's reason enough for us to trust you?" answered Wolf, now highly suspicious of these Sea-People.

"I want out of this place just as much as you do," responded Surilia boldly.

"What makes you think that we need your help?" asked Amergen.

"Because you will never get out of here without it," she answered coldly.

"So why do you need us?" probed Blade, sensing that the sea-woman had a hidden agenda. "Surely you could escape from here on your own?"

"I may need your help to get past the guards," admitted Surilia after a moment. "But you will certainly need my help with everything else, or you will never make it out of here alive."

"Where are your people now?" asked Arrow gently, trying to ease the tense silence that had filled the room.

"Our territory lies off the southwest coast of Ireland. I was seized from there when I was very young."

"Will you go back there if you get free of this place?" questioned Blade.

"It's all that I dream of," answered Surilia with sincerity.

"I reckon that we can trust her, Captain," offered O'Sullivan quietly. "It's not like we have much choice."

"Or much time either," added Amergen ruefully.

Wolf knew that Amergen was right. O'Sullivan too, for that matter. But the thought of Nemer's planned treachery made him very wary of this peculiar race.

"How many guards?" quizzed Wolf, wanting to hear more details.

"There are usually two sentries at the entrance to each

cave," answered Surilia, and then she seemed to pause.

"What aren't you telling us?" pressed Wolf, noting her hesitation.

"They only leave two guards if there is a hunting party going out," clarified Surilia. "But it would be best if we were gone before the hunters' return, as they may increase the guard on their way back."

"What do they hunt for?"

"Food, captives and plunder from sunken ships — whatever they can find."

"How many are in the hunting party?"

"Thirty-five warriors, maybe more," speculated Surilia. "But that's not the kind of information that Nemer tends to share with me."

"You don't like him very much, do you?" ventured Wolf, detecting the bitterness in her tone whenever she mentioned the king.

"He's an animal," was all that she would say, the determined look in her eyes masking the rest.

"Very well, tell us of this plan of yours," softened Wolf, in no doubt that Surilia's hatred for Nemer was real and an obvious benefit to them. "Perhaps we can find a way to help each other."

*

Surilia's shape-shifting plan had sounded fantastical, impossible and downright dangerous. And yet there they all stood waist-high in the cavern pool, draped in the dark grey cloaks that they had stolen from their room, a faint tingling sensation emanating from the strange robes. They had been reluctant to part with their arms, but Surilia had said that the weight of their weapons would be too great and would only drag them down to their deaths. But she had allowed them to carry their daggers.

"You must do exactly as I have told you," stressed Surilia, her eyes boring into the seven fugitives in the amber light, "or you will not survive what lies ahead. Remember, you will be able to hold your breath for much longer in your temporary form, but we dare not delay. Always keep your cloak tightly around you and it will serve its purpose. Open it before you have resurfaced and you will surely drown," she concluded ominously. Then she raised her hood, wrapped her cloak tightly around her, took several deep breaths and plunged beneath the water and was gone.

"We must be mad!" said Blade, voicing what the most of them certainly felt. Riona alone seemed excited at the perilous prospect.

"Probably," agreed Wolf, but it seemed that they had no other way out of this underwater world in which they were trapped. So they donned their hoods, secured their cloaks about them, then drew down several precious breaths and quickly followed Surilia underneath the surface.

*

Led by a dark grey female, a pod of seal-like creatures darted out from the entrance of a sea cave which was located at the base of a sheer underwater cliff. Most of the strange seals struggled to adapt to the water pressure at that depth, and some were disorientated by the darkness of the gloomy green waters as they were buffeted by the strong currents that swept along the bottom of the rock face. But Surilia quickly turned back and went among her fellow seals and appeared to reassure them before slowly leading the seven up along the steep wall, which was bedecked with a profusion of soft corals, white anemones and vibrant orange sponges.

Shafts of sunlight penetrated the water as Surilia led the seal-like creatures to the top of the undersea cliff and guided them across the shallow sea that stretched out above it. She coursed effortlessly through the forests of unruly brown kelp, which were dotted with bursts of bright green seaweed, weaving her way swiftly across a seabed that was strewn with enormous boulders interspersed with pockets of crisp cream sand. Startled crabs raised defiant claws towards her as she passed above them. Lobsters, too, crept backwards into their burrows, wary of her sudden shadow as it swept by. A boisterous bottlenose dolphin suddenly drifted in beside Surilia and swam alongside her for a while. Having no time for play, she soon brushed him aside, so the dolphin happily banked away to chase a young wrasse who had foolishly broken cover.

As they approached the shoreline, Surilia led the pod of seal-like creatures to the entrance of another sea cave which was located at the foot of a sheer headland. They moved stealthily now, fanning out as they entered the large pool within the cavern just as they had planned. Two of the other female 'seals' continued on towards the gently sloping shore which lay before them. They loosened their cloaks and pushed back their hoods as their heads cautiously broke the surface of the water, their eyes quickly readjusting to the soft amber light.

"Halt! Who goes there?" challenged the startled sentry who had been guarding the entrance to a cave within the cavern, fumbling for his short spear as the two women walked towards him out of the shallows, their daggers well concealed beneath their long cloaks.

"Can you help us?" pleaded Blade.

"Stay where you are!" ordered the second guard angrily, grabbing his spear more decisively and stepping aggressively towards the short shoreline.

"Our ship sank, and we are lost," added Arrow helplessly as they slowly approached the sandy shore, steadily closing the distance between themselves and the sentries.

"Land-People?" said the second guard suspiciously. "How do you come to be down here?" he demanded.

"It's a strange story," said Wolf as he softly stepped up behind the sentry and rested his dagger upon the man's shoulder. The other guard went to react but found Ferret's blade pressed against his neck and thought better of it. "We could spare you, or not," considered Wolf aloud as Blade and Arrow gently eased the spears out of the sentries' yielding hands. "Tell Nemer that we are grateful for his hospitality," said Wolf amiably as the Rangers marched the two men into the pool at the points of their own spears. "But we suspect that the king's food is off!" added Wolf coldly as the two scowling guards raised their hoods, pulled their cloaks about them and slipped silently beneath the water.

Retaining her own cloak, Surilia set about collecting the dark grey capes from each of them, carefully draping the precious cloaks across a large boulder near the entrance to the cave.

"They would hunt you high and low for it," said Surilia gently, seeing Ferret's eyes wild with want, his hands locked possessively about the magical robe. But Surilia's soft words proved to be enough, and Ferret sheepishly handed over the supernatural cloak, ashamed of his sudden burst of avarice.

"How is any of this possible?" asked Wolf, staring in wonder at the strange garment as he reluctantly handed it back.

"The world is far stranger than you will ever know," replied Surilia cryptically. "But know this, all of you: you cannot talk about these cloaks to anyone, and you must never speak of the Sea-People. They value their secrecy above all else."

"But why?" asked Amergen, truly fascinated by all that he had learned and keen to share his incredible story.

"The Land-People mistrust what they do not understand and tend to destroy those things that they secretly fear," warned Surilia. Then she walked off towards the entrance to the cave and beckoned them to follow her. "Come, we don't have much time."

The cave soon led them into a natural cavern that reached high up into the hard grey rock, its rough walls and craggy dome peppered with amber rocks which softly shed their orange light into the large, open cavern. There were a handful of tunnels leading off in all directions, and Surilia slowly walked past each one, carefully sniffing the air as she went, her face set in a mask of concentration. Suddenly, she stopped at one tunnel and drew down a deep draft through her nostrils, and then turned to them with a broad smile.

"It's this one."

*

The weird amber rocks embedded in the dank walls of the tunnel sprang to light as the eight escapees clambered past, slipping and sliding, falling and cursing as they climbed up through the cold, slick cave. Time seemed to have no place in their subterranean world, or sound other than that of their own making. Surilia did pause once to listen intently to something down below, a sound that only her sharp hearing was able to detect.

"Is it the hunting party?" asked Wolf with concern.

"No, it's not them," was all that she was prepared to say on the matter, keeping her suspicions firmly to herself. "But we must hurry!"

They noticed the smells at first, earthy smells: the aroma of the woods, the scent of wildflowers and the salty tang of the sea, all of which were carried down on copious drafts of cool, fresh air. And then they saw a glimpse of light and their pace quickened, and the light grew stronger. The final section of the tunnel was a blur, cuts and bruises all but forgotten. Instinctively, they held their hands up to shield their eyes as they cautiously stepped out of the sandy entrance to the cave, the sound of the sea lapping contentedly against the shore, music to their ears.

"I know this place," said Ferret quietly, looking up at the cliff that overshadowed the entrance to the cave. Then he rushed out onto the strand beyond the obscuring headland and pointed landward with delight. "The Dublin Mountains, I knew it!" he yelled. "We're back in Ireland, Captain!"

"We will find you, Surilia," came an ominous voice, drifting up from the tunnel.

"Styr?" asked Wolf.

"I thought that I had heard him earlier, but I wasn't sure," confessed Surilia. "I must hurry now and seek the protection of my people."

"Thank you for all your help, Surilia," said Wolf,

offering his hand. "I'm not sure that we would have made it without you."

"We have served each other well, Captain Wolf," answered Surilia, briefly taking hold of his hand before turning and heading quickly towards the sea.

"Wait!" called O'Sullivan anxiously. "Will I ever see you again?"

Surilia paused and considered his words for a moment.

"Look for me on the rocks near Blackrock reef at sun-up and sundown. One day I will be there," she said with conviction.

"I know those rocks well. I used to fish near there when I was a young boy," recalled O'Sullivan fondly.

"I know," replied Surilia enigmatically, slipping up her hood. Then she waded out into the breaking surf, pulled her cloak about her, and dived beneath the waves and was gone.

Chapter Thirty-Six

PARTINGS

The soft light of a new moon seeped down upon Dublin's empty streets. Most of the town's residents had taken to their beds, but a few hard-pressed whores still made a meagre living in the seedy alleyways down along the docks.

Now and then the stillness of the night was broken by a barking dog or a noisy drunk mumbling and stumbling as he found his way home. In the shadows of a side street, the sound of a muffled struggle briefly punctured the quiet as some unfortunate soul fought hard to retain his precious purse. The wind that whipped across the River Liffey was a little sharper these days as autumn drew to a close, the bite of the harsh breeze quickening the step of those who were still abroad on Dublin's deserted backstreets.

Rearmed and dressed in fresh green buckskins, the Rangers had discreetly gathered in a dimly lit warehouse near the wharf to settle accounts and take care of any unfinished business. The men had been handsomely paid, each according to their rank, so spirits were high as the Rangers revelled in their newfound wealth. Boru had been true to his word and generous, with all talk of outlawing those who had taken part in the sorry ambush at Eagle's Pass consigned to the past.

Also decked out in Ranger greens, Arrow was there too. The Rangers had insisted that she also received a full share despite her protestations and Amergen's reservations regarding a Thomond princess. Riona and Niamh, now dressed in fine clothing and draped with warm cloaks, had also been allowed to attend the assembly, which was unusual for such gatherings. But Commander Sten had been moved to make this rare exception, for it was clear that the bonds of friendship within the well-tested company were very strong indeed.

"I hear that Boru finally made his move," said Wolf as he and Sten stepped into a quiet corner of the warehouse.

"He devastated Limerick," answered Sten, clearly impressed by the audacious move. "It seems that Boru was so incensed by the number of Irish children being held there for slavery that he killed every Dane that was fit for war and enslaved the rest."

"Not a man to anger," responded Wolf, making a mental note of Boru's short temper — clearly not a man to cross. "And what of Ivar?"

"That canny rat escaped," replied the commander. "He's holed up on an island in the middle of the River Shannon with a handful of his men."

"Will his Irish allies come to his aid?"

"Not a chance. They don't like the jarl's silver that much," said Sten with a wry smile.

"What will become of O'Mahony and O'Donovan without the Danes at their backs?" wondered Wolf aloud. "Surely they'll be hunted men now?"

"You would think so," agreed Sten, "but rumour has it that that damned fool Mahon has gone off to search out the Irish traitors in order to make the peace."

"Ever the peace maker," sighed Wolf.

"Perhaps so, but not everyone in this world wants to make peace," answered the commander ruefully. "You would think that the king might have learned that by now."

"Still, Princess Aoife can be returned to her home now

that the threat from Ivar has been removed?" said Wolf, switching the subject, keen to conclude the whole twisted business.

"In theory, yes," replied Sten cautiously, steering Wolf further into the darkened corner as the talk in the warehouse grew louder. "But Boru doesn't want a large party of Rangers taking the girl back. Just you and another Ranger are to escort the princess to Thomond."

"Are the Connaught men still waspish?" speculated Wolf.

"Aye, they're pretty sore after that massacre in the badlands and still keen for revenge," explained Sten. "But the O'Kennedys have somehow managed to buy off the Connaught king. So it's not necessarily O'Connor that you need to worry about now; it's the dead men's kin. That's why Boru wants you to keep a low profile. He doesn't want things getting stirred up again, especially between the Irish."

"It would be best to get her back to Thomond before the winter weather sets in," suggested Wolf, observing her warmly as he spoke. The princess had become a valued member of their team and a firm favourite among the men.

"And it would be even better to get her out of Dublin before Jarl Kanarvan learns of her presence here," answered Sten, his voice holding a note of concern.

"Why? Would he try to hold her for ransom?"

"Or maybe keep her as another concubine," ventured Sten. "The horny old bastard is quite partial to royal flesh these days, has a bevy of beauties at his disposal. So he's hardly likely to turn his nose up at a young princess trapped within his walls."

"We could leave tonight," said Wolf without

hesitation.

"I thought that you might say that," said the commander with a small smile. "I have horses, equipment and supplies ready for you beyond the rampart. My guide will show you to a hidden gap in the palisade, well out of view of the sentries. All that remains to be answered now is what Ranger to take with you, Captain."

"I think that decision has already been made, Commander," answered Wolf, watching Ferret and Riona deep in conversation. "Princess Aoife is not the only girl that I must return to her homeland, and it seems that Riona has already chosen her escort."

"What is the story with that peculiar looking girl?" asked Sten as they walked back towards the gathered Rangers.

"It's a long one, Commander," replied Wolf evasively, and he hurried off to relate how matters stood to his leading men.

"I don't like it, Captain," responded Godfridsson after carefully chewing over Wolf's words. "It could well be a trap."

"If it is a trap, Lieutenant, whether I have two Rangers or twenty with me, it won't make much of a difference," reasoned Wolf. "This way, at least, I can travel fast and stay in the shadows."

"Perhaps," relented Godfrid after a moment. As an officer, he knew better than most that some orders were harder to swallow than others. "If you do find yourself in trouble, Captain, try and get word to me somehow," said Godfridsson as they briefly shook hands. "I'll be in Dublin for a while longer. I still have some leave to finish," added the lieutenant with a roguish grin then he slipped out a side door without any fuss.

*

O'Neill was obviously angry at being left behind, but Wolf thought that he was trying hard to hide it. "Maybe I'm getting too old for all this capering about anyway," he lamented, half in jest and part in earnest.

"You say that after every mission, Sergeant," countered Wolf with a friendly smile.

"Aye, maybe I do, Captain," agreed O'Neill. "But perhaps the time is right for me to try something new," he lightened, patting the gold coins stuffed into his pockets.

"You have obviously given it some thought," coaxed Wolf, keen to hear O'Neill's plans.

"I've always fancied having a tavern of my own. A place where I could charge high prices and tell tall tales," said O'Neill with a twinkle in his eye.

"I don't doubt your capacity to do either, Sergeant," laughed Wolf.

"With what we have now, I think that we could do it, Captain," said O'Neill with enthusiasm.

"We?" asked Wolf innocently.

"Blade and me," continued O'Neill in high spirits until he saw the confused look on Wolf's face. "I'm sorry, Captain, but I thought that you already knew about us," faltered the sergeant. "You don't mind, Wolf, do you?"

"Of course I don't mind, O'Neill," answered Wolf, recovering swiftly. "You just caught me by surprise. First I've heard of it, that's all. I have been a little preoccupied of late."

"Why, of course you have, Captain," went on O'Neill quickly. "But she's happy to take me as I am, and that's saying something. And I think that I understand her too, well, most of the time anyway. Don't get me wrong,

Wolf, I know that she could be up and gone in the morning. But that's a chance I'm prepared to take. And while it lasts, I'll be a happy man."

"What are you two conspiring about?" quizzed Blade as she sauntered towards them.

"I have just been telling the captain about our plans. About us," added O'Neill meekly.

"You don't mind, Wolf?" asked Blade with a hint of concern, stepping up close to him.

"I'm very pleased for you both," he replied with complete sincerity.

"I'm so glad," responded Blade happily and kissed Wolf softly on the cheek. "That means the world to me," she whispered into his ear. And then she drew back and stood beside O'Neill. "You must come and visit us in our new tavern whenever you're passing our way."

"I'd be delighted to raise a horn of ale to your success," smiled Wolf. "And how am I to find this place?"

"That will be easy; ours will be the tavern named the Sea Eagle, miles away from any sea," explained Blade with a straight face. And then the three of them burst into a bout of hearty laughter.

"Captain, we'll be off now," said a voice behind him. And Wolf turned to find Kelly with Niamh standing next to him. "We wanted to thank you, Captain, for all you've done, for getting Niamh and me out of that horrible place. I'm going back to my farmstead near Carlingford — Niamh and me," he continued hurriedly. "We're going to give farming another go. But we'll always have one eye on the sea and a weapon close by. We'll be ready for those sea pirates the next time, Captain," finished Kelly and then looked to Niamh, who hesitantly stepped forward.

"I will never be able to thank you enough for getting me away from those animals," said Niamh, trying to keep her voice steady as her eyes welled up. "But always know that you will have a bed beneath our roof and a place at our table, should you ever need it," added the young woman with passion. Then she squeezed his arm, and the couple quickly left.

*

Wolf took a quiet moment to enjoy the animated talk of the Rangers about him, glad to see the men content after their many trials. Godfridsson's section had gathered in a knot in one corner of the warehouse, and O'Carroll and McMahon were arguing over something, which was nothing new for them. Thorsten appeared to be bored with Ferguson's talk of buying back stolen relics for the church, while Hansen kept his own counsel in the shadows, as was his way.

Wolf's men had gravitated towards the opposite corner, where the O'Donnell brothers were busy telling Farrell about the fishing vessel that they planned to buy and were trying to persuade him to come in on the venture as a full partner, saying that the seas off the northwest coast of Ireland simply teemed with fish. Berg and O'Byrne were gearing up for a night of whoring, drinking and brawling and were determined to enlist their erstwhile drinking buddy to join the campaign. But O'Sullivan seemed strangely detached from the merriment, making feeble excuses about his sudden need to return swiftly to his small holding along the southwestern seaboard.

“She haunts my thoughts, Captain,” whispered O’Sullivan in a secretive tone as he paused beside Wolf.

“Surilia?” asked Wolf quietly, checking that no one was listening to their conversation.

“Aye, Captain,” responded O’Sullivan, still clearly unsettled by their surreal experience with the sea-maid. Then he walked off, eased out the door and went into the night.

*

Grateful for the cooling air, Wolf had stepped out of the warehouse for a quiet moment as the Rangers said their final farewells.

“Hey, Irish, are you still alive?” came a perky voice from above, and Wolf wheeled around to find the tavern boy, Toke, perched up on the moonlit roof.

“It seems that I am, old friend,” smiled Wolf. “Are you working for Commander Sten these days?”

“Sometimes, in between my other business interests, but I will start my Ranger training very soon,” answered Toke, puffing up with pride.

“It’s a dangerous profession,” cautioned Wolf after a moment’s reflection.

“Dangerous! Try living in this rats’ nest,” scoffed the tavern boy, gesturing towards the sprawling town.

“A dangerous place, for sure,” agreed Wolf, finding no fault with the boy’s assessment of Dublin. “For your training!” he added as he tossed a gold coin up towards the boy. “You’ll need it.” Toke snatched the spinning coin out of the air with ease, held it in the palm of his hand and briefly marvelled at its warm allure.

“Perhaps we will work together again someday,”

smiled Toke as he slipped the coin inside his grubby tunic.

"I'd like that," answered Wolf as he assessed the waning moon above them. Then he slipped back inside the warehouse to quickly gather up what little now remained of his dwindling pack.

Chapter Thirty-Seven

HOMEWARD

Wolf and his small party stole through the empty backstreets of Dublin in the dead of night, their sidearms concealed beneath their long dark green cloaks. Toke had proved to be a capable guide. The street urchin had kept the group moving swiftly through a maze of filthy alleys, where large rats moved reluctantly aside as they scoured the ground for discarded scraps, squealing and fighting over the choicest morsels. The few men that the group encountered simply swept them with nasty looks, while some simply went on pissing where they stood. One surly woman remained squatting and spat loudly at their feet as they hurried past.

Toke suddenly stopped at a large barrel stuffed with old straw and fresh horse droppings which stood tight against the town's timber palisade. The big container appeared immovable, but Toke thrust his hand down into the middle of the steaming pile and seemed to search about for something. Having quickly found the handle of the lid which had been placed just beneath the mucky layer, he then slowly lifted the top off the barrel and carefully put the circular tray, still heaped with dung, to one side.

"Empty!" said Toke with a bright smile as he tapped the hollow cask, and then quickly rolled the barrel to one side. "The jarl has his business, and we have ours. My friends will replace the barrel when we are gone," added their guide as he stepped towards the gap in timber uprights and slipped through the narrow opening in the defensive wall.

Arrow and Riona squeezed through the breach with ease, but Wolf, Amergen and Ferret had to pass through their swords, side-axes and daggers first to have any chance of fitting through the tight gap. The outside of the opening was well concealed by a sprawling gorse bush on top of a rise, screening any sudden movement from the sentries who manned the palisade. Down below the bush was a deep gully which kept them well hidden as they hurried away from the sleeping town. The shallow cleft in the ground soon petered out at the foot of a gentle slope, and Toke signalled for them all to hunker down around him.

"Your horses await you in that small grove up on the knoll," whispered Toke, pointing towards the darkened copse of trees standing stark against the moonlit sky. "This is as far as I go," he added, offering his mucky hand and then thinking better of it. "Sorry, Captain, I had forgotten where it's been! Next time," he said with an impish smile and then slipped back through the hollow.

*

Wolf gave a soft raven call as he approached the tree line and was relieved when a Ranger's throaty caw answered.

"Captain," called a familiar voice. "It's me, Hakon," said the corporal softly, stepping quietly from the shadows.

"Who else is with you?" asked Wolf, sensing that someone else was in the trees.

"Ranger Campbell is with the horses. He has a way with the beasts and can manage to keep them settled," replied Hakon as he led them to their animals.

Balor began pawing the ground as his master

approached, and Wolf had to quickly fish out an apple to calm the big stallion.

"He's been as good as gold, Captain," said Campbell affectionately, patting Balor's neck.

"You and Hakon drew the short straw on this detail," smiled Wolf as he dug out another apple for his horse.

"Not to worry, Captain, I'm sure that the lads will have plenty of fresh ale and warm women waiting for us when we get back," grinned Campbell.

"Commander Sten supervised the packing of the horses himself, so you should have everything that you need," said the corporal, handing Wolf a small leather purse. "I've put three bowstrings in that, Captain. But you will probably find more in your saddlebags if I know the commander. By the way," added Hakon as he went to leave, "the longbows are fairly new, so they might need a little breaking in."

"What does the future hold for you now, Corporal?" asked Wolf, mindful that Hakon was now also a wealthy man. Corporal Hakon paused to consider his answer, much to the irritation of Campbell, who appeared eager to be gone.

"More of the same, I reckon, Captain," answered Hakon after a moment. "Sure, what else would I do? A Ranger's life is the only one that I know."

*

The five riders had travelled hard that first night and several more after that, striking out across the midlands in the darkness and resting up during the daylight hours. Without the strength of numbers, Wolf had to rely on stealth. He avoided the Great Road west, as large parts of the timber causeway were exposed to open country and ever watchful eyes, and where bands of outlaws could make short work of unwary travellers. Instead, he chose the back roads, forest tracks, marshy trails and broken scrubland, guiding his small pack through the moonlit nights as best he could. Their shrunken band was too few in number to spare a forward scout. But Riona had proved to be a surprisingly efficient replacement and had alerted them on several occasions to large parties of men that were gathered in the woodlands up ahead. Wolf took no chances and assumed that they were outlaw camps with outlying sentries, and he gave their territory a wide berth.

"How do you know about the presence of these men?" Wolf had asked her once.

"The animals tell me," Riona had replied simply.

"The animals?"

"The bats are happy because the men light big fires to keep the cold at bay, which attracts many moths, so the bats have plenty to eat," she explained. "But the foxes are not so pleased because the noisy men scare away all their prey, while the rooks complain bitterly."

"And why do the rooks complain?"

"Because of the smell, of course," she had responded as if such a fact was obvious to everyone.

The past three nights had been cold and mostly wet as they had ridden ever westward. But the days had appeared even colder as they sat huddled silently in their damp cloaks, munching on dried stores and waiting for nightfall and the chance to stretch their stiff limbs. Autumn was well advanced now and the russet foliage was flush with seeds, acorns and red and indigo berries, the unmistakable barb of winter putting a definite edge on the blustery breeze.

The mood within their diminished group had become strangely subdued. Ferret never strayed far from Riona's side, and the young man seemed to grow ever more detached from the rest of the party with each passing day. Arrow and Amergen had gravitated towards the familiarity of each other, and if the princess was pleased to be returning home, she certainly didn't show it. When Wolf had eventually got an opportunity to casually ask her if she was happy to be heading back home, Aoife had simply said, "One half of me is content to be going home, but another part of me wants to turn this horse around and get as far away as I can."

"Get far away from what?" Wolf had asked, mystified by the statement.

"From a life that is not of my own making, Captain," she had spat bitterly, and then she spurred her horse on ahead.

*

Towards the end of the fourth night, they made camp in a pine grove beside Lough Ree near a belt of mixed woodland. Wolf took the first watch as dawn tinged the eastern sky, and the rest of the group curled up in their wet woollen cloaks and tried to sleep as best they could. Wolf was glad to have a moment alone to gather his thoughts and consider their options, for they had now arrived at the River Shannon. Bridges were few and far between across the mighty river and usually guarded. But they could use the one nearby at the monastery of Clonmacnoise and then strike swiftly southwest for the kingdom of Thomond although that would mean cutting through the territory of Connaught, which might prove to be a dangerous move given the Rangers' last bloody visit to the province. On the other hand, they could try following the Shannon southwards in the hope of finding a crossing still shallow enough to ford. But at this time of year and with all the heavy rain, that was highly unlikely.

The white heron will guide you, said an old, familiar voice in Wolf's head. *He will show you where to cross the river.*

Midir? Answered Wolf with the mind-speech, instinctively looking towards the nearby tree line, where a shadowy figure stood at the edge of the woods in the dawn light.

Follow the white heron, repeated Midir. *The bridges and fords are not safe for you, Wolf. The men of Connaught and the Kavanagh clan still thirst for your blood.*

Have I been betrayed?

Yes.

By the O'Kennedys?

No, they have not betrayed you, reassured Midir.

Then who has delivered me up to my enemies? persisted Wolf.

That matters little now. Suffice to say that a royal court has many spies, countless loose tongues and a score of greedy hearts.

What do they know of me? Wolf pressed, trying to gauge the extent of the damage, as anonymity was everything in his dangerous profession.

They know only that you are an Irish mercenary, nothing more than that. But now the Connaught men are suspicious of everyone that they do not know and are alert to strangers entering into their territory without good reason. So you must cross the Shannon only where the white heron shows you.

Wolf reflected upon Midir's troubling words for a moment and then set them aside for more pressing matters.

Have you come for the girl? asked Wolf, sensing that Riona was already getting ready to leave.

It is time. And it is good for the Land of the Ever-living Ones that she has been returned to us. But it is even better for the fertile soil of Ireland, said Midir ominously.

I owe you and Banba much.

There may come a time when you can repay us, responded Midir enigmatically.

My sword is yours, answered Wolf without hesitation.

Riona patted her horse affectionately, smiled softly at them all and went to leave. But then she turned and walked up to Amergen and gently touched his white hair, then headed off towards Midir. Halfway there, Riona paused to examine a plant for a brief moment and then glanced back towards Ferret before continuing on towards the trees.

"I think that I will go and stay with her a while," blurted Ferret as he sprang to his feet, having appeared dumbstruck as Riona walked away.

"Remember that time moves much differently there, Ferret. You must not linger in that place," warned Wolf. "A year in our lifetime can appear to be little more than a handful of days in that strange land."

"I know, Captain," responded Ferret vaguely as he walked off after her like a man in a trance. And it was clear that he was lost to them all now, for he had fallen completely under Riona's enchanted spell.

Do not linger at Beal Boru after you have returned the girl. There are turbulent times ahead for the kingdom of Thomond, and strangers will not be welcomed there, warned Midir as Riona and Ferret came to stand beside him at the tree line.

And where am I to go? Wolf asked, sensing that Midir already knew the answer.

You must go deep into the wilds of Thomond where you are at your strongest and at your safest, where the wolves can be your eyes and ears. Your enemies will not follow you into that fastness. There you should remain until the turmoil passes, advised Midir.

Turmoil? quizzed Wolf.

Midir said nothing for a long moment and seemed to be carefully considering his next words as Riona and Ferret drifted into the forest behind him.

King Mahon is to be assassinated by O'Mahony and O'Donovan, and there will be much bloodshed and upheaval in the province of Munster as a result of this low act, said Midir eventually. *After his brother's murder, Brian will be crowned the next king of Thomond. At that time, he may well require your services again.*

Wolf's gaze drifted towards Princess Aoife, and he found himself wondering how she would cope with the news of her brother's loss.

You must speak of this to no one! said Midir sternly, as if reading Wolf's thoughts. *The Morrigna have measured out Mahon's lifespan, and they have severed the thread of his worldly existence. It is done,* he concluded cryptically and then quietly stepped back into the shadows beneath the trees and was gone.

"What did he say to you?" asked Amergen, coming to

stand alongside Wolf.

"That we are to be guided by the white heron," said Wolf without any further elaboration, finally tearing his gaze away from the tree line, only to be stunned by what he saw.

"What are you staring at?" demanded Amergen defensively.

"Your hair!" answered Wolf with surprise.

"What about it?"

"It isn't white anymore, it's fair!" Amergen smiled towards the tree line as he took hold of a lock of his long golden hair and held it up to his eyes.

"Thank you, Riona," he sighed and briefly raised his other hand towards the trees.

Chapter Thirty-Eight

RETURN

Midir's words had troubled Wolf, but he tried to put them aside and get some rest as they waited out the daylight hours, hidden in a small cluster of pines. A light morning mist had begun to settle, and with Arrow taking the first watch, he wrapped himself in his damp cloak, then hunkered down against the base of a pine tree to get a little sleep.

The squawk was insistent and it was irritating, one long sonorous call and then a lengthy silence followed by another persistent caw. Wolf finally relented and forced open his heavy eyelids, directing his weary sight towards the offending noise, and there it was: a snow-white heron perched upon the branch of a barren tree. Of course, a white heron was not unheard of, but it certainly was a rarity in these bleak lands. And this particular bird had an incredible white hue which made it stand out even more starkly against the drab, misty landscape. The heron stared boldly at him for a long moment, and certain that it had his attention, the brazen bird then flew off towards the south, and Wolf sprang to his feet.

Using the two abandoned mounts as pack animals, Wolf, Amergen and Arrow hurriedly broke camp at noon. Munching handfuls of dried rations and washing it down with mouthfuls of tepid water, they hastily set off after the white bird in the grey morning light. Wolf felt uneasy moving about during the daylight hours after their nocturnal travels. But the light mist did shield them somewhat, which helped to ease his concerns.

The heron didn't follow the winding course of the

Shannon but took a direct course south, resting occasionally on isolated trees to allow the trio time to catch up with him. The terrain along the river was marshy and dotted with clumps of willow, bramble and alder, which provided them with some cover, but the horses found the mucky ground very hard going. Towards evening, the white heron turned west towards the nearby river, and they pushed on their heavy-legged horses through the boggy ground, following after the big bird as best they could.

"There!" shouted Arrow as they hurried towards the riverbank, pointing towards a dash of white standing motionless in the middle of a narrow ford.

"I never knew that there was a ford here," said Amergen, looking about him in disbelief as they approached the pristine bank. "Are you sure that we can trust this Midir?" he asked sceptically as the white heron stepped stealthily through the shallows in search of an unwary fish.

"I have never had any reason to doubt him," retorted Wolf. But he too was surprised to find a ford there, especially one with no territorial markings or sentries posted on either side of such a strategic crossing.

"Can we cross here?" asked Arrow dubiously.

"And can we trust this white bird?" piped in Amergen.

"A lone horseman!" called out Wolf suddenly, his keen senses picking up the faint thrum of pounding hooves in the near distance. "It looks like we're going to have to," answered Wolf, firing Amergen a sharp look before pushing Balor down the unblemished bank and splashing into the shallows. Arrow and Amergen coaxed their horses and the spare mounts down the bank and into the cold water and followed Wolf carefully across the narrow ford, quickly scrambling up the far bank before darting for cover in a nearby grove of alders.

Wolf grabbed his longbow and quiver as Amergen and Arrow swiftly led their horses deep into the thicket. Then he hastily took cover at the edge of the trees, where he quietly waited. The lone horseman approached the ford cautiously, and it was clear by the way that he scanned the ground below him as he went that the scout had most likely been tracking them for some time.

The scout went slowly towards the point where their horses had gone down the bank and crossed the ford, and Wolf gripped his bow tighter and pressed his thumb against the groove of the nocked arrow. The horseman paused at the edge of the riverbank and seemed a little perplexed by the hoof prints leading into the Shannon. He urged his mount down towards the river, and it was clear that the animal was nervous, whinnying and snorting as the water reached above its front fetlocks. The scout pushed his horse onwards, but the terrified animal finally balked, wheeled away from the river and clambered back up the bank. After settling his shivering mount, the horseman stared hard at the ford for a long moment, and then he peered intently into the stand of alders as if he suspected that someone lay in waiting for him. Appearing disgusted at his failure to traverse the shallow crossing, the scout spat at the river, turned his horse away from the ford and went back the way that he had come.

Curious at the horseman's hesitation to cross what was a shallow, narrow ford, Wolf waited until he heard the scout's horse some way off before cautiously making his way towards the riverbank in the fading light. But to Wolf's astonishment, the pinched shallow crossing was now completely gone and in its place was a wide, fast-flowing river, its deep, dark waters brimming with menace. Wolf scanned the surrounding area for any sign of the unusual heron, but it too had disappeared. Suspecting that there were strange forces at play here, Wolf offered a silent thanks to Midir for bringing them safely across the Shannon and into the territory of north Thomond. Then he made his way back quietly towards the trees.

Wary of the lone scout, they pushed on southwards into Thomond during the night, resting up along the western shores of Lough Derg in the small hours of the morning. At dawn, they finished off most of their supplies, watered their horses at the lough and then struck out on the last leg of their journey to Beal Boru. Arrow was content to travel through the kingdom of Thomond in the broad light of day. Not knowing who was friend and who was foe as yet, Wolf had his reservations, but he let the princess have her way, for this was Aoife's homeland.

*

Bedraggled and travel weary, the three riders approached Beal Boru as a cold breeze swept across the Shannon and a salmon-coloured dusk began to settle in the western sky. Passersby who travelled on the causeway to and from the large circular fort stared at the windswept trio with wary eyes and gave them a wide berth as they went by.

"Halt! Who goes there?" called a sentry from the high rampart perched behind the palisade as the three riders approached the closed gates.

"Is that you, Fergal?" shouted up Arrow as they stopped before the tall gates. "It's me, Princess Aoife."

The guard seemed uncertain of what to make of the girl in grubby green buckskins claiming to be the princess, and so he remained silent as he considered his options.

"Do you still have that scar on your chin that I gave you when we were sparring?" asked Aoife with a smile. The sentry instinctively touched his chin and then gave her a wry grin.

"The damned thing still plays havoc with my beard, Princess," said Fergal warmly, and then he called down to open up the gates.

Princess Aoife led Wolf and Amergen boldly into the great hall and up towards the throne, instantly ending all talk among the few leading men who had gathered around the seated Boru.

"Leave us," said Brian simply as he saw his sister approach. "All of you!" he called out towards the servants in the shadows and the two guards that were still standing by the main doors. "Aoife," said Brian with a warm smile as he stepped down from the raised dais to embrace his sister. Their reunion was a tender one, but Wolf sensed that there was tension there too.

"Is King Mahon here?" asked Aoife, standing back from her brother's arms.

"The king has gone on a fool's errand," answered Boru bitterly. "He's chasing after those two traitors, O'Mahony and O'Donovan, to offer them the hand of friendship."

Aoife could sense that Brian was deeply concerned for the safety of their brother and the security of the king, so she quickly changed the subject.

"Amergen, I believe you already know," said Aoife, gesturing towards her companions. "And this is Captain

Wolf."

"It's good to have you back, old friend," said Brian as he squeezed Amergen's hand. "And I just so happen to have a delicate task that needs your immediate attention," he added, and then he noticed the colour in his counsellor's hair. "What happened to your hair?"

"It's a long story, Commander, that will take a little time to tell," answered Amergen, looking uncomfortable about all the focus on his hair.

"I look forward to hearing it. You can tell me all tonight, Counsellor. But first I need some privacy with my long-lost sister," said Boru smoothly.

"Of course, Commander," replied Amergen, then gave a curt nod and left the hall.

"Captain Wolf, you have my deepest thanks for returning our sister to us," said Brian cordially as he firmly shook Wolf's hand. "But I urgently need a quiet moment with my sister. I'm sure that you understand."

"He can stay!" said Aoife forcefully as Wolf turned to leave, startling Boru's two wolfhounds, which sprang to their feet, sensing the tension in the hall, and began to circle Wolf with menace.

"To the fire!" ordered Brian, and the two gangly hounds loped off and flopped down near the open flame. "Their hearts are bigger than their brains," offered Boru as he gently led Aoife to a corner of the hall.

Wolf had no idea of the content of their conversation, but it was intense. And each gave the other as good as they got as the exchanges grew ever more heated.

"Damn it all, Aoife, if you won't do it for us, then do it for them. Do it for him!" blasted Brian as he glanced over at Wolf, his short temper starting to get the better of him. Boru's harsh words seemed to strike a chord within

Aoife, and she remained quiet for a long moment as she considered her brother's request. Then her shoulders seemed to slump a little, and she gave a small, dejected nod. The princess then appeared to gather herself up and square her shoulders as Brian rested a gentle hand on her arm and spoke some soothing words, bringing their sharp conversation to an end.

"It appears that I am to be wed to the Prince of Connaught!" said Aoife with false gusto as she strode back towards Wolf. "It seems that this is the royal deal that my brothers have struck to restore the peace and save you and your men, Captain," added the princess, her voice laced with bitterness.

"That is not a trade that I would ask you to make on my behalf," answered Wolf coldly, keeping his smouldering anger in check as he stared hard at Brian.

"I know it's not, Captain," responded Aoife calmly, casting a harsh look towards her brother as she walked over to Wolf and embraced him affectionately. "Thank you for bringing me home," added the princess and kissed him softly on the cheek. Then she headed towards the single door at the back of the hall as Wolf struggled to find some words of comfort for Aoife before she left.

"Arrow!" called Wolf as Aoife opened the door to leave. "Once a Ranger, always a Ranger."

She turned and gave him a thin smile.

"I will always remember that," replied the princess as she went to leave, but then she paused. "Someday you may need help in my world, Captain," she concluded cryptically and then she slipped out the door and was gone.

"My sister has told me that you handled yourself well on that raid into the north lands," said Boru, wearily sitting down on the throne.

"You should know that Sergeant Mac Namara made possible our escape," stated Wolf, keen to have Mac Namara's heroics acknowledged.

"Captain Mac Namara was a good man," reflected Brian. "His reputation will not be tarnished, and his family will not want."

"The ambush at Eagle's Pass..."

"Did not go as either of us would have wished, Captain," interjected Boru. "Let's just leave it at that."

"And what of the Connaught men?" pressed Wolf.

"King O'Connor will let the matter rest with this marriage between his son and Aoife," explained Brian. "But watch your back. The Kavanaghs have black hearts and long memories," he warned, appearing eager to conclude their conversation. "My sister says I am to give you whatever it is you want and that you have certainly earned it. Well, what is it that you want, Captain?"

"Only that which I was promised," answered Wolf simply.

"Which was what, exactly?" asked Brian shrewdly.

"The right to hunt on Thomond land and protection for the wolves that live there," responded Wolf.

"The first boon is easily granted, but the second request is a little unusual, to say the least," answered Boru, studying Wolf closely. "But then you strike me as an unusual man, so your wolves may have my protection. Is there anything else, Captain?" asked Brian as he rose to leave.

"Only that these agreements be put in writing," asked Wolf calmly.

"Is my word not good enough for you?" growled Boru.

"I meant no offence, Commander," placated Wolf. "But great men come, and great men go, and their words go with them sometimes, but the written word lives on long after they have gone."

Brian waved what looked like his consent as he stood. Then he headed for the door at the back of the hall.

"Don't stray too far, Captain. I may need your services again," said Boru as he paused at the open door. "This war is far from over," he added gravely, then went through the doorway and was gone.

Chapter Thirty-Nine

ENDINGS

Wolf and Amergen had shared a woodland track heading south since leaving Beal Boru that blustery morning. The deciduous trees appeared almost bare now, their discarded russet leaves careering madly about them at the mercy of every petulant gust. Wolf had stabled Balor at a safe house the day before, a farmstead with two young mares and a small orchard full of apple trees, so the big stallion would be well distracted until Wolf could risk a return. A horse would be of little use to Wolf in the wild, rugged lands of west Thomond, and besides, Balor's trail would be too easy to track, especially across any marshy terrain. And despite King O'Connor's fine words of peace to Brian Boru, Wolf was certain that there were a few vengeful Connaught men who were still keen to hunt him down. Amergen had also chosen to travel on foot, saying only that the task assigned to him by Boru was a delicate one and that stealth was essential.

The sullen sky and biting breeze had done little to lift Amergen's pensive mood, piquing Wolf's curiosity as they travelled deeper into the forest.

"Is the princess glad to be home?" ventured Wolf, trying to get to the source of Amergen's persistent brooding.

"She enjoyed what little she saw of it. They whisked her off right away to a nearby convent for a right royal scrubbing and a spiritual pruning in preparation for her upcoming nuptials," quipped Amergen, appearing to be content with the proposed betrothal.

"Why was Boru so early in the saddle?" asked Wolf

brazenly, having heard a troop of horsemen hurry from the fort before dawn as he lightly slept in a spare bunk in the guardhouse by the gates.

"You don't miss much, Captain," answered Amergen with a sliver of surprise as he paused to consider his next words. Then he added, "The one thing that's sure to put any war leader quickly into his saddle, night or day, and that's trouble."

It was clear that the counsellor was prepared to say no more on the matter, so Wolf probed no further. But secretly he wondered if that very trouble concerned King Mahon. Still, he heeded Midir's words and kept his thoughts firmly to himself.

They entered a small clearing in a swathe of pine trees near noon, and Amergen went to sit on the trunk of a fallen tree as he reached for his water skin.

"I see that your friends are back," said Amergen as he undid the stopper, gesturing towards the wolves that were patrolling along the tree line, watching their every move.

"They picked up my scent the moment that we entered the woods," answered Wolf with a sense of pride, glad to see the familiar outlines of Willow and Shadow at the head of a sizeable pack.

"Too much wine last night," confessed Amergen and then guzzled down several mouthfuls of warmish water. "We talked late into the night. Boru wanted to know every detail of our adventure. I told him most of it, but not all. Some details of our trip appear a little vague to me now, while other things seem quite unbelievable. A few of the darker memories from that strange otherworld will haunt my dreams for ever. I thought it best to leave out the more peculiar sections of our story altogether."

"Probably for the best," agreed Wolf.

"He wanted to know all about you, and your Rangers," continued Amergen. "I think that he was impressed. Don't be surprised if he offers you more work in these uncertain times."

"That's for another day, Counsellor," replied Wolf evasively, keen not to swiftly fall into another of Amergen's cunning traps.

"If you are a wise man, you won't refuse him, Captain," cautioned Amergen. "Boru could be a good ally to have in this troubled land, as he is sure to become a very powerful man in this country one day."

"We shall see," returned Wolf indifferently, eager to say his final farewells and make his own way into the wilds of the west.

"You never did ask me what I might have learned about your past," pointed out Amergen as he put the stopper back in the water skin.

"I reckoned that you would get around to that sooner or later," answered Wolf without much enthusiasm as he prepared to hear Amergen's report, wedging the foot of his bow against a rock and gently resting his hands on the other end.

"You will of course remember the Fort of the Two Ravens?" began Amergen.

"Yes, I recall the place," replied Wolf cautiously.

"Well, it seems that this hill fort was mysteriously attacked some years ago, and most of its inhabitants were killed," explained Amergen. "And what appeared to be just as bizarre as the great slaughter itself was the fact that those who raided the fort had no interest in seizing slaves or goods but had simply killed all the Christian inhabitants and left as suddenly as they had come."

"And what has any of this got to do with me?" asked

Wolf, strangely unsettled by this particular subject.

"Well, it appears as if a young boy may have survived the raid and fled into a nearby forest," related Amergen. "And as chance would have it, it seems as if a pack of wolves may have taken in the child and reared him as one of their own."

"Go on," prodded Wolf warily.

"Local villagers who had seen the boy running with the wolves in the woods tried to rescue the child. But the lad just simply disappeared and was never seen in the area again."

"And you think that this boy could have been me?" ventured Wolf.

"Well, could it?"

"For some reason, I have no recollection of that time in my life," replied Wolf after reflecting upon it for a long moment. "That part of my life is a blur, just fragments of vague, peculiar memories and a string of strange thoughts."

"But it might have been you?" pressed Amergen.

"It's possible, I suppose. What of it?"

"Because there is more to the story of the Fort of the Two Ravens than meets the eye, much more," continued Amergen in earnest, "for it seems that there was an ancient prophecy relating to this fort which stated that 'a boy from the Fort of the Two Ravens will sway the contest between the White Dragon and the Red Dragon'. If you were indeed this boy, I think it's fair to say that you have already swayed that battle. And who knows, perhaps you may be called upon to do so again."

"You speak of dragons?"

"The Druids of old talked often about this ongoing struggle: the war between the Nordic people, or the White

Dragon, and the Celtic race — the tribes of the Red Dragon," elaborated Amergen.

"All this talk of dragons and prophecies seems a little far-fetched to me," admitted Wolf after some thought.

"Perhaps, but someone obviously thought that the prophecy was not so unbelievable and had the inhabitants of the fort slaughtered because of it."

"Who would do such a callous act over a few hollow words?"

"I believe that your mother gave the order, Captain."

Wolf stared intently at Amergen, trying to make some sense of his outlandish claims, half expecting one of the counsellor's twisted tricks, but Amergen appeared to be completely serious.

"Why would she do such a thing?" asked Wolf, compelled to hear the rest of the harsh truth.

"From what I can piece together, your mother was a pagan priestess who was vehemently opposed to the rapid rise of Christianity in this country. So she sought guidance from a demon medium, and it was this malevolent spirit that gave her the prophecy about the fort and also arranged the assistance of another dark ally."

"What aren't you telling me?" asked Wolf coldly, sensing that Amergen was holding something back.

"It appears as if your mother believed that the prophecy pertained to your older brother..."

"So I was expendable," finished off Wolf.

"Something like that," replied Amergen meekly.

"Where are they now?"

"No one knows. After destroying the fort to cover her tracks, your mother took your older brother and fled into the night on a waiting ship with her secret accomplice, and she has never been seen in Ireland again."

"And how do you know so much about all this, Counsellor?" quizzed Wolf suspiciously.

"'There isn't a slaughter that one man doesn't come out of to tell the tale'," quoted Amergen. "A terrified survivor sought sanctuary in Saint Finbarr's monastery in Cork, and he's been doing penance there ever since; that's how I learned of the story. He said that he had been ordered to kill the younger brother, but he couldn't bring himself to cut the child's throat. So he tossed the boy over the palisade to let nature do the dirty work and reported the foul deed done. Fearing that the witch might learn of the henchman's lie through her sorcery, he refused to board the waiting ship and fled into the night in search of a safe place on holy ground."

Wolf remained stony-faced and silent as he thought long and hard on Amergen's brutal words.

"Maybe I was that boy and maybe not, but I have no recollection of those events. In any case, it matters little now who my people were or where I came from. For these wolves are my clan now, and this is where I belong," responded Wolf evenly, shouldering his longbow and preparing to take his leave.

"So it would seem," concluded Amergen, getting to his feet. "But remember this, Captain: this battle has only begun, and it appears that your mother and brother already stand with our enemies. Your paths are bound to cross, perhaps your swords too?"

"Perhaps," conceded Wolf but would not be drawn any further on the thorny matter.

"Your reputation is well deserved, Wolf," said Amergen, offering his hand, keen to move past the awkward moment.

“It has been interesting, Counsellor,” replied Wolf as he gripped Amergen’s hand.

“Next time, I’ll know where to find you!” called Amergen as Wolf headed towards the tree line, and Wolf paused and half-turned.

“Next time, I might not be so easy to find, old man,” answered Wolf with a wry smile, then he disappeared into the trees as the wolves of the forest sang out, for their leader had returned. Wolf had come home.

THE END

AUTHOR'S NOTE:

If certain aspects of this story appear unresolved, that's for good reason, as this twisted tale is far from over.

HISTORICAL NOTE:

Historically, (raid aside), the 'nuts and bolts' of this story are fairly accurate, although Aoife is a fictional character. The mythological elements herein are also a fair reflection of accepted Irish folklore (including the concept of the mermaid's magical cloak) while the legend of 'The Blue Mermen of Minch' is also well established in Scottish folklore.

The concept of 'The Rangers', I borrowed from another place and time, namely the Province of New Hampshire, USA, in and around the 1750s. Raised and trained by Major Robert Rogers and attached to the British Army during the Seven Years' War, (French and Indian War), 'Rogers' Rangers' were a light infantry force who conducted special operations against distant targets. They were well known by their distinctive green buckskins, which allowed them to blend in well with their woodland terrain. One standing order epitomized their stealthy strategy: 'When you're on the march, act the way you would if you was sneaking up on a deer. See the enemy first.'

I drew my inspiration for the sea kayak raid from 'Operation Frankton', a commando raid by a small Royal Marines' canoe team on German ships docked in Bordeaux in German occupied France during WW2.

Also, a similar kayak raid, ‘Operation Jaywick’, by Australian Special Forces on Japanese naval ships docked at Singapore in WW2.

ACKNOWLEDGEMENTS:

Firstly, I would like to mention my secondary school English teacher, Miss Gilmore, (Birr, Co. Offaly), who spotted some raw talent in me many years ago and duly encouraged it. I would also like to thank my first trusty proofreader, Kathleen Duffy, (Dundalk, Co. Louth), who carefully scrutinized my first fledgling articles. I would also like to pay tribute to the Irish Celtic/rock band 'Horslips', whose haunting tunes and intriguing lyrics led me to explore Ireland's magical past, an era that many of my generation knew very little about! I would also like to thank the team at the 'Writing Magazine', most especially Lesley Eames. I would also like to recognise the great many wonderful writers in my genre who have both entertained and educated me over the years, starting with the master himself, Bernard Cornwell. Also, and in no particular order, Kenneth Roberts, Stephen Lawhead, Michael Scott, Tim Severn, Robert Low, Giles Kristan, Raymond E. Feist, Ursula Le Guin, Jack Vance, Morgan Llywelyn, David Gemmel, Justin Hill and Nikolai Tolstoy, to name but a few. Of course, no such list would be complete without a word about our great mentor, J.R.R. Tolkien, who started many of us on a journey: one that some of us are still on today!

Finally, I would like to take this opportunity to salute the real Rangers, past and present: the men and women of the United States Army Rangers, and the Irish Army Ranger Wing, who initially drew their training from their US counterparts. In many ways, the Rangers strive to embody some of mankind's better traits — toughness, tenacity, stealth and daring —admirable abilities indeed.

About The Author

Don lives in Ireland, where he feels a deep connection to the land. He is married and a father of two, a daughter and a son. Don has been writing for over forty years and has a healthy portfolio, mostly feature articles and short stories (two of which were prize winners — 'The Sea-maid' and 'Deep Thoughts', a result of his deep fascination with the sea). He is also a regular contributor to several Irish national magazines, including 'Ireland's Own', 'Ireland's Eye', 'The Irish Mountain Log' and 'Subsea,' supplying them all with a variety of articles on Vikings, mermaids, wildlife, mountains and history, while all four magazines have also published his short stories. Don also regularly publishes feature articles in both of his local newspapers, 'The Dundalk Democrat' and 'The Argus'.

Don is an avid hill walker and scuba diver, and he draws great inspiration from both the mountains and the sea as, he notes, did the poet William Wordsworth. "Two voices are there; One is of the Sea, One of the Mountains; Each a mighty Voice..." (1807) Don is also an Advanced Adventure Sport Instructor, reflecting his passion for outdoor adventure activities.

Besides his background in construction, Don has also completed several courses in English, Creative Writing, Short Story Writing and Freelance Journalism. He also served for three years in the Irish Permanent Defence Forces, serving with the 27th Battalion along the Irish border. Don also did a six-month peacekeeping tour of duty with the 46th Irish Battalion with the U.N. in the troubled lands of south Lebanon.

Don writes full-time now, having closed down his construction business and taken early retirement so that he could finally focus on what has always been his primary goal: writing!

'Wolf's Quest' is Don's first novel.

www.blossomspringpublishing.com

Printed in Great Britain
by Amazon

56725135R00209